FATHER BROWN

G. K. CHESTERTON

FATHER BROWN

THE ESSENTIAL TALES

Introduction by P. D. James

THE MODERN LIBRARY

NEW YORK

2005 Modern Library Paperback Edition

LIBRARY OF CONGRESS CATALOGING-IN-PUBLICATION DATA
Chesterton, G. K. (Gilbert Keith)
Father Brown: the essential tales / G. K. Chesterton;
with an introduction by P. D. James
p. cm.
Contents: The blue cross—The secret garden—The queer feet—The flying
stars—The invisible man—The honour of israel gow—The sins of prince
saradine—The hammer of god—The three tools of death—The absence of
mr. glass—The paradise of thieves—The man in the passage—The head of
caesar—The purple wig—The strange crime of john boulnois.
ISBN 0-8129-7222-8
1. Brown, Father (Fictitious character)—Fiction. 2. Detective and
mystery stories, English. 3. Catholics—Fiction. 4. England—Fiction.
5. Clergy—Fiction. I. James, P. D. II. Title.
PR4453.C4A6 2005
823'.912—dc22   2004059535

Modern Library website address: www.modernlibrary.com

Printed in the United States of America

8   9

G. K. CHESTERTON

Gilbert Keith Chesterton, the genial and prolific writer who presided over the world of English letters during the first decades of the twentieth century, was born in London on May 29, 1874, into a cultivated middle-class family. Chesterton, while at St. Paul's School, was singled out as a student with distinct literary promise for his ability to recite long passages from Dickens, Scott, and Shakespeare. He later attended the Slade School of Art and University College, London, but abandoned his studies in 1895 to read manuscripts for a London publisher and eventually found work as a freelance journalist. Over the next decades Chesterton's weekly articles in the *Daily News,* the *Illustrated London News,* the *Daily Herald,* and the *New Witness* established his reputation as a witty and provocative social critic who was a master of irreverent paradox. Long hailed as Fleet Street's reincarnation of Dr. Samuel Johnson, he began publishing his own journal of public opinion, *G. K.'s Weekly,* in 1925. George Bernard Shaw deemed Chesterton "a man of colossal genius" and prompted him to write the play *Magic,* which was produced on the London stage in 1913. With *What's Wrong with the World* (1910) he achieved recognition as a leading exponent of Distributism, a decentralized economic system in which private property would be divided into the smallest possible units. Chesterton's conversion to Catholicism in 1922 occasioned his writing the biographies *St. Francis of Assisi* (1923) and *St. Thomas Aquinas* (1933), as well as *The Everlasting Man* (1925), perhaps the highest expression of his mysticism. Some of his earlier religious views were expressed in *Heretics* (1905) and *Orthodoxy* (1908). G. K. Chesterton completed his celebrated *Autobiography* (1936) less than two months before his death in Beaconsfield, near London, on June 14, 1936.

"To follow Chesterton's mind and its expression is an introduction to the English soul," remarked his friend, the writer Hilaire Belloc. "He is a mirror of England." Chesterton initially gained prominence as a poet and literary biographer. His first published work, *Greybeards at Play* (1900), contains pure nonsense verse in the tradition of Lewis Carroll and W. S. Gilbert. "I cannot think of a single comic poem by Chesterton that is not a triumphant success," said W. H. Auden. His next collection, *The Wild Knight and Other Poems* (1900), marked the real beginning of Chesterton's career as a poet. *The Ballad of the White Horse* (1911), a long narrative poem that retells the story of King Alfred the Great's fight to keep the pagan Norsemen from taking over Christian England, is generally regarded as his greatest serious verse. Chesterton showcased much of his so-called political poetry in *Wine, Water and Song* (1915) and presented his poems of World War I in *The Ballad of St. Barbara and Other Verses* (1922). *Charles Dickens,* his acclaimed critical biography of the great Victorian novelist, was published in 1906. "It is conventional to say that Chesterton's book on Dickens is the best thing he ever wrote," reflected V. S. Pritchett. "It is not merely good; it is a masterpiece and contains, among other things, the most enlightening portrait of Dickens himself that I have ever read." Likewise T. S. Eliot stated that "there is no better critic of Dickens living than Mr. Chesterton." Chesterton produced several other masterful works that artfully meld literary criticism with biography: *Robert Browning* (1903), *George Bernard Shaw* (1909), *William Blake* (1910), *Robert Louis Stevenson* (1927), and *Chaucer* (1932). *The Victorian Age in Literature,* perhaps his most famous work of literary criticism, appeared in 1913.

"[Chesterton] had a genius simply for having original ideas," noted Wilfrid Sheed in discussing his brilliance as an essayist. "It is hardly possible to read a page of Chesterton without finding an unexpected idea, at best wise, at worst fiendishly ingenious. . . . The spillover of his thinking leaves us a body of aphorisms universal enough to belong to literature." During the course of his career Chesterton compiled hundreds of essays in a score of collections, including *The Defendant* (1901), *Twelve Types* (1902), *All Things Considered* (1908), *Tremendous Trifles* (1909), *Alarms and Discursions* (1910), *A Miscellany of Men* (1912), *The Barbarism of Berlin* (1914), *The Uses of Diversity* (1920), *Fancies Versus Fads* (1923), *Come to Think of It* (1930), *All Is Grist* (1931), *All I Survey* (1933), *Avowals and Denials* (1934), *The Well and the Shallows* (1935), and *As I Was Saying* (1936). "Chesterton inherited from the aesthetes of the 1880s and 1890s the conviction that a writer should be continuously 'bright' and epigrammatic," observed W. H. Auden. "When he is really enthralled by a subject he is brilliant, without any doubt one of the finest aphorists in English literature." In addition, several volumes of essays culled from his papers have appeared posthumously, namely *The Common Man* (1950), *A Handful of Authors* (1953), *The Glass Walking-Stick* (1955), *Chesterton on Shakespeare* (1971), and *The Apostle and the Wild Ducks* (1975).

Chesterton also enjoyed success as a novelist and short-story writer. "[It] is in his fiction that I find Chesterton's genius best and most characteristically displayed," said Kingsley Amis. "The novels and stories dramatize virtually the whole range of the themes and interests met in his other work." He made his debut as a novelist with *The Napoleon of Notting Hill* (1904), a futuristic tale set in 1984. *The Man Who Was Thursday* (1908), his next novel, was hailed by C. S. Lewis as "a powerful picture of the loneliness and bewilderment which each of us encounters in his (apparently) single-handed struggle with the universe." His subsequent fiction includes *The Ball and the Cross* (1910), *Manalive* (1912), *The Flying Inn* (1914), and *The Return of Don Quixote* (1927). As Anthony Burgess commented: "His best novels—*The Napoleon of Notting Hill*, *The Man Who Was Thursday*, and *The Flying Inn*—are as entertaining as when they were first written, and the substructure of the farce and fantasy—a concern with free will, Western civilization, and the ultimate mysteries of religion—is not less valid in the age of superstates and nuclear deterrents and brainwashing than it was in Chesterton's more innocent heyday."

Today Chesterton is perhaps best remembered for his detective stories featuring Father Brown, a seemingly absent-minded cleric who possesses a profound understanding of evil. Originally published in the *Saturday Evening Post,* the stories were collected in *The Innocence of Father Brown* (1911), *The Wisdom of Father Brown* (1914), *The Incredulity of Father Brown* (1926), *The Secret of Father Brown* (1927), and *The Scandal of Father Brown* (1935). "[Father Brown] is one of the greatest of all great detective figures," said Kingsley Amis. "For many, he will always be *the* greatest. . . . His field of knowledge is human nature, and his skills are observation, reason and common sense." Chesterton created several other amateur sleuths—notably Basil Grant, Horne Fisher, Gabriel Gale, and Mr. Pond—who appeared in *The Club of Queer Trades* (1905), *The Man Who Knew Too Much* (1922), *The Poet and the Lunatics* (1929), and *The Paradoxes of Mr. Pond* (1937). "A reading of Chesterton reinforces the truth that the best detective stories have been written by artists and not by artisans," reflected critic Julian Symons.

"Chesterton belonged to an age when literary men could be public figures, just like politicians," observed Anthony Burgess. "His immense range was essentially that of the professional writer who would be ashamed to reject any literary challenge. He could write biography, *belles lettres,* literary criticism, history, philosophy, drama, as well as novels, detective fiction, and verse. . . . He was spontaneously witty, but he could also be carefully epigrammatic. He thought of words not as neutral rational counters, but as confetti, bonbons, artillery." His friend and biographer Maisie Ward agreed: "Few writers have as much vitality as G.K.C., and one of its manifestations is the endless variety of his work. . . . The man is so exuberant, so disrespectful to the learned, so deadsure, so comic where he is most serious. This is the real paradox of Chesterton." And Wilfrid Sheed concluded: "Chesterton was a brilliant philosophical journalist. . . . The range of [his] talent was almost alarming. . . . [He] was simply what the word 'genius' meant."

Contents

Father Brown
The Essential Tales

INTRODUCTION

P. D. James

Gilbert Keith Chesterton, who was born on Camden Hill in London in 1874 and died in 1936, can be described in terms which are hardly ever used of a writer today; he was a man of letters. All his life he earned his living by his pen and he was as versatile as he was prolific. After his education at the intellectually prestigious St. Paul's School, he went on to study at the Slade School of Art and was talented as an illustrator, particularly of the novels of his life-long friend, Hilaire Belloc. Chesterton gained a reputation as a novelist, essayist, critic, journalist, and poet, and although much of this copious output, particularly on social, political, and religious subjects, has proved ephemeral, his book about Charles Dickens, published in 1906, remains an influential work, and a few of his poems, including "The Donkey," the vigorous narrative poem "Lepanto," and "The Rolling English Road," continue to appear in anthologies of popular verse.

But although much has been lost, what remain in the public imagination, and are still read with pleasure and admiration, are his detective short stories featuring a Roman Catholic priest, Father Brown. These first appeared in *The Innocence of Father Brown*, published in 1911, and were followed by four further volumes, *The Wis-*

dom *of Father Brown* (1914), *The Incredulity of Father Brown* (1926), *The Secret of Father Brown* (1927), and *The Scandal of Father Brown* (1935). The character is based on a friend of Chesterton's, Father John O'Connor of St. Cuthbert's Church in Bradford, to whom *The Secret of Father Brown* was dedicated.

All G. K. Chesterton's writings, including the Father Brown stories, show, however subtly, the influence of his religious faith (he was received into the Roman Catholic Church in 1922) and of his image of the world. He had a great romantic view of England, an almost medieval nostalgia for a simpler, rural and happy land, remote from technology, materialistic big business, and monolithic state power. It was a view that he shared with Hilaire Belloc, earning them from George Bernard Shaw the twin nickname of Chesterbelloc. Their England conjures a picture of happy contented villagers, of old men drinking with friends outside the pub, of the rolling English road, and of a simple unexamined patriotism. And from this view of the world, from his deeply held religious faith, and from his teeming imagination, G. K. Chesterton created a unique amateur detective who has gained an assured place in the canon of mystery writing.

Physically, Father Brown could not be more unlike the conventional romantic, handsome, and confident amateur detectives of the Golden Age of mystery writing. In the story "The Blue Cross," we see him through the eyes of Valentin, described as the head of the Paris police. Admittedly at the time, Father Brown, for purposes of his own, was exaggerating his apparent innocuousness, but we can be sure that what Valentin saw, so did other characters who encountered Father Brown. We are told that in the railway carriage the two were sharing was a very short Roman Catholic priest going up from a small Essex village, who seemed to Valentin to be "the essence of those Eastern flats; he had a face as round and dull as a Norfolk dumpling; he had eyes as empty as the North Sea; he had several brown paper parcels, which he was quite incapable of collecting. . . . He had a large, shabby umbrella, which constantly fell on the floor. He did not seem to know which was the right end of his return ticket."

Valentin was not the only person to be taken in by this seeming innocence and simplicity. The bumbling exterior hides one of the most acute brains in the history of fictional detection, and those apparently empty eyes miss nothing. Unlike most of the Golden Age heroes of detective fiction, essentially he works alone. He has no professional supporter to do the routine legwork or provide additional police support when required, as has Lord Peter Wimsey in Inspector Parker. He is not bizarrely eccentric, as is Agatha Christie's Poirot. Unlike Sherlock Holmes, he has no Watson to ask questions which the more simple-minded readers might like to put and whose purpose is to demonstrate the great detective's brilliance and superior intellect. Naturally, given the decades in which he operates, he has no scientific advice available, indeed no official person whose help he can readily enlist in moments of crisis. He solves crimes by a mixture of common sense, observation, and deduction, and by his knowledge of the human heart. After years of hearing confessions, he knows the best and worst of which human beings are capable even though those secrets are locked in his heart. As he says to Flambeau, the master thief whom he outwits in "The Blue Cross" and whom he restores to honesty, "Has it never struck you that a man who does next to nothing but hear men's real sins is not likely to be wholly unaware of human evil?" And he has another advantage in being a priest, of never being required precisely to explain his presence since it is assumed he is occupied with his priestly function, and of being a man in whom many might naturally confide.

Although we are told that Father Brown was parish priest in Cobhole in Essex before moving to London, we meet him in other and very different places, in England and overseas and in a variety of settings and company across the whole social and economic spectrum. Nothing and no one is alien to him. We never encounter him in the daily routine of his pastoral duties at Cobhole, never learn where exactly he lives, who housekeeps for him, what kind of church he has or his relationship with his bishop. We are not told his age, whether his parents are still living or even his Christian name. In each of the stories he makes his quiet appearance unannounced, as much at home with the poor and humble as he is with the rich and famous, and applying to all situations his own immutable spirituality. But he is always a rationalist with a dislike of superstition, which he sees as inimical to his faith. Like the other characters in the stories—and like us, the readers—he sees the physical facts of the case, but only he, by a process of deduction, interprets them correctly. We see what is apparently obvious however bizarre; he sees what is true. Chesterton loved paradox and, because we encounter Father Brown often in incongruous or bizarre company and he comes unencumbered by his past, the little priest is himself a paradox, at once mundane and unthreatening, but also mysterious and iconic.

In a book entitled *A Century of Detective Stories*, published by Hutchinson between the wars (the precise date is nowhere mentioned in the volume), G. K. Chesterton wrote the introduction. After paying tribute to Edgar Allan Poe and Sherlock Holmes, he sets out the advantages and disadvantages of the short mystery story as compared with the longer novel. He points out that "the long story is more successful in one not unimportant point: that it is sometimes possible to realise that a man is alive before we realise that he is dead." In the short story "the narrative is so brief that often the living characters may be left at the end looking rather like conventional corpses." But although the police novel can be used for a fuller development of character, Chesterton comments that "it is not always filled with life, but rather padded as something else." His own short stories are always filled with life. In *A Century of Detective Stories* Chesterton included one of his own, "The Secret Garden." We can therefore assume that it is one he himself particularly valued, and it seems right to include it in this new edition.

With such a large output, it would be unreasonable to expect all of the more than fifty Father Brown stories to be equal in quality and readers will have their own favorites. But even if a single story slightly disappoints, the quality of the writing never does. Chesterton never wrote an inelegant or clumsy sentence. The Father Brown stories are brilliantly written in a style richly complex, imaginative, vigorous, poetic, and spiced with paradoxes. He was an artist as well as a writer and he sees life with an artist's eye. He wanted his readers to share that poetic vision, to see the romance and numinousness in commonplace things.

> Men lived among mighty mountains and eternal forests for ages before they realised they were poetical; it may reasonably be inferred that some of our descendants may see the chimney-pots as rich a purple as the mountain-peaks, and find the lamp-posts as old and natural as the trees ("A Defence of the Detective Stories").

His characters are vividly described and stand before us in all their eccentric diversity. He is particularly skilled at evoking the effect of changing light on landscape, its power to transmogrify and beguile, so that the seemingly mundane and familiar become pregnant with mystery:

> Outside, the last edges of the sunset still clung to the corners of the green square but inside a lamp had already been kindled; and in the mingling of the two lights the coloured globe glowed like some monstrous jewel and the fantastic outlines of the fiery fishes seemed to give it indeed something of the mystery of a talisman; like strange shapes seen by a seer in the crystal of doom ("The Song of the Flying Fish").

With so rich a literary feast it has been suggested that the stories are best savored a few at a time, rather than gulped at a single sitting.

In one respect G. K. Chesterton was ahead of his time. He was one of the first writers of detective fiction to realize that this popular genre could be a vehicle for exploring and exposing the condition of society and of saying something true about human nature. Before he even planned the Father Brown stories, Chesterton wrote that "the only thrill, even of a common thriller, is concerned somehow with the conscience and the will." We read the Father Brown stories for a variety of pleasures, including their ingenuity, their wit and intelligence, and for the brilliance of the writing. But they provide more. Chesterton was concerned with the greatest of all problems, the vagaries of the human heart. It is because of this all-embracing humanity that the Father Brown stories will continue to entrance, entertain, and solace readers inhabiting a world infinitely more complex and dangerous than was the England in which Chesterton wrote. It is not surprising that eminent historians of the mystery genre have for decades agreed that, at their best, the Father Brown stories are among the finest crime stories ever written.

———

P. D. JAMES is the bestselling author of celebrated literary mystery novels, many of them featuring her poet-detective, Commander Adam Dalgliesh of New Scotland Yard. Recent books include *A Certain Justice, Death in Holy Orders,* and *The Murder Room.* Previously she served in the police and criminal justice departments of Great Britain's Home Office. She has received honorary doctorates from seven universities, and in 1991 was made a life peer as Baroness James of Holland Park. She lives in London and Oxford.

A NOTE ON THE TEXT

Originally published in the United States by *The Saturday Evening Post*, G. K. Chesterton's popular short stories featuring Father Brown were collected in *The Innocence of Father Brown* (1911), *The Wisdom of Father Brown* (1914), *The Incredulity of Father Brown* (1926), *The Secret of Father Brown* (1927), and *The Scandal of Father Brown* (1935). This Modern Library Paperback Classic was set from the first American editions of *The Innocence of Father Brown* and *The Wisdom of Father Brown*. Selections for *Father Brown: The Essential Tales* were made in cooperation with the American Chesterton Society; please visit the society's website at http://www.chesterton.org/ to learn more about G. K. Chesterton and his work.

FATHER BROWN

THE BLUE CROSS

Between the silver ribbon of morning and the green glittering ribbon of sea, the boat touched Harwich and let loose a swarm of folk like flies, among whom the man we must follow was by no means conspicuous—nor wished to be. There was nothing notable about him, except a slight contrast between the holiday gaiety of his clothes and the official gravity of his face. His clothes included a slight, pale grey jacket, a white waistcoat, and a silver straw hat with a grey-blue ribbon. His lean face was dark by contrast, and ended in a curt black beard that looked Spanish and suggested an Elizabethan ruff. He was smoking a cigarette with the seriousness of an idler. There was nothing about him to indicate the fact that the grey jacket covered a loaded revolver, that the white waistcoat covered a police card, or that the straw hat covered one of the most powerful intellects in Europe. For this was Valentin himself, the head of the Paris police and the most famous investigator of the world; and he was coming from Brussels to London to make the greatest arrest of the century.

Flambeau was in England. The police of three countries had tracked the great criminal at last from Ghent to Brussels, from Brussels to the Hook of Holland; and it was conjectured that he would take some advantage of the unfamiliarity and confusion of the Eucharistic Congress, then taking place in London. Probably he would travel as some minor clerk or secretary connected with it; but, of course, Valentin could not be certain; nobody could be certain about Flambeau.

It is many years now since this colossus of crime suddenly ceased, keeping the world in a turmoil; and when he ceased, as they said after the death of Roland, there was a great quiet upon the earth. But in his best days (I mean, of course, his worst) Flambeau was a figure as statuesque and international as the Kaiser. Almost every morning the daily paper announced that he had escaped the consequences of one extraordinary crime by committing another. He was a Gascon of gigantic stature and bodily daring; and the wildest tales were told of his outbursts of athletic humour; how he turned the *juge d'instruction* upside down and stood him on his head, "to clear his mind"; how he ran down the Rue de Rivoli with a policeman under each arm. It is due to him to say that his fantastic physical strength was generally employed in such bloodless though undignified scenes; his real crimes were chiefly those of ingenious and wholesale robbery. But each of his thefts was almost a new sin, and would make a story by itself. It was he who ran the great Tyrolean Dairy Company in London, with no dairies, no cows, no carts, no milk, but with some thousand subscribers. These he served by the simple operation of moving the little milk cans outside people's doors to the doors of his own customers. It was he who had kept up an unaccountable and close correspondence with a young lady whose whole letter-bag was intercepted, by the extraordinary trick of photographing his messages infinitesimally small upon the slides of a microscope. A sweeping simplicity, however, marked many of his experiments. It is said that he once repainted all the numbers in a street in the dead of night merely to divert one traveller into a trap. It is quite certain that he invented a portable pillar-box, which he put up at corners in quiet suburbs on the chance of strangers dropping postal orders into it. Lastly, he was known to be a startling acrobat; despite his huge figure, he could leap like a grasshopper and melt into the tree-tops like a monkey.

Hence the great Valentin, when he set out to find Flambeau, was perfectly aware that his adventures would not end when he had found him.

But how was he to find him? On this the great Valentin's ideas were still in process of settlement.

There was one thing which Flambeau, with all his dexterity of disguise, could not cover, and that was his singular height. If Valentin's quick eye had caught a tall apple-woman, a tall grenadier, or even a tolerably tall duchess, he might have arrested them on the spot. But all along his train there was nobody that could be a disguised Flambeau, any more than a cat could be a disguised giraffe. About the people on the boat he had already satisfied himself; and the people picked up at Harwich or on the journey limited themselves with certainty to six. There was a short railway official travelling up to the terminus, three fairly short market gardeners picked up two stations afterwards, one very short widow lady going up from a small Essex town, and a very short Roman Catholic priest going up from a small Essex village. When it came to the last case, Valentin gave it up and almost laughed. The little priest was so much the essence of those Eastern flats; he had a face as round and dull as a Norfolk dumpling; he had eyes as empty as the North Sea; he had several brown paper parcels, which he was quite incapable of collecting. The Eucharistic Congress had doubtless sucked out of their local stagnation many such creatures, blind and helpless, like moles disinterred. Valentin was a sceptic in the severe style of France, and could have no love for priests. But he could have pity for them, and this one might have provoked pity in anybody. He had a large, shabby umbrella, which constantly fell on the floor. He did not seem to know which was the right end of his return ticket. He explained with a moon-calf simplicity to everybody in the carriage that he had to be careful, because he had something made of real silver "with blue stones" in one of his brown paper parcels. His quaint blending of Essex flatness with saintly simplicity continuously amused the Frenchman till the priest arrived (somehow) at Tottenham with all his parcels, and came back for his umbrella. When he did the last, Valentin even had the good nature to warn him not to take care of the silver by telling everybody about it. But to whomever he talked, Valentin kept his eye open for someone else; he looked out steadily for anyone, rich or poor, male or female, who was well up to six feet; for Flambeau was four inches above it.

He alighted at Liverpool Street, however, quite conscientiously secure that he had not missed the criminal so far. He then went to Scotland Yard to regularise his position and arrange for help in case of need; he then lit another cigarette and went for a long stroll in the streets of London. As he was walking in the streets and squares beyond Victoria, he paused suddenly and stood. It was a quaint, quiet square, very typical of London, full of an accidental stillness. The tall, flat houses round looked at once prosperous and uninhabited; the square of shrubbery in the centre looked as deserted as a green Pacific islet. One of the four sides was much higher than the rest, like a dais; and the line of this side was broken by one of London's admirable accidents—a restaurant that looked as if it had strayed from Soho. It was an unreasonably attractive object, with dwarf plants in pots and long, striped blinds of lemon yellow and white. It stood specially high above the street, and in the usual patchwork way of London, a flight of steps from the street ran up to meet the front door almost as a fire-escape might run up to a first-floor window. Valentin stood and smoked in front of the yellow-white blinds and considered them long.

The most incredible thing about miracles is that they happen. A few clouds in heaven do come together into the staring shape of one human eye. A tree does stand up in the landscape of a doubtful journey in the exact and elaborate shape of a note of interrogation. I have seen both these things myself within the last few days. Nelson does die in the instant of victory; and a man named Williams does quite accidentally murder a man named Williamson; it sounds like a sort of infanticide. In short, there is in life an element of elfin coincidence which people reckoning on the prosaic may perpetually miss. As it has been well expressed in the paradox of Poe, wisdom should reckon on the unforeseen.

Aristide Valentin was unfathomably French; and the French in-

telligence is intelligence specially and solely. He was not "a thinking machine"; for that is a brainless phrase of modern fatalism and
materialism. A machine only *is* a machine because it cannot think.
But he was a thinking man, and a plain man at the same time. All his
wonderful successes, that looked like conjuring, had been gained by
plodding logic, by clear and commonplace French thought. The
French electrify the world not by starting any paradox, they electrify it by carrying out a truism. They carry a truism so far—as in
the French Revolution. But exactly because Valentin understood
reason, he understood the limits of reason. Only a man who knows
nothing of motors talks of motoring without petrol; only a man
who knows nothing of reason talks of reasoning without strong,
undisputed first principles. Here he had no strong first principles.
Flambeau had been missed at Harwich; and if he was in London at
all, he might be anything from a tall tramp on Wimbledon Common to a tall toastmaster at the Hôtel Métropole. In such a naked
state of nescience, Valentin had a view and a method of his own.

In such cases he reckoned on the unforeseen. In such cases, when
he could not follow the train of the reasonable, he coldly and carefully followed the train of the unreasonable. Instead of going to the
right places—banks, police stations, rendezvous—he systematically went to the wrong places; knocked at every empty house,
turned down every *cul de sac*, went up every lane blocked with rubbish, went round every crescent that led him uselessly out of the
way. He defended this crazy course quite logically. He said that if
one had a clue this was the worst way; but if one had no clue at all
it was the best, because there was just the chance that any oddity
that caught the eye of the pursuer might be the same that had
caught the eye of the pursued. Somewhere a man must begin, and
it had better be just where another man might stop. Something
about that flight of steps up to the shop, something about the quietude and quaintness of the restaurant, roused all the detective's
rare romantic fancy and made him resolve to strike at random. He
went up the steps, and sitting down at a table by the window, asked
for a cup of black coffee.

It was half-way through the morning, and he had not breakfasted; the slight litter of other breakfasts stood about on the table to remind him of his hunger; and adding a poached egg to his order, he proceeded musingly to shake some white sugar into his coffee, thinking all the time about Flambeau. He remembered how Flambeau had escaped, once by a pair of nail scissors, and once by a house on fire; once by having to pay for an unstamped letter, and once by getting people to look through a telescope at a comet that might destroy the world. He thought his detective brain as good as the criminal's, which was true. But he fully realised the disadvantage. "The criminal is the creative artist; the detective only the critic," he said with a sour smile, and lifted his coffee cup to his lips slowly, and put it down very quickly. He had put salt in it.

He looked at the vessel from which the silvery powder had come; it was certainly a sugar-basin; as unmistakably meant for sugar as a champagne-bottle for champagne. He wondered why they should keep salt in it. He looked to see if there were any more orthodox vessels. Yes; there were two salt-cellars quite full. Perhaps there was some speciality in the condiment in the salt-cellars. He tasted it; it was sugar. Then he looked round at the restaurant with a refreshed air of interest, to see if there were any other traces of that singular artistic taste which puts the sugar in the salt-cellars and the salt in the sugar-basin. Except for an odd splash of some dark fluid on one of the white-papered walls, the whole place appeared neat, cheerful and ordinary. He rang the bell for the waiter.

When that official hurried up, fuzzy-haired and somewhat bleary-eyed at that early hour, the detective (who was not without an appreciation of the simpler forms of humour) asked him to taste the sugar and see if it was up to the high reputation of the hotel. The result was that the waiter yawned suddenly and woke up.

"Do you play this delicate joke on your customers every morning?" inquired Valentin. "Does changing the salt and sugar never pall on you as a jest?"

The waiter, when this irony grew clearer, stammeringly assured him that the establishment had certainly no such intention; it must be a most curious mistake. He picked up the sugar-basin and looked at it; he picked up the salt-cellar and looked at that, his face growing more and more bewildered. At last he abruptly excused himself, and hurrying away, returned in a few seconds with the proprietor. The proprietor also examined the sugar-basin and then the salt-cellar; the proprietor also looked bewildered.

Suddenly the waiter seemed to grow inarticulate with a rush of words.

"I zink," he stuttered eagerly, "I zink it is those two clergymen."

"What two clergymen?"

"The two clergymen," said the waiter, "that threw soup at the wall."

"Threw soup at the wall?" repeated Valentin, feeling sure this must be some singular Italian metaphor.

"Yes, yes," said the attendant excitedly, and pointing at the dark splash on the white paper; "threw it over there on the wall."

Valentin looked his query at the proprietor, who came to his rescue with fuller reports.

"Yes, sir," he said, "it's quite true, though I don't suppose it has anything to do with the sugar and salt. Two clergymen came in and drank soup here very early, as soon as the shutters were taken down. They were both very quiet, respectable people; one of them paid the bill and went out; the other, who seemed a slower coach altogether, was some minutes longer getting his things together. But he went at last. Only, the instant before he stepped into the street he deliberately picked up his cup, which he had only half emptied, and threw the soup slap on the wall. I was in the back room myself, and so was the waiter; so I could only rush out in time to find the wall splashed and the shop empty. It don't do any particular damage, but it was confounded cheek; and I tried to catch the men in the street. They were too far off though; I only noticed they went round the next corner into Carstairs Street."

The detective was on his feet, hat settled and stick in hand. He had already decided that in the universal darkness of his mind he could only follow the first odd finger that pointed; and this finger was odd enough. Paying his bill and clashing the glass doors behind him, he was soon swinging round into the other street.

It was fortunate that even in such fevered moments his eye was cool and quick. Something in a shop-front went by him like a mere flash; yet he went back to look at it. The shop was a popular greengrocer and fruiterer's, an array of goods set out in the open air and plainly ticketed with their names and prices. In the two most prominent compartments were two heaps, of oranges and of nuts respectively. On the heap of nuts lay a scrap of cardboard, on which was written in bold, blue chalk, "Best tangerine oranges, two a penny." On the oranges was the equally clear and exact description, "Finest Brazil nuts, 4d. a lb." M. Valentin looked at these two placards and fancied he had met this highly subtle form of humour before, and that somewhat recently. He drew the attention of the red-faced fruiterer, who was looking rather sullenly up and down the street, to this inaccuracy in his advertisements. The fruiterer said nothing, but sharply put each card into its proper place. The detective, leaning elegantly on his walking-cane, continued to scrutinise the shop. At last he said, "Pray excuse my apparent irrelevance, my good sir, but I should like to ask you a question in experimental psychology and the association of ideas."

The red-faced shopman regarded him with an eye of menace; but he continued gaily, swinging his cane, "Why," he pursued, "why are two tickets wrongly placed in a greengrocer's shop like a shovel hat that has come to London for a holiday? Or, in case I do not make myself clear, what is the mystical association which connects the idea of nuts marked as oranges with the idea of two clergymen, one tall and the other short?"

The eyes of the tradesman stood out of his head like a snail's; he really seemed for an instant likely to fling himself upon the stranger. At last he stammered angrily: "I don't know what you 'ave to do with it, but if you're one of their friends, you can tell 'em from me that I'll knock their silly 'eads off, parsons or no parsons, if they upset my apples again."

"Indeed?" asked the detective, with great sympathy. "Did they upset your apples?"

"One of 'em did," said the heated shopman; "rolled 'em all over the street. I'd 'ave caught the fool but for havin' to pick 'em up."

"Which way did these parsons go?" asked Valentin.

"Up that second road on the left-hand side, and then across the square," said the other promptly.

"Thanks," replied Valentin, and vanished like a fairy. On the other side of the second square he found a policeman, and said: "This is urgent, constable; have you seen two clergymen in shovel hats?"

The policeman began to chuckle heavily. "I 'ave, sir; and if you arst me, one of 'em was drunk. He stood in the middle of the road that bewildered that——"

"Which way did they go?" snapped Valentin.

"They took one of them yellow buses over there," answered the man; "them that go to Hampstead."

Valentin produced his official card and said very rapidly: "Call up two of your men to come with me in pursuit," and crossed the road with such contagious energy that the ponderous policeman was moved to almost agile obedience. In a minute and a half the French detective was joined on the opposite pavement by an inspector and a man in plain clothes.

"Well, sir," began the former, with smiling importance, "and what may——?"

Valentin pointed suddenly with his cane. "I'll tell you on the top of that omnibus," he said, and was darting and dodging across the tangle of the traffic. When all three sank panting on the top seats of the yellow vehicle, the inspector said: "We could go four times as quick in a taxi."

"Quite true," replied their leader placidly, "if we only had an idea of where we were going."

"Well, where *are* you going?" asked the other, staring.

Valentin smoked frowningly for a few seconds; then, removing his cigarette, he said: "If you *know* what a man's doing, get in front of him; but if you want to guess what he's doing, keep behind him. Stray when he strays; stop when he stops; travel as slowly as he. Then you may see what he saw and may act as he acted. All we can do is to keep our eyes skinned for a queer thing."

"What sort of queer thing do you mean?" asked the inspector.

"Any sort of queer thing," answered Valentin, and relapsed into obstinate silence.

The yellow omnibus crawled up the northern roads for what seemed like hours on end; the great detective would not explain further, and perhaps his assistants felt a silent and growing doubt of his errand. Perhaps, also, they felt a silent and growing desire for lunch, for the hours crept long past the normal luncheon hour, and the long roads of the North London suburbs seemed to shoot out into length after length like an infernal telescope. It was one of those journeys on which a man perpetually feels that now at last he must have come to the end of the universe, and then finds he has only come to the beginning of Tufnell Park. London died away in draggled taverns and dreary scrubs, and then was unaccountably born again in blazing high streets and blatant hotels. It was like passing through thirteen separate vulgar cities all just touching each other. But though the winter twilight was already threatening the road ahead of them, the Parisian detective still sat silent and watchful, eyeing the frontage of the streets that slid by on either side. By the time they had left Camden Town behind, the policemen were nearly asleep; at least, they gave something like a jump as Valentin leapt erect, struck a hand on each man's shoulder, and shouted to the driver to stop.

They tumbled down the steps into the road without realising why they had been dislodged; when they looked round for enlightenment they found Valentin triumphantly pointing his finger towards a window on the left side of the road. It was a large window, forming part of the long façade of a gilt and palatial public-house; it was the part reserved for respectable dining, and labelled "Restaurant." This window, like all the rest along the frontage of the hotel, was of frosted and figured glass; but in the middle of it was a big, black smash, like a star in the ice.

"Our cue at last," cried Valentin, waving his stick; "the place with the broken window."

"What window? What cue?" asked his principal assistant. "Why, what proof is there that this has anything to do with them?"

Valentin almost broke his bamboo stick with rage.

"Proof!" he cried. "Good God! the man is looking for proof! Why, of course, the chances are twenty to one that it has *nothing* to do with them. But what else can we do? Don't you see we must either follow one wild possibility or else go home to bed?" He banged his way into the restaurant, followed by his companions, and they were soon seated at a late luncheon at a little table, and looking at the star of smashed glass from the inside. Not that it was very informative to them even then.

"Got your window broken, I see," said Valentin to the waiter as he paid the bill.

"Yes, sir," answered the attendant, bending busily over the change, to which Valentin silently added an enormous tip. The waiter straightened himself with mild but unmistakable animation.

"Ah, yes, sir," he said. "Very odd thing, that sir."

"Indeed? Tell us about it," said the detective with careless curiosity.

"Well, two gents in black came in," said the waiter; "two of those foreign parsons that are running about. They had a cheap and quiet little lunch, and one of them paid for it and went out. The other was just going out to join him when I looked at my change again and found he'd paid me more than three times too much. 'Here,' I says to the chap who was nearly out of the door, 'you've paid too much.' 'Oh,' he says, very cool, 'have we?' 'Yes,' I says, and picks up the bill to show him. Well, that was a knock-out."

"What do you mean?" asked his interlocutor.

"Well, I'd have sworn on seven Bibles that I'd put 4s. on that bill. But now I saw I'd put 14s., as plain as paint."

"Well?" cried Valentin, moving slowly, but with burning eyes, "and then?"

"The parson at the door he says all serene, 'Sorry to confuse your accounts, but it'll pay for the window.' 'What window?' I says. 'The one I'm going to break,' he says, and smashed that blessed pane with his umbrella."

All three inquirers made an exclamation; and the inspector said under his breath, "Are we after escaped lunatics?" The waiter went on with some relish for the ridiculous story:

"I was so knocked silly for a second, I couldn't do anything. The man marched out of the place and joined his friend just round the corner. Then they went so quick up Bullock Street that I couldn't catch them, though I ran round the bars to do it."

"Bullock Street," said the detective, and shot up that thoroughfare as quickly as the strange couple he pursued.

Their journey now took them through bare brick ways like tunnels; streets with few lights and even with few windows; streets that seemed built out of the blank backs of everything and everywhere. Dusk was deepening, and it was not easy even for the London policemen to guess in what exact direction they were treading. The inspector, however, was pretty certain that they would eventually strike some part of Hampstead Heath. Abruptly one bulging gas-lit window broke the blue twilight like a bull's-eye lantern; and Valentin stopped an instant before a little garish sweetstuff shop. After an instant's hesitation he went in; he stood amid the gaudy colours of the confectionery with entire gravity and bought thirteen chocolate cigars with a certain care. He was clearly preparing an opening; but he did not need one.

An angular, elderly young woman in the shop had regarded his elegant appearance with a merely automatic inquiry; but when she saw the door behind him blocked with the blue uniform of the inspector, her eyes seemed to wake up.

"Oh," she said, "if you've come about that parcel, I've sent it off already."

"Parcel!" repeated Valentin; and it was his turn to look inquiring.

"I mean the parcel the gentleman left—the clergyman gentleman."

"For goodness' sake," said Valentin, leaning forward with his first real confession of eagerness, "for Heaven's sake tell us what happened exactly."

"Well," said the woman a little doubtfully, "the clergymen came in about half an hour ago and bought some peppermints and talked a bit, and then went off towards the Heath. But a second after, one of them runs back into the shop and says, 'Have I left a parcel?' Well, I looked everywhere and couldn't see one; so he says, 'Never mind; but if it should turn up, please post it to this address,' and he left me the address and a shilling for my trouble. And sure enough, though I thought I'd looked everywhere, I found he'd left a brown paper parcel, so I posted it to the place he said. I can't remember the address now; it was somewhere in Westminster. But as the thing seemed so important, I thought perhaps the police had come about it."

"So they have," said Valentin shortly. "Is Hampstead Heath near here?"

"Straight on for fifteen minutes," said the woman, "and you'll come right out on the open." Valentin sprang out of the shop and began to run. The other detectives followed him at a reluctant trot.

The street they threaded was so narrow and shut in by shadows that when they came out unexpectedly into the void common and vast sky they were startled to find the evening still so light and clear. A perfect dome of peacock-green sank into gold amid the blackening trees and the dark violet distances. The glowing green tint was just deep enough to pick out in points of crystal one or two stars. All that was left of the daylight lay in a golden glitter across the edge of Hampstead and that popular hollow which is called the Vale of Health. The holiday makers who roam this region had not wholly dispersed; a few couples sat shapelessly on benches; and here and there a distant girl still shrieked in one of the swings. The glory of heaven deepened and darkened around the sublime vulgarity of man; and standing on the slope and looking across the valley, Valentin beheld the thing which he sought.

Among the black and breaking groups in that distance was one especially black which did not break—a group of two figures clerically clad. Though they seemed as small as insects, Valentin could see that one of them was much smaller than the other. Though the other had a student's stoop and an inconspicuous manner, he could see that the man was well over six feet high. He shut his teeth and went forward, whirling his stick impatiently. By the time he had substantially diminished the distance and magnified the two black figures as in a vast microscope, he had perceived something else; something which startled him, and yet which he had somehow expected. Whoever was the tall priest, there could be no doubt about the identity of the short one. It was his friend of the Harwich train, the stumpy little *curé* of Essex whom he had warned about his brown paper parcels.

Now, so far as this went, everything fitted in finally and rationally enough. Valentin had learned by his inquiries that morning that a Father Brown from Essex was bringing up a silver cross with sapphires, a relic of considerable value, to show some of the foreign priests at the congress. This undoubtedly was the "silver with blue stones"; and Father Brown undoubtedly was the little greenhorn in the train. Now there was nothing wonderful about the fact that what Valentin had found out Flambeau had also found out; Flambeau found out everything. Also there was nothing wonderful in the fact that when Flambeau heard of a sapphire cross he should try to steal it; that was the most natural thing in all natural history. And most certainly there was nothing wonderful about the fact that Flambeau should have it all his own way with such a silly sheep as the man with the umbrella and the parcels. He was the sort of man whom anybody could lead on a string to the North Pole; it was not surprising that an actor like Flambeau, dressed as another priest, could lead him to Hampstead Heath. So far the crime seemed clear enough; and while the detective pitied the priest for his helplessness, he almost despised Flambeau for condescending to so gullible a victim. But when Valentin thought of all that had happened in between, of all that had led him to his triumph, he racked his brains for the smallest rhyme or reason in it. What had the stealing of a blue-and-silver cross from a priest from Essex to do with chucking soup at wall paper? What had it to do with calling nuts oranges, or with paying for windows first and breaking them afterwards? He had come to the end of his chase; yet somehow he had missed the middle of it. When he failed (which was seldom), he had usually grasped the clue, but nevertheless missed the criminal. Here he had grasped the criminal, but still he could not grasp the clue.

The two figures that they followed were crawling like black flies across the huge green contour of a hill. They were evidently sunk in conversation, and perhaps did not notice where they were going; but they were certainly going to the wilder and more silent heights of the Heath. As their pursuers gained on them, the latter had to use the undignified attitudes of the deer-stalker, to crouch behind clumps of trees and even to crawl prostrate in deep grass. By these ungainly ingenuities the hunters even came close enough to the quarry to hear the murmur of the discussion, but no word could be distinguished except the word "reason" recurring frequently in a high and almost childish voice. Once over an abrupt dip of land and a dense tangle of thickets, the detectives actually lost the two figures they were following. They did not find the trail again for an agonising ten minutes, and then it led round the brow of a great dome of hill overlooking an amphitheatre of rich and desolate sunset scenery. Under a tree in this commanding yet neglected spot was an old ramshackle wooden seat. On this seat sat the two priests still in serious speech together. The gorgeous green and gold still clung to the darkening horizon; but the dome above was turning slowly from peacock-green to peacock-blue, and the stars detached themselves more and more like solid jewels. Mutely motioning to his followers, Valentin contrived to creep up behind the big branching tree, and, standing there in deathly silence, heard the words of the strange priests for the first time.

After he had listened for a minute and a half, he was gripped by a devilish doubt. Perhaps he had dragged the two English policemen to the wastes of a nocturnal heath on an errand no saner than seeking figs on its thistles. For the two priests were talking exactly like priests, piously, with learning and leisure, about the most aerial enigmas of theology. The little Essex priest spoke the more simply, with his round face turned to the strengthening stars; the other talked with his head bowed, as if he were not even worthy to look at them. But no more innocently clerical conversation could have been heard in any white Italian cloister or black Spanish cathedral.

The first he heard was the tail of one of Father Brown's sentences, which ended: ". . . what they really meant in the Middle Ages by the heavens being incorruptible."

The taller priest nodded his bowed head and said:

"Ah, yes, these modern infidels appeal to their reason; but who can look at those millions of worlds and not feel that there may well be wonderful universes above us where reason is utterly unreasonable?"

"No," said the other priest; "reason is always reasonable, even in the last limbo, in the lost borderland of things. I know that people charge the Church with lowering reason, but it is just the other way.

Alone on earth, the Church makes reason really supreme. Alone on earth, the Church affirms that God himself is bound by reason."

The other priest raised his austere face to the spangled sky and said:

"Yet who knows if in that infinite universe——?"

"Only infinite physically," said the little priest, turning sharply in his seat, "not infinite in the sense of escaping from the laws of truth."

Valentin behind his tree was tearing his fingernails with silent fury. He seemed almost to hear the sniggers of the English detectives whom he had brought so far on a fantastic guess only to listen to the metaphysical gossip of two mild old parsons. In his impatience he lost the equally elaborate answer of the tall cleric, and when he listened again it was again Father Brown who was speaking:

"Reason and justice grip the remotest and the loneliest star. Look at those stars. Don't they look as if they were single diamonds and sapphires? Well, you can imagine any mad botany or geology you please. Think of forests of adamant with leaves of brilliants. Think the moon is a blue moon, a single elephantine sapphire. But don't fancy that all that frantic astronomy would make the smallest difference to the reason and justice of conduct. On plains of opal, under cliffs cut out of pearl, you would still find a notice-board, 'Thou shalt not steal.'"

Valentin was just in the act of rising from his rigid and crouching attitude and creeping away as softly as might be, felled by the one great folly of his life. But something in the very silence of the tall priest made him stop until the latter spoke. When at last he did speak, he said simply, his head bowed and his hands on his knees:

"Well, I still think that other worlds may perhaps rise higher than our reason. The mystery of heaven is unfathomable, and I for one can only bow my head."

Then, with brow yet bent and without changing by the faintest shade his attitude or voice, he added:

"Just hand over that sapphire cross of yours, will you? We're all alone here, and I could pull you to pieces like a straw doll."

The utterly unaltered voice and attitude added a strange violence to that shocking change of speech. But the guarder of the relic only seemed to turn his head by the smallest section of the compass. He seemed still to have a somewhat foolish face turned to the stars. Perhaps he had not understood. Or, perhaps, he had understood and sat rigid with terror.

"Yes," said the tall priest, in the same low voice and in the same still posture, "yes, I am Flambeau."

Then, after a pause, he said:

"Come, will you give me that cross?"

"No," said the other, and the monosyllable had an odd sound.

Flambeau suddenly flung off all his pontifical pretensions. The great robber leaned back in his seat and laughed low but long.

"No," he cried, "you won't give it me, you proud prelate. You won't give it me, you little celibate simpleton. Shall I tell you why you won't give it me? Because I've got it already in my own breast-pocket."

The small man from Essex turned what seemed to be a dazed face in the dusk, and said, with the timid eagerness of "The Private Secretary":

"Are—are you sure?"

Flambeau yelled with delight.

"Really, you're as good as a three-act farce," he cried. "Yes, you turnip, I am quite sure. I had the sense to make a duplicate of the right parcel, and now, my friend, you've got the duplicate and I've got the jewels. An old dodge, Father Brown—a very old dodge."

"Yes," said Father Brown, and passed his hand through his hair with the same strange vagueness of manner. "Yes, I've heard of it before."

The colossus of crime leaned over to the little rustic priest with a sort of sudden interest.

"*You* have heard of it?" he asked. "Where have *you* heard of it?"

"Well, I mustn't tell you his name, of course," said the little man simply. "He was a penitent, you know. He had lived prosperously for about twenty years entirely on duplicate brown paper parcels. And so, you see, when I began to suspect you, I thought of this poor chap's way of doing it at once."

"Began to suspect me?" repeated the outlaw with increased intensity. "Did you really have the gumption to suspect me just because I brought you up to this bare part of the heath?"

"No, no," said Brown with an air of apology. "You see, I suspected you when we first met. It's that little bulge up the sleeve where you people have the spiked bracelet."

"How in Tartarus," cried Flambeau, "did you ever hear of the spiked bracelet?"

"Oh, one's little flock, you know!" said Father Brown, arching his eyebrows rather blankly. "When I was a curate in Hartlepool, there were three of them with spiked bracelets. So, as I suspected you from the first, don't you see, I made sure that the cross should go safe, anyhow. I'm afraid I watched you, you know. So at last I saw you change the parcels. Then, don't you see, I changed them back again. And then I left the right one behind."

"Left it behind?" repeated Flambeau, and for the first time there was another note in his voice beside his triumph.

"Well, it was like this," said the little priest, speaking in the same unaffected way. "I went back to that sweet-shop and asked if I'd left a parcel, and gave them a particular address if it turned up. Well, I knew I hadn't; but when I went away again I did. So, instead of running after me with that valuable parcel, they have sent it flying to a friend of mine in Westminster." Then he added rather sadly: "I learnt that, too, from a poor fellow in Hartlepool. He used to do it with handbags he stole at railway stations, but he's in a monastery now. Oh, one gets to know, you know," he added, rubbing his head again with the same sort of desperate apology. "We can't help being priests. People come and tell us these things."

Flambeau tore a brown paper parcel out of his inner pocket and rent it in pieces. There was nothing but paper and sticks of lead inside it. He sprang to his feet with a gigantic gesture, and cried:

"I don't believe you. I don't believe a bumpkin like you could manage all that. I believe you've still got the stuff on you, and if you don't give it up—why, we're all alone, and I'll take it by force!"

"No," said Father Brown simply, and stood up also, "you won't take it by force. First, because I really haven't still got it. And, second, because we are not alone."

Flambeau stopped in his stride forward.

"Behind that tree," said Father Brown, pointing, "are two strong policemen and the greatest detective alive. How did they come here, do you ask? Why, I brought them, of course! How did I do it? Why, I'll tell you if you like! Lord bless you, we have to know twenty such things when we work among the criminal classes! Well, I wasn't sure you were a thief, and it would never do to make a scandal against one of our own clergy. So I just tested you to see if anything would make you show yourself. A man generally makes a small scene if he finds salt in his coffee; if he doesn't, he has some reason for keeping quiet. I changed the salt and sugar, and *you* kept quiet. A man generally objects if his bill is three times too big. If he pays it, he has some motive for passing unnoticed. I altered your bill, and *you* paid it."

The world seemed waiting for Flambeau to leap like a tiger. But he was held back as by a spell; he was stunned with the utmost curiosity.

"Well," went on Father Brown, with lumbering lucidity, "as you wouldn't leave any tracks for the police, of course somebody had to. At every place we went to, I took care to do something that would get us talked about for the rest of the day. I didn't do much harm—a splashed wall, spilt apples, a broken window; but I saved the cross, as the cross will always be saved. It is at Westminster by now. I rather wonder you didn't stop it with the Donkey's Whistle."

"With the what?" asked Flambeau.

"I'm glad you've never heard of it," said the priest, making a face. "It's a foul thing. I'm sure you're too good a man for a Whistler. I couldn't have countered it even with the Spots myself; I'm not strong enough in the legs."

"What on earth are you talking about?" asked the other.

"Well, I did think you'd know the Spots," said Father Brown, agreeably surprised. "Oh, you can't have gone so very wrong yet!"

"How in blazes do you know all these horrors?" cried Flambeau.

The shadow of a smile crossed the round, simple face of his clerical opponent.

"Oh, by being a celibate simpleton, I suppose," he said. "Has it never struck you that a man who does next to nothing but hear men's real sins is not likely to be wholly unaware of human evil? But, as a matter of fact, another part of my trade, too, made me sure you weren't a priest."

"What?" asked the thief, almost gaping.

"You attacked reason," said Father Brown. "It's bad theology."

And even as he turned away to collect his property, the three policemen came out from under the twilight trees. Flambeau was an artist and a sportsman. He stepped back and swept Valentin a great bow.

"Do not bow to me, *mon ami*," said Valentin with silver clearness. "Let us both bow to our master."

And they both stood an instant uncovered while the little Essex priest blinked about for his umbrella.

THE SECRET GARDEN

Aristide Valentin, Chief of the Paris Police, was late for his dinner, and some of his guests began to arrive before him. These were, however, reassured by his confidential servant, Ivan, the old man with a scar, and a face almost as grey as his moustaches, who always sat at a table in the entrance hall—a hall hung with weapons. Valentin's house was perhaps as peculiar and celebrated as its master. It was an old house, with high walls and tall poplars almost overhanging the Seine; but the oddity—and perhaps the police value—of its architecture was this: that there was no ultimate exit at all except through this front door, which was guarded by Ivan and the armoury. The garden was large and elaborate, and there were many exits from the house into the garden. But there was no exit from the garden into the world outside; all round it ran a tall, smooth, unscalable wall with special spikes at the top; no bad garden, perhaps, for a man to reflect in whom some hundred criminals had sworn to kill.

As Ivan explained to the guests, their host had telephoned that he was detained for ten minutes. He was, in truth, making some last arrangements about executions and such ugly things; and though these duties were rootedly repulsive to him, he always performed them with precision. Ruthless in the pursuit of criminals, he was very mild about their punishment. Since he had been supreme over French—and largely over European—policial methods, his great influence had been honourably used for the mitigation of sentences and the purification of prisons. He was one of the great humanitarian French freethinkers; and the only thing wrong with them is that they make mercy even colder than justice.

When Valentin arrived he was already dressed in black clothes and the red rosette—an elegant figure, his dark beard already streaked with grey. He went straight through his house to his study, which opened on the grounds behind. The garden door of it was open, and after he had carefully locked his box in its official place, he stood for a few seconds at the open door looking out upon the garden. A sharp moon was fighting with the flying rags and tatters of a storm, and Valentin regarded it with a wistfulness unusual in such scientific natures as his. Perhaps such scientific natures have some psychic prevision of the most tremendous problem of their lives. From any such occult mood, at least, he quickly recovered, for he knew he was late, and that his guests had already begun to arrive. A glance at his drawing-room when he entered it was enough to make certain that his principal guest was not there, at any rate. He saw all the other pillars of the little party; he saw Lord Galloway, the English Ambassador—a choleric old man with a russet face like an apple, wearing the blue ribbon of the Garter. He saw Lady Galloway, slim and threadlike, with silver hair and a face sensitive and superior. He saw her daughter, Lady Margaret Graham, a pale and pretty girl with an elfish face and copper-coloured hair. He saw the Duchess of Mont St. Michel, black-eyed and opulent, and with her her two daughters, black-eyed and opulent also. He saw Dr. Simon, a typical French scientist, with glasses, a pointed brown beard, and a forehead barred with those parallel wrinkles which are the penalty of superciliousness, since they come through constantly elevating the eyebrows. He saw Father Brown, of Cobhole, in Essex, whom he had recently met in England. He saw—perhaps with more interest than any of these—a tall man in uniform, who had bowed to the Galloways without receiving any very hearty acknowledgment, and who now advanced alone to pay his respects to his host. This was Commandant O'Brien, of the French Foreign Legion. He was a slim yet somewhat swaggering figure, clean-shaven, dark-haired, and blue-eyed, and, as seemed natural in an officer of that famous regiment of victorious failures and successful suicides, he had an air at once dashing and melancholy. He was by birth an Irish gentleman, and in boyhood had known the Galloways—especially Margaret Graham. He had left his country after some crash of debts, and now expressed his complete freedom from British etiquette by swinging about in uniform, sabre and spurs. When he bowed to the Ambassador's family, Lord and Lady Galloway bent stiffly, and Lady Margaret looked away.

But for whatever old causes such people might be interested in each other, their distinguished host was not specially interested in them. No one of them at least was in his eyes the guest of the evening. Valentin was expecting, for special reasons, a man of world-wide fame, whose friendship he had secured during some of his great detective tours and triumphs in the United States. He was expecting Julius K. Brayne, that multi-millionaire whose colossal and even crushing endowments of small religions have occasioned so much easy sport and easier solemnity for the American and English papers. Nobody could quite make out whether Mr. Brayne was an atheist or a Mormon or a Christian Scientist; but he was ready to pour money into any intellectual vessel, so long as it was an untried vessel. One of his hobbies was to wait for the American Shakespeare—a hobby more patient than angling. He admired Walt Whitman, but thought that Luke P. Tanner, of Paris, Pa., was more "progressive" than Whitman any day. He liked anything that he thought "progressive." He thought Valentin "progressive," thereby doing him a grave injustice.

The solid appearance of Julius K. Brayne in the room was as decisive as a dinner bell. He had this great quality, which very few of us can claim, that his presence was as big as his absence. He was a huge fellow, as fat as he was tall, clad in complete evening black, without so much relief as a watch-chain or a ring. His hair was white and well brushed back like a German's; his face was red, fierce and cherubic, with one dark tuft under the lower lip that threw up that otherwise infantile visage with an effect theatrical and even Mephistophelean. Not long, however, did that *salon* merely stare at the celebrated American; his lateness had already become a domestic problem, and he was sent with all speed into the dining-room with Lady Galloway on his arm.

Except on one point the Galloways were genial and casual enough. So long as Lady Margaret did not take the arm of that adventurer O'Brien, her father was quite satisfied; and she had not done so, she had decorously gone in with Dr. Simon. Nevertheless, old Lord Galloway was restless and almost rude. He was diplomatic enough during dinner, but when, over the cigars, three of the younger men—Simon the doctor, Brown the priest, and the detrimental O'Brien, the exile in a foreign uniform—all melted away to mix with the ladies or smoke in the conservatory, then the English diplomatist grew very undiplomatic indeed. He was stung every sixty seconds with the thought that the scamp O'Brien might be signalling to Margaret somehow; he did not attempt to imagine how. He was left over the coffee with Brayne, the hoary Yankee who believed in all religions, and Valentin, the grizzled Frenchman who believed in none. They could argue with each other, but neither could appeal to him. After a time this "progressive" logomachy had reached a crisis of tedium; Lord Galloway got up also and sought the drawing-room. He lost his way in long passages for some six or eight minutes: till he heard the high-pitched, didactic voice of the doctor, and then the dull voice of the priest, followed by general laughter. They also, he thought with a curse, were probably arguing about "science and religion." But the instant he opened the *salon* door he saw only one thing—he saw what was not there. He saw that Commandant O'Brien was absent, and that Lady Margaret was absent too.

Rising impatiently from the drawing-room, as he had from the dining-room, he stamped along the passage once more. His notion of protecting his daughter from the Irish-Algerian ne'er-do-well had become something central and even mad in his mind. As he went towards the back of the house, where was Valentin's study, he was surprised to meet his daughter, who swept past with a white, scornful face, which was a second enigma. If she had been with

O'Brien, where was O'Brien? If she had not been with O'Brien, where had she been? With a sort of senile and passionate suspicion he groped his way to the dark back parts of the mansion, and eventually found a servants' entrance that opened on to the garden. The moon with her scimitar had now ripped up and rolled away all the storm-wrack. The argent light lit up all four corners of the garden. A tall figure in blue was striding across the lawn towards the study door; a glint of moonlit silver on his facings picked him out as Commandant O'Brien.

He vanished through the French windows into the house, leaving Lord Galloway in an indescribable temper, at once virulent and vague. The blue-and-silver garden, like a scene in a theatre, seemed to taunt him with all that tyrannic tenderness against which his worldly authority was at war. The length and grace of the Irishman's stride enraged him as if he were a rival instead of a father; the moonlight maddened him. He was trapped as if by magic into a garden of troubadours, a Watteau fairyland; and, willing to shake off such amorous imbecilities by speech, he stepped briskly after his enemy. As he did so he tripped over some tree or stone in the grass; looked down at it first with irritation and then a second time with curiosity. The next instant the moon and the tall poplars looked at an unusual sight—an elderly English diplomatist running hard and crying or bellowing as he ran.

His hoarse shouts brought a pale face to the study door, the beaming glasses and worried brow of Dr. Simon, who heard the nobleman's first clear words. Lord Galloway was crying: "A corpse in the grass—a blood-stained corpse." O'Brien at least had gone utterly out of his mind.

"We must tell Valentin at once," said the doctor, when the other had brokenly described all that he had dared to examine. "It is fortunate that he is here"; and even as he spoke the great detective entered the study, attracted by the cry. It was almost amusing to note his typical transformation; he had come with the common concern of a host and a gentleman, fearing that some guest or servant was ill. When he was told the gory fact, he turned with all his gravity instantly bright and businesslike; for this, however abrupt and awful, was his business.

"Strange, gentlemen," he said as they hurried out into the garden, "that I should have hunted mysteries all over the earth, and now one comes and settles in my own back-yard. But where is the place?" They crossed the lawn less easily, as a slight mist had begun to rise from the river; but under the guidance of the shaken Galloway they found the body sunken in deep grass—the body of a very tall and broad-shouldered man. He lay face downwards, so they could only see that his big shoulders were clad in black cloth, and that his big head was bald, except for a wisp or two of brown hair that clung to his skull like wet seaweed. A scarlet serpent of blood crawled from under his fallen face.

"At least," said Simon, with a deep and singular intonation, "he is none of our party."

"Examine him, doctor," cried Valentin rather sharply. "He may not be dead."

The doctor bent down. "He is not quite cold, but I am afraid he is dead enough," he answered. "Just help me to lift him up."

They lifted him carefully an inch from the ground, and all doubts as to his being really dead were settled at once and frightfully. The head fell away. It had been entirely sundered from the body; whoever had cut his throat had managed to sever the neck as well. Even Valentin was slightly shocked. "He must have been as strong as a gorilla," he muttered.

Not without a shiver, though he was used to anatomical abortions, Dr. Simon lifted the head. It was slightly slashed about the neck and jaw, but the face was substantially unhurt. It was a ponderous, yellow face, at once sunken and swollen, with a hawk-like nose and heavy lids—the face of a wicked Roman emperor, with, perhaps, a distant touch of a Chinese emperor. All present seemed to look at it with the coldest eye of ignorance. Nothing else could be noted about the man except that, as they had lifted his body, they had seen underneath it the white gleam of a shirt-front defaced with a red gleam of blood. As Dr. Simon said, the man had never been of their party. But he might very well have been trying to join it, for he had come dressed for such an occasion.

Valentin went down on his hands and knees and examined with his closest professional attention the grass and ground for some twenty yards round the body, in which he was assisted less skilfully by the doctor, and quite vaguely by the English lord. Nothing rewarded their grovellings except a few twigs, snapped or chopped into very small lengths, which Valentin lifted for an instant's examination and then tossed away.

"Twigs," he said gravely; "twigs, and a total stranger with his head cut off; that is all there is on this lawn."

There was an almost creepy stillness, and then the unnerved Galloway called out sharply:

"Who's that? Who's that over there by the garden wall?"

A small figure with a foolishly large head drew waveringly near them in the moonlit haze; looked for an instant like a goblin, but turned out to be the harmless little priest whom they had left in the drawing-room.

"I say," he said meekly, "there are no gates to this garden, do you know."

Valentin's black brows had come together somewhat crossly, as they did on principle at the sight of the cassock. But he was far too just a man to deny the relevance of the remark. "You are right," he said. "Before we find out how he came to be killed, we may have to find out how he came to be here. Now listen to me, gentlemen. If it can be done without prejudice to my position and duty, we shall all agree that certain distinguished names might well be kept out of this. There are ladies, gentlemen, and there is a foreign ambassador. If we must mark it down as a crime, then it must be followed up as a crime. But till then I can use my own discretion. I am the head of the police; I am so public that I can afford to be private. Please Heaven, I will clear every one of my own guests before I call in my men to look for anybody else. Gentlemen, upon your honour, you will none of you leave the house till to-morrow at noon; there are bedrooms for all. Simon, I think you know where to find my man, Ivan, in the front hall; he is a confidential man. Tell him to leave another servant on guard and come to me at once. Lord Galloway, you are certainly the best person to tell the ladies what has happened, and prevent a panic. They also must stay. Father Brown and I will remain with the body."

When this spirit of the captain spoke in Valentin he was obeyed like a bugle. Dr. Simon went through to the armoury and routed out Ivan, the public detective's private detective. Galloway went to the drawing-room and told the terrible news tactfully enough, so that by the time the company assembled there the ladies were already startled and already soothed. Meanwhile the good priest and the good atheist stood at the head and foot of the dead man motionless in the moonlight, like symbolic statues of their two philosophies of death.

Ivan, the confidential man with the scar and the moustaches, came out of the house like a cannon ball, and came racing across the lawn to Valentin like a dog to his master. His livid face was quite lively with the glow of this domestic detective story, and it was with almost unpleasant eagerness that he asked his master's permission to examine the remains.

"Yes; look, if you like, Ivan," said Valentin, "but don't be long. We must go in and thrash this out in the house."

Ivan lifted the head, and then almost let it drop.

"Why," he gasped, "it's—no, it isn't; it can't be. Do you know this man, sir?"

"No," said Valentin indifferently; "we had better go inside."

Between them they carried the corpse to a sofa in the study, and then all made their way to the drawing-room.

The detective sat down at a desk quietly, and even with hesitation; but his eye was the iron eye of a judge at assize. He made a few rapid notes upon paper in front of him, and then said shortly: "Is everybody here?"

"Not Mr. Brayne," said the Duchess of Mont St. Michel, looking round.

"No," said Lord Galloway in a hoarse, harsh voice. "And not Mr. Neil O'Brien, I fancy. I saw that gentleman walking in the garden when the corpse was still warm."

"Ivan," said the detective, "go and fetch Commandant O'Brien and Mr. Brayne. Mr. Brayne, I know, is finishing a cigar in the dining-room; Commandant O'Brien, I think, is walking up and down the conservatory. I am not sure."

The faithful attendant flashed from the room, and before anyone could stir or speak Valentin went on with the same soldierly swiftness of exposition.

"Everyone here knows that a dead man has been found in the garden, his head cut clean from his body. Dr. Simon, you have examined it. Do you think that to cut a man's throat like that would need great force? Or, perhaps, only a very sharp knife?"

"I should say that it could not be done with a knife at all," said the pale doctor.

"Have you any thought," resumed Valentin, "of a tool with which it could be done?"

"Speaking within modern probabilities, I really haven't," said the doctor, arching his painful brows. "It's not easy to hack a neck through even clumsily, and this was a very clean cut. It could be done with a battle-axe or an old headsman's axe, or an old two-handed sword."

"But, good heavens!" cried the Duchess, almost in hysterics, "there aren't any two-handed swords and battle-axes round here."

Valentin was still busy with the paper in front of him. "Tell me," he said, still writing rapidly, "could it have been done with a long French cavalry sabre?"

A low knocking came at the door, which, for some unreasonable reason, curdled everyone's blood like the knocking in Macbeth. Amid that frozen silence Dr. Simon managed to say: "A sabre—yes, I suppose it could."

"Thank you," said Valentin. "Come in, Ivan."

The confidential Ivan opened the door and ushered in Commandant Neil O'Brien, whom he had found at last pacing the garden again.

The Irish officer stood up disordered and defiant on the threshold. "What do you want with me?" he cried.

"Please sit down," said Valentin in pleasant, level tones. "Why, you aren't wearing your sword. Where is it?"

"I left it on the library table," said O'Brien, his brogue deepening in his disturbed mood. "It was a nuisance, it was getting——"

"Ivan," said Valentin, "please go and get the Commandant's sword from the library." Then, as the servant vanished, "Lord Galloway says he saw you leaving the garden just before he found the corpse. What were you doing in the garden?"

The Commandant flung himself recklessly into a chair. "Oh," he cried in pure Irish, "admirin' the moon. Communing with Nature, me bhoy."

A heavy silence sank and endured, and at the end of it came again that trivial and terrible knocking. Ivan reappeared, carrying an empty steel scabbard. "This is all I can find," he said.

"Put it on the table," said Valentin, without looking up.

There was an inhuman silence in the room, like that sea of inhuman silence round the dock of the condemned murderer. The Duchess's weak exclamations had long ago died away. Lord Galloway's swollen hatred was satisfied and even sobered. The voice that came was quite unexpected.

"I think I can tell you," cried Lady Margaret, in that clear, quivering voice with which a courageous woman speaks publicly. "I can tell you what Mr. O'Brien was doing in the garden, since he is bound to silence. He was asking me to marry him. I refused; I said in my family circumstances I could give him nothing but my respect. He was a little angry at that; he did not seem to think much of my respect. I wonder," she added, with rather a wan smile, "if he will care at all for it now. For I offer it him now. I will swear anywhere that he never did a thing like this."

Lord Galloway had edged up to his daughter, and was intimidating her in what he imagined to be an undertone. "Hold your tongue, Maggie," he said in a thunderous whisper. "Why should you shield the fellow? Where's his sword? Where's his confounded cavalry——"

He stopped because of the singular stare with which his daughter was regarding him, a look that was indeed a lurid magnet for the whole group.

"You old fool!" she said, in a low voice without pretence of piety, "what do you suppose you are trying to prove? I tell you this man was innocent while with me. But if he wasn't innocent, he was still with me. If he murdered a man in the garden, who was it who must have seen—who must at least have known? Do you hate Neil so much as to put your own daughter——"

Lady Galloway screamed. Everyone else sat tingling at the touch of those satanic tragedies that have been between lovers before now. They saw the proud, white face of the Scotch aristocrat and her lover, the Irish adventurer, like old portraits in a dark house. The long silence was full of formless historical memories of murdered husbands and poisonous paramours.

In the centre of this morbid silence an innocent voice said: "Was it a very long cigar?"

The change of thought was so sharp that they had to look round to see who had spoken.

"I mean," said little Father Brown, from the corner of the room, "I mean that cigar Mr. Brayne is finishing. It seems nearly as long as a walking-stick."

Despite the irrelevance there was assent as well as irritation in Valentin's face as he lifted his head.

"Quite right," he remarked sharply. "Ivan, go and see about Mr. Brayne again, and bring him here at once."

The instant the factotum had closed the door, Valentin addressed the girl with an entirely new earnestness.

"Lady Margaret," he said, "we all feel, I am sure, both gratitude and admiration for your act in rising above your lower dignity and explaining the Commandant's conduct. But there is a hiatus still. Lord Galloway, I understand, met you passing from the study to the drawing-room, and it was only some minutes afterwards that he found the garden and the Commandant still walking there."

"You have to remember," replied Margaret, with a faint irony in her voice, "that I had just refused him, so we should scarcely have come back arm in arm. He is a gentleman, anyhow; and he loitered behind—and so got charged with murder."

"In those few moments," said Valentin gravely, "he might really——"

The knock came again, and Ivan put in his scarred face.

"Beg pardon, sir," he said, "but Mr. Brayne has left the house."

"Left!" cried Valentin, and rose for the first time to his feet.

"Gone. Scooted. Evaporated," replied Ivan, in humorous French. "His hat and coat are gone, too, and I'll tell you something to cap it all. I ran outside the house to find any traces of him, and I found one, and a big trace, too."

"What do you mean?" asked Valentin.

"I'll show you," said his servant, and reappeared with a flashing naked cavalry sabre, streaked with blood about the point and edge. Everyone in the room eyed it as if it were a thunderbolt; but the experienced Ivan went on quite quietly:

"I found this," he said, "flung among the bushes fifty yards up the road to Paris. In other words, I found it just where your respectable Mr. Brayne threw it when he ran away."

There was again a silence, but of a new sort. Valentin took the sabre, examined it, reflected with unaffected concentration of thought, and then turned a respectful face to O'Brien. "Commandant," he said, "we trust you will always produce this weapon if it is wanted for police examination. Meanwhile," he added, slapping the steel back in the ringing scabbard, "let me return you your sword."

At the military symbolism of the action the audience could hardly refrain from applause.

For Neil O'Brien, indeed, that gesture was the turning-point of existence. By the time he was wandering in the mysterious garden again in the colours of the morning the tragic futility of his ordinary mien had fallen from him; he was a man with many reasons for happiness. Lord Galloway was a gentleman, and had offered him an apology. Lady Margaret was something better than a lady, a woman at least, and had perhaps given him something better than an apology, as they drifted among the old flower-beds before breakfast. The whole company was more light-hearted and humane, for though the riddle of the death remained, the load of suspicion was lifted off them all, and sent flying off to Paris with the strange millionaire—a man they hardly knew. The devil was cast out of the house—he had cast himself out.

Still, the riddle remained; and when O'Brien threw himself on a garden seat beside Dr. Simon, that keenly scientific person at once resumed it. He did not get much talk out of O'Brien, whose thoughts were on pleasanter things.

"I can't say it interests me much," said the Irishman frankly, "especially as it seems pretty plain now. Apparently Brayne hated this stranger for some reason; lured him into the garden, and killed him with my sword. Then he fled to the city, tossing the sword away as he went. By the way, Ivan tells me the dead man had a Yankee dollar in his pocket. So he was a countryman of Brayne's, and that seems to clinch it. I don't see any difficulties about the business."

"There are five colossal difficulties," said the doctor quietly; "like high walls within walls. Don't mistake me. I don't doubt that Brayne did it; his flight, I fancy, proves that. But as to how he did it. First difficulty: Why should a man kill another man with a great hulking sabre, when he can almost kill him with a pocket knife and put it back in his pocket? Second difficulty: Why was there no noise or outcry? Does a man commonly see another come up waving a scimitar and offer no remarks? Third difficulty: A servant watched the front door all the evening; and a rat cannot get into Valentin's garden anywhere. How did the dead man get into the garden? Fourth difficulty: Given the same conditions, how did Brayne get out of the garden?"

"And the fifth," said Neil, with eyes fixed on the English priest who was coming slowly up the path.

"Is a trifle, I suppose," said the doctor, "but I think an odd one. When I first saw how the head had been slashed, I supposed the assassin had struck more than once. But on examination I found many cuts across the truncated section; in other words, they were struck *after* the head was off. Did Brayne hate his foe so fiendishly that he stood sabring his body in the moonlight?"

"Horrible!" said O'Brien, and shuddered.

The little priest, Brown, had arrived while they were talking, and had waited, with characteristic shyness, till they had finished. Then he said awkwardly:

"I say, I'm sorry to interrupt. But I was sent to tell you the news!"

"News?" repeated Simon, and stared at him rather painfully through his glasses.

"Yes, I'm sorry," said Father Brown mildly. "There's been another murder, you know."

Both men on the seat sprang up, leaving it rocking.

"And, what's stranger still," continued the priest, with his dull eye on the rhododendrons, "it's the same disgusting sort; it's another beheading. They found the second head actually bleeding into the river, a few yards along Brayne's road to Paris; so they suppose that he——"

"Great Heaven!" cried O'Brien. Is Brayne a monomaniac?"

"There are American vendettas," said the priest impassively. Then he added: "They want you to come to the library and see it."

Commandant O'Brien followed the others towards the inquest, feeling decidedly sick. As a soldier, he loathed all this secretive carnage; where were these extravagant amputations going to stop? First one head was hacked off, and then another; in this case (he told himself bitterly) it was not true that two heads were better than one. As he crossed the study he almost staggered at a shocking coincidence. Upon Valentin's table lay the coloured picture of yet a third bleeding head; and it was the head of Valentin himself. A second glance showed him it was only a Nationalist paper, called *The Guillotine*, which every week showed one of its political opponents with rolling eyes and writhing features just after execution; for Valentin was an anti-clerical of some note. But O'Brien was an Irishman, with a kind of chastity even in his sins; and his gorge rose against that great brutality of the intellect which belongs only to France. He felt Paris as a whole, from the grotesques on the Gothic churches to the gross caricatures in the newspapers. He remembered the gigantic jests of the Revolution. He saw the whole city as one ugly energy, from the sanguinary sketch lying on Valentin's table up to where, above a mountain and forest of gargoyles, the great devil grins on Notre Dame.

The library was long, low, and dark; what light entered it shot from under low blinds and had still some of the ruddy tinge of morning. Valentin and his servant Ivan were waiting for them at the upper end of a long, slightly-sloping desk, on which lay the mortal remains, looking enormous in the twilight. The big black figure and yellow face of the man found in the garden confronted them essentially unchanged. The second head, which had been fished from among the river reeds that morning, lay streaming and dripping beside it; Valentin's men were still seeking to recover the rest of this second corpse, which was supposed to be afloat. Father Brown, who did not seem to share O'Brien's sensibilities in the least, went up to the second head and examined it with his blinking care. It was little more than a mop of wet white hair, fringed with silver fire in the red and level morning light; the face, which seemed of an ugly, empurpled and perhaps criminal type, had been much battered against trees or stones as it tossed in the water.

"Good morning, Commandant O'Brien," said Valentin, with quiet cordiality. "You have heard of Brayne's last experiment in butchery, I suppose?"

Father Brown was still bending over the head with white hair, and he said, without looking up:

"I suppose it is quite certain that Brayne cut off this head, too."

"Well, it seems common sense," said Valentin, with his hands in his pockets. "Killed in the same way as the other. Found within a few yards of the other. And sliced by the same weapon which we know he carried away."

"Yes, yes; I know," replied Father Brown submissively. "Yet, you know, I doubt whether Brayne could have cut off this head."

"Why not?" inquired Dr. Simon, with a rational stare.

"Well, doctor," said the priest, looking up blinking, "can a man cut off his own head? I don't know."

O'Brien felt an insane universe crashing about his ears; but the doctor sprang forward with impetuous practicality and pushed back the wet white hair.

"Oh, there's no doubt it's Brayne," said the priest quietly. "He had exactly that chip in the left ear."

The detective, who had been regarding the priest with steady and glittering eyes, opened his clenched mouth and said sharply: "You seem to know a lot about him, Father Brown."

"I do," said the little man simply. "I've been about with him for some weeks. He was thinking of joining our church."

The star of the fanatic sprang into Valentin's eyes; he strode towards the priest with clenched hands. "And, perhaps," he cried, with a blasting sneer, "perhaps he was also thinking of leaving all his money to your church."

"Perhaps he was," said Brown stolidly; "it is possible."

"In that case," cried Valentin, with a dreadful smile, "you may indeed know a great deal about him. About his life and about his——"

Commandant O'Brien laid a hand on Valentin's arm. "Drop that slanderous rubbish, Valentin," he said, "or there may be more swords yet."

But Valentin (under the steady, humble gaze of the priest) had already recovered himself. "Well," he said shortly, "people's private opinions can wait. You gentlemen are still bound by your promise to stay; you must enforce it on yourselves—and on each other. Ivan here will tell you anything more you want to know; I must get to business and write to the authorities. We can't keep this quiet any longer. I shall be writing in my study if there is any more news."

"Is there any more news, Ivan?" asked Dr. Simon, as the chief of police strode out of the room.

"Only one more thing, I think, sir," said Ivan, wrinkling up his grey old face, "but that's important, too, in its way. There's that old buffer you found on the lawn," and he pointed without pretence of reverence at the big black body with the yellow head. "We've found out who he is, anyhow."

"Indeed!" cried the astonished doctor, "and who is he?"

"His name was Arnold Becker," said the under-detective, "though he went by many aliases. He was a wandering sort of scamp, and is known to have been in America; so that was where Brayne got his knife into him. We didn't have much to do with him ourselves, for he worked mostly in Germany. We've communicated, of course, with the German police. But, oddly enough, there was a twin brother of his, named Louis Becker, whom we had a great deal to do with. In fact, we found it necessary to guillotine him only yesterday. Well, it's a rum thing, gentlemen, but when I saw that fellow flat on the lawn I had the greatest jump of my life. If I hadn't seen Louis Becker guillotined with my own eyes, I'd have sworn it was Louis Becker lying there in the grass. Then, of course, I remembered his twin brother in Germany, and following up the clue——"

The explanatory Ivan stopped, for the excellent reason that nobody was listening to him. The Commandant and the doctor were both staring at Father Brown, who had sprung stiffly to his feet, and was holding his temples tight like a man in sudden and violent pain.

"Stop, stop, stop!" he cried; "stop talking a minute, for I see half. Will God give me strength? Will my brain make the one jump and see all? Heaven help me! I used to be fairly good at thinking. I could paraphrase any page in Aquinas once. Will my head split—or will it see? I see half—I only see half."

He buried his head in his hands, and stood in a sort of rigid torture of thought or prayer, while the other three could only go on staring at this last prodigy of their wild twelve hours.

When Father Brown's hands fell they showed a face quite fresh and serious, like a child's. He heaved a huge sigh, and said: "Let us get this said and done with as quickly as possible. Look here, this will be the quickest way to convince you all of the truth." He turned to the doctor. "Dr. Simon," he said, "you have a strong headpiece, and I heard you this morning asking the five hardest questions about this business. Well, if you will ask them again, I will answer them."

Simon's pince-nez dropped from his nose in his doubt and wonder, but he answered at once. "Well, the first question, you know, is why a man should kill another with a clumsy sabre at all when a man can kill with a bodkin?"

"A man cannot behead with a bodkin," said Brown calmly, "and for *this* murder beheading was absolutely necessary."

"Why?" asked O'Brien, with interest.

"And the next question?" asked Father Brown.

"Well, why didn't the man cry out or anything?" asked the doctor; "sabres in gardens are certainly unusual."

"Twigs," said the priest gloomily, and turned to the window which looked on the scene of death. "No one saw the point of the twigs. Why should they lie on that lawn (look at it) so far from any tree? They were not snapped off; they were chopped off. The murderer occupied his enemy with some tricks with the sabre, showing how he could cut a branch in mid-air, or whatnot. Then, while his enemy bent down to see the result, a silent slash, and the head fell."

"Well," said the doctor slowly, "that seems plausible enough. But my next two questions will stump anyone."

The priest still stood looking critically out of the window and waited.

"You know how all the garden was sealed up like an air-tight chamber," went on the doctor. "Well, how did the strange man get into the garden?"

Without turning round, the little priest answered: "There never was any strange man in the garden."

There was a silence, and then a sudden cackle of almost childish laughter relieved the strain. The absurdity of Brown's remark moved Ivan to open taunts.

"Oh!" he cried; "then we didn't lug a great fat corpse on to a sofa last night? He hadn't got into the garden, I suppose?"

"Got into the garden?" repeated Brown reflectively. "No, not entirely."

"Hang it all," cried Simon, "a man gets into a garden, or he doesn't."

"Not necessarily," said the priest, with a faint smile. "What is the next question, doctor?"

"I fancy you're ill," exclaimed Dr. Simon sharply; "but I'll ask the next question if you like. How did Brayne get out of the garden?"

"He didn't get out of the garden," said the priest, still looking out of the window.

"Didn't get out of the garden?" exploded Simon.

"Not completely," said Father Brown.

Simon shook his fists in a frenzy of French logic. "A man gets out of a garden, or he doesn't," he cried.

"Not always," said Father Brown.

Dr. Simon sprang to his feet impatiently. "I have no time to spare on such senseless talk," he cried angrily. "If you can't understand a man being on one side of a wall or the other, I won't trouble you further."

"Doctor," said the cleric very gently, "we have always got on very pleasantly together. If only for the sake of old friendship, stop and tell me your fifth question."

The impatient Simon sank into a chair by the door and said

briefly: "The head and shoulders were cut about in a queer way. It seemed to be done after death."

"Yes," said the motionless priest, "it was done so as to make you assume exactly the one simple falsehood that you did assume. It was done to make you take for granted that the head belonged to the body."

The borderland of the brain, where all the monsters are made, moved horribly in the Gaelic O'Brien. He felt the chaotic presence of all the horse-men and fish-women that man's unnatural fancy has begotten. A voice older than his first fathers seemed saying in his ear: "Keep out of the monstrous garden where grows the tree with double fruit. Avoid the evil garden where died the man with two heads." Yet, while these shameful symbolic shapes passed across the ancient mirror of his Irish soul, his Frenchified intellect was quite alert, and was watching the odd priest as closely and incredulously as all the rest.

Father Brown had turned round at last, and stood against the window with his face in dense shadow; but even in that shadow they could see it was pale as ashes. Nevertheless, he spoke quite sensibly, as if there were no Gaelic souls on earth.

"Gentlemen," he said, "you did not find the strange body of Becker in the garden. You did not find any strange body in the garden. In face of Dr. Simon's rationalism, I still affirm that Becker was only partly present. Look here!" (pointing to the black bulk of the mysterious corpse) "you never saw that man in your lives. Did you ever see this man?"

He rapidly rolled away the bald, yellow head of the unknown, and put in its place the white-maned head beside it. And there, complete, unified, unmistakable, lay Julius K. Brayne.

"The murderer," went on Brown quietly, "hacked off his enemy's head and flung the sword far over the wall. But he was too clever to fling the sword only. He flung the *head* over the wall also. Then he had only to clap on another head to the corpse, and (as he insisted on a private inquest) you all imagined a totally new man."

"Clap on another head!" said O'Brien staring.

"What other head? Heads don't grow on garden bushes, do they?"

"No," said Father Brown huskily, and looking at his boots; "there is only one place where they grow. They grow in the basket of the guillotine, beside which the chief of Police, Aristide Valentin, was standing not an hour before the murder. Oh, my friends, hear me a minute more before you tear me in pieces. Valentin is an honest man, if being mad for an arguable cause is honesty. But did you never see in that cold, grey eye of his that he is mad? He would do anything, *anything,* to break what he calls the superstition of the Cross. He has fought for it and starved for it, and now he has murdered for it. Brayne's crazy millions had hitherto been scattered among so many sects that they did little to alter the balance of things. But Valentin heard a whisper that Brayne, like so many scatter-brained sceptics, was drifting to us; and that was quite a different thing. Brayne would pour supplies into the impoverished and pugnacious Church of France; he would support six Nationalist newspapers like *The Guillotine.* The battle was already balanced on a point, and the fanatic took flame at the risk. He resolved to destroy the millionaire, and he did it as one would expect the greatest of detectives to commit his only crime. He abstracted the severed head of Becker on some criminological excuse, and took it home in his official box. He had that last argument with Brayne, that Lord Galloway did not hear the end of; that failing, he led him out into the sealed garden, talked about swordsmanship, used twigs and a sabre for illustration, and——"

Ivan of the Scar sprang up. "You lunatic," he yelled; "you'll go to my master now, if I take you by——"

"Why, I was going there," said Brown heavily; "I must ask him to confess, and all that."

Driving the unhappy Brown before them like a hostage or sacrifice, they rushed together into the sudden stillness of Valentin's study.

The great detective sat at his desk apparently too occupied to hear their turbulent entrance. They paused a moment, and then something in the look of that upright and elegant back made the doctor run forward suddenly. A touch and a glance showed him that there was a small box of pills at Valentin's elbow, and that Valentin was dead in his chair; and on the blind face of the suicide was more than the pride of Cato.

THE QUEER FEET

If you meet a member of that select club, The Twelve True Fishermen, entering the Vernon Hotel for the annual club dinner, you will observe, as he takes off his overcoat, that his evening coat is green and not black. If (supposing that you have the star-defying audacity to address such a being) you ask him why, he will probably answer that he does it to avoid being mistaken for a waiter. You will then retire crushed. But you will leave behind you a mystery as yet unsolved and a tale worth telling.

If (to pursue the same vein of improbable conjecture) you were to meet a mild, hard-working little priest, named Father Brown, and were to ask him what he thought was the most singular luck of his life, he would probably reply that upon the whole his best stroke was at the Vernon Hotel, where he had averted a crime and, perhaps, saved a soul, merely by listening to a few footsteps in a passage. He is perhaps a little proud of this wild and wonderful guess of his, and it is possible that he might refer to it. But since it is immeasurably unlikely that you will ever rise high enough in the social world to find The Twelve True Fishermen, or that you will ever sink low enough among slums and criminals to find Father Brown, I fear you will never hear the story at all unless you hear it from me.

The Vernon Hotel at which The Twelve True Fishermen held their annual dinners was an institution such as can only exist in an oligarchical society which has almost gone mad on good manners. It was that topsy-turvy product—an "exclusive" commercial enterprise. That is, it was a thing which paid not by attracting people, but actually by turning people away. In the heart of a plutocracy tradesmen become cunning enough to be more fastidious than their customers. They positively create difficulties so that their wealthy and weary clients may spend money and diplomacy in overcoming them. If there were a fashionable hotel in London which no man could enter who was under six foot, society would meekly make up parties of six-foot men to dine in it. If there were an expensive restaurant which by a mere caprice of its proprietor was only open on Thursday afternoon, it would be crowded on Thursday afternoon. The Vernon Hotel stood, as if by accident, in the corner of a square in Belgravia. It was a small hotel; and a very inconvenient one. But its very inconveniences were considered as walls protecting a particular class. One inconvenience, in particular, was held to be of vital importance: the fact that practically only twenty-four people could dine in the place at once. The only big dinner table was the celebrated terrace table, which stood open to the air on a sort of veranda overlooking one of the most exquisite old gardens in London. Thus it happened that even the twenty-four seats at this table could only be enjoyed in warm weather; and this making the enjoyment yet more difficult made it yet more desired. The existing owner of the hotel was a Jew named Lever; and he made nearly a million out of it, by making it difficult to get into. Of course he combined with this limitation in the scope of his enterprise the most careful polish in its performance. The wines and cooking were really as good as any in Europe, and the demeanour of the attendants exactly mirrored the fixed mood of the English upper class. The proprietor knew all his waiters like the fingers on his hand; there were only fifteen of them all told. It was much easier to become a Member of Parliament than to become a waiter in that hotel. Each waiter was trained in terrible silence and smoothness, as if he were a gentleman's servant. And, indeed, there was generally at least one waiter to every gentleman who dined.

The club of The Twelve True Fishermen would not have consented to dine anywhere but in such a place, for it insisted on a luxurious privacy; and would have been quite upset by the mere thought that any other club was even dining in the same building. On the occasion of their annual dinner the Fishermen were in the habit of exposing all their treasures, as if they were in a private house, especially the celebrated set of fish knives and forks which were, as it were, the insignia of the society, each being exquisitely wrought in silver in the form of a fish, and each loaded at the hilt with one large pearl. These were always laid out for the fish course, and the fish course was always the most magnificent in that magnificent repast. The society had a vast number of ceremonies and observances, but it had no history and no object; that was where it was so very aristocratic. You did not have to be anything in order to be one of the Twelve Fishers; unless you were already a certain sort of person, you never even heard of them. It had been in existence twelve years. Its president was Mr. Audley. Its vice-president was the Duke of Chester.

If I have in any degree conveyed the atmosphere of this appalling hotel, the reader may feel a natural wonder as to how I came to know anything about it, and may even speculate as to how so ordinary a person as my friend Father Brown came to find himself in that golden galley. As far as that is concerned, my story is simple, or even vulgar. There is in the world a very aged rioter and demagogue who breaks into the most refined retreats with the dreadful information that all men are brothers, and wherever this leveller went on his pale horse it was Father Brown's trade to follow. One of the waiters, an Italian, had been struck down with a paralytic stroke that afternoon; and his Jewish employer, marvelling mildly at such superstitions, had consented to send for the nearest Popish priest. With what the waiter confessed to Father Brown we are not concerned, for the excellent reason that that cleric kept it to himself; but apparently it involved him in writing out a note or statement for the conveying of some message or the righting of some wrong. Father Brown, therefore, with a meek impudence which he would have shown equally in Buckingham Palace, asked to be provided with a room and writing materials. Mr. Lever was torn in two. He was a kind man, and had also that bad imitation of kindness, the dislike of any difficulty or scene. At the same time the presence of one unusual stranger in his hotel that evening was like a speck of dirt on something just cleaned. There was never any borderland or anteroom in the Vernon Hotel, no people waiting in the hall, no customers coming in on chance. There were fifteen waiters. There were twelve guests. It would be as startling to find a new guest in the hotel that night as to find a new brother taking breakfast or tea in one's own family. Moreover, the priest's appearance was second-rate and his clothes muddy; a mere glimpse of him afar off might precipitate a crisis in the club. Mr. Lever at last hit on a plan to cover, since he might not obliterate, the disgrace. When you enter (as you never will) the Vernon Hotel, you pass down a short passage decorated with a few dingy but important pictures, and come to the main vestibule and lounge which opens on your right into passages leading to the public rooms, and on your left to a similar passage pointing to the kitchens and offices of the hotel. Immediately on your left hand is the corner of a glass office, which abuts upon the lounge—a house within a house, so to sepak, like the old hotel bar which probably once occupied its place.

In this office sat the representative of the proprietor (nobody in this place ever appeared in person if he could help it), and just beyond the office, on the way to the servants' quarters, was the gentlemen's cloak room, the last boundary of the gentlemen's domain. But between the office and the cloak room was a small private room without other outlet, sometimes used by the proprietor for delicate and important matters, such as lending a duke a thousand pounds or declining to lend him sixpence. It is a mark of the magnificent tolerance of Mr. Lever that he permitted this holy place to be for about half an hour profaned by a mere priest, scribbling away on a piece of paper. The story which Father Brown was writing down was very likely a much better story than this one, only it will never be known. I can merely state that it was very nearly as long, and that the last two or three paragraphs of it were the least exciting and absorbing.

For it was by the time that he had reached these that the priest began a little to allow his thoughts to wander and his animal senses, which were commonly keen, to awaken. The time of darkness and dinner was drawing on; his own forgotten little room was without a light, and perhaps the gathering gloom, as occasionally happens, sharpened the sense of sound. As Father Brown wrote the last and least essential part of his document, he caught himself writing to the rhythm of a recurrent noise outside, just as one sometimes thinks to the tune of a railway train. When he became conscious of the thing he found what it was: only the ordinary patter of feet passing the door, which in an hotel was no very unlikely matter. Nevertheless, he stared at the darkened ceiling, and listened to the sound. After he had listened for a few seconds dreamily, he got to his feet and listened intently, with his head a little on one side. Then he sat down again and buried his brow in his hands, now not merely listening, but listening and thinking also.

The footsteps outside at any given moment were such as one might hear in any hotel; and yet, taken as a whole, there was something very strange about them. There were no other footsteps. It was always a very silent house, for the few familiar guests went at once to their own apartments, and the well-trained waiters were told to be almost invisible until they were wanted. One could not conceive any place where there was less reason to apprehend anything irregular. But these footsteps were so odd that one could not decide to call them regular or irregular. Father Brown followed them with his finger on the edge of the table, like a man trying to learn a tune on the piano.

First, there came a long rush of rapid little steps, such as a light man might make in winning a walking race. At a certain point they stopped and changed to a sort of slow, swinging stamp, numbering not a quarter of the steps, but occupying about the same time. The moment the last echoing stamp had died away would come again the run or ripple of light, hurrying feet, and then again the thud of the heavier walking. It was certainly the same pair of boots, partly because (as has been said) there were no other boots about, and partly because they had a small but unmistakable creak in them. Father Brown had the kind of head that cannot help asking questions; and on this apparently trivial question his head almost split. He had seen men run in order to jump. He had seen men run in order to slide. But why on earth should a man run in order to walk? Or, again, why should he walk in order to run? Yet no other description would cover the antics of this invisible pair of legs. The man was either walking very fast down one-half of the corridor in order to walk very slow down the other half; or he was walking very slow at one end to have the rapture of walking fast at the other. Neither suggestion seemed to make much sense. His brain was growing darker and darker, like his room.

Yet, as he began to think steadily, the very blackness of his cell seemed to make his thoughts more vivid; he began to see as in a kind of vision the fantastic feet capering along the corridor in unnatural or symbolic attitudes. Was it a heathen religious dance? Or some entirely new kind of scientific exercise? Father Brown began to ask himself with more exactness what the steps suggested. Taking the slow step first: it certainly was not the step of the proprietor. Men of his type walk with a rapid waddle, or they sit still. It could not be any servant or messenger waiting for directions. It did not sound like it. The poorer orders (in an oligarchy) sometimes lurch about when they are slightly drunk, but generally, and especially in such gorgeous scenes, they stand or sit in constrained attitudes. No; that heavy yet springy step, with a kind of careless emphasis, not specially noisy, yet not caring what noise it made, belonged to only one of the animals of this earth. It was a gentleman of western Europe, and probably one who had never worked for his living.

Just as he came to this solid certainty, the step changed to the quicker one, and ran past the door as feverishly as a rat. The listener remarked that though this step was much swifter it was also much more noiseless, almost as if the man were walking on tiptoe. Yet it was not associated in his mind with secrecy, but with something else—something that he could not remember. He was maddened by one of those half-memories that make a man feel half-witted. Surely he had heard that strange, swift walking somewhere. Suddenly he sprang to his feet with a new idea in his head, and walked to the door. His room had no direct outlet on the passage, but let on one side into the glass office, and on the other into the cloak room beyond. He tried the door into the office, and found it locked. Then he looked at the window, now a square pane full of purple cloud cleft by livid sunset, and for an instant he smelt evil as a dog smells rats.

The rational part of him (whether the wiser or not) regained its supremacy. He remembered that the proprietor had told him that he should lock the door, and would come later to release him. He told himself that twenty things he had not thought of might explain the eccentric sounds outside; he reminded himself that there was just enough light left to finish his own proper work. Bringing his paper to the window so as to catch the last stormy evening light, he resolutely plunged once more into the almost completed record. He had written for about twenty minutes, bending closer and closer to his paper in the lessening light; then suddenly he sat upright. He had heard the strange feet once more.

This time they had a third oddity. Previously the unknown man had walked, with levity indeed and lightning quickness, but he had walked. This time he ran. One could hear the swift, soft, bounding steps coming along the corridor, like the pads of a fleeing and leaping panther. Whoever was coming was a very strong, active man, in still yet tearing excitement. Yet, when the sound had swept up to the office like a sort of whispering whirlwind, it suddenly changed again to the old slow, swaggering stamp.

Father Brown flung down his paper, and, knowing the office door to be locked, went at once into the cloak room on the other side. The attendant of this place was temporarily absent, probably because the only guests were at dinner and his office was a sinecure. After groping through a grey forest of overcoats, he found that the dim cloak room opened on the lighted corridor in the form of a sort of counter of half-door, like most of the counters across which we have all handed umbrellas and received tickets. There was a light immediately above the semicircular arch of this opening. It threw little illumination on Father Brown himself, who seemed a mere dark outline against the dim sunset window behind him. But it threw an almost theatrical light on the man who stood outside the cloak room in the corridor.

He was an elegant man in very plain evening dress; tall, but with an air of not taking up much room; one felt that he could have slid along like a shadow where many smaller men would have been obvious and obstructive. His face, now flung back in the lamplight, was swarthy and vivacious, the face of a foreigner. His figure was good, his manners good humoured and confident; a critic could only say that his black coat was a shade below his figure and manners, and even bulged and bagged in an odd way. The moment he caught sight of Brown's black silhouette against the sunset, he tossed down a scrap of paper with a number and called out with amiable authority: "I want my hat and coat, please; I find I have to go away at once."

Father Brown took the paper without a word, and obediently went to look for the coat; it was not the first menial work he had done in his life. He brought it and laid it on the counter; meanwhile, the strange gentleman who had been feeling in his waistcoat pocket, said laughing: "I haven't got any silver; you can keep this." And he threw down half a sovereign, and caught up his coat.

Father Brown's figure remained quite dark and still; but in that instant he had lost his head. His head was always most valuable when he had lost it. In such moments he put two and two together and made four million. Often the Catholic Church (which is wedded to common sense) did not approve of it. Often he did not approve of it himself. But it was real inspiration—important at rare crises—when whosoever shall lose his head the same shall save it.

"I think, sir," he said civilly, "that you have some silver in your pocket."

The tall gentleman stared. "Hang it," he cried, "if I choose to give you gold, why should you complain?"

"Because silver is sometimes more valuable than gold," said the priest mildly; "that is, in large quantities."

The stranger looked at him curiously. Then he looked still more curiously up the passage towards the main entrance. Then he looked back at Brown again, and then he looked very carefully at the window beyond Brown's head, still coloured with the afterglow of the storm. Then he seemed to make up his mind. He put one hand on the counter, vaulted over as easily as an acrobat and

towered above the priest, putting one tremendous hand upon his collar.

"Stand still," he said, in a hacking whisper. "I don't want to threaten you, but——"

"I do want to threaten you," said Father Brown, in a voice like a rolling drum, "I want to threaten you with the worm that dieth not, and the fire that is not quenched."

"You're a rum sort of cloak-room clerk," said the other.

"I am a priest, Monsieur Flambeau," said Brown, "and I am ready to hear your confession."

The other stood gasping for a few moments, and then staggered back into a chair.

The first two courses of the dinner of The Twelve True Fishermen had proceeded with placid success. I do not possess a copy of the menu; and if I did it would not convey anything to anybody. It was written in a sort of super-French employed by cooks, but quite unintelligible to Frenchmen. There was a tradition in the club that the *hors d'œuvres* should be various and manifold to the point of madness. They were taken seriously because they were avowedly useless extras, like the whole dinner and the whole club. There was also a tradition that the soup course should be light and unpretending— a sort of simple and austere vigil for the feast of fish that was to come. The talk was that strange, slight talk which governs the British Empire, which governs it in secret, and yet would scarcely enlighten an ordinary Englishman even if he could overhear it. Cabinet ministers on both sides were alluded to by their Christian names with a sort of bored benignity. The Radical Chancellor of the Exchequer, whom the whole Tory party was supposed to be cursing for his extortions, was praised for his minor poetry, or his saddle in the hunting field. The Tory leader, whom all Liberals were supposed to hate as a tyrant, was discussed and, on the whole, praised—as a Liberal. It seemed somehow that politicians were very important. And yet, anything seemed important about them except their politics. Mr. Audley, the chairman, was an amiable, elderly man who still wore Gladstone collars; he was a kind of symbol of all that phantasmal and yet fixed society. He had never done anything—not even anything wrong. He was not fast; he was not even particularly rich. He was simply in the thing; and there was an end of it. No party could ignore him, and if he had wished to be in the Cabinet he certainly would have been put there. The Duke of Chester, the vice-president, was a young and rising politician. That is to say, he was a pleasant youth, with flat, fair hair and a freckled face, with moderate intelligence and enormous estates. In public his appearances were always successful and his principle was simple enough. When he thought of a joke he made it, and was called brilliant. When he could not think of a joke he said that this was no time for trifling, and was called able. In private, in a club of his own class, he was simply quite pleasantly frank and silly, like a schoolboy. Mr. Audley, never having been in politics, treated them a little more seriously. Sometimes he even embarrassed the company by phrases suggesting that there was some difference between a Liberal and a Conservative. He himself was a Conservative, even in private life. He had a roll of grey hair over the back of his collar, like certain old-fashioned statesmen, and seen from behind he looked like the man the empire wants. Seen from the front he looked like a mild, self-indulgent bachelor, with rooms in the Albany—which he was.

As has been remarked, there were twenty-four seats at the terrace table, and only twelve members of the club. Thus they could occupy the terrace in the most luxurious style of all, being ranged along the inner side of the table, with no one opposite, commanding an uninterrupted view of the garden, the colours of which were still vivid, though evening was closing in somewhat luridly for the time of year. The chairman sat in the centre of the line, and the vice-president at the right-hand end of it. When the twelve guests first trooped into their seats it was the custom (for some unknown reason) for all the fifteen waiters to stand lining the wall like troops presenting arms to the king, while the fat proprietor stood and bowed to the club with radiant surprise, as if he had never heard of them before. But before the first chink of knife and fork this army of retainers had vanished, only the one or two required to collect and distribute the plates darting about in deathly silence. Mr. Lever, the proprietor, of course had disappeared in convulsions of courtesy long before. It would be exaggerative, indeed irreverent, to say that he ever positively appeared again. But when the important course, the fish course, was being brought on, there was—how shall I put it?—a vivid shadow, a projection of his personality, which told that he was hovering near. The sacred fish course consisted (to the eyes of the vulgar) in a sort of monstrous pudding, about the size and shape of a wedding cake, in which some considerable number of interesting fishes had finally lost the shapes which God had given to them. The Twelve True Fishermen took up their celebrated fish knives and fish forks, and approached it as gravely as if every inch of the pudding cost as much as the silver fork it was eaten with. So it did, for all I know. This course was dealt with in eager and devouring silence; and it was only when his plate was nearly empty that the young duke made the ritual remark: "They can't do this anywhere but here."

"Nowhere," said Mr. Audley, in a deep bass voice, turning to the speaker and nodding his venerable head a number of times. "Nowhere, assuredly, except here. It was represented to me that at the Café Anglais——"

Here he was interrupted and even agitated for a moment by the removal of his plate, but he recaptured the valuable thread of his thoughts. "It was represented to me that the same could be done at the Café Anglais. Nothing like it, sir," he said, shaking his head ruthlessly, like a hanging judge. "Nothing like it."

"Overrated place," said a certain Colonel Pound, speaking (by the look of him) for the first time for some months.

"Oh, I don't know," said the Duke of Chester, who was an optimist, "it's jolly good for some things. You can't beat it at——"

A waiter came swiftly along the room, and then stopped dead. His stoppage was as silent as his tread; but all those vague and kindly gentlemen were so used to the utter smoothness of the unseen machinery which surrounded and supported their lives, that a waiter doing anything unexpected was a start and a jar. They felt as you and I would feel if the inanimate world disobeyed—if a chair ran away from us.

The waiter stood staring a few seconds, while there deepened on every face at table a strange shame which is wholly the product of our time. It is the combination of modern humanitarianism with the horrible modern abyss between the souls of the rich and poor. A genuine historic aristocrat would have thrown things at the waiter, beginning with empty bottles, and very probably ending with money. A genuine democrat would have asked him, with a comrade-like clearness of speech, what the devil he was doing. But these modern plutocrats could not bear a poor man near to them, either as a slave or as a friend. That something had gone wrong with the servants was merely a dull, hot embarrassment. They did not want to be brutal, and they dreaded the need to be benevolent. They wanted the thing, whatever it was, to be over. It was over. The waiter, after standing for some seconds rigid, like a cataleptic, turned round and ran madly out of the room.

When he reappeared in the room, or rather in the doorway, it was in company with another waiter, with whom he whispered and gesticulated with southern fierceness. Then the first waiter went away, leaving the second waiter, and reappeared with a third waiter. By the time a fourth waiter had joined this hurried synod, Mr. Audley felt it necessary to break the silence in the interests of Tact. He used a very loud cough, instead of a presidential hammer, and said: "Splendid work young Moocher's doing in Burmah. Now, no other nation in the world could have——"

A fifth waiter had sped towards him like an arrow, and was whispering in his ear: "So sorry. Important! Might the proprietor speak to you?"

The chairman turned in disorder, and with a dazed stare saw Mr. Lever coming towards them with his lumbering quickness. The gait of the good proprietor was indeed his usual gait, but his face was by no means usual. Generally it was a genial copper-brown; now it was a sickly yellow.

"You will pardon me, Mr. Audley," he said, with asthmatic breathlessness. "I have great apprehensions. Your fish-plates, they are cleared away with the knife and fork on them!"

"Well, I hope so," said the chairman, with some warmth.

"You see him?" panted the excited hotel keeper; "you see the waiter who took them away? You know him?"

"Know the waiter?" answered Mr. Audley indignantly. "Certainly not!"

Mr. Lever opened his hands with a gesture of agony. "I never send him," he said. "I know not when or why he come. I send my waiter to take away the plates, and he find them already away."

Mr. Audley still looked rather too bewildered to be really the man the empire wants; none of the company could say anything except the man of wood—Colonel Pound—who seemed galvanised into an unnatural life. He rose rigidly from his chair, leaving all the rest sitting, screwed his eyeglass into his eye, and spoke in a raucous undertone as if he had half-forgotten how to speak. "Do you mean," he said, "that somebody has stolen our silver fish service?"

The proprietor repeated the open-handed gesture with even greater helplessness; and in a flash all the men at the table were on their feet.

"Are all your waiters here?" demanded the colonel, in his low, harsh accent.

"Yes; they're all here. I noticed it myself," cried the young duke, pushing his boyish face into the inmost ring. "Always count 'em as I come in; they look so queer standing up against the wall."

"But surely one cannot exactly remember," began Mr. Audley, with heavy hesitation.

"I remember exactly, I tell you," cried the duke excitedly. "There never have been more than fifteen waiters at this place, and there were no more than fifteen to-night, I'll swear; no more and no less."

The proprietor turned upon him, quaking in a kind of palsy of surprise. "You say—you say," he stammered, "that you see all my fifteen waiters?"

"As usual," assented the duke. "What is the matter with that?"

"Nothing," said Lever, with a deepening accent, "only you did not. For one of zem is dead upstairs."

There was a shocking stillness for an instant in that room. It may be (so supernatural is the word death) that each of those idle men looked for a second at his soul, and saw it as a small dried pea. One of them—the duke, I think—even said with the idiotic kindness of wealth: "Is there anything we can do?"

"He has had a priest," said the Jew, not untouched.

Then, as to the clang of doom, they awoke to their own position. For a few weird seconds they had really felt as if the fifteenth waiter might be the ghost of the dead man upstairs. They had been dumb under that oppression, for ghosts were to them an embarrassment, like beggars. But the remembrance of the silver broke the spell of the miraculous; broke it abruptly and with a brutal reaction. The colonel flung over his chair and strode to the door. "If there was a fifteenth man here, friends," he said, "that fifteenth fellow was a thief. Down at once to the front and back doors and secure everything; then we'll talk. The twenty-four pearls of the club are worth recovering."

Mr. Audley seemed at first to hesitate about whether it was gentlemanly to be in such a hurry about anything; but, seeing the duke dash down the stairs with youthful energy, he followed with a more mature motion.

At the same instant a sixth waiter ran into the room, and declared that he had found the pile of fish-plates on a sideboard, with no trace of the silver.

The crowd of diners and attendants that tumbled helter-skelter down the passages divided into two groups. Most of the Fishermen followed the proprietor to the front room to demand news of any exit. Colonel Pound, with the chairman, the vice-president, and one or two others, darted down the corridor leading to the servants' quarters, as the more likely line of escape. As they did so they passed the dim alcove or cavern of the cloak room, and saw a short, black-coated figure, presumably an attendant, standing a little way back in the shadow of it.

"Hallo, there!" called out the duke. "Have you seen anyone pass?"

The short figure did not answer the question directly, but merely said: "Perhaps I have got what you are looking for, gentlemen."

They paused, wavering and wondering, while he quietly went to the back of the cloak room, and came back with both hands full of shining silver, which he laid out on the counter as calmly as a salesman. It took the form of a dozen quaintly shaped forks and knives.

"You—you——" began the colonel, quite thrown off his balance at last. Then he peered into the dim little room and saw two things: first, that the short, black-clad man was dressed like a clergyman; and, second, that the window of the room behind him was burst, as if someone had passed violently through.

"Valuable things to deposit in a cloak room, aren't they?" remarked the clergyman, with cheerful composure.

"Did—did you steal those things?" stammered Mr. Audley, with staring eyes.

"If I did," said the cleric pleasantly, "at least I am bringing them back again."

"But you didn't," said Colonel Pound, still staring at the broken window.

"To make a clean breast of it, I didn't," said the other, with some humour. And he seated himself quite gravely on a stool.

"But you know who did," said the colonel.

"I don't know his real name," said the priest placidly, "but I know something of his fighting weight, and a great deal about his spiritual difficulties. I formed the physical estimate when he was trying to throttle me, and the moral estimate when he repented."

"Oh, I say—repented!" cried young Chester, with a sort of crow of laughter.

Father Brown got to his feet, putting his hands behind him. "Odd, isn't it," he said, "that a thief and a vagabond should repent, when so many who are rich and secure remain hard and frivolous, and without fruit for God or man? But there, if you will excuse me, you trespass a little upon my province. If you doubt the penitence as a practical fact, there are your knives and forks. You are the Twelve True Fishers, and there are all your silver fish. But He has made me a fisher of men."

"Did you catch this man?" asked the colonel, frowning.

Father Brown looked him full in his frowning face. "Yes," he said, "I caught him, with an unseen hook and an invisible line which is long enough to let him wander to the ends of the world, and still to bring him back with a twitch upon the thread."

There was a long silence. All the other men present drifted away to carry the recovered silver to their comrades, or to consult the proprietor about the queer condition of affairs. But the grim-faced colonel still sat sideways on the counter, swinging his long, lank legs and biting his dark moustache.

At last he said quietly to the priest: "He must have been a clever fellow, but I think I know a cleverer."

"He was a clever fellow," answered the other, "but I am not quite sure of what other you mean."

"I mean you," said the colonel, with a short laugh. "I don't want to get the fellow jailed; make yourself easy about that. But I'd give a good many silver forks to know exactly how you fell into this affair, and how you got the stuff out of him. I reckon you're the most up-to-date devil of the present company."

Father Brown seemed rather to like the saturnine candour of the soldier. "Well," he said, smiling, "I mustn't tell you anything of the man's identity, or his own story, of course; but there's no particular reason why I shouldn't tell you of the mere outside facts which I found out for myself."

He hopped over the barrier with unexpected activity, and sat beside Colonel Pound, kicking his short legs like a little boy on a gate. He began to tell the story as easily as if he were telling it to an old friend by a Christmas fire.

"You see, colonel," he said, "I was shut up in that small room there doing some writing, when I heard a pair of feet in this passage doing a dance that was as queer as the dance of death. First came quick, funny little steps, like a man walking on tiptoe for a wager; then came slow, careless, creaking steps, as of a big man walking about with a cigar. But they were both made by the same feet, I swear, and they came in rotation; first the run and then the walk, and then the run again. I wondered at first idly and then wildly why a man should act these two parts at once. One walk I knew; it was just like yours, colonel. It was the walk of a well-fed gentleman waiting for something, who strolls about rather because he is physically alert than because he is mentally impatient. I knew that I knew the other walk, too, but I could not remember what it was. What wild creature had I met on my travels that tore along on tiptoe in that extraordinary style? Then I heard a clink of plates some-where; and the answer stood up as plain as St. Peter's. It was the walk of a waiter—that walk with the body slanted forward, the eyes looking down, the ball of the toe spurning away the ground, the coat tails and napkin flying. Then I thought for a minute and a half more. And I believe I saw the manner of the crime, as clearly as if I were going to commit it."

Colonel Pound looked at him keenly, but the speaker's mild grey eyes were fixed upon the ceiling with almost empty wistfulness.

"A crime," he said slowly, "is like any other work of art. Don't look surprised; crimes are by no means the only works of art that come from an infernal workshop. But every work of art, divine or diabolic, has one indispensable mark—I mean, that the centre of it is simple, however much the fulfilment may be complicated. Thus, in *Hamlet*, let us say, the grotesqueness of the grave-digger, the flowers of the mad girl, the fantastic finery of Osric, the pallor of the ghost and the grin of the skull are all oddities in a sort of tan-gled wreath round one plain tragic figure of a man in black. Well, this also," he said, getting slowly down from his seat with a smile, "this also is the plain tragedy of a man in black. Yes," he went on, seeing the colonel look up in some wonder, "the whole of this tale turns on a black coat. In this, as in *Hamlet*, there are the rococo excrescences—yourselves, let us say. There is the dead waiter, who was there when he could not be there. There is the invisible hand that swept your table clear of silver and melted into air. But every clever crime is founded ultimately on some one quite simple fact—some fact that is not itself mysterious. The mystification comes in covering it up, in leading men's thoughts away from it. This large and subtle and (in the ordinary course) most profitable crime, was built on the plain fact that a gentleman's evening dress is the same as a waiter's. All the rest was acting, and thundering good acting, too."

"Still," said the colonel, getting up and frowning at his boots, "I am not sure that I understand."

"Colonel," said Father Brown, "I tell you that this archangel of impudence who stole your forks walked up and down this passage twenty times in the blaze of all the lamps, in the glare of all the eyes. He did not go and hide in dim corners where suspicion might have searched for him. He kept constantly on the move in the lighted corridors, and everywhere that he went he seemed to be there by right. Don't ask me what he was like; you have seen him yourself six or seven times to-night. You were waiting with all the other grand people in the reception room at the end of the passage there, with the terrace just beyond. Whenever he came among you gentlemen, he came in the lightning style of a waiter, with bent head, flapping napkin and flying feet. He shot out on to the terrace, did something to the table cloth, and shot back again towards the office and the waiters' quarters. By the time he had come under the eye of the office clerk and the waiters he had become another man in every inch of his body, in every instinctive gesture. He strolled among the servants with the absent-minded insolence which they have all seen in their patrons. It was no new thing to them that a swell from the dinner party should pace all parts of the house like an animal at the Zoo; they know that nothing marks the Smart Set more than a habit of walking where one chooses. When he was magnificently weary of walking down that particular passage he would wheel round and pace back past the office; in the shadow of the arch just beyond he was altered as by a blast of magic, and went hurrying forward again among the Twelve Fishermen, an obsequious attendant. Why should the gentlemen look at a chance waiter? Why should the waiters suspect a first-rate walking gentleman? Once or twice he played the coolest tricks. In the proprietor's private quarters he called out breezily for a syphon of soda water, saying he was thirsty. He said genially that he would carry it himself, and he did; he carried it quickly and correctly through the thick of you, a waiter with an obvious errand. Of course, it could not have been kept up long, but it only had to be kept up till the end of the fish course.

"His worst moment was when the waiters stood in a row; but even then he contrived to lean against the wall just round the corner in such a way that for that important instant the waiters thought him a gentleman, while the gentlemen thought him a waiter. The rest went like winking. If any waiter caught him away from the table, that waiter caught a languid aristocrat. He had only to time himself two minutes before the fish was cleared, become a swift servant, and clear it himself. He put the plates down on a sideboard, stuffed the silver in his breast pocket, giving it a bulgy look, and ran like a hare (I heard him coming) till he came to the cloak room. There he had only to be a plutocrat again—a plutocrat called away suddenly on business. He had only to give his ticket to the cloak-room attendant, and go out again elegantly as he had come in. Only—only I happened to be the cloak-room attendant."

"What did you do to him?" cried the colonel, with unusual intensity. "What did he tell you?"

"I beg your pardon," said the priest immovably, "that is where the story ends."

"And the interesting story begins," muttered Pound. "I think I understand his professional trick. But I don't seem to have got hold of yours."

"I must be going," said Father Brown.

They walked together along the passage to the entrance hall, where they saw the fresh, freckled face of the Duke of Chester, who was bounding buoyantly along towards them.

"Come along, Pound," he cried breathlessly. "I've been looking for you everywhere. The dinner's going again in spanking style, and old Audley has got to make a speech in honour of the forks being saved. We want to start some new ceremony, don't you know, to commemorate the occasion. I say, you really got the goods back, what do you suggest?"

"Why," said the colonel, eyeing him with a certain sardonic approval, "I should suggest that henceforward we wear green coats, instead of black. One never knows what mistakes may arise when one looks so like a waiter."

"Oh, hang it all!" said the young man, "a gentleman never looks like a waiter."

"Nor a waiter like a gentleman, I suppose," said Colonel Pound, with the same lowering laughter on his face. "Reverend sir, your friend must have been very smart to act the gentleman."

Father Brown buttoned up his commonplace overcoat to the neck, for the night was stormy, and took his commonplace umbrella from the stand.

"Yes," he said; "it must be very hard work to be a gentleman; but, do you know, I have sometimes thought that it may be almost as laborious to be a waiter."

And saying "Good evening," he pushed open the heavy doors of that palace of pleasures. The golden gates closed behind him, and he went at a brisk walk through the damp, dark streets in search of a penny omnibus.

THE FLYING STARS

"The most beautiful crime I ever committed," Flambeau would say in his highly moral old age, "was also, by a singular coincidence, my last. It was committed at Christmas. As an artist I had always attempted to provide crimes suitable to the special season or landscapes in which I found myself, choosing this or that terrace or garden for a catastrophe, as if for a statuary group. Thus squires should be swindled in long rooms panelled with oak; while Jews, on the other hand, should rather find themselves unexpectedly penniless among the lights and screens of the Café Riche. Thus, in England, if I wished to relieve a dean of his riches (which is not so easy as you might suppose), I wished to frame him, if I make myself clear, in the green lawns and grey towers of some cathedral town. Similarly, in France, when I had got money out of a rich and wicked peasant (which is almost impossible), it gratified me to get his indignant head relieved against a grey line of clipped poplars, and those solemn plains of Gaul over which broods the mighty spirit of Millet.

"Well, my last crime was a Christmas crime, a cheery, cosy, English middle-class crime; a crime of Charles Dickens. I did it in a good old middle-class house near Putney, a house with a crescent of carriage drive, a house with a stable by the side of it, a house with the name on the two outer gates, a house with a monkey tree. Enough, you know the species. I really think my imitation of Dickens's style was dexterous and literary. It seems almost a pity I repented the same evening."

Flambeau would then proceed to tell the story from the inside; and even from the inside it was odd. Seen from the outside it was perfectly incomprehensible, and it is from the outside that the stranger must study it. From this standpoint the drama may be said to have begun when the front doors of the house with the stable opened on the garden with the monkey tree, and a young girl came out with bread to feed the birds on the afternoon of Boxing Day. She had a pretty face, with brave brown eyes; but her figure was beyond conjecture, for she was so wrapped up in brown furs that it was hard to say which was hair and which was fur. But for the attractive face she might have been a small toddling bear.

The winter afternoon was reddening towards evening, and already a ruby light was rolled over the bloomless beds, filling them, as it were, with the ghosts of the dead roses. On one side of the house stood the stable, on the other an alley or cloister of laurels led to the larger garden behind.

The young lady, having scattered bread for the birds (for the fourth or fifth time that day, because the dog ate it), passed unobtrusively down the lane of laurels and into a glimmering plantation of evergreens behind. Here she gave an exclamation of wonder, real or ritual, and looking up at the high garden wall above her, beheld it fantastically bestridden by a somewhat fantastic figure.

"Oh, don't jump, Mr. Crook," she called out in some alarm; "it's much too high."

The individual riding the party wall like an aerial horse was a tall, angular young man, with dark hair sticking up like a hair brush, intelligent and even distinguished lineaments, but a sallow and almost alien complexion. This showed the more plainly because he wore an aggressive red tie, the only part of his costume of which he seemed to take any care. Perhaps it was a symbol. He took no notice of the girl's alarmed adjuration, but leapt like a grasshopper to the ground beside her, where he might very well have broken his legs.

"I think I was meant to be a burglar," he said placidly, "and I have no doubt I should have been if I hadn't happened to be born in that nice house next door. I can't see any harm in it, anyhow."

"How can you say such things?" she remonstrated.

"Well," said the young man, "if you're born on the wrong side of the wall, I can't see that it's wrong to climb over it."

"I never know what you will say or do next," she said.

"I don't often know myself," replied Mr. Crook; "but then I am on the right side of the wall now."

"And which is the right side of the wall?" asked the young lady, smiling.

"Whichever side you are on," said the young man named Crook.

As they went together through the laurels towards the front garden a motor horn sounded thrice, coming nearer and nearer, and a car of splendid speed, great elegance, and a pale green colour swept up to the front doors like a bird and stood throbbing.

"Hullo, hullo!" said the young man with the red tie, "here's somebody born on the right side, anyhow. I didn't know, Miss Adams, that your Santa Claus was so modern as this."

"Oh, that's my godfather, Sir Leopold Fischer. He always comes on Boxing Day."

Then, after an innocent pause, which unconsciously betrayed some lack of enthusiasm, Ruby Adams added:

"He is very kind."

John Crook, journalist, had heard of that eminent City magnate; and it was not his fault if the City magnate had not heard of him; for in certain articles in *The Clarion* or *The New Age* Sir Leopold had been dealt with austerely. But he said nothing and grimly watched the unloading of the motor-car, which was rather a long process. A large, neat chauffeur in green got out from the front, and a small, neat man-servant in grey got out from the back, and between them they deposited Sir Leopold on the doorstep and began to unpack him, like some very carefully protected parcel. Rugs enough to stock a bazaar, furs of all the beasts of the forest, and scarves of all the colours of the rainbow were unwrapped one by one, till they revealed something resembling the human form; the form of a friendly, but foreign-looking old gentleman, with a grey goat-like beard and a beaming smile, who rubbed his big fur gloves together.

Long before this revelation was complete the two big doors of the porch had opened in the middle, and Colonel Adams (father of the furry young lady) had come out himself to invite his eminent guest inside. He was a tall, sunburnt, and very silent man, who wore a red smoking-cap like a fez, making him look like one of the English Sirdars or Pashas in Egypt. With him was his brother-in-law, lately come from Canada, a big and rather boisterous young gentleman-farmer, with a yellow beard, by name James Blount. With him also was the more insignificant figure of the priest from the neighbouring Roman Church; for the colonel's late wife had been a Catholic, and the children, as is common in such cases, had been trained to follow her. Everything seemed undistinguished about the priest, even down to his name, which was Brown; yet the colonel had always found something companionable about him, and frequently asked him to such family gatherings.

In the large entrance hall of the house there was ample room even for Sir Leopold and the removal of his wraps. Porch and vestibule, indeed, were unduly large in proportion to the house, and formed, as it were, a big room with the front door at one end, and the bottom of the staircase at the other. In front of the large hall fire, over which hung the colonel's sword, the process was completed and the company, including the saturnine Crook, presented to Sir Leopold Fischer. That venerable financier, however, still seemed struggling with portions of his well-lined attire, and at length produced from a very interior tail-coat pocket, a black oval case which he radiantly explained to be his Christmas present for his goddaughter. With an unaffected vain-glory that had something disarming about it he held out the case before them all; it flew open at a touch and half-blinded them. It was just as if a crystal fountain had spurted in their eyes. In a nest of orange velvet lay like three eggs, three white and vivid diamonds that seemed to set the very air on fire all round them. Fischer stood beaming benevolently and drinking deep of the astonishment and ecstasy of the girl, the grim admiration and gruff thanks of the colonel, the wonder of the whole group.

"I'll put 'em back now, my dear," said Fischer, returning the case to the tails of his coat. "I had to be careful of 'em coming down. They're the three great African diamonds called 'The Flying Stars,' because they've been stolen so often. All the big criminals are on the track; but even the rough men about in the streets and hotels could hardly have kept their hands off them. I might have lost them on the road here. It was quite possible."

"Quite natural, I should say," growled the man in the red tie. "I shouldn't blame 'em if they had taken 'em. When they ask for bread, and you don't even give them a stone, I think they might take the stone for themselves."

"I won't have you talking like that," cried the girl, who was in a curious glow. "You've only talked like that since you became a horrid what's-his-name. You know what I mean. What do you call a man who wants to embrace the chimney-sweep?"

"A saint," said Father Brown.

"I think," said Sir Leopold, with a supercilious smile, "that Ruby means a Socialist."

"A radical does not mean a man who lives on radishes," remarked Crook, with some impatience; "and a Conservative does not mean a man who preserves jam. Neither, I assure you, does a Socialist mean a man who desires a social evening with the chimney-sweep. A Socialist means a man who wants all the chimneys swept and all the chimney-sweeps paid for it."

"But who won't allow you," put in the priest in a low voice, "to own your own soot."

Crook looked at him with an eye of interest and even respect. "Does one want to own soot?" he asked.

"One might," answered Brown, with speculation in his eye. "I've heard that gardeners use it. And I once made six children happy at Christmas when the conjuror didn't come, entirely with soot— applied externally."

"Oh, splendid," cried Ruby. "Oh, I wish you'd do it to this company."

The boisterous Canadian, Mr. Blount, was lifting his loud voice in applause, and the astonished financier his (in some considerable deprecation), when a knock sounded at the double front doors. The priest opened them, and they showed again the front garden of evergreens, monkey tree and all, now gathering gloom against a gorgeous violet sunset. The scene thus framed was so coloured and quaint, like a back scene in a play, that they forgot a moment the insignificant figure standing in the door. He was dusty-looking and in a frayed coat, evidently a common messenger. "Any of you gentlemen Mr. Blount?" he asked, and held forward a letter doubtfully. Mr. Blount started, and stopped in his shout of assent. Ripping up the envelope with evident astonishment he read it; his face clouded a little, and then cleared, and he turned to his brother-in-law and host.

"I'm sick at being such a nuisance, colonel," he said, with the cheery colonial convention; "but would it upset you if an old acquaintance called on me here to-night on business? In point of fact it's Florian, that famous French acrobat and comic actor; I knew him years ago out West (he was a French-Canadian by birth), and he seems to have business for me, though I hardly guess what."

"Of course, of course," replied the colonel carelessly. "My dear chap, any friend of yours. No doubt he will prove an acquisition."

"He'll black his face, if that's what you mean," cried Blount, laughing. "I don't doubt he'd black everyone else's eyes. I don't care; I'm not refined. I like the jolly old pantomime where a man sits on his top hat."

"Not on mine, please," said Sir Leopold Fischer, with dignity.

"Well, well," observed Crook, airily, "don't let's quarrel. There are lower jokes than sitting on a top hat."

Dislike of the red-tied youth, born of his predatory opinions and evident intimacy with the pretty godchild, led Fischer to say, in his most sarcastic, magisterial manner: "No doubt you have found something much lower than sitting on a top hat. What is it, pray?"

"Letting a top hat sit on you, for instance," said the Socialist.

"Now, now, now," cried the Canadian farmer with his barbarian benevolence, "don't let's spoil a jolly evening. What I say is, let's do something for the company to-night. Not blacking faces or sitting on hats, if you don't like those—but something of the sort. Why couldn't we have a proper old English pantomime—clown, columbine, and so on. I saw one when I left England at twelve years old, and it's blazed in my brain like a bonfire ever since. I came back to the old country only last year, and I find the thing's extinct. Nothing but a lot of snivelling fairy plays. I want a hot poker and a policeman made into sausages, and they give me princesses moralising by moonlight, Blue Birds, or something. Blue Beard's more in my line, and him I like best when he turned into the pantaloon."

"I'm all for making a policeman into sausages," said John Crook. "It's a better definition of Socialism than some recently given. But surely the get-up would be too big a business."

"Not a scrap," cried Blount, quite carried away. "A harle-quinade's the quickest thing we can do, for two reasons. First, one can gag to any degree; and, second, all the objects are household things—tables and towel-horses and washing baskets, and things like that."

"That's true," admitted Crook, nodding eagerly and walking about. "But I'm afraid I can't have my policeman's uniform? Haven't killed a policeman lately."

Blount frowned thoughtfully a space, and then smote his thigh. "Yes, we can!" he cried. "I've got Florian's address here, and he knows every *costumier* in London. I'll 'phone him to bring a police dress when he comes." And he went bounding away to the telephone.

"Oh, it's glorious, godfather," cried Ruby, almost dancing. "I'll be columbine and you shall be pantaloon."

The millionaire held himself stiff with a sort of heathen solemnity. "I think, my dear," he said, "you must get someone else for pantaloon."

"I will be pantaloon, if you like," said Colonel Adams, taking his cigar out of his mouth, and speaking for the first and last time.

"You ought to have a statue," cried the Canadian, as he came back, radiant, from the telephone. "There, we are all fitted. Mr. Crook shall be clown; he's a journalist and knows all the oldest jokes. I can be harlequin, that only wants long legs and jumping about. My friend Florian 'phones he's bringing the police costume; he's changing on the way. We can act it in this very hall, the audience sitting on those broad stairs opposite, one row above another. These front doors can be the back scene, either open or shut. Shut, you see an English interior. Open, a moonlit garden. It all goes by magic." And snatching a chance piece of billiard chalk from his pocket, he ran it across the hall floor, half-way between the front door and the staircase, to mark the line of the footlights.

How even such a banquet of bosh was got ready in the time remained a riddle. But they went at it with that mixture of recklessness and industry that lives when youth is in a house; and youth was in that house that night, though not all may have isolated the two faces and hearts from which it flamed. As always happens, the invention grew wilder and wilder through the very tameness of the *bourgeois* conventions from which it had to create. The columbine looked charming in an outstanding skirt that strangely resembled the large lamp-shade in the drawing-room. The clown and pantaloon made themselves white with flour from the cook, and red with rouge from some other domestic, who remained (like all true Christian benefactors) anonymous. The harlequin, already clad in silver paper out of cigar boxes, was, with difficulty, prevented from smashing the old Victorian lustre chandeliers, that he might cover himself with resplendent crystals. In fact he would certainly have done so, had not Ruby unearthed some old pantomime paste jewels she had worn at a fancy dress party as the Queen of Diamonds. Indeed, her uncle, James Blount, was getting almost out of hand in his excitement; he was like a schoolboy. He put a paper donkey's head unexpectedly on Father Brown, who bore it patiently, and even found some private manner of moving his ears. He even essayed to put the paper donkey's tail to the coat tails of Sir Leopold Fischer. This, however, was frowned down. "Uncle is too absurd," cried Ruby to Crook, round whose shoulders she had seriously placed a string of sausages. "Why is he so wild?"

"He is harlequin to your columbine," said Crook. "I am only the clown who makes the old jokes."

"I wish you were the harlequin," she said, and left the string of sausages swinging.

Father Brown, though he knew every detail done behind the

scenes, and had even evoked applause by his transformation of a pillow into a pantomime baby, went round to the front and sat among the audience with all the solemn expectation of a child at his first matinée. The spectators were few, relations, one or two local friends, and the servants; Sir Leopold sat in the front seat, his full and still fur-collared figure largely obscuring the view of the little cleric behind him; but it has never been settled by artistic authorities whether the cleric lost much. The pantomime was utterly chaotic, yet not contemptible; there ran through it a rage of improvisation which came chiefly from Crook the clown. Commonly he was a clever man, and he was inspired to-night with a wild omniscience, a folly wiser than the world, that which comes to a young man who has seen for an instant a particular expression on a particular face. He was supposed to be the clown, but he was really almost everything else, the author (so far as there was an author), the prompter, the scene-painter, the scene-shifter, and, above all, the orchestra. At abrupt intervals in the outrageous performance he would hurl himself in full costume at the piano and bang out some popular music equally absurd and appropriate.

The climax of this, as of all else, was the moment when the two front doors at the back of the scene flew open, showing the lovely moonlit garden, but showing more prominently the famous professional guest; the great Florian, dressed up as a policeman. The clown at the piano played the constabulary chorus in the "Pirates of Penzance," but it was drowned in the deafening applause, for every gesture of the great comic actor was an admirable though restrained version of the carriage and manner of the police. The harlequin leapt upon him and hit him over the helmet; the pianist playing "Where did you get that hat?" he faced about in admirably simulated astonishment, and then the leaping harlequin hit him again (the pianist suggesting a few bars of "Then we had another one"). Then the harlequin rushed right into the arms of the policeman and fell on top of him, amid a roar of applause. Then it was that the strange actor gave that celebrated imitation of a dead man, of which the fame still lingers round Putney. It was almost impossible to believe that a living person could appear so limp.

The athletic harlequin swung him about like a sack or twisted or tossed him like an Indian club; all the time to the most maddeningly ludicrous tunes from the piano. When the harlequin heaved the comic constable heavily off the floor the clown played "I arise from dreams of thee." When he shuffled him across his back, "With my bundle on my shoulder," and when the harlequin finally let fall the policeman with a most convincing thud, the lunatic at the instrument struck into a jingling measure with some words which are still believed to have been, "I sent a letter to my love and on the way I dropped it."

At about this limit of mental anarchy Father Brown's view was obscured altogether; for the City magnate in front of him rose to his full height and thrust his hands savagely into all his pockets. Then he sat down nervously, still fumbling, and then stood up again. For an instant it seemed seriously likely that he would stride across the footlights; then he turned a glare at the clown playing the piano; and then he burst in silence out of the room.

The priest had only watched for a few more minutes the absurd but not inelegant dance of the amateur harlequin over his splendidly unconscious foe. With real though rude art, the harlequin danced slowly backwards out of the door into the garden, which was full of moonlight and stillness. The vamped dress of silver paper and paste, which had been too glaring in the footlights, looked more and more magical and silvery as it danced away under a brilliant moon. The audience was closing in with a cataract of applause, when Brown felt his arm abruptly touched, and he was asked in a whisper to come into the colonel's study.

He followed his summoner with increasing doubt, which was not dispelled by a solemn comicality in the scene of the study. There sat Colonel Adams, still unaffectedly dressed as a pantaloon, with the knobbed whalebone nodding above his brow, but with his poor old eyes sad enough to have sobered a Saturnalia. Sir Leopold Fischer was leaning against the mantelpiece and heaving with all the importance of panic.

"This is a very painful matter, Father Brown," said Adams. "The truth is, those diamonds we all saw this afternoon seem to have vanished from my friend's tail-coat pocket. And as you——"

"As I," supplemented Father Brown, with a broad grin, "was sitting just behind him——"

"Nothing of the sort shall be suggested," said Colonel Adams, with a firm look at Fischer, which rather implied that some such thing *had* been suggested. "I only ask you to give me the assistance that any gentleman might give."

"Which is turning out his pockets," said Father Brown, and proceeded to do so, displaying seven and sixpence, a return ticket, a small silver crucifix, a small breviary, and a stick of chocolate.

The colonel looked at him long, and then said, "Do you know, I should like to see the inside of your head more than the inside of your pockets. My daughter is one of your people, I know; well, she has lately——" and he stopped.

"She has lately," cried out old Fischer, "opened her father's house to a cut-throat Socialist, who says openly he would steal anything from a richer man. This is the end of it. Here is the richer man—and none the richer."

"If you want the inside of my head you can have it," said Brown rather wearily. "What it's worth you can say afterwards. But the first thing I find in that disused pocket is this; that men who mean to steal diamonds don't talk Socialism. They are more likely," he added demurely, "to denounce it."

Both the others shifted sharply and the priest went on:

"You see, we know these people, more or less. That Socialist would no more steal a diamond than a Pyramid. We ought to look at once to the one man we don't know. The fellow acting the policeman—Florian. Where is he exactly at this minute, I wonder."

The pantaloon sprang erect and strode out of the room. An interlude ensued, during which the millionaire stared at the priest, and the priest at his breviary; then the pantaloon returned and said, with *staccato* gravity, "The policeman is still lying on the stage. The curtain has gone up and down six times; he is still lying there."

Father Brown dropped his book and stood staring with a look of blank mental ruin. Very slowly a light began to creep in his grey eyes, and then he made the scarcely obvious answer.

"Please forgive me, colonel, but when did your wife die?"

"Wife!" replied the staring soldier, "she died this year two months. Her brother James arrived just a week too late to see her."

The little priest bounded like a rabbit shot. "Come on!" he cried in quite unusual excitement. "Come on! We've got to go and look at that policeman!"

They rushed on to the now curtained stage, breaking rudely past the columbine and clown (who seemed whispering quite contentedly), and Father Brown bent over the prostrate comic policeman.

"Chloroform," he said as he rose; "I only guessed it just now."

There was a startled stillness, and then the colonel said slowly, "Please say seriously what all this means."

Father Brown suddenly shouted with laughter, then stopped, and only struggled with it for instants during the rest of his speech. "Gentlemen," he gasped, "there's not much time to talk. I must run after the criminal. But this great French actor who played the policeman—this clever corpse the harlequin waltzed with and dandled and threw about—he was——" His voice again failed him, and he turned his back to run.

"He was?" called Fischer inquiringly.

"A real policeman," said Father Brown, and ran away into the dark.

There were hollows and bowers at the extreme end of that leafy garden, in which the laurels and other immortal shrubs showed against sapphire sky and silver moon, even in that midwinter, warm colours as of the south. The green gaiety of the waving laurels, the rich purple indigo of the night, the moon like a monstrous crystal, make an almost irresponsibly romantic picture; and among the top branches of the garden trees a strange figure is climbing, who looks not so much romantic as impossible. He sparkles from head to heel, as if clad in ten million moons; the real moon catches him at every movement and sets a new inch of him on fire. But he swings, flashing and successful, from the short tree in this garden to the tall, rambling tree in the other, and only stops there because a shade has slid under the smaller tree and has unmistakably called up to him.

"Well, Flambeau," says the voice, "you really look like a Flying Star; but that always means a Falling Star at last."

The silver, sparkling figure above seems to lean forward in the laurels and, confident of escape, listens to the little figure below.

"You never did anything better, Flambeau. It was clever to come from Canada (with a Paris ticket, I suppose) just a week after Mrs. Adams died, when no one was in a mood to ask questions. It was cleverer to have marked down the Flying Stars and the very day of Fischer's coming. But there's no cleverness, but mere genius, in what followed. Stealing the stones, I suppose, was nothing to you. You could have done it by sleight of hand in a hundred other ways besides that pretence of putting a paper donkey's tail to Fischer's coat. But in the rest you eclipsed yourself."

The silvery figure among the green leaves seems to linger as if hypnotised, though his escape is easy behind him; he is staring at the man below.

"Oh, yes," says the man below, "I know all about it. I know you not only forced the pantomime, but put it to a double use. You were going to steal the stones quietly; news came by an accomplice that you were already suspected, and a capable police officer was coming to rout you up that very night. A common thief would have been thankful for the warning and fled; but you are a poet. You already had the clever notion of hiding the jewels in a blaze of false stage jewellery. Now, you saw that if the dress were a harlequin's the appearance of a policeman would be quite in keeping. The worthy officer started from Putney police station to find you, and walked into the queerest trap ever set in this world. When the front door opened he walked straight on to the stage of a Christmas pantomime, where he could be kicked, clubbed, stunned, and drugged by the dancing harlequin, amid roars of laughter from all the most respectable people in Putney. Oh, you will never do anything better. And now, by the way, you might give me back those diamonds."

The green branch on which the glittering figure swung, rustled as if in astonishment; but the voice went on:

"I want you to give them back, Flambeau, and I want you to give up this life. There is still youth and honour and humour in you; don't fancy they will last in that trade. Men may keep a sort of level of good, but no man has ever been able to keep on one level of evil.

That road goes down and down. The kind man drinks and turns cruel; the frank man kills and lies about it. Many a man I've known started like you to be an honest outlaw, a merry robber of the rich, and ended stamped into slime. Maurice Blum started out as an anarchist of principle, a father of the poor; he ended a greasy spy and tale-bearer that both sides used and despised. Harry Burke started his free money movement sincerely enough; now he's sponging on a half-starved sister for endless brandies and sodas. Lord Amber went into wild society in a sort of chivalry; now he's paying blackmail to the lowest vultures in London. Captain Barillon was the great gentleman-apache before your time; he died in a madhouse, screaming with fear of the "narks" and receivers that had betrayed him and hunted him down. I know the woods look very free behind you, Flambeau; I know that in a flash you could melt into them like a monkey. But some day you will be an old grey monkey, Flambeau. You will sit up in your free forest cold at heart and close to death, and the tree-tops will be very bare."

Everything continued still, as if the small man below held the other in the tree in some long invisible leash; and he went on:

"Your downward steps have begun. You used to boast of doing nothing mean, but you are doing something mean to-night. You are leaving suspicion on an honest boy with a good deal against him already; you are separating him from the woman he loves and who loves him. But you will do meaner things than that before you die."

Three flashing diamonds fell from the tree to the turf. The small man stooped to pick them up, and when he looked up again the green cage of the tree was emptied of its silver bird.

The restoration of the gems (accidentally picked up by Father Brown, of all people) ended the evening in uproarious triumph; and Sir Leopold, in his height of good humour, even told the priest that though he himself had broader views, he could respect those whose creed required them to be cloistered and ignorant of this world.

THE INVISIBLE MAN

In the cool blue twilight of two steep streets in Camden Town, the shop at the corner, a confectioner's, glowed like the butt of a cigar. One should rather say, perhaps, like the butt of a firework, for the light was of many colours and some complexity, broken up by many mirrors and dancing on many gilt and gaily-coloured cakes and sweetmeats. Against this one fiery glass were glued the noses of many gutter-snipes, for the chocolates were all wrapped in those red and gold and green metallic colours which are almost better than chocolate itself; and the huge white wedding-cake in the window was somehow at once remote and satisfying, just as if the whole North Pole were good to eat. Such rainbow provocations could naturally collect the youth of the neighbourhood up to the ages of ten or twelve. But this corner was also attractive to youth at a later stage; and a young man, not less than twenty-four, was staring into the same shop window. To him, also, the shop was of fiery charm, but this attraction was not wholly to be explained by chocolates; which, however, he was far from despising.

He was a tall, burly, red-haired young man, with a resolute face but a listless manner. He carried under his arm a flat, grey portfolio of black-and-white sketches, which he had sold with more or less success to publishers ever since his uncle (who was an admiral) had disinherited him for Socialism, because of a lecture which he had delivered against that economic theory. His name was John Turnbull Angus.

Entering at last, he walked through the confectioner's shop to the back room, which was a sort of pastry-cook restaurant, merely raising his hat to the young lady who was serving there. She was a dark, elegant, alert girl in black, with a high colour and very quick, dark eyes; and after the ordinary interval she followed him into the inner room to take his order.

His order was evidently a usual one. "I want, please," he said with precision, "one halfpenny bun and a small cup of black coffee." An instant before the girl could turn away he added, "Also, I want you to marry me."

The young lady of the shop stiffened suddenly and said, "Those are jokes I don't allow."

The red-haired young man lifted grey eyes of an unexpected gravity.

"Really and truly," he said, "it's as serious—as serious as the halfpenny bun. It is expensive, like the bun; one pays for it. It is indigestible, like the bun. It hurts."

The dark young lady had never taken her dark eyes off him, but seemed to be studying him with almost tragic exactitude. At the end of her scrutiny she had something like the shadow of a smile, and she sat down in a chair.

"Don't you think," observed Angus, absently, "that it's rather cruel to eat these halfpenny buns? They might grow up into penny buns. I shall give up these brutal sports when we are married."

The dark young lady rose from her chair and walked to the window, evidently in a state of strong but not unsympathetic cogitation. When at last she swung round again with an air of resolution she was bewildered to observe that the young man was carefully laying out on the table various objects from the shop-window. They included a pyramid of highly coloured sweets, several plates of sandwiches, and the two decanters containing that mysterious port and sherry which are peculiar to pastry-cooks. In the middle of this neat arrangement he had carefully let down the enormous load of white sugared cake which had been the huge ornament of the window.

"What on earth are you doing?" she asked.

"Duty, my dear Laura," he began.

"Oh, for the Lord's sake, stop a minute," she cried, "and don't talk to me in that way. I mean, what is all that?"

"A ceremonial meal, Miss Hope."

"And what is *that*?" she asked impatiently, pointing to the mountain of sugar.

"The wedding-cake, Mrs. Angus," he said.

The girl marched to that article, removed it with some clatter, and put it back in the shop window; she then returned, and, putting her elegant elbows on the table, regarded the young man not unfavourably but with considerable exasperation.

"You don't give me any time to think," she said.

"I'm not such a fool," he answered; "that's my Christian humility."

She was still looking at him; but she had grown considerably graver behind the smile.

"Mr. Angus," she said steadily, "before there is a minute more of this nonsense I must tell you something about myself as shortly as I can."

"Delighted," replied Angus gravely. "You might tell me something about myself, too, while you are about it."

"Oh, do hold your tongue and listen," she said. "It's nothing that I'm ashamed of, and it isn't even anything that I'm specially sorry about. But what would you say if there were something that is no business of mine and yet is my nightmare?"

"In that case," said the man seriously, "I should suggest that you bring back the cake."

"Well, you must listen to the story first," said Laura, persistently. "To begin with, I must tell you that my father owned the inn called the 'Red Fish' at Ludbury, and I used to serve people in the bar."

"I have often wondered," he said, "why there was a kind of a Christian air about this one confectioner's shop."

"Ludbury is a sleepy, grassy little hole in the Eastern Counties, and the only kind of people who ever came to the 'Red Fish' were occasional commercial travellers, and for the rest, the most awful people you can see, only you've never seen them. I mean little, loungy men, who had just enough to live on and had nothing to do but lean about in bar-rooms and bet on horses, in bad clothes that were just too good for them. Even these wretched young rotters were not very common at our house; but there were two of them that were a lot too common—common in every sort of way. They both lived on money of their own, and were wearisomely idle and over-dressed. But yet I was a bit sorry for them, because I half believe they slunk into our little empty bar because each of them had a slight deformity; the sort of thing that some yokels laugh at. It wasn't exactly a deformity either; it was more an oddity. One of them was a surprisingly small man, something like a dwarf, or at least like a jockey. He was not at all jockeyish to look at, though; he had a round black head and a well-trimmed black beard, bright eyes like a bird's; he jingled money in his pockets; he jangled a great gold watch chain; and he never turned up except dressed just too much like a gentleman to be one. He was no fool though, though a futile idler; he was curiously clever at all kinds of things that couldn't be the slightest use; a sort of impromptu conjuring; making fifteen matches set fire to each other like a regular firework; or cutting a banana or some such thing into a dancing doll. His name was Isidore Smythe; and I can see him still, with his little dark face, just coming up to the counter, making a jumping kangaroo out of five cigars.

"The other fellow was more silent and more ordinary; but somehow he alarmed me much more than poor little Smythe. He was very tall and slight, and light-haired; his nose had a high bridge, and he might almost have been handsome in a spectral sort of way; but he had one of the most appalling squints I have ever seen or heard of. When he looked straight at you, you didn't know where you were yourself, let alone what he was looking at. I fancy this sort of disfigurement embittered the poor chap a little; for while Smythe was ready to show off his monkey tricks anywhere, James

Welkin (that was the squinting man's name) never did anything except soak in our bar parlour, and go for great walks by himself in the flat, grey country all round. All the same, I think Smythe, too, was a little sensitive about being so small, though he carried it off more smartly. And so it was that I was really puzzled, as well as startled, and very sorry, when they both offered to marry me in the same week.

"Well, I did what I've since thought was perhaps a silly thing. But, after all, these freaks were my friends in a way; and I had a horror of their thinking I refused them for the real reason, which was that they were so impossibly ugly. So I made up some gas of another sort, about never meaning to marry anyone who hadn't carved his way in the world. I said it was a point of principle with me not to live on money that was just inherited like theirs. Two days after I had talked in this well-meaning sort of way, the whole trouble began. The first thing I heard was that both of them had gone off to seek their fortunes, as if they were in some silly fairy tale.

"Well, I've never seen either of them from that day to this. But I've had two letters from the little man called Smythe, and really they were rather exciting."

"Ever heard of the other man?" asked Angus.

"No, he never wrote," said the girl, after an instant's hesitation. "Smythe's first letter was simply to say that he had started out walking with Welkin to London; but Welkin was such a good walker that the little man dropped out of it, and took a rest by the roadside. He happened to be picked up by some travelling show, and, partly because he was nearly a dwarf, and partly because he was really a clever little wretch, he got on quite well in the show business, and was soon sent up to the Aquarium, to do some tricks that I forget. That was his first letter. His second was much more of a startler, and I only got it last week."

The man called Angus emptied his coffee-cup and regarded her with mild and patient eyes. Her own mouth took a slight twist of laughter as she resumed, "I suppose you've seen on the hoardings all about this 'Smythe's Silent Service'? Or you must be the only person that hasn't. Oh, I don't know much about it, it's some clock-work invention for doing all the housework by machinery. You know the sort of thing: 'Press a Button—A Butler Who Never Drinks.' 'Turn a Handle—Ten Housemaids Who Never Flirt.' You must have seen the advertisements. Well, whatever these machines are, they are making pots of money; and they are making it all for that little imp whom I knew down in Ludbury. I can't help feeling pleased the poor little chap has fallen on his feet; but the plain fact is, I'm in terror of his turning up any minute and telling me he's carved his way in the world—as he certainly has."

"And the other man?" repeated Angus with a sort of obstinate quietude.

Laura Hope got to her feet suddenly. "My friend," she said, "I think you are a witch. Yes, you are quite right. I have not seen a line of the other man's writing; and I have no more notion than the dead of what or where he is. But it is of him that I am frightened. It is he who is all about my path. It is he who has half driven me mad. Indeed, I think he has driven me mad; for I have felt him where he could not have been, and I have heard his voice when he could not have spoken."

"Well, my dear," said the young man, cheerfully, "if he were Satan himself, he is done for now you have told somebody. One goes mad all alone, old girl. But when was it you fancied you felt and heard our squinting friend?"

"I heard James Welkin laugh as plainly as I hear you speak," said the girl, steadily. "There was nobody there, for I stood just outside the shop at the corner, and could see down both streets at once. I had forgotten how he laughed, though his laugh was as odd as his squint. I had not thought of him for nearly a year. But it's a solemn truth that a few seconds later the first letter came from his rival."

"Did you ever make the spectre speak or squeak, or anything?" asked Angus, with some interest.

Laura suddenly shuddered, and then said, with an unshaken voice, "Yes. Just when I had finished reading the second letter from Isidore Smythe announcing his success, just then, I heard Welkin say, 'He shan't have you, though.' It was quite plain, as if he were in the room. It is awful; I think I must be mad."

"If you really were mad," said the young man, "you would think you must be sane. But certainly there seems to me to be something a little rum about this unseen gentleman. Two heads are better than one—I spare you allusions to any other organs—and really, if you would allow me, as a sturdy, practical man, to bring back the wedding-cake out of the window——"

Even as he spoke, there was a sort of steely shriek in the street outside, and a small motor, driven at devilish speed, shot up to the door of the shop and stuck there. In the same flash of time a small man in a shiny top hat stood stamping in the outer room.

Angus, who had hitherto maintained hilarious ease from motives of mental hygiene, revealed the strain of his soul by striding abruptly out of the inner room and confronting the new-comer. A glance at him was quite sufficient to confirm the savage guesswork of a man in love. This very dapper but dwarfish figure, with the spike of black beard carried insolently forward, the clever unrestful eyes, the neat but very nervous fingers, could be none other than the man just described to him: Isidore Smythe, who made dolls out of banana skins and match-boxes; Isidore Smythe, who made millions out of undrinking butlers and unflirting housemaids of metal. For a moment the two men, instinctively understanding each other's air of possession, looked at each other with that curious cold generosity which is the soul of rivalry.

Mr. Smythe, however, made no allusion to the ultimate ground of their antagonism, but said simply and explosively. "Has Miss Hope seen that thing on the window?"

"On the window?" repeated the staring Angus.

"There's no time to explain other things," said the small millionaire shortly. "There's some tomfoolery going on here that has to be investigated."

He pointed his polished walking-stick at the window, recently depleted by the bridal preparations of Mr. Angus; and that gentleman was astonished to see along the front of the glass a long strip of paper pasted, which had certainly not been on the window when he had looked through it some time before. Following the energetic Smythe outside into the street, he found that some yard and a half of stamp paper had been carefully gummed along the glass outside, and on this was written in straggly characters, "If you marry Smythe, he will die."

"Laura," said Angus, putting his big red head into the shop, "you're not mad."

"It's the writing of that fellow Welkin," said Smythe gruffly. "I haven't seen him for years, but he's always bothering me. Five times in the last fortnight he's had threatening letters left at my flat, and I can't even find out who leaves them, let alone if it is Welkin himself. The porter of the flats swears that no suspicious characters have been seen, and here he has pasted up a sort of dado on a public shop window, while the people in the shop——"

"Quite so," said Angus modestly, "while the people in the shop were having tea. Well, sir, I can assure you I appreciate your common sense in dealing so directly with the matter. We can talk about other things afterwards. The fellow cannot be very far off yet, for I swear there was no paper there when I went last to the window, ten or fifteen minutes ago. On the other hand, he's too far off to be chased, as we don't even know the direction. If you'll take my advice, Mr. Smythe, you'll put this at once in the hands of some energetic inquiry man, private rather than public. I know an extremely clever fellow, who has set up in business five minutes from here in your car. His name's Flambeau, and though his youth was a bit stormy, he's a strictly honest man now, and his brains are worth money. He lives in Lucknow Mansions, Hampstead."

"That is odd," said the little man, arching his black eyebrows. "I live, myself, in Himylaya Mansions, round the corner. Perhaps you might care to come with me; I can go to my rooms and sort out these queer Welkin documents, while you run round and get your friend the detective."

"You are very good," said Angus politely. "Well, the sooner we act the better."

Both men, with a queer kind of impromptu fairness, took the same sort of formal farewell of the lady, and both jumped into the brisk little car. As Smythe took the handles and they turned the great corner of the street, Angus was amused to see a gigantesque poster of "Smythe's Silent Service," with a picture of a huge headless iron doll, carrying a saucepan with the legend, "A Cook Who Is Never Cross."

"I use them in my own flat," said the little black-bearded man, laughing, "partly for advertisements, and partly for real convenience. Honestly, and all above board, those big clockwork dolls of mine do bring you coals or claret or a time-table quicker than any live servants I've ever known, if you know which knob to press. But I'll never deny, between ourselves, that such servants have their disadvantages, too."

"Indeed?" said Angus; "is there something they can't do?"

"Yes," replied Smythe coolly; "they can't tell me who left those threatening letters at my flat."

The man's motor was small and swift like himself; in fact, like his domestic service, it was of his own invention. If he was an advertising quack, he was one who believed in his own wares. The sense of something tiny and flying was accentuated as they swept up long white curves of road in the dead but open daylight of evening. Soon the white curves came sharper and dizzier; they were upon ascending spirals, as they say in the modern religions. For, indeed, they were cresting a corner of London which is almost as precipitous as Edinburgh, if not quite so picturesque. Terrace rose above terrace, and the special tower of flats they sought, rose above them all to almost Egyptian height, gilt by the level sunset. The change, as they turned the corner and entered the crescent known as Himylaya Mansions, was as abrupt as the opening of a window; for they found that pile of flats sitting above London as above a green sea of slate. Opposite to the mansions, on the other side of the gravel crescent, was a bushy enclosure more like a steep hedge or dyke than a garden, and some way below that ran a strip of artificial water, a sort of canal, like the moat of that embowered fortress. As the car swept round the crescent it passed, at one corner, the stray stall of a man selling chestnuts; and right away at the other end of the curve, Angus could see a dim blue policeman walking slowly. These were the only human shapes in that high suburban solitude; but he had an irrational sense that they expressed the speechless poetry of London. He felt as if they were figures in a story.

The little car shot up to the right house like a bullet, and shot out its owner like a bomb shell. He was immediately inquiring of a tall commissionaire in shining braid, and a short porter in shirt sleeves, whether anybody or anything had been seeking his apartments. He was assured that nobody and nothing had passed these officials since his last inquiries; whereupon he and the slightly bewildered Angus were shot up in the lift like a rocket, till they reached the top floor.

"Just come in for a minute," said the breathless Smythe. "I want to show you those Welkin letters. Then you might run round the corner and fetch your friend." He pressed a button concealed in the wall, and the door opened of itself.

It opened on a long, commodious ante-room, of which the only arresting features, ordinarily speaking, were the rows of tall half-human mechanical figures that stood up on both sides like tailors' dummies. Like tailors' dummies they were headless; and like tailors' dummies they had a handsome unnecessary humpiness in the shoulders, and a pigeon-breasted protuberance of chest; but barring this, they were not much more like a human figure than any automatic machine at a station that is about the human height. They had two great hooks like arms, for carrying trays; and they were painted pea-green, or vermillion, or black for convenience of distinction; in every other way they were only automatic machines and nobody would have looked twice at them. On this occasion, at least, nobody did. For between the two rows of these domestic dummies lay something more interesting than most of the mechanics of the world. It was a white, tattered scrap of paper scrawled with red ink; and the agile inventor had snatched it up almost as soon as the door flew open. He handed it to Angus without a word. The red ink on it actually was not dry, and the message ran, "If you have been to see her to-day, I shall kill you."

There was a short silence, and then Isidore Smythe said quietly, "Would you like a little whisky? I rather feel as if I should."

"Thank you; I should like a little Flambeau," said Angus,

gloomily. "This business seems to me to be getting rather grave. I'm going round at once to fetch him."

"Right you are," said the other, with admirable cheerfulness. "Bring him round here as quick as you can."

But as Angus closed the front door behind him he saw Smythe push back a button, and one of the clockwork images glided from its place and slid along a groove in the floor carrying a tray with syphon and decanter. There did seem something a trifle weird about leaving the little man alone among those dead servants, who were coming to life as the door closed.

Six steps down from Smythe's landing the man in shirt sleeves was doing something with a pail. Angus stopped to extract a promise, fortified with a prospective bribe, that he would remain in that place until the return with the detective, and would keep count of any kind of stranger coming up those stairs. Dashing down to the front hall he then laid similar charges of vigilance on the commissionaire at the front door, from whom he learned the simplifying circumstances that there was no back door. Not content with this, he captured the floating policeman and induced him to stand opposite the entrance and watch it; and finally paused an instant for a pennyworth of chestnuts, and an inquiry as to the probable length of the merchant's stay in the neighbourhood.

The chestnut seller, turning up the collar of his coat, told him he should probably be moving shortly, as he thought it was going to snow. Indeed, the evening was growing grey and bitter, but Angus, with all his eloquence, proceeded to nail the chestnut man to his post.

"Keep yourself warm on your own chestnuts," he said earnestly. "Eat up your whole stock; I'll make it worth your while. I'll give you a sovereign if you'll wait here till I come back, and then tell me whether any man, woman, or child has gone into that house where the commissionaire is standing."

He then walked away smartly, with a last look at the besieged tower.

"I've made a ring round that room, anyhow," he said. "They can't all four of them be Mr. Welkin's accomplices."

Lucknow Mansions were, so to speak, on a lower platform of

that hill of houses, of which Himylaya Mansions might be called the peak. Mr. Flambeau's semi-official flat was on the ground floor, and presented in every way a marked contrast to the American machinery and cold hotel-like luxury of the flat of the Silent Service. Flambeau, who was a friend of Angus, received him in a rococo artistic den behind his office, of which the ornaments were sabres, harquebuses, Eastern curiosities, flasks of Italian wine, savage cooking-pots, a plumy Persian cat, and a small dusty-looking Roman Catholic priest, who looked particularly out of place.

"This is my friend Father Brown," said Flambeau. "I've often wanted you to meet him. Splendid weather, this; a little cold for Southerners like me."

"Yes, I think it will keep clear," said Angus, sitting down on a violet-striped Eastern ottoman.

"No," said the priest quietly, "it has begun to snow."

And, indeed, as he spoke, the first few flakes, foreseen by the man of chestnuts, began to drift across the darkening window-pane.

"Well," said Angus heavily. "I'm afraid I've come on business, and rather jumpy business at that. The fact is, Flambeau, within a stone's throw of your house is a fellow who badly wants your help; he's perpetually being haunted and threatened by an invisible enemy—a scoundrel whom nobody has even seen." As Angus proceeded to tell the whole tale of Smythe and Welkin, beginning with Laura's story, and going on with his own, the supernatural laugh at the corner of two empty streets, the strange distinct words spoken in an empty room, Flambeau grew more and more vividly concerned, and the little priest seemed to be left out of it, like a piece of furniture. When it came to the scribbled stamp paper pasted on the window, Flambeau rose, seeming to fill the room with his huge shoulders.

"If you don't mind," he said, "I think you had better tell me the rest on the nearest road to this man's house. It strikes me, somehow, that there is no time to be lost."

"Delighted," said Angus, rising also, "though he's safe enough for the present, for I've set four men to watch the only hole to his burrow."

They turned out into the street, the small priest trundling after them with the docility of a small dog. He merely said, in a cheerful way, like one making conversation, "How quick the snow gets thick on the ground."

As they threaded the steep side streets already powdered with silver, Angus finished his story; and by the time they reached the crescent with the towering flats, he had leisure to turn his attention to the four sentinels. The chestnut seller, both before and after receiving a sovereign, swore stubbornly that he had watched the door and seen no visitor enter. The policeman was even more emphatic. He said he had had experience of crooks of all kinds, in top hats and in rags; he wasn't so green as to expect suspicious characters to look suspicious; he looked out for anybody, and, so help him, there had been nobody. And when all three men gathered round the gilded commissionaire, who still stood smiling astride of the porch, the verdict was more final still.

"I've got a right to ask any man, duke or dustman, what he wants in these flats," said the genial and gold-laced giant, "and I'll swear there's been nobody to ask since this gentleman went away."

The unimportant Father Brown, who stood back, looking modestly at the pavement, here ventured to say meekly, "Has nobody been up and down stairs, then, since the snow began to fall? It began while we were all round at Flambeau's."

"Nobody's been in here, sir, you can take it from me," said the official, with beaming authority.

"Then I wonder what that is?" said the priest, and stared at the ground blankly like a fish.

The others all looked down also; and Flambeau used a fierce exclamation and a French gesture. For it was unquestionably true that down the middle of the entrance guarded by the man in gold lace, actually between the arrogant, stretched legs of that colossus, ran a stringy pattern of grey footprints stamped upon the white snow.

"God!" cried Angus involuntarily, "the Invisible Man!"

Without another word he turned and dashed up the stairs, with Flambeau following; but Father Brown still stood looking about him in the snow-clad street as if he had lost interest in his query.

Flambeau was plainly in a mood to break down the door with his big shoulders, but the Scotchman, with more reason, if less intuition, fumbled about on the frame of the door till he found the invisible button; and the door swung slowly open.

It showed substantially the same serried interior; the hall had grown darker, though it was still struck here and there with the last crimson shafts of sunset, and one or two of the headless machines had been moved from their places for this or that purpose, and stood here and there about the twilit place. The green and red of their coats were all darkened in the dusk; and their likeness to human shapes slightly increased by their very shapelessness. But in the middle of them all, exactly where the paper with the red ink had lain, there lay something that looked like red ink spilt out of its bottle. But it was not red ink.

With a French combination of reason and violence Flambeau simply said "Murder!" and, plunging into the flat, had explored every corner and cupboard of it in five minutes. But if he expected to find a corpse he found none. Isidore Smythe was not in the place, either dead or alive. After the most tearing search the two men met each other in the outer hall, with streaming faces and staring eyes. "My friend," said Flambeau, talking French in his excitement, "not only is your murderer invisible, but he makes invisible also the murdered man."

Angus looked round at the dim room full of dummies, and in some Celtic corner of his Scotch soul a shudder started. One of the life-size dolls stood immediately overshadowing the blood stain, summoned, perhaps, by the slain man an instant before he fell. One of the high-shouldered hooks that served the thing for arms, was a little lifted, and Angus had suddenly the horrid fancy that poor Smythe's own iron child had struck him down. Matter had rebelled, and these machines had killed their master. But even so, what had they done with him?

"Eaten him?" said the nightmare at his ear; and he sickened for an instant at the idea of rent, human remains absorbed and crushed into all that acephalous clockwork.

He recovered his mental health by an emphatic effort, and said to Flambeau, "Well, there it is. The poor fellow has evaporated like a cloud and left a red streak on the floor. The tale does not belong to this world."

"There is only one thing to be done," said Flambeau, "whether it belongs to this world or the other, I must go down and talk to my friend."

They descended, passing the man with the pail, who again asseverated that he had let no intruder pass, down to the commissionaire and the hovering chestnut man, who rigidly reasserted their own watchfulness. But when Angus looked round for his fourth confirmation he could not see it, and called out with some nervousness, "Where is the policeman?"

"I beg your pardon," said Father Brown; "that is my fault. I just sent him down the road to investigate something—that I just thought worth investigating."

"Well, we want him back pretty soon," said Angus abruptly, "for the wretched man upstairs has not only been murdered, but wiped out."

"How?" asked the priest.

"Father," said Flambeau, after a pause, "upon my soul I believe it is more in your department than mine. No friend or foe has entered the house, but Smythe is gone, as if stolen by the fairies. If that is not supernatural, I——"

As he spoke they were all checked by an unusual sight; the big blue policeman came round the corner of the crescent, running. He came straight up to Brown.

"You're right, sir," he panted, "they've just found poor Mr. Smythe's body in the canal down below."

Angus put his hand wildly to his head. "Did he run down and drown himself?" he asked.

"He never came down, I'll swear," said the constable, "and he wasn't drowned either, for he died of a great stab over the heart."

"And yet you saw no one enter?" said Flambeau in a grave voice.

"Let us walk down the road a little," said the priest.

As they reached the other end of the crescent he observed abruptly, "Stupid of me! I forgot to ask the policeman something. I wonder if they found a light brown sack."

"Why a light brown sack?" asked Angus, astonished.

"Because if it was any other coloured sack, the case must begin over again," said Father Brown; "but if it was a light brown sack, why, the case is finished."

"I am pleased to hear it," said Angus with hearty irony. "It hasn't begun, so far as I am concerned."

"You must tell us all about it," said Flambeau with a strange heavy simplicity, like a child.

Unconsciously they were walking with quickening steps down the long sweep of road on the other side of the high crescent, Father Brown leading briskly, though in silence. At last he said with an almost touching vagueness, "Well, I'm afraid you'll think it so prosy. We always begin at the abstract end of things, and you can't begin this story anywhere else.

"Have you ever noticed this—that people never answer what you say? They answer what you mean—or what they think you mean. Suppose one lady says to another in a country house, 'Is anybody staying with you?' the lady doesn't answer 'Yes; the butler, the three footmen, the parlourmaid, and so on,' though the parlourmaid may be in the room, or the butler behind her chair. She says 'There is *nobody* staying with us,' meaning nobody of the sort you mean. But suppose a doctor inquiring into an epidemic asks, 'Who is staying in the house?' then the lady will remember the butler, parlourmaid, and the rest. All language is used like that; you never get a question answered literally, even when you get it answered truly. When those four quite honest men said that no man had gone into the Mansions, they did not really mean that *no man* had gone into them. They meant no man whom they could suspect of being your man. A man did go into the house, and did come out of it, but they never noticed him."

"An invisible man?" inquired Angus, raising his red eyebrows.

"A mentally invisible man," said Father Brown.

A minute or two after he resumed in the same unassuming voice, like a man thinking his way. "Of course you can't think of such a man, until you do think of him. That's where his cleverness comes in. But I came to think of him through two or three little things in the tale Mr. Angus told us. First, there was the fact that this Welkin went for long walks. And then there was the vast lot of stamp paper on the window. And then, most of all, there were the two things the young lady said—things that couldn't be true. Don't get annoyed," he added hastily, noting a sudden movement of the Scotchman's head; "she thought they were true. A person *can't* be quite alone in a street a second before she receives a letter. She can't be quite alone in a street when she starts reading a letter just received. There must be somebody pretty near her; he must be mentally invisible."

"Why must there be somebody near her?" asked Angus.

"Because," said Father Brown, "barring carrier-pigeons, somebody must have brought her the letter."

"Do you really mean to say," asked Flambeau, with energy, "that Welkin carried his rival's letters to his lady?"

"Yes," said the priest. "Welkin carried his rival's letters to his lady. You see, he had to."

"Oh, I can't stand much more of this," exploded Flambeau. "Who is this fellow? What does he look like. What is the usual get-up of a mentally invisible man?"

"He is dressed rather handsomely in red, blue, and gold," replied the priest promptly with precision, "and in this striking, and even showy, costume he entered Himylaya Mansions under eight human eyes; he killed Smythe in cold blood, and came down into the street again carrying the dead body in his arms——"

"Reverend sir," cried Angus, standing still, "are you raving mad, or am I?"

"You are not mad," said Brown, "only a little unobservant. You have not noticed such a man as this, for example."

He took three quick strides forward, and put his hand on the shoulder of an ordinary passing postman who had bustled by them unnoticed under the shade of the trees.

"Nobody ever notices postmen somehow," he said thoughtfully; "yet they have passions like other men, and even carry large bags where a small corpse can be stowed quite easily."

The postman, instead of turning naturally, had ducked and tumbled against the garden fence. He was a lean fair-bearded man of very ordinary appearance, but as he turned an alarmed face over his shoulder, all three men were fixed with an almost fiendish squint.

Flambeau went back to his sabres, purple rugs, and Persian cat, having many things to attend to. John Turnbull Angus went back to the lady at the shop, with whom that imprudent young man contrives to be extremely comfortable. But Father Brown walked those snow-covered hills under the stars for many hours with a murderer, and what they said to each other will never be known.

The Honour of Israel Gow

A stormy evening of olive and silver was closing in, as Father Brown, wrapped in a grey Scotch plaid, came to the end of a grey Scotch valley and beheld the strange castle of Glengyle. It stopped one end of the glen or hollow like a blind alley; and it looked like the end of the world. Rising in steep roofs and spires of seagreen slate in the manner of the old French-Scotch châteaux, it reminded an Englishman of the sinister steeple-hats of witches in fairy tales; and the pine-woods that rocked round the green turrets looked, by comparison, as black as numberless flocks of ravens. This note of a dreamy, almost a sleepy devilry, was no mere fancy from the landscape. For there did rest on the place one of those clouds of pride and madness and mysterious sorrow which lie more heavily on the noble houses of Scotland than on any other of the children of men. For Scotland has a double dose of the poison called heredity; the sense of blood in the aristocrat, and the sense of doom in the Calvinist.

The priest had snatched a day from his business at Glasgow to meet his friend Flambeau, the amateur detective, who was at Glengyle Castle with another more formal officer investigating the life and death of the late Earl of Glengyle. That mysterious person was the last representative of a race whose valour, insanity, and violent cunning had made them terrible even among the sinister nobility of their nation in the sixteenth century. None were deeper in that labyrinthine ambition, in chamber within chamber of that palace of lies that was built up around Mary Queen of Scots.

The rhyme in the country-side attested the motive and the result of their machinations candidly:

> *As green sap to the simmer trees*
> *Is red gold to the Ogilvies.*

For many centuries there had never been a decent lord in Glengyle Castle; and with the Victorian era one would have thought that all eccentricities were exhausted. The last Glengyle, however, satisfied his tribal tradition by doing the only thing that was left for him to do; he disappeared. I do not mean that he went abroad; by all accounts he was still in the castle, if he was anywhere. But though his name was in the church register and the big red Peerage, nobody ever saw him under the sun.

If anyone saw him it was a solitary man-servant, something between a groom and a gardener. He was so deaf that the more business-like assumed him to be dumb; while the more penetrating declared him to be half-witted. A gaunt, red-haired labourer, with a dogged jaw and chin, but quite blank blue eyes, he went by the name of Israel Gow, and was the one silent servant on that deserted estate. But the energy with which he dug potatoes, and the regularity with which he disappeared into the kitchen gave people an impression that he was providing for the meals of a superior, and that the strange earl was still concealed in the castle. If society needed any further proof that he was there, the servant persistently asserted that he was not at home. One morning the provost and the minister (for the Glengyes were Presbyterian) were summoned to the castle. There they found that the gardener, groom, and cook had added to his many professions that of an undertaker, and had nailed up his noble master in a coffin. With how much or how little further inquiry this odd fact was passed, did not as yet very plainly appear; for the thing had never been legally investigated till Flambeau had gone north two or three days before. By then the body of Lord Glengyle (if it was the body) had lain for some time in the little churchyard on the hill.

As Father Brown passed through the dim garden and came under the shadow of the château, the clouds were thick and the whole air damp and thundery. Against the last stripe of the green-gold sunset he saw a black human silhouette; a man in a chimney-pot hat, with a big spade over his shoulder. The combination was queerly suggestive of a sexton; but when Brown remembered the deaf servant who dug potatoes, he thought it natural enough. He knew something of the Scotch peasant; he knew the respectability which might well feel it necessary to wear "blacks" for an official inquiry; he knew also the economy that would not lose an hour's digging for that. Even the man's start and suspicious stare as the priest went by were consonant enough with the vigilance and jealousy of such a type.

The great door was opened by Flambeau himself, who had with him a lean man with iron-grey hair and papers in his hand: Inspector Craven from Scotland Yard. The entrance hall was mostly stripped and empty; but the pale, sneering faces of one or two of the wicked Ogilvies looked down out of black periwigs and blackening canvas.

Following them into an inner room, Father Brown found that the allies had been seated at a long oak table, of which their end was covered with scribbled papers, flanked with whisky and cigars. Through the whole of its remaining length it was occupied by detached objects arranged at intervals; objects about as inexplicable as any objects could be. One looked like a small heap of glittering broken glass. Another looked like a high heap of brown dust. A third appeared to be a plain stick of wood.

"You seem to have a sort of geological museum here," he said, as he sat down, jerking his head briefly in the direction of the brown dust and the crystalline fragments.

"Not a geological museum," replied Flambeau; "say a psychological museum."

"Oh, for the Lord's sake," cried the police detective laughing, "don't let's begin with such long words."

"Don't you know what psychology means?" asked Flambeau with friendly surprise. "Psychology means being off your chump."

"Still I hardly follow," replied the official.

"Well," said Flambeau, with decision, "I mean that we've only found out one thing about Lord Glengyle. He was a maniac."

The black silhouette of Gow with his top hat and spade passed the window, dimly outlined against the darkening sky. Father Brown stared passively at it and answered:

"I can understand there must have been something odd about the man, or he wouldn't have buried himself alive—nor been in such a hurry to bury himself dead. But what makes you think it was lunacy?"

"Well," said Flambeau, "you just listen to the list of things Mr. Craven has found in the house."

"We must get a candle," said Craven, suddenly, "A storm is getting up, and it's too dark to read."

"Have you found any candles," asked Brown smiling, "among your oddities?"

Flambeau raised a grave face, and fixed his dark eyes on his friend.

"That is curious, too," he said. "Twenty-five candles, and not a trace of a candlestick."

In the rapidly darkening room and rapidly rising wind, Brown went along the table to where a bundle of wax candles lay among the other scrappy exhibits. As he did so he bent accidentally over the heap of red-brown dust; and a sharp sneeze cracked the silence.

"Hullo!" he said, "snuff!"

He took one of the candles, lit it carefully, came back and stuck it in the neck of the whisky bottle. The unrestful night air, blowing through the crazy window, waved the long flame like a banner. And on every side of the castle they could hear the miles and miles of black pine-wood seething like a black sea around a rock.

"I will read the inventory," began Craven gravely, picking up one of the papers, "the inventory of what we found loose and unexplained in the castle. You are to understand that the place generally was dismantled and neglected; but one or two rooms had plainly been inhabited in a simple but not squalid style by somebody; somebody who was not the servant Gow. The list is as follows:

"First item. A very considerable hoard of precious stones, nearly all diamonds, and all of them loose, without any setting whatever. Of course, it is natural that the Ogilvies should have family jewels; but those are exactly the jewels that are almost always set in particular articles of ornament. The Ogilvies would seem to have kept theirs loose in their pockets, like coppers.

"Second item. Heaps and heaps of loose snuff, not kept in a horn, or even a pouch, but lying in heaps on the mantlepieces, on the sideboard, on the piano, anywhere. It looks as if the old gentleman would not take the trouble to look in a pocket or lift a lid.

"Third item. Here and there about the house curious little heaps of minute pieces of metal, some like steel springs and some in the form of microscopic wheels. As if they had gutted some mechanical toy.

"Fourth item. The wax candles, which have to be stuck in bottle necks because there is nothing else to stick them in. Now I wish you to note how very much queerer all this is than anything we anticipated. For the central riddle we are prepared; we have all seen at a glance that there was something wrong about the last earl. We have come here to find out whether he really lived here, whether he really died here, whether that red-haired scarecrow who did his burying had anything to do with his dying. But suppose the worst in all this, the most lurid or melodramatic solution you like. Suppose the servant really killed the master, or suppose the master isn't really dead, or suppose the master is dressed up as the servant, or suppose the servant is buried for the master; invent what Wilkie Collins' tragedy you like, and you still have not explained a candle without a candlestick, or why an elderly gentleman of good family should habitually spill snuff on the piano. The core of the tale we could imagine; it is the fringes that are mysterious. By no stretch of fancy can the human mind connect together snuff and diamonds and wax and loose clockwork."

"I think I see the connexion," said the priest. "This Glengyle was mad against the French Revolution. He was an enthusiast for the *ancien régime,* and was trying to re-enact literally the family life of the last Bourbons. He had snuff because it was the eighteenth-century luxury; wax candles, because they were the eighteenth-century lighting; the mechanical bits of iron represent the locksmith hobby of Louis XVI; the diamonds are for the Diamond Necklace of Marie Antoinette."

Both the other men were staring at him with round eyes. "What a perfectly extraordinary notion!" cried Flambeau. "Do you really think that is the truth?"

"I am perfectly sure it isn't," answered Father Brown, "only you said that nobody could connect snuff and diamonds and clockwork and candles. I give you that connexion off-hand. The real truth, I am very sure, lies deeper."

He paused a moment and listened to the wailing of the wind in the turrets. Then he said, "The late Earl of Glengyle was a thief. He lived a second and darker life as a desperate housebreaker. He did not have any candlesticks because he only used these candles cut short in the little lantern he carried. The snuff he employed as the fiercest French criminals have used pepper: to fling it suddenly in dense masses in the face of a captor or pursuer. But the final proof is in the curious coincidence of the diamonds and the small steel wheels. Surely that makes everything plain to you? Diamonds and small steel wheels are the only two instruments with which you can cut out a pane of glass."

The bough of a broken pine-tree lashed heavily in the blast against the windowpane behind them, as if in parody of a burglar, but they did not turn round. Their eyes were fastened on Father Brown.

"Diamonds and small wheels," repeated Craven ruminating. "Is that all that makes you think it the true explanation?"

"I don't think it the true explanation," replied the priest placidly; "but you said that nobody could connect the four things. The true tale, of course, is something much more humdrum. Glengyle had found, or thought he had found, precious-stones on his estate. Somebody had bamboozled him with those loose brilliants, saying they were found in the castle caverns. The little wheels are some diamond-cutting affair. He had to do the thing very roughly and in a small way, with the help of a few shepherds or rude fellows on these hills. Snuff is the one great luxury of such Scotch shepherds; it's the one thing with which you can bribe them. They didn't have candlesticks because they didn't want them; they held the candles in their hands when they explored the caves."

"Is that all?" asked Flambeau after a long pause. "Have we got to the dull truth at last?"

"Oh, no," said Father Brown.

As the wind died in the most distant pine-woods with a long hoot as of mockery Father Brown, with an utterly impassive face, went on:

"I only suggested that because you said one could not plausibly connect snuff with clockwork or candles with bright stones. Ten false philosophies will fit the universe; ten false theories will fit Glengyle Castle. But we want the real explanation of the castle and the universe. But are there no other exhibits?"

Craven laughed, and Flambeau rose smiling to his feet and strolled down the long table.

"Items five, six, seven, etc.," he said, "and certainly more varied than instructive. A curious collection, not of lead pencils, but of the lead out of lead pencils. A senseless stick of bamboo, with the top rather splintered. It might be the instrument of the crime. Only, there isn't any crime. The only other things are a few old missals and little Catholic pictures, which the Ogilvies kept, I suppose, from the Middle Ages—their family pride being stronger than their Puritanism. We only put them in the museum because they seem curiously cut about and defaced."

The heady tempest without drove a dreadful wrack of clouds across Glengyle and threw the long room into darkness as Father Brown picked up the little illuminated pages to examine them. He spoke before the drift of darkness had passed; but it was the voice of an utterly new man.

"Mr. Craven," said he, talking like a man ten years younger, "you have got a legal warrant, haven't you, to go up and examine that grave? The sooner we do it the better, and get to the bottom of this horrible affair. If I were you I should start now."

"Now," repeated the astonished detective, "and why now?"

"Because this is serious," answered Brown; "this is not split snuff or loose pebbles, that might be there for a hundred reasons. There is only one reason I know of for *this* being done; and the reason goes down to the roots of the world. These religious pictures are not just dirtied or torn or scrawled over, which might be done in idleness or bigotry, by children or by Protestants. These have been treated very carefully—and very queerly. In every place where the great ornamented name of God comes in the old illuminations it has been elaborately taken out. The only other thing that has been removed is the halo round the head of the Child Jesus. Therefore, I say, let us get our warrant and our spade and our hatchet, and go up and break open that coffin."

"What *do* you mean?" demanded the London officer.

"I mean," answered the little priest, and his voice seemed to rise slightly in the roar of the gale. "I mean that the great devil of the universe may be sitting on the top tower of this castle at this moment, as big as a hundred elephants, and roaring like the Apocalypse. There is black magic somewhere at the bottom of this."

"Black magic," repeated Flambeau in a low voice, for he was too enlightened a man not to know of such things; "but what can these other things mean?"

"Oh, something damnable, I suppose," replied Brown impatiently. "How should I know? How can I guess all their mazes down below? Perhaps you can make a torture out of snuff and bamboo. Perhaps lunatics lust after wax and steel filings. Perhaps there is a maddening drug made of lead pencils! Our shortest cut to the mystery is up the hill to the grave."

His comrades hardly knew that they had obeyed and followed him till a blast of the night wind nearly flung them on their faces in the garden. Nevertheless they had obeyed him like automata; for Craven found a hatchet in his hand, and the warrant in his pocket; Flambeau was carrying the heavy spade of the strange gardener; Father Brown was carrying the little gilt book from which had been torn the name of God.

The path up the hill to the churchyard was crooked but short; only under that stress of wind it seemed laborious and long. Far as the eye could see, farther and farther as they mounted the slope, were seas beyond seas of pines, now all aslope one way under the wind. And that universal gesture seemed as vain as it was vast, as vain as if that wind were whistling about some unpeopled and pur-poseless planet. Through all that infinite growth of grey-blue forests sang, shrill and high, that ancient sorrow that is in the heart of all heathen things. One could fancy that the voices from the under world of unfathomable foliage were cries of the lost and wandering pagan gods: gods who had gone roaming in that irra-tional forest, and who will never find their way back to heaven.

"You see," said Father Brown in a low but easy tone, "Scotch people before Scotland existed were a curious lot. In fact, they're a curious lot still. But in the prehistoric times I fancy they really wor-shipped demons. That," he added genially, "is why they jumped at the Puritan theology."

"My friend," said Flambeau, turning in a kind of fury, "what does all that snuff mean?"

"My friend," replied Brown, with equal seriousness, "there is one mark of all genuine religions: materialism. Now, devil-worship is a perfectly genuine religion."

They had come up on the grassy scalp of the hill, one of the few bald spots that stood clear of the crashing and roaring pine forest. A mean enclosure, partly timber and partly wire, rattled in the tempest to tell them the border of the graveyard. But by the time Inspector Craven had come to the corner of the grave, and Flam-beau had planted his spade point downwards and leaned on it, they were both almost as shaken as the shaky wood and wire. At the foot of the grave grew great tall thistles, grey and silver in their decay. Once or twice, when a ball of thistledown broke under the breeze and flew past him, Craven jumped slightly as if it had been an arrow.

Flambeau drove the blade of his spade through the whistling grass into the wet clay below. Then he seemed to stop and lean on it as on a staff.

"Go on," said the priest very gently. "We are only trying to find the truth. What are you afraid of?"

"I am afraid of finding it," said Flambeau.

The London detective spoke suddenly in a high crowing voice that was meant to be conversational and cheery. "I wonder why he really did hide himself like that. Something nasty, I suppose; was he a leper?"

"Something worse than that," said Flambeau.

"And what do you imagine," asked the other, "would be worse than a leper?"

"I don't imagine it," said Flambeau.

He dug for some dreadful minutes in silence, and then said in a choked voice, "I'm afraid of his not being the right shape."

"Nor was that piece of paper, you know," said Father Brown quietly, "and we survived even that piece of paper."

Flambeau dug on with a blind energy. But the tempest had shouldered away the choking grey clouds that clung to the hills like smoke and revealed grey fields of faint starlight before he cleared the shape of a rude timber coffin, and somehow tipped it up upon the turf. Craven stepped forward with his axe; a thistle-top touched him, and he flinched. Then he took a firmer stride, and hacked and wrenched with an energy like Flambeau's till the lid was torn off, and all that was there lay glimmering in the grey starlight.

"Bones," said Craven; and then he added, "but it is a man," as if that were something unexpected.

"Is he," asked Flambeau in a voice that went oddly up and down, "is he all right?"

"Seems so," said the officer huskily, bending over the obscure and decaying skeleton in the box. "Wait a minute."

A vast heave went over Flambeau's huge figure. "And now I come to think of it," he cried, "why in the name of madness shouldn't he be all right? What is it gets hold of a man on these cursed cold mountains? I think it's the black, brainless repetition; all these forests, and over all an ancient horror of unconsciousness. It's like the dream of an atheist. Pine-trees and more pine-trees and millions more pine-trees——"

"God!" cried the man by the coffin, "but he hasn't got a head."

While the others stood rigid the priest, for the first time, showed a leap of startled concern.

"No head!" he repeated. *"No head?"* as if he had almost expected some other deficiency.

Half-witted visions of a headless baby born to Glengyle, of a headless youth hiding himself in the castle, of a headless man pacing those ancient halls or that gorgeous garden, passed in panorama through their minds. But even in that stiffened instant the tale took no root in them and seemed to have no reason in it. They stood listening to the loud woods and the shrieking sky quite foolishly, like exhausted animals. Thought seemed to be something enormous that had suddenly slipped out of their grasp.

"There are three headless men," said Father Brown, "standing round this open grave."

The pale detective from London opened his mouth to speak, and left it open like a yokel, while a long scream of wind tore the sky; then he looked at the axe in his hands as if it did not belong to him, and dropped it.

"Father," said Flambeau in that infantile and heavy voice he used very seldom, "what are we to do?"

His friend's reply came with the pent promptitude of a gun going off.

"Sleep!" cried Father Brown. "Sleep. We have come to the end of the ways. Do you know what sleep is? Do you know that every man who sleeps believes in God? It is a sacrament; for it is an act of faith and it is a food. And we need a sacrament, if only a natural one. Something has fallen on us that falls very seldom on men; perhaps the worst thing that can fall on them."

Craven's parted lips came together to say, "What do you mean?"

The priest had turned his face to the castle as he answered:

"We have found the truth; and the truth makes no sense."

He went down the path in front of them with a plunging and reckless step very rare with him, and when they reached the castle again he threw himself upon sleep with the simplicity of a dog.

Despite his mystic praise of slumber, Father Brown was up earlier than anyone else except the silent gardener; and was found smoking a big pipe and watching that expert at his speechless labours in the kitchen garden. Towards daybreak the rocking storm had ended in roaring rains, and the day came with a curious freshness. The gardener seemed even to have been conversing, but at sight of the detectives he planted his spade sullenly in a bed and, saying something about his breakfast, shifted along the lines of cabbages and shut himself in the kitchen. "He's a valuable man, that," said Father Brown. "He does the potatoes amazingly. Still," he added, with a dispassionate charity, "he has his faults; which of us hasn't? He doesn't dig this bank quite regularly. There, for instance," and he stamped suddenly on one spot. "I'm really very doubtful about that potato."

"And why?" asked Craven, amused with the little man's hobby.

"I'm doubtful about it," said the other, "because old Gow was doubtful about it himself. He put his spade in methodically in every place but just this. There must be a mighty fine potato just here."

Flambeau pulled up the spade and impetuously drove it into the place. He turned up, under a load of soil, something that did not look like a potato, but rather like a monstrous, over-domed mushroom. But it struck the spade with a cold click; it rolled over like a ball, and grinned up at them.

"The Earl of Glengyle," said Brown sadly, and looked down heavily at the skull.

Then, after a momentary meditation, he plucked the spade from Flambeau, and, saying "We must hide it again," clamped the skull down in the earth. Then he leaned his little body and huge head on the great handle of the spade, that stood up stiffly in the earth, and his eyes were empty and his forehead full of wrinkles. "If one could only conceive," he muttered, "the meaning of this last monstrosity." And leaning on the large spade handle, he buried his brows in his hands, as men do in church.

All the corners of the sky were brightening into blue and silver; the birds were chattering in the tiny garden trees; so loud it seemed as if the trees themselves were talking. But the three men were silent enough.

"Well, I give it all up," said Flambeau at last boisterously. "My brain and this world don't fit each other; and there's an end of it. Snuff, spoilt Prayer Books, and the insides of musical boxes— what——"

Brown threw up his bothered brow and rapped on the spade handle with an intolerance quite unusual with him. "Oh, tut, tut, tut, tut!" he cried. "All that is as plain as a pikestaff. I understood the snuff and clockwork, and so on, when I first opened my eyes this morning. And since then I've had it out with old Gow, the gardener, who is neither so deaf nor so stupid as he pretends. There's nothing amiss about the loose items. I was wrong about the torn mass-book, too; there's no harm in that. But it's this last business. Desecrating graves and stealing dead men's heads—surely there's harm in that? Surely there's black magic still in that? That doesn't fit in to the quite simple story of the snuff and the candles." And, striding about again, he smoked moodily.

"My friend," said Flambeau, with a grim humour, "you must be careful with me and remember I was once a criminal. The great advantage of that estate was that I always made up the story myself, and acted it as quick as I chose. This detective business of waiting about is too much for my French impatience. All my life, for good or evil, I have done things at the instant; I always fought duels the next morning; I always paid bills on the nail; I never even put off a visit to the dentist——"

Father Brown's pipe fell out of his mouth and broke into three pieces on the gravel path. He stood rolling his eyes, the exact picture of an idiot. "Lord, what a turnip I am!" he kept saying. "Lord, what a turnip!" Then, in a somewhat groggy kind of way, he began to laugh.

"The dentist!" he repeated. "Six hours in the spiritual abyss, and all because I never thought of the dentist! Such a simple, such a beautiful and peaceful thought! Friends, we have passed a night in hell; but now the sun is risen, the birds are singing, and the radiant form of the dentist consoles the world."

"I will get some sense out of this," cried Flambeau, striding forward, "if I use the tortures of the Inquisition."

Father Brown repressed what appeared to be a momentary disposition to dance on the now sunlit lawn and cried quite piteously, like a child, "Oh, let me be silly a little. You don't know how un-happy I have been. And now I know that there has been no deep sin in this business at all. Only a little lunacy, perhaps—and who minds that?"

He spun round once more, then faced them with gravity.

"This is not a story of crime," he said; "rather it is the story of a strange and crooked honesty. We are dealing with the one man on earth, perhaps, who has taken no more than his due. It is a study in the savage living logic that has been the religion of this race.

"That old local rhyme about the house of Glengyle—

'As green sap to the simmer trees
Is red gold to the Ogilvies'—

was literal as well as metaphorical. It did not merely mean that the Glengyles sought for wealth; it was also true that they literally gathered gold; they had a huge collection of ornaments and uten-sils in that metal. They were, in fact, misers whose mania took that turn. In the light of that fact, run through all the things we found in the castle. Diamonds without their gold rings; candles without their gold candlesticks; snuff without the gold snuff-boxes; pencil-leads without the gold pencil-cases; a walking-stick with-out its gold top; clockwork without the gold clocks—or rather watches. And, mad as it sounds, because the halos and the name of God in the old missals were of real gold; these also were taken away."

The garden seemed to brighten, the grass to grow gayer in the strengthening sun, as the crazy truth was told. Flambeau lit a ciga-rette as his friend went on.

"Were taken away," continued Father Brown; "were taken away—but not stolen. Thieves would never have left this mystery. Thieves would have taken the gold snuff-boxes, snuff and all; the gold pencil-cases, lead and all. We have to deal with a man with a peculiar conscience, but certainly a conscience. I found that mad moralist this morning in the kitchen garden yonder, and I heard the whole story.

"The late Archibald Ogilvie was the nearest approach to a good man ever born at Glengyle. But his bitter virtue took the turn of the misanthrope; he moped over the dishonesty of his ancestors, from which, somehow, he generalised a dishonesty of all men. More especially he distrusted philanthropy or free-giving; and he swore if he could find one man who took his exact rights he should have all the gold of Glengyle. Having delivered this defiance to humanity he shut himself up, without the smallest expectation of its being answered. One day, however, a deaf and seemingly senseless lad from a distant village brought him a belated telegram; and Glengyle, in his acrid pleasantry, gave him a new farthing. At least he thought he had done so, but when he turned over his change he found the new farthing still there and a sovereign gone. The accident offered him vistas of sneering speculation. Either way, the boy would show the greasy greed of the species. Either he would vanish, a thief stealing a coin; or he would sneak back with it virtuously, a snob seeking a reward. In the middle of that night Lord Glengyle was knocked up out of his bed—for he lived alone—and forced to open the door to the deaf idiot. The idiot brought with him, not the sovereign, but exactly nineteen shillings and elevenpence three-farthings in change.

"Then the wild exactitude of this action took hold of the mad lord's brain like fire. He swore he was Diogenes, that had long sought an honest man, and at last had found one. He made a new will, which I have seen. He took the literal youth into his huge, neglected house, and trained him up as his solitary servant and—after an odd manner—his heir. And whatever that queer creature understands, he understood absolutely his lord's two fixed ideas: first, that the letter of right is everything; and second, that he himself was to have the gold of Glengyle. So far, that is all; and that is simple. He has stripped the house of gold, and taken not a grain that was not gold; not so much as a grain of snuff. He lifted the gold leaf off an old illumination, fully satisfied that he left the rest unspoilt. All that I understood; but I could not understand this skull business. I was really uneasy about that human head buried among the potatoes. It distressed me—till Flambeau said the word.

"It will be all right. He will put the skull back in the grave, when he has taken the gold out of the tooth."

And, indeed, when Flambeau crossed the hill that morning, he saw that strange being, the just miser, digging at the desecrated grave, the plaid round his throat thrashing out in the mountain wind; the sober top hat on his head.

THE SINS OF PRINCE SARADINE

When Flambeau took his month's holiday from his office in Westminster he took it in a small sailing-boat, so small that it passed much of its time as a rowing-boat. He took it, moreover, in little rivers in the Eastern counties, rivers so small that the boat looked like a magic boat, sailing on land through meadows and cornfields. The vessel was just comfortable for two people; there was room only for necessities, and Flambeau had stocked it with such things as his special philosophy considered necessary. They reduced themselves, apparently, to four essentials: tins of salmon, if he should want to eat; loaded revolvers, if he should want to fight; a bottle of brandy, presumably in case he should faint; and a priest, presumably in case he should die. With this light luggage he crawled down the little Norfolk rivers, intending to reach the Broads at last, but meanwhile delighting in the overhanging gardens and meadows, the mirrored mansions or villages, lingering to fish in the pools and corners, and in some sense hugging the shore.

Like a true philosopher, Flambeau had no aim in his holiday; but, like a true philosopher, he had an excuse. He had a sort of half purpose, which he took just so seriously that its success would crown the holiday, but just so lightly that its failure would not spoil it. Years ago, when he had been a king of thieves and the most famous figure in Paris, he had often received wild communications of approval, denunciation, or even love; but one had, somehow, stuck in his memory. It consisted simply of a visiting-card, in an envelope with an English postmark. On the back of the card was written in French and in green ink: "If you ever retire and become respectable, come and see me. I want to meet you, for I have met all the other great men of my time. That trick of yours of getting one detective to arrest the other was the most splendid scene in French history." On the front of the card was engraved in the formal fashion, "Prince Saradine, Reed House, Reed Island, Norfolk."

He had not troubled much about the prince then, beyond ascertaining that he had been a brilliant and fashionable figure in southern Italy. In his youth, it was said, he had eloped with a married woman of high rank; the escapade was scarcely startling in his social world, but it had clung to men's minds because of an additional tragedy: the alleged suicide of the insulted husband, who appeared to have flung himself over a precipice in Sicily. The prince then lived in Vienna for a time, but his more recent years seemed to have been passed in perpetual and restless travel. But when Flambeau, like the prince himself, had left European celebrity and settled in England, it occurred to him that he might pay a surprise visit to this eminent exile in the Norfolk Broads. Whether he should find the place he had no idea; and, indeed, it was sufficiently small and forgotten. But, as things fell out, he found it much sooner than he expected.

They had moored their boat one night under a bank veiled in high grasses and short pollarded trees. Sleep, after heavy sculling, had come to them early, and by a corresponding accident they awoke before it was light. To speak more strictly, they awoke before it was daylight; for a large lemon moon was only just setting in the forest of high grass above their heads, and the sky was of a vivid violet-blue, nocturnal but bright. Both men had simultaneously a reminiscence of childhood, of the elfin and adventurous time when tall weeds close over us like woods. Standing up thus against the large low moon, the daisies really seemed to be giant daisies, the dandelions to be giant dandelions. Somehow it reminded them of the dado of a nursery wall paper. The drop of the river-bed sufficed to sink them under the roots of all shrubs and flowers and make them gaze upwards at the grass.

"By Jove!" said Flambeau, "it's like being in fairyland."

Father Brown sat bolt upright in the boat and crossed himself. His movement was so abrupt that his friend asked him, with a mild stare, what was the matter.

"The people who wrote the medieval ballads," answered the priest, "knew more about fairies than you do. It isn't only nice things that happen in fairyland."

"Oh, bosh!" said Flambeau. "Only nice things could happen under such an innocent moon. I am for pushing on now and seeing what does really come. We may die and rot before we ever see again such a moon or such a mood."

"All right," said Father Brown. "I never said it was always wrong to enter fairyland. I only said it was always dangerous."

They pushed slowly up the brightening river; the glowing violet of the sky and the pale gold of the moon grew fainter and fainter, and faded into that vast colourless cosmos that precedes the colours of the dawn. When the first faint stripes of red and gold and grey split the horizon from end to end they were broken by the black bulk of a town or village which sat on the river just ahead of them. It was already an easy twilight, in which all things were visible, when they came under the hanging roofs and bridges of this riverside hamlet. The houses, with their long, low, stooping roofs, seemed to come down to drink at the river, like huge grey and red cattle. The broadening and whitening dawn had already turned to working daylight before they saw any living creature on the wharves and bridges of that silent town. Eventually they saw a very placid and prosperous man in his shirt sleeves, with a face as round as the recently sunken moon, and rays of red whisker around the low arc of it, who was leaning on a post above the sluggish tide. By an impulse not to be analysed, Flambeau rose to his full height in the swaying boat and shouted at the man to ask if he knew Reed Island or Reed House. The prosperous man's smile grew slightly more expansive, and he simply pointed up the river towards the next bend of it. Flambeau went ahead without further speech.

The boat took many such grassy corners and followed many such reedy and silent reaches of river; but before the search had become monotonous they had swung round a specially sharp angle and come into the silence of a sort of pool or lake, the sight of which instinctively arrested them. For in the middle of this wider piece of water, fringed on every side with rushes, lay a long, low islet, along which ran a long, low house or bungalow built of bamboo or some kind of tough tropic cane. The upstanding rods of bamboo which made the walls were pale yellow, the sloping rods that made the roof were of darker red or brown, otherwise the long house was a thing of repetition and monotony. The early morning breeze rustled the reeds round the island and sang in the strange ribbed house as in a giant pan-pipe.

"By George!" cried Flambeau; "here is the place, after all! Here is Reed Island, if ever there was one. Here is Reed House, if it is anywhere. I believe that fat man with whiskers was a fairy."

"Perhaps," remarked Father Brown impartially. "If he was, he was a bad fairy."

But even as he spoke the impetuous Flambeau had run his boat ashore in the rattling reeds, and they stood in the long, quaint islet beside the odd and silent house.

The house stood with its back, as it were, to the river and the only landing-stage; the main entrance was on the other side, and looked down the long island garden. The visitors approached it, therefore, by a small path running round nearly three sides of the house, close under the low eaves. Through three different windows on three different sides they looked in on the same long, well-lit room, panelled in light wood, with a large number of looking-glasses, and laid out as for an elegant lunch. The front door, when they came round to it at last, was flanked by two turquoise-blue flower pots. It was opened by a butler of the drearier type—long, lean, grey, and listless—who murmured that Prince Saradine was from home at present, but was expected hourly; the house being kept ready for him and his guests. The exhibition of the card with the scrawl of green ink awoke a flicker of life in the parchment face of the depressed retainer, and it was with a certain shaky courtesy that he suggested that the strangers should remain. "His Highness may be here any minute," he said, "and would be distressed to have just missed any gentleman he had invited. We have orders always to keep a little cold lunch for him and his friends, and I am sure he would wish it to be offered."

Moved with curiosity to this minor adventure, Flambeau assented gracefully, and followed the old man, who ushered him ceremoniously into the long, lightly panelled room. There was nothing very notable about it, except the rather unusual alternation of many long, low windows with many long, low oblongs of looking-glass, which gave a singular air of lightness and unsubstantialness to the place. It was somehow like lunching out of doors. One or two pictures of a quiet kind hung in the corners, one a large grey photograph of a very young man in uniform, another a red chalk sketch of two long-haired boys. Asked by Flambeau whether the soldierly person was the prince, the butler answered shortly in the negative; it was the prince's younger brother, Captain Stephen Saradine, he said. And with that the old man seemed to dry up suddenly and lose all taste for conversation.

After lunch had tailed off with exquisite coffee and liqueurs, the guests were introduced to the garden, the library, and the housekeeper—a dark, handsome lady, of no little majesty, and rather like a plutonic Madonna. It appeared that she and the butler were the only survivors of the prince's original foreign *ménage*, all the other servants now in the house being new and collected in Norfolk by the housekeeper. This latter lady went by the name of Mrs. Anthony, but she spoke with a slight Italian accent, and Flambeau did not doubt that Anthony was a Norfolk version of some more Latin name. Mr. Paul, the butler, also had a faintly foreign air, but he was in tongue and training English, as are many of the most polished men-servants of the cosmopolitan nobility.

Pretty and unique as it was, the place had about it a curious luminous sadness. Hours passed in it like days. The long, well-windowed rooms were full of daylight, but it seemed a dead daylight. And through all other incidental noises, the sound of talk, the clink of glasses, or the passing feet of servants, they could hear on all sides of the house the melancholy noise of the river.

"We have taken a wrong turning, and come to a wrong place," said Father Brown, looking out of the window at the grey-green sedges and the silver flood. "Never mind; one can sometimes do good by being the right person in the wrong place."

Father Brown, though commonly a silent, was an oddly sympathetic little man, and in those few but endless hours he unconsciously sank deeper into the secrets of Reed House than his professional friend. He had that knack of friendly silence which is so essential to gossip; and saying scarcely a word, he probably obtained from his new acquaintances all that in any case they would have told. The butler indeed was naturally uncommunicative. He betrayed a sullen and almost animal affection for his master; who, he said, had been very badly treated. The chief offender seemed to be his highness's brother, whose name alone would lengthen the old man's lantern jaws and pucker his parrot nose into a sneer. Captain Stephen was a ne'er-do-well, apparently, and had drained his benevolent brother of hundreds and thousands; forced him to fly from fashionable life and live quietly in this retreat. That was all Paul, the butler, would say, and Paul was obviously a partisan.

The Italian housekeeper was somewhat more communicative, being, as Brown fancied, somewhat less content. Her tone about her master was faintly acid; though not without a certain awe. Flambeau and his friend were standing in the room of the looking-glasses examining the red sketch of the two boys, when the housekeeper swept in swiftly on some domestic errand. It was a peculiarity of this glittering, glass-panelled place that anyone entering was reflected in four or five mirrors at once; and Father Brown, without turning round, stopped in the middle of a sentence of family criticism. But Flambeau, who had his face close up to the picture was already saying in a loud voice, "The brothers Saradine, I suppose. They both look innocent enough. It would be hard to say which is the good brother and which the bad." Then, realising the lady's presence, he turned the conversation with some triviality, and strolled out into the garden. But Father Brown still gazed steadily at the red crayon sketch; and Mrs. Anthony still gazed steadily at Father Brown.

She had large and tragic brown eyes, and her olive face glowed darkly with a curious and painful wonder—as of one doubtful of a stranger's identity or purpose. Whether the little priest's coat and creed touched some southern memories of confession, or whether she fancied he knew more than he did, she said to him in a low voice as to a fellow plotter, "He is right enough in one way, your friend. He says it would be hard to pick out the good and bad brothers. Oh, it would be hard, it would be mighty hard, to pick out the good one."

"I don't understand you," said Father Brown, and began to move away.

The woman took a step nearer to him, with thunderous brows and a sort of savage stoop, like a bull lowering his horns.

"There isn't a good one," she hissed. "There was badness enough in the captain taking all that money, but I don't think there was much goodness in the prince giving it. The captain's not the only one with something against him."

A light dawned on the cleric's averted face, and his mouth formed silently the word "blackmail." Even as he did so the woman turned an abrupt white face over her shoulder and almost fell. The door had opened soundlessly and the pale Paul stood like a ghost in the doorway. By the weird trick of the reflecting walls, it seemed as if five Pauls had entered by five doors simultaneously.

"His Highness," he said, "has just arrived."

In the same flash the figure of a man had passed outside the first window, crossing the sunlit pane like a lighted stage. An instant later he passed at the second window and the many mirrors repainted in successive frames the same eagle profile and marching figure. He was erect and alert, but his hair was white and his complexion of an odd ivory yellow. He had that short, curved Roman nose which generally goes with long, lean cheeks and chin, but these were partly masked by moustache and imperial. The moustache was much darker than the beard, giving an effect slightly theatrical, and he was dressed up to the same dashing part, having a white top hat, an orchid in his coat, a yellow waistcoat and yellow gloves which he flapped and swung as he walked. When he came round to the front door they heard the stiff Paul open it, and heard the new arrival say cheerfully, "Well, you see I have come." The stiff Mr. Paul bowed and answered in his inaudible manner; for a few minutes their conversation could not be heard. Then the butler said, "Everything is at your disposal"; and the glove-flapping Prince Saradine came gaily into the room to greet them. They beheld once more that spectral scene—five princes entering a room with five doors.

The prince put the white hat and yellow gloves on the table and offered his hand quite cordially.

"Delighted to see you here, Mr. Flambeau," he said. "Knowing you very well by reputation, if that's not an indiscreet remark."

"Not at all," answered Flambeau, laughing. "I am not sensitive. Very few reputations are gained by unsullied virtue."

The prince flashed a sharp look at him to see if the retort had any personal point; then he laughed also and offered chairs to everyone, including himself.

"Pleasant little place, this, I think," he said with a detached air. "Not much to do, I fear; but the fishing is really good."

The priest, who was staring at him with the grave stare of a baby, was haunted by some fancy that escaped definition. He looked at the grey, carefully curled hair, yellow white visage, and slim, somewhat foppish figure. These were not unnatural, though perhaps a shade *pronouncé*, like the outfit of a figure behind the footlights. The nameless interest lay in something else, in the very framework of the face; Brown was tormented with a half memory of having seen it somewhere before. The man looked like some old friend of his dressed up. Then he suddenly remembered the mirrors, and put his fancy down to some psychological effect of that multiplication of human masks.

Prince Saradine distributed his social attentions between his guests with great gaiety and tact. Finding the detective of a sporting turn and eager to employ his holiday, he guided Flambeau and

Flambeau's boat down to the best fishing spot in the stream, and was back in his own canoe in twenty minutes to join Father Brown in the library and plunge equally politely into the priest's more philosophic pleasures. He seemed to know a great deal both about the fishing and the books, though of these not the most edifying; he spoke five or six languages, though chiefly the slang of each. He had evidently lived in varied cities and very motley societies, for some of his cheerfullest stories were about gambling hells and opium dens, Australian bushrangers or Italian brigands. Father Brown knew that the once celebrated Saradine had spent his last few years in almost ceaseless travel, but he had not guessed that the travels were so disreputable or so amusing.

Indeed, with all his dignity of a man of the world, Prince Saradine radiated to such sensitive observers as the priest, a certain atmosphere of the restless and even the unreliable. His face was fastidious, but his eye was wild; he had little nervous ticks, like a man shaken by drink or drugs, and he neither had, nor professed to have, his hand on the helm of household affairs. All these were left to the two old servants, especially to the butler, who was plainly the central pillar of the house. Mr. Paul, indeed, was not so much a butler as a sort of steward or, even, chamberlain; he dined privately, but with almost as much pomp as his master; he was feared by all the servants; and he consulted with the prince decorously, but somewhat unbendingly—rather as if he were the prince's solicitor. The sombre housekeeper was a mere shadow in comparison; indeed, she seemed to efface herself and wait only on the butler, and Brown heard no more of those volcanic whispers which had half told him of the younger brother who blackmailed the elder. Whether the prince was really being thus bled by the absent captain, he could not be certain, but there was something insecure and secretive about Saradine that made the tale by no means incredible.

When they went once more into the long hall with the windows and the mirrors, yellow evening was dropping over the waters and the willowy banks; and a bittern sounded in the distance like an elf upon his dwarfish drum. The same singular sentiment of some sad and evil fairyland crossed the priest's mind again like a little grey cloud. "I wish Flambeau were back," he muttered.

"Do you believe in doom?" asked the restless Prince Saradine suddenly.

"No," answered his guest. "I believe in Doomsday."

The prince turned from the window and stared at him in a singular manner, his face in shadow against the sunset. "What do you mean?" he asked.

"I mean that we here are on the wrong side of the tapestry," answered Father Brown. "The things that happen here do not seem to mean anything; they mean something somewhere else. Somewhere else retribution will come on the real offender. Here it often seems to fall on the wrong person."

The prince made an inexplicable noise like an animal; in his shadowed face the eyes were shining queerly. A new and shrewd thought exploded silently in the other's mind. Was there another meaning in Saradine's blend of brilliancy and abruptness? Was the prince—— Was he perfectly sane? He was repeating, "The wrong person—the wrong person," many more times than was natural in a social exclamation.

Then Father Brown awoke tardily to a second truth. In the mirrors before him he could see the silent door standing open, and the silent Mr. Paul standing in it, with his usual pallid impassiveness.

"I thought it better to announce at once," he said, with the same stiff respectfulness as of an old family lawyer, "a boat rowed by six men has come to the landing-stage, and there's a gentleman sitting in the stern."

"A boat!" repeated the prince; "a gentleman?" and he rose to his feet.

There was a startled silence punctuated only by the odd noise of the bird in the sedge; and then, before anyone could speak again, a new face and figure passed in profile round the three sunlit windows, as the prince had passed an hour or two before. But except for the accident that both outlines were aquiline, they had little in common. Instead of the new white topper of Saradine, was a black one of antiquated or foreign shape; under it was a young and very solemn face, clean shaven, blue about its resolute chin, and carrying a faint suggestion of the young Napoleon. The association was assisted by something old and odd about the whole get-up, as of a man who had never troubled to change the fashions of his fathers. He had a shabby blue frock coat, a red, soldierly looking waistcoat, and a kind of coarse white trousers common among the early Victorians, but strangely incongruous to-day. From all this old clothes-shop his olive face stood out strangely young and monstrously sincere.

"The deuce!" said Prince Saradine, and clapping on his white hat he went to the front door himself, flinging it open on the sunset garden.

By that time the new-comer and his followers were drawn up on the lawn like a small stage army. The six boatmen had pulled the boat well up on shore, and were guarding it almost menacingly, holding their oars erect like spears. They were swarthy men, and some of them wore earrings. But one of them stood forward beside the olive-faced young man in the red waistcoat, and carried a large black case of unfamiliar form.

"Your name," said the young man, "is Saradine?"

Saradine assented rather negligently.

The new-comer had dull, dog-like brown eyes, as different as possible from the restless and glittering grey eyes of the prince. But once again Father Brown was tortured with a sense of having seen somewhere a replica of the face; and once again he remembered the repetitions of the glass-panelled room, and put down the coincidence to that. "Confound this crystal palace!" he muttered. "One sees everything too many times. It's like a dream."

"If you are Prince Saradine," said the young man, "I may tell you that my name is Antonelli."

"Antonelli," repeated the prince languidly. "Somehow I remember the name."

"Permit me to present myself," said the young Italian.

With his left hand he politely took off his old-fashioned top hat; with his right he caught Prince Saradine so ringing a crack across the face that the white top hat rolled down the steps and one of the blue flower-pots rocked upon its pedestal.

The prince, whatever he was, was evidently not a coward; he

sprang at his enemy's throat and almost bore him backwards to the grass. But his enemy extricated himself with a singularly inappropriate air of hurried politeness.

"That is all right," he said, panting and in halting English. "I have insulted. I will give satisfaction. Marco, open the case."

The man beside him with the earrings and the big black case proceeded to unlock it. He took out of it two long Italian rapiers, with splendid steel hilts and blades, which he planted point downwards in the lawn. The strange young man standing facing the entrance with his yellow and vindictive face, the two swords standing up in the turf like two crosses in a cemetery, and the line of the ranked towers behind, gave it all an odd appearance of being some barbaric court of justice. But everything else was unchanged, so sudden had been the interruption. The sunset gold still glowed on the lawn, and the bittern still boomed as announcing some small but dreadful destiny.

"Prince Saradine," said the man called Antonelli, "when I was an infant in the cradle you killed my father and stole my mother; my father was the more fortunate. You did not kill him fairly, as I am going to kill you. You and my wicked mother took him driving to a lonely pass in Sicily, flung him down a cliff, and went on your way. I could imitate you if I chose, but imitating you is too vile. I have followed you all over the world, and you have always fled from me. But this is the end of the world—and of you. I have you now, and I give you the chance you never gave my father. Choose one of those swords."

Prince Saradine, with contracted brows, seemed to hesitate a moment, but his ears were still singing with the blow, and he sprang forward and snatched at one of the hilts. Father Brown had also sprung forward, striving to compose the dispute; but he soon found his personal presence made matters worse. Saradine was a French freemason and a fierce atheist, and a priest moved him by the law of contraries. And for the other man neither priest nor layman moved him at all. This young man with the Bonaparte face and the brown eyes was something far sterner than a puritan—a pagan. He was a simple slayer from the morning of the earth; a man of the stone age—a man of stone.

One hope remained, the summoning of the household; and Father Brown ran back into the house. He found, however, that all the under servants had been given a holiday ashore by the autocrat Paul, and that only the sombre Mrs. Anthony moved uneasily about the long rooms. But the moment she turned a ghastly face upon him, he resolved one of the riddles of the house of mirrors. The heavy brown eyes of Antonelli were the heavy brown eyes of Mrs. Anthony; and in a flash he saw half the story.

"Your son is outside," he said without wasting words; "either he or the prince will be killed. Where is Mr. Paul?"

"He is at the landing-stage," said the woman faintly. "He is—he is—signalling for help."

"Mrs. Anthony," said Father Brown seriously, "there is no time for nonsense. My friend has his boat down the river fishing. Your son's boat is guarded by your son's men. There is only this one canoe; what is Mr. Paul doing with it?"

"Santa Maria! I do not know," she said; and swooned all her length on the matted floor.

Father Brown lifted her to a sofa, flung a pot of water over her, shouted for help, and then rushed down to the landing-stage of the little island. But the canoe was already in mid-stream, and old Paul was pulling and pushing it up the river with an energy incredible at his years.

"I will save my master," he cried, his eyes blazing maniacally. "I will save him yet!"

Father Brown could do nothing but gaze after the boat as it struggled up-stream and pray that the old man might waken the little town in time.

"A duel is bad enough," he muttered, rubbing up his rough dust-coloured hair, "but there's something wrong about this duel, even as a duel. I feel it in my bones. But what can it be?"

As he stood staring at the water, a wavering mirror of sunset, he heard from the other end of the island garden a small but unmistakable sound—the cold concussion of steel. He turned his head.

Away on the farthest cape or headland of the long islet, on a strip of turf beyond the last rank of roses, the duellists had already crossed swords. Evening above them was a dome of virgin gold, and, distant as they were, every detail was picked out. They had cast off their coats, but the yellow waistcoat and white hair of Saradine, the red waistcoat and white trousers of Antonelli, glittered in the level light like the colours of the dancing clockwork dolls. The two swords sparkled from point to pommel like two diamond pins. There was something frightful in the two figures appearing so little and so gay. They looked like two butterflies trying to pin each other to a cork.

Father Brown ran as hard as he could, his little legs going like a wheel. But when he came to the field of combat he found he was both too late and too early—too late to stop the strife, under the shadow of the grim Sicilians leaning on their oars, and too early to anticipate any disastrous issue of it. For the two men were singularly well matched, the prince using his skill with a sort of cynical confidence, the Sicilian using his with a murderous care. Few finer fencing matches can ever have been seen in crowded amphitheatres than that which tinkled and sparkled on that forgotten island in the reedy river. The dizzy fight was balanced so long that hope began to revive in the protesting priest; by all common probability Paul must soon come back with the police. It would be some comfort even if Flambeau came back from his fishing, for Flambeau, physically speaking, was worth four other men. But there was no sign of Flambeau, and, what was much queerer, no sign of Paul or the police. No other raft or stick was left to float on; in that lost island in that vast nameless pool, they were cut off as on a rock in the Pacific.

Almost as he had the thought the ringing of the rapiers quickened to a rattle, the prince's arms flew up, and the point shot out behind between his shoulder-blades. He went over with a great whirling movement, almost like one throwing the half of a boy's cart-wheel. The sword flew from his hand like a shooting star, and dived into the distant river. And he himself sank with so earth-shaking a subsidence that he broke a big rose-tree with his body and shook up into the sky a cloud of red earth—like the smoke of some heathen sacrifice. The Sicilian had made blood-offering to the ghost of his father.

The priest was instantly on his knees by the corpse; but only to make too sure that it was a corpse. As he was still trying some last hopeless tests he heard for the first time voices from farther up the river, and saw a police boat shoot up to the landing-stage, with constables and other important people, including the excited Paul. The little priest rose with a distinctly dubious grimace.

"Now, why on earth," he muttered, "why on earth couldn't he have come before?"

Some seven minutes later the island was occupied by an invasion of townsfolk and police, and the latter had put their hands on the victorious duellist, ritually reminding him that anything he said might be used against him.

"I shall not say anything," said the monomaniac, with a wonderful and peaceful face. "I shall never say anything more. I am very happy, and I only want to be hanged."

Then he shut his mouth as they led him away, and it is the strange but certain truth that he never opened it again in this world, except to say "Guilty" at his trial.

Father Brown had stared at the suddenly crowded garden, the arrest of the man of blood, the carrying away of the corpse after its examination by the doctor, rather as one watches the breakup of some ugly dream; he was motionless, like a man in a nightmare. He gave his name and address as a witness, but declined their offer of a boat to the shore, and remained alone in the island garden, gazing at the broken rose bush and the whole green theatre of that swift and inexplicable tragedy. The light died along the river; mist rose in the marshy banks; a few belated birds flitted fitfully across.

Stuck stubbornly in his sub-consciousness (which was an unusually lively one) was an unspeakable certainty that there was something still unexplained. This sense that had clung to him all day could not be fully explained by his fancy about "looking-glass land." Somehow he had not seen the real story, but some game or masque. And yet people do not get hanged or run through the body for the sake of a charade.

As he sat on the steps of the landing-stage ruminating he grew conscious of the tall, dark streak of a sail coming silently down the shining river, and sprang to his feet with such a backrush of feeling that he almost wept.

"Flambeau!" he cried, and shook his friend by both hands again and again, much to the astonishment of that sportsman, as he came on shore with his fishing tackle. "Flambeau," he said, "so you're not killed?"

"Killed!" repeated the angler in great astonishment. "And why should I be killed?"

"Oh, because nearly everybody else is," said his companion rather wildly. "Saradine got murdered, and Antonelli wants to be hanged, and his mother's fainted, and I, for one, don't know whether I'm in this world or the next. But, thank God, you're in the same one." And he took the bewildered Flambeau's arm.

As they turned from the landing-stage they came under the eaves of the low bamboo house, and looked in through one of the windows, as they had done on their first arrival. They beheld a lamp-lit interior well calculated to arrest their eyes. The table in the long dining-room had been laid for dinner when Saradine's destroyer had fallen like a storm-bolt on the island. And the dinner was now in placid progress, for Mrs. Anthony sat somewhat sullenly at the foot of the table, while at the head of it was Mr. Paul, the *major domo*, eating and drinking of the best, his bleared, bluish eyes standing queerly out of his face, his gaunt countenance inscrutable, but by no means devoid of satisfaction.

With a gesture of powerful impatience, Flambeau rattled at the window, wrenched it open, and put an indignant head into the lamp-lit room.

"Well," he cried. "I can understand you may need some refreshment, but really to steal your master's dinner while he lies murdered in the garden——"

"I have stolen a great many things in a long and pleasant life," replied the strange old gentleman placidly; "this dinner is one of the few things I have not stolen. This dinner and this house and garden happen to belong to me."

A thought flashed across Flambeau's face. "You mean to say," he began, "that the will of Prince Saradine——"

"I am Prince Saradine," said the old man, munching a salted almond.

Father Brown, who was looking at the birds outside, jumped as if he were shot, and put in at the window a pale face like a turnip.

"You are *what?*" he repeated in a shrill voice.

"Paul, Prince Saradine, *à vos ordres,*" said the venerable person politely, lifting a glass of sherry. "I live here very quietly, being a domestic kind of fellow; and for the sake of modesty I am called Mr. Paul, to distinguish me from my unfortunate brother Mr. Stephen. He died, I hear, recently—in the garden. Of course, it is not my fault if enemies pursue him to this place. It is owing to the regrettable irregularity of his life. He was not a domestic character."

He relapsed into silence, and continued to gaze at the opposite wall just above the bowed and sombre head of the woman. They saw plainly the family likeness that had haunted them in the dead man. Then his old shoulders began to heave and shake a little, as if he were choking, but his face did not alter.

"My God!" cried Flambeau after a pause, "he's laughing!"

"Come away," said Father Brown, who was quite white. "Come away from this house of hell. Let us get into an honest boat again."

Night had sunk on rushes and river by the time they had pushed off from the island, and they went down-stream in the dark, warming themselves with two big cigars that glowed like crimson ships' lanterns. Father Brown took his cigar out of his mouth and said:

"I suppose you can guess the whole story now? After all, it's a primitive story. A man had two enemies. He was a wise man. And so he discovered that two enemies are better than one."

"I do not follow that," answered Flambeau.

"Oh, it's really simple," rejoined his friend. "Simple, though anything but innocent. Both the Saradines were scamps, but the prince, the elder, was the sort of scamp that gets to the top, and the younger, the captain, was the sort that sinks to the bottom. This squalid officer fell from beggar to blackmailer, and one ugly day he got his hold upon his brother, the prince. Obviously it was for no light matter, for Prince Paul Saradine was frankly 'fast,' and had no reputation to lose as to the mere sins of society. In plain fact, it was a hanging matter, and Stephen literally had a rope round his brother's neck. He had somehow discovered the truth about the Sicilian affair, and could prove that Paul murdered old Antonelli in the mountains. The captain raked in the hush money heavily for ten years, until even the prince's splendid fortune began to look a little foolish.

"But Prince Saradine bore another burden besides his blood-sucking brother. He knew that the son of Antonelli, a mere child at the time of the murder, had been trained in savage Sicilian loyalty, and lived only to avenge his father, not with the gibbet (for he lacked Stephen's legal proof), but with the old weapons of vendetta. The boy had practised arms with a deadly perfection, and about the time that he was old enough to use them Prince Saradine began, as the society papers said, to travel. The fact is that he began to flee for his life, passing from place to place like a hunted criminal; but with one relentless man upon his trail. That was Prince Paul's position, and by no means a pretty one. The more money he spent on eluding Antonelli the less he had to silence Stephen. The more he gave to silence Stephen the less chance there was of finally escaping Antonelli. Then it was that he showed himself a great man—a genius like Napoleon.

"Instead of resisting his two antagonists, he surrendered suddenly to both of them. He gave way like a Japanese wrestler, and his foes fell prostrate before him. He gave up the race round the world, and he gave up his address to young Antonelli; then he gave up everything to his brother. He sent Stephen money enough for smart clothes and easy travel, with a letter saying roughly: 'This is all I have left. You have cleaned me out. I still have a little house in Norfolk, with servants and a cellar, and if you want more from me you must take that. Come and take possession if you like, and I will live there quietly as your friend or agent or anything.' He knew that the Sicilian had never seen the Saradine brothers save, perhaps, in pictures; he knew they were somewhat alike, both having grey, pointed beards. Then he shaved his own face and waited. The trap worked. The unhappy captain, in his new clothes, entered the house in triumph as a prince, and walked upon the Sicilian's sword.

"There was one hitch, and it is to the honour of human nature.

Evil spirits like Saradine often blunder by never expecting the virtues of mankind. He took it for granted that the Italian's blow, when it came, would be dark, violent and nameless, like the blow it avenged; that the victim would be knifed at night, or shot from behind a hedge, and so die without speech. It was a bad minute for Prince Paul when Antonelli's chivalry proposed a formal duel, with all its possible explanations. It was then that I found him putting off in his boat with wild eyes. He was fleeing, bareheaded, in an open boat before Antonelli should learn who he was.

"But, however agitated, he was not hopeless. He knew the adventurer and he knew the fanatic. It was quite probable that Stephen, the adventurer, would hold his tongue, through his mere histrionic pleasure in playing a part, his lust for clinging to his new cosy quarters, his rascal's trust in luck, and his fine fencing. It was certain that Antonelli, the fanatic, would hold his tongue, and be hanged without telling tales of his family. Paul hung about on the river till he knew the fight was over. Then he roused the town, brought the police, saw his two vanquished enemies taken away forever, and sat down smiling to his dinner."

"Laughing, God help us!" said Flambeau with a strong shudder. "Do they get such ideas from Satan?"

"He got that idea from you," answered the priest.

"God forbid!" ejaculated Flambeau. "From me? What do you mean?"

The priest pulled a visiting-card from his pocket and held it up in the faint glow of his cigar; it was scrawled with green ink.

"Don't you remember his original invitation to you?" he asked, "and the compliment to your criminal exploit? 'That trick of yours,' he says, 'of getting one detective to arrest the other?' He has just copied your trick. With an enemy on each side of him, he slipped swiftly out of the way and let them collide and kill each other."

Flambeau tore Prince Saradine's card from the priest's hands and rent it savagely in small pieces.

"There's the last of that old skull and crossbones," he said as he scattered the pieces upon the dark and disappearing waves of the stream; "but I should think it would poison the fishes."

The last gleam of white card and green ink was drowned and

darkened; a faint and vibrant colour as of morning changed the sky, and the moon behind the grasses grew paler. They drifted in silence.

"Father," said Flambeau suddenly, "do you think it was all a dream?"

The priest shook his head, whether in dissent or agnosticism, but remained mute. A smell of hawthorn and of orchards came to them through the darkness, telling them that a wind was awake; the next moment it swayed their little boat and swelled their sail, and carried them onward down the winding river to happier places and the homes of harmless men.

THE HAMMER OF GOD

The little village of Bohun Beacon was perched on a hill so steep that the tall spire of its church seemed only like the peak of a small mountain. At the foot of the church stood a smithy, generally red with fires and always littered with hammers and scraps of iron; opposite to this, over a rude cross of cobbled paths, was "The Blue Boar," the only inn of the place. It was upon this crossway, in the lifting of a leaden and silver daybreak, that two brothers met in the street and spoke; though one was beginning the day and the other finishing it. The Rev. and Hon. Wilfred Bohun was very devout, and was making his way to some austere exercises of prayer or contemplation at dawn. Colonel the Hon. Norman Bohun, his elder brother, was by no means devout, and was sitting in evening dress on the bench outside "The Blue Boar," drinking what the philosophic observer was free to regard either as his last glass on Tuesday or his first on Wednesday. The colonel was not particular.

The Bohuns were one of the very few aristocratic families really dating from the Middle Ages, and their pennon had actually seen Palestine. But it is a great mistake to suppose that such houses stand high in chivalric tradition. Few except the poor preserve traditions. Aristocrats live not in traditions but in fashions. The Bohuns had been Mohocks under Queen Anne and Mashers under Queen Victoria. But like more than one of the really ancient houses, they had rotted in the last two centuries into mere drunkards and dandy degenerates, till there had even come a whisper of insanity. Certainly there was something hardly human about the colonel's wolfish pursuit of pleasure, and his chronic resolution not to go home till morning had a touch of the hideous clarity of insomnia. He was a tall, fine animal, elderly, but with hair still startlingly yellow. He would have looked merely blond and leonine, but his blue eyes were sunk so deep in his face that they looked black. They were a little too close together. He had very long yellow moustaches; on each side of them a fold or furrow from nostril to jaw, so that a sneer seemed cut into his face. Over his evening clothes he wore a curious pale yellow coat that looked more like a very light dressing gown than an overcoat, and on the back of his head was stuck an extraordinary broad-brimmed hat of a bright green colour, evidently some oriental curiosity caught up at random. He was proud of appearing in such incongruous attires—proud of the fact that he always made them look congruous.

His brother the curate had also the yellow hair and the elegance, but he was buttoned up to the chin in black, and his face was clean-shaven, cultivated, and a little nervous. He seemed to live for nothing but his religion; but there were some who said (notably the blacksmith, who was a Presbyterian) that it was a love of Gothic architecture rather than of God, and that his haunting of the church like a ghost was only another and purer turn of the almost morbid thirst for beauty which sent his brother raging after women and wine. This charge was doubtful, while the man's practical piety was indubitable. Indeed, the charge was mostly an ignorant misunderstanding of the love of solitude and secret prayer, and was founded on his being often found kneeling, not before the altar, but in peculiar places, in the crypts or gallery, or even in the belfry. He was at the moment about to enter the church through the yard of the smithy, but stopped and frowned a little as he saw his brother's cavernous eyes staring in the same direction. On the hypothesis that the colonel was interested in the church he did not waste any speculations. There only remained the blacksmith's shop, and though the blacksmith was a Puritan and none of his people, Wilfred Bohun had heard some scandals about a beautiful and rather celebrated wife. He flung a suspicious look across the shed, and the colonel stood up laughing to speak to him.

"Good morning, Wilfred," he said. "Like a good landlord I am watching sleeplessly over my people. I am going to call on the blacksmith."

Wilfred looked at the ground, and said: "The blacksmith is out. He is over at Greenford."

"I know," answered the other with silent laughter; "that is why I am calling on him."

"Norman," said the cleric, with his eye on a pebble in the road, "are you ever afraid of thunderbolts?"

"What do you mean?" asked the colonel. "Is your hobby meteorology?"

"I mean," said Wilfred, without looking up, "do you ever think that God might strike you in the street?"

"I beg your pardon," said the colonel; "I see your hobby is folklore."

"I know your hobby is blasphemy," retorted the religious man, stung in the one live place of his nature. "But if you do not fear God, you have good reason to fear man."

The elder raised his eyebrows politely. "Fear man?" he said.

"Barnes the blacksmith is the biggest and strongest man for forty miles round," said the clergyman sternly. "I know you are no coward or weakling, but he could throw you over the wall."

This struck home, being true, and the lowering line by mouth and nostril darkened and deepened. For a moment he stood with the heavy sneer on his face. But in an instant Colonel Bohun had recovered his own cruel good humour and laughed, showing two dog-like front teeth under his yellow moustache. "In that case, my dear Wilfred," he said quite carelessly, "it was wise for the last of the Bohuns to come out partially in armour."

And he took off the queer round hat covered with green, showing that it was lined within with steel. Wilfred recognised it indeed as a light Japanese or Chinese helmet torn down from a trophy that hung in the old family hall.

"It was the first hat to hand," explained his brother airily; "always the nearest hat—and the nearest woman."

"The blacksmith is away at Greenford," said Wilfred quietly; "the time of his return is unsettled."

And with that he turned and went into the church with bowed head, crossing himself like one who wishes to be quit of an unclean spirit. He was anxious to forget such grossness in the cool twilight of his tall Gothic cloisters; but on that morning it was fated that his still round of religious exercises should be everywhere arrested by small shocks. As he entered the church, hitherto always empty at that hour, a kneeling figure rose hastily to its feet and came towards the full daylight of the doorway. When the curate saw it he stood still with surprise. For the early worshipper was none other than the village idiot, a nephew of the blacksmith, one who neither would nor could care for the church or for anything else. He was always called "Mad Joe," and seemed to have no other name; he was a dark, strong, slouching lad, with a heavy white face, dark straight hair, and a mouth always open. As he passed the priest, his moon-calf countenance gave no hint of what he had been doing or thinking of. He had never been known to pray before. What sort bf prayers was he saying now? Extraordinary prayers surely.

Wilfred Bohun stood rooted to the spot long enough to see the idiot go out into the sunshine, and even to see his dissolute brother hail him with a sort of avuncular jocularity. The last thing he saw was the colonel throwing pennies at the open mouth of Joe, with the serious appearance of trying to hit it.

This ugly sunlight picture of the stupidity and cruelty of the earth sent the ascetic finally to his prayers for purification and new thoughts. He went up to a pew in the gallery, which brought him under a coloured window which he loved and always quieted his spirit; a blue window with an angel carrying lilies. There he began to think less about the half-wit, with his livid face and mouth like a fish. He began to think less of his evil brother, pacing like a lean lion in his horrible hunger. He sank deeper and deeper into those cold and sweet colours of silver blossoms and sapphire sky.

In this place half an hour afterwards he was found by Gibbs, the village cobbler, who had been sent for him in some haste. He got to his feet with promptitude, for he knew that no small matter would have brought Gibbs into such a place at all. The cobbler was, as in many villages, an atheist, and his appearance in church was a shade more extraordinary than Mad Joe's. It was a morning of theological enigmas.

"What is it?" asked Wilfred Bohun rather stiffly, but putting out a trembling hand for his hat.

The atheist spoke in a tone that, coming from him, was quite startlingly respectful, and even, as it were, huskily sympathetic.

"You must excuse me, sir," he said in a hoarse whisper, "but we didn't think it right not to let you know at once. I'm afraid a rather dreadful thing has happened, sir. I'm afraid your brother——"

Wilfred clenched his frail hands. "What devilry has he done now?" he cried in involuntary passion.

"Why, sir," said the cobbler, coughing, "I'm afraid he's done nothing, and won't do anything. I'm afraid he's done for. You had really better come down, sir."

The curate followed the cobbler down a short winding stair which brought them out at an entrance rather higher than the street. Bohun saw the tragedy in one glance, flat underneath him like a plan. In the yard of the smithy were standing five or six men mostly in black, one in an inspector's uniform. They included the doctor, the Presbyterian minister, and the priest from the Roman Catholic chapel, to which the blacksmith's wife belonged. The latter was speaking to her, indeed, very rapidly, in an undertone, as she, a magnificent woman with red-gold hair, was sobbing blindly on a bench. Between these two groups, and just clear of the main heap of hammers, lay a man in evening dress, spread-eagled and flat on his face. From the height above Wilfred could have sworn to every item of his costume and appearance, down to the Bohun rings upon his fingers; but the skull was only a hideous splash, like a star of blackness and blood.

Wilfred Bohun gave but one glance, and ran down the steps into the yard. The doctor, who was the family physician, saluted him, but he scarcely took any notice. He could only stammer out: "My brother is dead. What does it mean? What is this horrible mystery?" There was an unhappy silence; and then the cobbler, the most outspoken man present, answered: "Plenty of horror, sir," he said; "but not much mystery."

"What do you mean?" asked Wilfred, with a white face.

"It's plain enough," answered Gibbs. "There is only one man for forty miles round that could have struck such a blow as that, and he's the man that had most reason to."

"We must not prejudge anything," put in the doctor, a tall, black-bearded man, rather nervously; "but it is competent for me to corroborate what Mr. Gibbs says about the nature of the blow, sir; it is an incredible blow. Mr. Gibbs says that only one man in this district could have done it. I should have said myself that nobody could have done it."

A shudder of superstition went through the slight figure of the curate. "I can hardly understand," he said.

"Mr. Bohun," said the doctor in a low voice, "metaphors literally fail me. It is inadequate to say that the skull was smashed to bits like an eggshell. Fragments of bone were driven into the body and the ground like bullets into a mud wall. It was the hand of a giant."

He was silent a moment, looking grimly through his glasses; then he added: "The thing has one advantage—that it clears most people of suspicion at one stroke. If you or I or any normally made man in the country were accused of this crime, we should be acquitted as an infant would be acquitted of stealing the Nelson column."

"That's what I say," repeated the cobbler obstinately; "there's only one man that could have done it, and he's the man that would have done it. Where's Simeon Barnes, the blacksmith?"

"He's over at Greenford," faltered the curate.

"More likely over in France," muttered the cobbler.

"No; he is in neither of those places," said a small and colourless voice, which came from the little Roman priest who had joined the group. "As a matter of fact, he is coming up the road at this moment."

The little priest was not an interesting man to look at, having stubbly brown hair and a round and stolid face. But if he had been as splendid as Apollo no one would have looked at him at that moment. Everyone turned round and peered at the pathway which wound across the plain below, along which was indeed walking, at his own huge stride and with a hammer on his shoulder, Simeon the smith. He was a bony and gigantic man, with deep, dark, sinister eyes and a dark chin beard. He was walking and talking quietly with two other men; and though he was never specially cheerful, he seemed quite at his ease.

"My God!" cried the atheistic cobbler, "and there's the hammer he did it with."

"No," said the inspector, a sensible-looking man with a sandy moustache, speaking for the first time. "There's the hammer he did it with over there by the church wall. We have left it and the body exactly as they are."

All glanced round and the short priest went across and looked down in silence at the tool where it lay. It was one of the smallest and the lightest of the hammers, and would not have caught the eye among the rest; but on the iron edge of it were blood and yellow hair.

After a silence the short priest spoke without looking up, and there was a new note in his dull voice. "Mr. Gibbs was hardly right," he said, "in saying that there is no mystery. There is at least the mystery of why so big a man should attempt so big a blow with so little a hammer."

"Oh, never mind that," cried Gibbs, in a fever. "What are we to do with Simeon Barnes?"

"Leave him alone," said the priest quietly. "He is coming here of himself. I know those two men with him. They are very good fellows from Greenford, and they have come over about the Presbyterian chapel."

Even as he spoke the tall smith swung round the corner of the church, and strode into his own yard. Then he stood there quite still, and the hammer fell from his hand. The inspector, who had preserved impenetrable propriety, immediately went up to him.

"I won't ask you, Mr. Barnes," he said, "whether you know anything about what has happened here. You are not bound to say. I hope you don't know, and that you will be able to prove it. But I must go through the form of arresting you in the King's name for the murder of Colonel Norman Bohun."

"You are not bound to say anything," said the cobbler in officious excitement. "They've got to prove everything. They haven't proved yet that it is Colonel Bohun, with the head all smashed up like that."

"That won't wash," said the doctor aside to the priest. "That's out of the detective stories. I was the colonel's medical man, and I knew his body better than he did. He had very fine hands, but quite peculiar oncs. The second and third fingers were the same length. Oh, that's the colonel right enough."

As he glanced at the brained corpse upon the ground the iron eyes of the motionless blacksmith followed them and rested there also.

"Is Colonel Bohun dead?" said the smith quite calmly. "Then he's damned."

"Don't say anything! Oh, don't say anything," cried the atheist cobbler, dancing about in an ecstasy of admiration of the English legal system. For no man is such a legalist as the good Secularist.

The blacksmith turned on him over his shoulder the august face of a fanatic.

"It's well for you infidels to dodge like foxes because the world's law favours you," he said; "but God guards His own in His pocket, as you shall see this day."

Then he pointed to the colonel and said: "When did this dog die in his sins?"

"Moderate your language," said the doctor.

"Moderate the Bible's language, and I'll moderate mine. When did he die?"

"I saw him alive at six o'clock this morning," stammered Wilfred Bohun.

"God is good," said the smith. "Mr. Inspector, I have not the slightest objection to being arrested. It is you who may object to arresting me. I don't mind leaving the court without a stain on my character. You do mind perhaps leaving the court with a bad setback in your career."

The solid inspector for the first time looked at the blacksmith with a lively eye; as did everybody else, except the short, strange priest, who was still looking down at the little hammer that had dealt the dreadful blow.

"There are two men standing outside this shop," went on the blacksmith with ponderous lucidity, "good tradesmen in Greenford whom you all know, who will swear that they saw me from before midnight till daybreak and long after in the committee-room of our Revival Mission, which sits all night, we save souls so fast. In Greenford itself twenty people could swear to me for all that time. If I were a heathen, Mr. Inspector, I would let you walk on to your downfall. But as a Christian man I feel bound to give you your chance, and ask you whether you will hear my alibi now or in court."

The inspector seemed for the first time disturbed, and said, "Of course I should be glad to clear you altogether now."

The smith walked out of his yard with the same long and easy stride, and returned to his two friends from Greenford, who were indeed friends of nearly everyone present. Each of them said a few words which no one ever thought of disbelieving. When they had spoken, the innocence of Simeon stood up as solid as the great church above them.

One of those silences struck the group which are more strange and insufferable than any speech. Madly, in order to make conversation, the curate said to the Catholic priest:

"You seem very much interested in that hammer, Father Brown."

"Yes, I am," said Father Brown; "why is it such a small hammer?"

The doctor swung round on him.

"By George, that's true," he cried; "who would use a little hammer with ten larger hammers lying about?"

Then he lowered his voice in the curate's ear and said: "Only the kind of person that can't lift a large hammer. It is not a question of force or courage between the sexes. It's a question of lifting power in the shoulders. A bold woman could commit ten murders with a light hammer and never turn a hair. She could not kill a beetle with a heavy one."

Wilfred Bohun was staring at him with a sort of hypnotised horror, while Father Brown listened with his head a little on one side, really interested and attentive. The doctor went on with more hissing emphasis:

"Why do these idiots always assume that the only person who hates the wife's lover is the wife's husband? Nine times out of ten the person who most hates the wife's lover is the wife. Who knows what insolence or treachery he had shown her—look there?"

He made a momentary gesture towards the red-haired woman on the bench. She had lifted her head at last and the tears were drying on her splendid face. But the eyes were fixed on the corpse with an electric glare that had in it something of idiocy.

The Rev. Wilfred Bohun made a limp gesture as if waving away all desire to know; but Father Brown, dusting off his sleeve some ashes blown from the furnace, spoke in his indifferent way.

"You are like so many doctors," he said; "your mental science is really suggestive. It is your physical science that is utterly impossible. I agree that the woman wants to kill the co-respondent much more than the petitioner does. And I agree that a woman will always pick up a small hammer instead of a big one. But the difficulty is one of physical impossibility. No woman ever born could have smashed a man's skull out flat like that." Then he added reflectively, after a pause: "These people haven't grasped the whole of it. The man was actually wearing an iron helmet, and the blow scattered it like broken glass. Look at that woman. Look at her arms."

Silence held them all up again, and then the doctor said rather sulkily: "Well, I may be wrong; there are objections to everything. But I stick to the main point. No man but an idiot would pick up that little hammer if he could use a big hammer."

With that the lean and quivering hands of Wilfred Bohun went up to his head and seemed to clutch his scanty yellow hair. After an instant they dropped, and he cried: "That was the word I wanted; you have said the word."

Then he continued, mastering his discomposure: "The words you said were, 'No man but an idiot would pick up the small hammer.'"

"Yes," said the doctor. "Well?"

"Well," said the curate, "no man but an idiot did." The rest stared at him with eyes arrested and riveted, and he went on in a febrile and feminine agitation.

"I am a priest," he cried unsteadily, "and a priest should be no shedder of blood. I—I mean that he should bring no one to the gallows. And I thank God that I see the criminal clearly now—because he is a criminal who cannot be brought to the gallows."

"You will not denounce him?" inquired the doctor.

"He would not be hanged if I did denounce him," answered Wilfred with a wild but curiously happy smile. "When I went into the church this morning I found a madman praying there—that poor Joe, who has been wrong all his life. God knows what he prayed; but with such strange folk it is not incredible to suppose that their prayers are all upside down. Very likely a lunatic would pray before killing a man. When I last saw poor Joe he was with my brother. My brother was mocking him."

"By Jove!" cried the doctor, "this is talking at last. But how do you explain——"

The Rev. Wilfred was almost trembling with the excitement of his own glimpse of the truth. "Don't you see; don't you see," he cried feverishly; "that is the only theory that covers both the queer things, that answers both the riddles. The two riddles are the little hammer and the big blow. The smith might have struck the big blow, but would not have chosen the little hammer. His wife would have chosen the little hammer, but she could not have struck the big blow. But the madman might have done both. As for the little hammer—why, he was mad and might have picked up anything. And for the big blow, have you never heard, doctor, that a maniac in his paroxysm may have the strength of ten men?"

The doctor drew a deep breath and then said, "By golly, I believe you've got it."

Father Brown had fixed his eyes on the speaker so long and steadily as to prove that his large grey, ox-like eyes were not quite so insignificant as the rest of his face. When silence had fallen he said with marked respect: "Mr. Bohun, yours is the only theory yet propounded which holds water every way and is essentially unassailable. I think, therefore, that you deserve to be told, on my positive knowledge, that it is not the true one." And with that the old little man walked away and stared again at the hammer.

"That fellow seems to know more than he ought to," whispered the doctor peevishly to Wilfred. "Those popish priests are deucedly sly."

"No, no," said Bohun, with a sort of wild fatigue. "It was the lunatic. It was the lunatic."

The group of the two clerics and the doctor had fallen away from the more official group containing the inspector and the man he had arrested. Now, however, that their own party had broken up, they heard voices from the others. The priest looked up quietly and then looked down again as he heard the blacksmith say in a loud voice:

"I hope I've convinced you, Mr. Inspector. I'm a strong man, as you say, but I couldn't have flung my hammer bang here from Greenford. My hammer hasn't got wings that it should come flying half a mile over hedges and fields."

The inspector laughed amicably and said: "No, I think you can be considered out of it, though it's one of the rummiest coincidences I ever saw. I can only ask you to give us all the assistance you can in finding a man as big and strong as yourself. By George! you might be useful, if only to hold him! I suppose you yourself have no guess at the man?"

"I may have a guess," said the pale smith, "but it is not at a man." Then, seeing the scared eyes turn towards his wife on the bench, he put his huge hand on her shoulder and said: "Nor a woman either."

"What do you mean?" asked the inspector jocularly. "You don't think cows use hammers, do you?"

"I think no thing of flesh held that hammer," said the blacksmith in a stifled voice; "mortally speaking, I think the man died alone."

Wilfred made a sudden forward movement and peered at him with burning eyes.

"Do you mean to say, Barnes," came the sharp voice of the cobbler, "that the hammer jumped up of itself and knocked the man down?"

"Oh, you gentlemen may stare and snigger," cried Simeon; "you clergymen who tell us on Sunday in what a stillness the Lord smote Sennacherib. I believe that One who walks invisible in every house defended the honour of mine, and laid the defiler dead before the door of it. I believe the force in that blow was just the force there is in earthquakes, and no force less."

Wilfred said, with a voice utterly undescribable: "I told Norman myself to beware of the thunderbolt."

"That agent is outside my jurisdiction," said the inspector with a slight smile.

"You are not outside His," answered the smith; "see you to it," and, turning his broad back, he went into the house.

The shaken Wilfred was led away by Father Brown, who had an easy and friendly way with him. "Let us get out of this horrid place, Mr. Bohun," he said. "May I look inside your church? I hear it's one of the oldest in England. We take some interest, you know," he added with a comical grimace, "in old English churches."

Wilfred Bohun did not smile, for humour was never his strong point. But he nodded rather eagerly, being only too ready to explain the Gothic splendours to someone more likely to be sympathetic than the Presbyterian blacksmith or the atheist cobbler.

"By all means," he said; "let us go in at this side." And he led the way into the high side entrance at the top of the flight of steps. Father Brown was mounting the first step to follow him when he felt a hand on his shoulder, and turned to behold the dark, thin figure of the doctor, his face darker yet with suspicion.

"Sir," said the physician harshly, "you appear to know some secrets in this black business. May I ask if you are going to keep them to yourself?"

"Why, doctor," answered the priest, smiling quite pleasantly, "there is one very good reason why a man of my trade should keep things to himself when he is not sure of them, and that is that it is so constantly his duty to keep them to himself when he is sure of them. But if you think I have been discourteously reticent with you or anyone, I will go to the extreme limit of my custom. I will give you two very large hints."

"Well, sir?" said the doctor gloomily.

"First," said Father Brown quietly, "the thing is quite in your own province. It is a matter of physical science. The blacksmith is mistaken, not perhaps in saying that the blow was divine, but certainly in saying that it came by a miracle. It was no miracle, doctor, except in so far as man is himself a miracle, with his strange and wicked and yet half-heroic heart. The force that smashed that skull was a force well known to scientists—one of the most frequently debated of the laws of nature."

The doctor, who was looking at him with frowning intentness, only said: "And the other hint?"

"The other hint is this," said the priest. "Do you remember the blacksmith, though he believes in miracles, talking scornfully of the impossible fairy tale that his hammer had wings and flew half a mile across country?"

"Yes," said the doctor, "I remember that."

"Well," added Father Brown, with a broad smile, "that fairy tale was the nearest thing to the real truth that has been said to-day." And with that he turned his back and stumped up the steps after the curate.

The Rev. Wilfred, who had been waiting for him, pale and impatient, as if this little delay were the last straw for his nerves, led him immediately to his favourite corner of the church, that part of the gallery closest to the carved roof and lit by the wonderful window with the angel. The little Latin priest explored and admired everything exhaustively, talking cheerfully but in a low voice all the time. When in the course of his investigation he found the side exit and the winding stair down which Wilfred had rushed to find his brother dead, Father Brown ran not down but up, with the agility of a monkey, and his clear voice came from an outer plat- form above.

"Come up here, Mr. Bohun," he called. "The air will do you good."

Bohun followed him, and came out on a kind of stone gallery or balcony outside the building, from which one could see the illim- itable plain in which their small hill stood, wooded away to the pur- ple horizon and dotted with villages and farms. Clear and square, but quite small beneath them, was the blacksmith's yard, where the inspector still stood taking notes and the corpse still lay like a smashed fly.

"Might be the map of the world, mightn't it?" said Father Brown.

"Yes," said Bohun very gravely, and nodded his head.

Immediately beneath and about them the lines of the Gothic building plunged outwards into the void with a sickening swift- ness akin to suicide. There is that element of Titan energy in the architecture of the Middle Ages that, from whatever aspect it be seen, it always seems to be rushing away, like the strong back of some maddened horse. This church was hewn out of ancient and silent stone, bearded with old fungoids and stained with the nests of birds. And yet, when they saw it from below, it sprang like a fountain at the stars; and when they saw it, as now, from above, it poured like a cataract into a voiceless pit. For these two men on the tower were left alone with the most terrible aspect of the Gothic; the monstrous foreshortening and disproportion, the dizzy perspectives, the glimpses of great things small and small things great; a topsy-turvydom of stone in the mid-air. Details of stone, enormous by their proximity, were relieved against a pattern of fields and farms, pygmy in their distance. A carved bird or beast at a corner seemed like some vast walking or flying dragon wasting the pastures and villages below. The whole atmosphere was dizzy and dangerous, as if men were upheld in air amid the gyrating wings of colossal genii; and the whole of that old church, as tall and rich as a cathedral, seemed to sit upon the sunlit country like a cloudburst.

"I think there is something rather dangerous about standing on these high places even to pray," said Father Brown. "Heights were made to be looked at, not to be looked from."

"Do you mean that one may fall over," asked Wilfred.

"I mean that one's soul may fall if one's body doesn't," said the other priest.

"I scarcely understand you," remarked Bohun indistinctly.

"Look at that blacksmith, for instance," went on Father Brown calmly; "a good man, but not a Christian—hard, imperious, unforgiving. Well, his Scotch religion was made up by men who prayed on hills and high crags, and learnt to look down on the world more than to look up at heaven. Humility is the mother of giants. One sees great things from the valley; only small things from the peak."

"But he—he didn't do it," said Bohun tremulously.

"No," said the other in an odd voice; "we know he didn't do it."

After a moment he resumed, looking tranquilly out over the plain with his pale grey eyes. "I knew a man," he said, "who began by worshipping with others before the altar, but who grew fond of high and lonely places to pray from, corners or niches in the belfry or the spire. And once in one of those dizzy places, where the whole world seemed to turn under him like a wheel, his brain turned also, and he fancied he was God. So that though he was a good man, he committed a great crime."

Wilfred's face was turned away, but his bony hands turned blue and white as they tightened on the parapet of stone.

"He thought it was given to *him* to judge the world and strike down the sinner. He would never have had such a thought if he had been kneeling with other men upon a floor. But he saw all men walking about like insects. He saw one especially strutting just below him, insolent and evident by a bright green hat—a poisonous insect."

Rooks cawed round the corners of the belfry; but there was no other sound till Father Brown went on.

"This also tempted him, that he had in his hand one of the most awful engines of nature; I mean gravitation, that mad and quickening rush by which all earth's creatures fly back to her heart when released. See, the inspector is strutting just below us in the smithy. If I were to toss a pebble over this parapet it would be something like a bullet by the time it struck him. If I were to drop a hammer—even a small hammer——"

Wilfred Bohun threw one leg over the parapet, and Father Brown had him in a minute by the collar.

"Not by that door," he said quite gently; "that door leads to hell."

Bohun staggered back against the wall, and stared at him with frightful eyes.

"How do you know all this?" he cried. "Are you a devil?"

"I am a man," answered Father Brown gravely; "and therefore have all devils in my heart. Listen to me," he said after a short pause. "I know what you did—at least, I can guess the great part of it. When you left your brother you were racked with no unrighteous rage, to the extent even that you snatched up a small hammer, half inclined to kill him with his foulness on his mouth. Recoiling, you thrust it under your buttoned coat instead, and rushed into the church. You pray wildly in many places, under the angel window, upon the platform above, and a higher platform still, from which you could see the colonel's Eastern hat like the back of a green beetle crawling about. Then something snapped in your soul, and you let God's thunderbolt fall."

Wilfred put a weak hand to his head, and asked in a low voice: "How did you know that his hat looked like a green beetle?"

"Oh, that," said the other with the shadow of a smile, "that was common sense. But hear me further. I say I know all this; but no one else shall know it. The next step is for you; I shall take no more steps; I will seal this with the seal of confession. If you ask me why, there are many reasons, and only one that concerns you. I leave things to you because you have not yet gone very far wrong, as assassins go. You did not help to fix the crime on the smith when it was easy; or on his wife, when that was easy. You tried to fix it on the imbecile because you knew that he could not suffer. That was one of the gleams that it is my business to find in assassins. And now come down into the village, and go your own way as free as the wind; for I have said my last word."

They went down the winding stairs in utter silence, and came out into the sunlight by the smithy. Wilfred Bohun carefully unlatched the wooden gate of the yard, and going up to the inspector, said: "I wish to give myself up; I have killed my brother."

THE THREE TOOLS OF DEATH

Both by calling and conviction Father Brown knew better than most of us, that every man is dignified when he is dead. But even he felt a pang of incongruity when he was knocked up at daybreak and told that Sir Aaron Armstrong had been murdered. There was something absurd and unseemly about secret violence in connexion with so entirely entertaining and popular a figure. For Sir Aaron Armstrong was entertaining to the point of being comic; and popular in such a manner as to be almost legendary. It was like hearing that Sunny Jim had hanged himself; or that Mr. Pickwick had died in Hanwell. For though Sir Aaron was a philanthropist, and thus dealt with the darker side of our society, he prided himself on dealing with it in the brightest possible style. His political and social speeches were cataracts of anecdotes and "loud laughter"; his bodily health was of a bursting sort; his ethics were all optimism; and he dealt with the Drink problem (his favourite topic) with that immortal or even monotonous gaiety which is so often a mark of the prosperous total abstainer.

The established story of his conversion was familiar on the more puritanic platforms and pulpits, how he had been, when only a boy, drawn away from Scotch theology to Scotch whisky, and how he had risen out of both and become (as he modestly put it) what he was. Yet his wide white beard, cherubic face, and sparkling spectacles, at the numberless dinners and congresses where they appeared, made it hard to believe, somehow, that he had ever been anything so morbid as either a dram-drinker or a Calvinist. He was, one felt, the most seriously merry of all the sons of men.

He had lived on the rural skirt of Hampstead in a handsome house, high but not broad, a modern and prosaic tower. The narrowest of its narrow sides overhung the steep green bank of a railway, and was shaken by passing trains. Sir Aaron Armstrong, as he boisterously explained, had no nerves. But if the train had often given a shock to the house, that morning the tables were turned, and it was the house that gave a shock to the train.

The engine slowed down and stopped just beyond that point where an angle of the house impinged upon the sharp slope of turf. The arrest of most mechanical things must be slow; but the living cause of this had been very rapid. A man clad completely in black, even (it was remembered) to the dreadful detail of black gloves, appeared on the ridge above the engine, and waved his black hands like some sable windmill. This in itself would hardly have stopped even a lingering train. But there came out of him a cry which was talked of afterwards as something utterly unnatural and new. It was one of those shouts that are horridly distinct even when we cannot hear what is shouted. The word in this case was "Murder!"

But the engine-driver swears he would have pulled up just the same if he had heard only the dreadful and definite accent and not the word.

The train once arrested, the most superficial stare could take in many features of the tragedy. The man in black on the green bank was Sir Aaron Armstrong's man-servant Magnus. The baronet in his optimism had often laughed at the black gloves of this dismal attendant; but no one was likely to laugh at him just now.

So soon as an inquirer or two had stepped off the line and across the smoky hedge, they saw, rolled down almost to the bottom of the bank, the body of an old man in a yellow dressing-gown with a very vivid scarlet lining. A scrap of rope seemed caught about his leg, entangled persumably in a struggle. There was a smear or so of blood, though very little; but the body was bent or broken into a posture impossible to any living thing. It was Sir Aaron Armstrong. A few more bewildered moments brought out a big fair-bearded man, whom some travellers could salute as the dead man's secretary, Patrick Royce, once well known in Bohemian society and even famous in the Bohemian arts. In a manner more vague, but even more convincing, he echoed the agony of the servant. By the time the third figure of that household, Alice Armstrong, daughter of the dead man, had come already tottering and wavering into the garden, the engine-driver had put a stop to his stoppage. The whistle had blown and the train had panted on to get help from the next station.

Father Brown had been thus rapidly summoned at the request of Patrick Royce, the big ex-Bohemian secretary. Royce was an Irishman by birth; and that casual kind of Catholic that never remembers his religion until he is really in a hole. But Royce's request might have been less promptly complied with if one of the official detectives had not been a friend and admirer of the unofficial Flambeau; and it was impossible to be a friend of Flambeau without hearing numberless stories about Father Brown. Hence, while the young detective (whose name was Merton) led the little priest across the fields to the railway, their talk was more confidential than could be expected between two total strangers.

"As far as I can see," said Mr. Merton candidly, "there is no sense to be made of it at all. There is nobody one can suspect. Magnus is a solemn old fool; far too much of a fool to be an assassin. Royce has been the baronet's best friend for years; and his daughter undoubtedly adored him. Besides, it's all too absurd. Who would kill such a cheery old chap as Armstrong? Who could dip his hands in the gore of an after-dinner speaker? It would be like killing Father Christmas."

"Yes, it was a cheery house," assented Father Brown. "It was a cheery house while he was alive. Do you think it will be cheery now he is dead?"

Merton started a little and regarded his companion with an enlivened eye. "Now he is dead?" he repeated.

"Yes," continued the priest stolidly, "*he* was cheerful. But did he communicate his cheerfulness? Frankly, was anyone else in the house cheerful but he?"

A window in Merton's mind let in that strange light of surprise in which we see for the first time things we have known all along. He had often been to the Armstrongs', on little police jobs of the philanthropist; and, now he came to think of it, it was in itself a depressing house. The rooms were very high and very cold; the decoration mean and provincial; the draughty corridors were lit by electricity that was bleaker than moonlight. And though the old man's scarlet face and silver beard had blazed like a bonfire in each room or passage in turn, it did not leave any warmth behind it. Doubtless this spectral discomfort in the place was partly due to the very vitality and exuberance of its owner; he needed no stoves or lamps, he would say, but carried his own warmth with him. But when Merton recalled the other inmates, he was compelled to confess that they also were as shadows of their lord. The moody manservant, with his monstrous black gloves, was almost a nightmare; Royce, the secretary, was solid enough, a big bull of a man, in tweeds, with a short beard; but the straw-coloured beard was startlingly salted with grey like the tweeds, and the broad forehead was barred with premature wrinkles. He was good-natured enough also, but it was a sad sort of good-nature, almost a heart-broken sort—he had the general air of being some sort of failure in life. As for Armstrong's daughter, it was almost incredible that she was his daughter; she was so pallid in colour and sensitive in outline. She was graceful, but there was a quiver in the very shape of her that was like the lines of an aspen. Merton had sometimes wondered if she had learnt to quail at the crash of the passing trains.

"You see," said Father Brown, blinking modestly, "I'm not sure that the Armstrong cheerfulness is so very cheerful—for other people. You say that nobody could kill such a happy old man, but I'm not sure; *ne nos inducas in tentationem*. If ever I murdered somebody," he added quite simply, "I dare say it might be an Optimist."

"Why?" cried Merton, amused. "Do you think people dislike cheerfulness?"

"People like frequent laughter," answered Father Brown, "but I don't think they like a permanent smile. Cheerfulness without humour is a very trying thing."

They walked some way in silence along the windy grassy bank by the rail, and just as they came under the far-flung shadow of the tall Armstrong house, Father Brown said suddenly, like a man throwing away a troublesome thought rather than offering it seriously: "Of course, drink is neither good nor bad in itself. But I can't help sometimes feeling that men like Armstrong want an occasional glass of wine, to sadden them."

Merton's official superior, a grizzled and capable detective named Gilder, was standing on the green bank waiting for the coroner, talking to Patrick Royce, whose big shoulders and bristly beard and hair towered above him. This was the more noticeable because Royce walked always with a sort of powerful stoop, and seemed to be going about his small clerical and domestic duties in a heavy and humbled style, like a buffalo drawing a go-cart.

He raised his head with unusual pleasure at the sight of the priest, and took him a few paces apart. Meanwhile Merton was addressing the older detective respectfully indeed, but not without a certain boyish impatience.

"Well, Mr. Gilder, have you got much farther with the mystery?"

"There is no mystery," replied Gilder, as he looked under dreamy eyelids at the rooks.

"Well, there is for me, at any rate," said Merton, smiling.

"It is simple enough, my boy," observed the senior investigator, stroking his grey, pointed beard. "Three minutes after you'd gone for Mr. Royce's parson the whole thing came out. You know that pasty-faced servant in the black gloves who stopped the train?"

"I should know him anywhere. Somehow he rather gave me the creeps."

"Well," drawled Gilder, "when the train had gone on again, that man had gone too. Rather a cool criminal, don't you think, to escape by the very train that went off for the police?"

"You're pretty sure, I suppose," remarked the young man, "that he really did kill his master?"

"Yes, my son, I'm pretty sure," replied Gilder drily, "for the trifling reason that he has gone off with twenty thousand pounds in papers that were in his master's desk. No, the only thing worth calling a difficulty is how he killed him. The skull seems broken as with some big weapon, but there's no weapon at all lying about, and the murderer would have found it awkward to carry it away, unless the weapon was too small to be noticed."

"Perhaps the weapon was too big to be noticed," said the priest, with an odd little giggle.

Gilder looked round at this wild remark, and rather sternly asked Brown what he meant.

"Silly way of putting it, I know," said Father Brown apologetically. "Sounds like a fairy tale. But poor Armstrong was killed with a giant's club, a great green club, too big to be seen, and which we call the earth. He was broken against this green bank we are standing on."

"How do you mean?" asked the detective quickly.

Father Brown turned his moon face up to the narrow façade of the house and blinked hopelessly up. Following his eyes, they saw that right at the top of this otherwise blind back quarter of the building, an attic window stood open.

"Don't you see," he explained, pointing a little awkwardly like a child, "he was thrown down from there?"

Gilder frowningly scrutinised the window, and then said: "Well, it is certainly possible. But I don't see why you are so sure about it."

Brown opened his grey eyes wide. "Why," he said, "there's a bit of rope round the dead man's leg. Don't you see that other bit of rope up there caught at the corner of the window?"

At that height the thing looked like the faintest particle of dust or hair, but the shrewd old investigator was satisfied. "You're quite right, sir," he said to Father Brown; "that is certainly one to you."

Almost as he spoke a special train with one carriage took the curve of the line on their left, and, stopping, disgorged another group of policemen, in whose midst was the hangdog visage of Magnus, the absconded servant.

"By Jove! they've got him," cried Gilder, and stepped forward with quite a new alertness.

"Have you got the money?" he cried to the first policeman.

The man looked him in the face with a rather curious expression and said: "No." Then he added: "At least, not here."

"Which is the inspector, please?" asked the man called Magnus.

When he spoke everyone instantly understood how this voice had stopped a train. He was a dull-looking man with flat black hair, a colourless face, and a faint suggestion of the East in the level slits in his eyes and mouth. His blood and name, indeed, had remained dubious, ever since Sir Aaron had "rescued" him from a waitership in a London restaurant, and (as some said) from more infamous things. But his voice was as vivid as his face was dead. Whether through exactitude in a foreign language, or in deference to his master (who had been somewhat deaf), Magnus's tones had a peculiarly ringing and piercing quality, and the whole group quite jumped when he spoke.

"I always knew this would happen," he said aloud with brazen blandness. "My poor old master made game of me for wearing black; but I always said I should be ready for his funeral."

And he made a momentary movement with his two dark-gloved hands.

"Sergeant," said Inspector Gilder, eyeing the black hands with wrath, "aren't you putting the bracelets on this fellow; he looks pretty dangerous."

"Well, sir," said the sergeant, with the same odd look of wonder, "I don't know that we can."

"What do you mean?" asked the other sharply. "Haven't you arrested him?"

A faint scorn widened the slit-like mouth, and the whistle of an approaching train seemed oddly to echo the mockery.

"We arrested him," replied the sergeant gravely, "just as he was coming out of the police station at Highgate, where he had deposited all his master's money in the care of Inspector Robinson."

Gilder looked at the man-servant in utter amazement. "Why on earth did you do that?" he asked of Magnus.

"To keep it safe from the criminal, of course," replied that person placidly.

"Surely," said Gilder, "Sir Aaron's money might have been safely left with Sir Aaron's family."

The tail of his sentence was drowned in the roar of the train as it went rocking and clanking; but through all the hell of noises to which that unhappy house was periodically subject, they could hear the syllables of Magnus's answer, in all their bell-like distinctness: "I have no reason to feel confidence in Sir Aaron's family."

All the motionless men had the ghostly sensation of the presence of some new person; and Merton was scarcely surprised when he looked up and saw the pale face of Armstrong's daughter over Father Brown's shoulder. She was still young and beautiful in a silvery style, but her hair was of so dusty and hueless a brown that in some shadows it seemed to have turned totally grey.

"Be careful what you say," said Royce gruffly, "you'll frighten Miss Armstrong."

"I hope so," said the man with the clear voice.

As the woman winced and everyone else wondered, he went on: "I am somewhat used to Miss Armstrong's tremors. I have seen her trembling off and on for years. And some said she was shaking with cold and some she was shaking with fear, but I know she was shaking with hate and wicked anger—fiends that have had their feast this morning. She would have been away by now with her lover and all the money but for me. Ever since my poor old master prevented her from marrying that tipsy blackguard——"

"Stop," said Gilder very sternly. "We have nothing to do with your family fancies or suspicions. Unless you have some practical evidence, your mere opinions——"

"Oh! I'll give you practical evidence," cut in Magnus, in his hacking accent. "You'll have to subpoena me, Mr. Inspector, and I shall have to tell the truth. And the truth is this: An instant after the old man was pitched bleeding out of the window, I ran into the attic, and found his daughter swooning on the floor with a red dagger still

in her hand. Allow me to hand that also to the proper authorities."
He took from his tail-pocket a long horn-hilted knife with a red
smear on it, and handed it politely to the sergeant. Then he stood
back again, and his slits of eyes almost faded from his face in one fat
Chinese sneer.

Merton felt an almost bodily sickness at the sight of him; and he
muttered to Gilder: "Surely you would take Miss Armstrong's word
against his?"

Father Brown suddenly lifted a face so absurdly fresh that it
looked somehow as if he had just washed it. "Yes," he said, radiating
innocence, "but is Miss Armstrong's word against his?"

The girl uttered a startled, singular little cry; everyone looked at
her. Her figure was rigid as if paralysed; only her face within its
frame of faint brown hair was alive with an appalling surprise. She
stood like one of a sudden lassooed and throttled.

"This man," said Mr. Gilder gravely, "actually says that you were
found grasping a knife, insensible, after the murder."

"He says the truth," answered Alice.

The next fact of which they were conscious was that Patrick
Royce strode with his great stooping head into their ring and uttered the singular words: "Well, if I've got to go, I'll have a bit of
pleasure first."

His huge shoulder heaved and he sent an iron fist smash into
Magnus's bland Mongolian visage, laying him on the lawn as flat as
a starfish. Two or three of the police instantly put their hands on
Royce; but to the rest it seemed as if all reason had broken up and
the universe were turning into a brainless harlequinade.

"None of that, Mr. Royce," Gilder had called out authoritatively.
"I shall arrest you for assault."

"No, you won't," answered the secretary in a voice like an iron
gong, "you will arrest me for murder."

Gilder threw an alarmed glance at the man knocked down; but
since that outraged person was already sitting up and wiping a little blood off a substantially uninjured face, he only said shortly:
"What do you mean?"

"It is quite true, as this fellow says," explained Royce, "that Miss

Armstrong fainted with a knife in her hand. But she had not snatched the knife to attack her father, but to defend him."

"To defend him," repeated Gilder gravely. "Against whom?"

"Against me," answered the secretary.

Alice looked at him with a complex and baffling face; then she said in a low voice: "After it all, I am still glad you are brave."

"Come upstairs," said Patrick Royce heavily, "and I will show you the whole cursed thing."

The attic, which was the secretary's private place (and rather a small cell for so large a hermit), had indeed all the vestiges of a violent drama. Near the centre of the floor lay a large revolver as if flung away; nearer to the left was rolled a whisky bottle, open but not quite empty. The cloth of the little table lay dragged and trampled, and a length of cord, like that found on the corpse, was cast wildly across the window-sill. Two vases were smashed on the mantelpiece and one on the carpet.

"I was drunk," said Royce; and this simplicity in the prematurely battered man somehow had the pathos of the first sin of a baby.

"You all know about me," he continued huskily; "everybody knows how my story began, and it may as well end like that too. I was called a clever man once, and might have been a happy one; Armstrong saved the remains of a brain and body from the taverns, and was always kind to me in his own way, poor fellow! Only he wouldn't let me marry Alice here; and it will always be said that he was right enough. Well, you can form your own conclusions, and you won't want me to go into details. That is my whisky bottle half emptied in the corner; that is my revolver quite emptied on the carpet. It was the rope from my box that was found on the corpse, and it was from my window the corpse was thrown. You need not set detectives to grub up my tragedy; it is a common enough weed in this world. I give myself to the gallows; and, by God, that is enough!"

At a sufficiently delicate sign, the police gathered round the large man to lead him away; but their unobtrusiveness was somewhat staggered by the remarkable appearance of Father Brown, who was on his hands and knees on the carpet in the doorway, as if engaged in some kind of undignified prayers. Being a person utterly insensible to the social figure he cut, he remained in this posture, but turned a bright round face up at the company, presenting the appearance of a quadruped with a very comic human head.

"I say," he said good-naturedly, "this really won't do at all, you know. At the beginning you said we'd found no weapon. But now we're finding too many; there's the knife to stab, and the rope to strangle, and the pistol to shoot; and after all he broke his neck by falling out of a window! It won't do. It's not economical." And he shook his head at the ground as a horse does grazing.

Inspector Gilder had opened his mouth with serious intentions, but before he could speak the grotesque figure on the floor had gone on quite volubly.

"And now three quite impossible things. First, these holes in the carpet, where the six bullets have gone in. Why on earth should anybody fire at the carpet? A drunken man lets fly at his enemy's head, the thing that's grinning at him. He doesn't pick a quarrel with his feet, or lay siege to his slippers. And then there's the rope"—and having done with the carpet the speaker lifted his hands and put them in his pocket, but continued unaffectedly on his knees—"in what conceivable intoxication would anybody try to put a rope round a man's neck and finally put it round his leg? Royce, anyhow, was not so drunk as that, or he would be sleeping like a log by now. And, plainest of all, the whisky bottle. You suggest a dipsomaniac fought for the whisky bottle, and then having won, rolled it away in a corner, spilling one half and leaving the other. That is the very last thing a dipsomaniac would do."

He scrambled awkwardly to his feet, and said to the self-accused murderer in tones of limpid penitence: "I'm awfully sorry, my dear sir, but your tale is really rubbish."

"Sir," said Alice Armstrong in a low tone to the priest, "can I speak to you alone for a moment?"

This request forced the communicative cleric out of the gangway, and before he could speak in the next room, the girl was talking with strange incisiveness.

"You are a clever man," she said, "and you are trying to save Patrick, I know. But it's no use. The core of all this is black, and the more things you find out the more there will be against the miserable man I love."

"Why?" asked Brown, looking at her steadily.

"Because," she answered equally steadily, "I saw him commit the crime myself."

"Ah!" said the unmoved Brown, "and what did he do?"

"I was in this room next to them," she explained; "both doors were closed, but I suddenly heard a voice, such as I had never heard on earth, roaring 'Hell, hell, hell,' again and again, and then the two doors shook with the first explosion of the revolver. Thrice again the thing banged before I got the two doors open and found the room full of smoke; but the pistol was smoking in my poor, mad Patrick's hand; and I saw him fire the last murderous volley with my own eyes. Then he leapt on my father, who was clinging in terror to the window-sill, and, grappling, tried to strangle him with the rope, which he threw over his head, but which slipped over his struggling shoulders to his feet. Then it tightened round one leg and Patrick dragged him along like a maniac. I snatched a knife from the mat, and, rushing between them, managed to cut the rope before I fainted."

"I see," said Father Brown, with the same wooden civility. "Thank you."

As the girl collapsed under her memories, the priest passed stiffly into the next room, where he found Gilder and Merton alone with Patrick Royce, who sat in a chair, handcuffed. There he said to the Inspector submissively:

"Might I say a word to the prisoner in your presence; and might he take off those funny cuffs for a minute?"

"He is a very powerful man," said Merton in an undertone. "Why do you want them taken off?"

"Why, I thought," replied the priest humbly, "that perhaps I might have the very great honour of shaking hands with him."

Both detectives stared, and Father Brown added: "Won't you tell them about it, sir?"

The man on the chair shook his tousled head, and the priest turned impatiently.

"Then I will," he said. "Private lives are more important than public reputations. I am going to save the living, and let the dead bury their dead."

He went to the fatal window, and blinked out of it as he went on talking.

"I told you that in this case there were too many weapons and only one death. I tell you now that they were not weapons, and were not used to cause death. All those grisly tools, the noose, the bloody knife, the exploding pistol, were instruments of a curious mercy. They were not used to kill Sir Aaron, but to save him."

"To save him!" repeated Gilder. "And from what?"

"From himself," said Father Brown. "He was a suicidal maniac."

"*What?*" cried Merton in an incredulous tone. "And the Religion of Cheerfulness——"

"It is a cruel religion," said the priest, looking out of the window. "Why couldn't they let him weep a little, like his fathers before him? His plans stiffened, his views grew cold; behind that merry mask was the empty mind of the atheist. At last, to keep up his hilarious public level, he fell back on that dram-drinking he had abandoned long ago. But there is this horror about alcoholism in a sincere teetotaler: that he pictures and expects that psychological inferno from which he has warned others. It leapt upon poor Armstrong prematurely, and by this morning he was in such a case that he sat here and cried he was in hell, in so crazy a voice that his daughter did not know it. He was mad for death, and with the monkey tricks of the mad he had scattered round him death in many shapes—a running noose and his friend's revolver and a knife. Royce entered accidentally and acted in a flash. He flung the knife on the mat behind him, snatched up the revolver, and having no time to unload it, emptied it shot after shot all over the floor. The suicide saw a fourth shape of death, and made a dash for the window. The rescuer did the only thing he could—ran after him with the rope and tried to tie him hand and foot. Then it was that the unlucky girl ran in, and misunderstanding the struggle, strove to slash her father free. At first she only slashed poor Royce's knuckles, from which has come all the little blood in this affair. But, of course, you noticed that he left blood, but no wound, on that servant's face? Only before the poor woman swooned, she did hack her father loose, so that he went crashing through that window into eternity."

There was a long stillness slowly broken by the metallic noises of Gilder unlocking the handcuffs of Patrick Royce, to whom he said: "I think I should have told the truth, sir. You and the young lady are worth more than Armstrong's obituary notices."

"Confound Armstrong's notices," cried Royce roughly. "Don't you see it was because she mustn't know?"

"Mustn't know what?" asked Merton.

"Why, that she killed her father, you fool!" roared the other. "He'd have been alive now but for her. It might craze her to know that."

"No, I don't think it would," remarked Father Brown, as he picked up his hat. "I rather think I should tell her. Even the most murderous blunders don't poison life like sins; anyhow, I think you may both be the happier now. I've got to go back to the Deaf School."

As he went out on to the gusty grass an acquaintance from High-gate stopped him and said:

"The coroner has arrived. The inquiry is just going to begin."

"I've got to get back to the Deaf School," said Father Brown. "I'm sorry I can't stop for the inquiry."

THE ABSENCE OF MR. GLASS

The consulting-rooms of Dr. Orion Hood, the eminent criminologist and specialist in certain moral disorders, lay along the sea-front at Scarborough, in a series of very large and well-lighted French windows, which showed the North Sea like one endless outer wall of blue-green marble. In such a place the sea had something of the monotony of a blue-green dado: for the chambers themselves were ruled throughout by a terrible tidiness not unlike the terrible tidiness of the sea. It must not be supposed that Dr. Hood's apartments excluded luxury, or even poetry. These things were there, in their place; but one felt that they were never allowed out of their place. Luxury was there: there stood upon a special table eight or ten boxes of the best cigars; but they were built upon a plan so that the strongest were always nearest the wall and the mildest nearest the window. A tantalus containing three kinds of spirit, all of a liqueur excellence, stood always on this table of luxury; but the fanciful have asserted that the whisky, brandy, and rum seemed always to stand at the same level. Poetry was there: the left-hand corner of the room was lined with as complete a set of English classics as the right hand could show of English and foreign physiologists. But if one took a volume of Chaucer or Shelley from that rank, its absence irritated the mind like a gap in a man's front teeth. One could not say the books were never read; probably they were, but there was a sense of their being chained to their places, like the Bibles in the old churches. Dr. Hood treated his private bookshelf as if it were a public library. And if this strict scientific intangibility steeped even the shelves laden with lyrics and ballads and the tables laden with drink and tobacco, it goes without saying that yet more of such heathen holiness protected the other shelves that held the specialist's library, and the other tables that sustained the frail and even fairy-like instruments of chemistry or mechanics.

Dr. Orion Hood paced the length of his string of apartments, bounded—as the boys' geographies say—on the east by the North Sea and on the west by the serried ranks of his sociological and criminologist library. He was clad in an artist's velvet, but with none of an artist's negligence; his hair was heavily shot with grey, but growing thick and healthy; his face was lean, but sanguine and expectant. Everything about him and his room indicated something at once rigid and restless, like that great Northern Sea by which (on pure principles of hygiene) he had built his home.

Fate, being in a funny mood, pushed the door open and introduced into those long, strict, sea-flanked apartments one who was perhaps the most startling opposite of them and their master. In answer to a curt but civil summons, the door opened inwards and there shambled into the room a shapeless little figure, which seemed to find its own hat and umbrella as unmanageable as a mass of luggage. The umbrella was a black and prosaic bundle long past repair, the hat was a broad-curved black hat, clerical but not common in England, the man was the very embodiment of all that is homely and helpless.

The doctor regarded the new-comer with a restrained astonishment, not unlike that he would have shown if some huge but obviously harmless sea-beast had crawled into his room. The new-comer regarded the doctor with that beaming but breathless geniality which characterises a corpulent charwoman who has just managed to stuff herself into an omnibus. It is a rich confusion of social self-congratulation and bodily disarray. His hat tumbled to the carpet, his heavy umbrella slipped between his knees with a thud; he reached after the one and ducked after the other, but with an unimpaired smile on his round face spoke simultaneously as follows:

"My name is Brown. Pray excuse me. I come about that business of the MacNabs. I have heard you often help people out of such troubles. Pray excuse me if I am wrong."

By this time he had sprawlingly recovered the hat, and made an odd little bobbing bow over it, as if setting everything quite right.

"I hardly understand you," replied the scientist, with a cold intensity of manner. "I fear you have mistaken the chambers. I am Dr. Hood, and my work is almost entirely literary and educational. It is true that I have sometimes been consulted by the police in cases of peculiar difficulty and importance, but——"

"Oh, this is of the greatest importance," broke in the little man called Brown. "Why, her mother won't let them get engaged." And he leaned back in his chair in radiant rationality.

The brows of Dr. Hood were drawn down darkly, but the eyes under them were bright with something that might be anger or might be amusement. "And still," he said, "I do not quite understand."

"You see, they want to get married," said the man with the clerical hat. "Maggie MacNab and young Todhunter want to get *married*. Now, what can be more important than that?"

The great Orion Hood's scientific triumphs had deprived him of many things—some said of his health, others of his God; but they had not wholly despoiled him of his sense of the absurd. At the last plea of the ingenuous priest a chuckle broke out of him from inside, and he threw himself into an arm-chair in an ironical attitude of the consulting physician.

"Mr. Brown," he said gravely, "it is quite fourteen and a half years since I was personally asked to test a personal problem: then it was the case of an attempt to poison the French President at a Lord Mayor's Banquet. It is now, I understand, a question of whether some friend of yours called Maggie is a suitable fiancée for some friend of hers called Todhunter. Well, Mr. Brown, I am a sportsman. I will take it on. I will give the MacNab family my best advice, as good as I gave the French Republic and the King of England—no, better: fourteen years better. I have nothing else to do this afternoon. Tell me your story."

The little clergyman called Brown thanked him with unquestionable warmth, but still with a queer kind of simplicity. It was rather as if he were thanking a stranger in a smoking-room for some trouble in passing the matches, than as if he were (as he was) practically thanking the Curator of Kew Gardens for coming with him into a field, to find a four-leaved clover. With scarcely a semi-colon after his hearty thanks, the little man began his recital:

"I told you my name was Brown; well, that's the fact, and I'm the priest of the little Catholic Church I dare say you've seen beyond those straggly streets, where the town ends towards the north. In the last and straggliest of those streets which runs along the sea like a sea-wall there is a very honest but rather sharp-tempered member of my flock, a widow called MacNab. She has one daughter, and she lets lodgings; and between her and the daughter, and between her and the lodgers—well, I dare say there is a great deal to be said on both sides. At present she has only one lodger, the young man called Todhunter; but he has given more trouble than all the rest, for he wants to marry the young woman of the house."

"And the young woman of the house," asked Dr. Hood, with huge and silent amusement, "what does she want?"

"Why, she wants to marry him," cried Father Brown, sitting up eagerly. "That is just the awful complication."

"It is indeed a hideous enigma," said Dr. Hood.

"This young James Todhunter," continued the cleric, "is a very decent man so far as I know; but then nobody knows very much. He is a bright, brownish little fellow, agile like a monkey, clean-shaven like an actor, and obliging like a born courier. He seems to have quite a pocketful of money, but nobody knows what his trade is. Mrs. MacNab, therefore (being of a pessimistic turn), is quite sure it is something dreadful, and probably connected with dynamite. The dynamite must be of a shy and noiseless sort, for the poor fellow only shuts himself up for several hours of the day and studies something behind a locked door. He declares his privacy is temporary and justified, and promises to explain before the wedding. That is all that anyone knows for certain, but Mrs. MacNab will tell you a great deal more than even she is certain of. You know how the tales grow like grass on such a patch of ignorance as that. There are tales of two voices heard talking in the room; though, when the door is opened, Todhunter is always found alone. There are tales of a mysterious tall man in a silk hat, who once came out of the sea-mists and apparently out of the sea, stepping softly across the sandy fields and through the small back garden at twilight, till he was heard talking to the lodger at his open back window. The colloquy seemed to end in a quarrel: Todhunter dashed down his window with violence, and the man in the high hat melted into the sea-fog again. This story is told by the family with the fiercest mystification, but I really think Mrs. MacNab prefers her own original tale: that the Other Man (or whatever it is) crawls out every night from the big box in the corner, which is kept locked all day. You see, therefore, how this sealed door of Todhunter's is treated as the gate of all the fancies and monstrosities of the *Thousand and One Nights.* And yet there is the little fellow in his respectable black jacket, as punctual and innocent as a parlour clock. He pays his rent to the tick; he is practically a teetotaller; he is tirelessly kind with the younger children, and can keep them amused for a day on end; and, last and most urgent of all, he has made himself equally popular with the eldest daughter, who is ready to go to church with him tomorrow."

A man warmly concerned with any large theories has always a relish for applying them to any triviality. The great specialist, having condescended to the priest's simplicity, condescended expansively. He settled himself with comfort in his arm-chair and began to talk in the tone of a somewhat absentminded lecturer:

"Even in a minute instance, it is best to look first to the main tendencies of Nature. A particular flower may not be dead in early winter, but the flowers are dying; a particular pebble may never be wetted with the tide, but the tide is coming in. To the scientific eye all human history is a series of collective movements, destructions or migrations, like the massacre of flies in winter or the return of birds in spring. Now the root fact in all history is Race. Race produces religion; Race produces legal and ethical wars. There is no stronger case than that of the wild, unworldly and perishing stock which we commonly call the Celts, of whom your friends the Mac-Nabs are specimens. Small, swarthy, and of this dreamy and drifting blood, they accept easily the superstitious explanation of any incidents, just as they still accept (you will excuse me for saying) that superstitious explanation of all incidents which you and your Church represent. It is not remarkable that such people, with the sea moaning behind them and the Church (excuse me again) droning in front of them, should put fantastic features into what are probably plain events. You, with your small parochial responsibilities, see only this particular Mrs. MacNab, terrified with this particular tale of two voices and a tall man out of the sea. But the man with the scientific imagination sees, as it were, the whole clan of MacNabs scattered over the whole world, in its ultimate average as uniform as a tribe of birds. He sees thousands of Mrs. MacNabs, in thousands of houses, dropping their little drop of morbidity in the tea-cups of their friends; he sees——"

Before the scientist could conclude his sentence, another and more impatient summons sounded from without; someone with swishing skirts was marshalled hurriedly down the corridor, and the door opened on a young girl, decently dressed but disordered and red-hot with haste. She had sea-blown blonde hair, and would have been entirely beautiful if her cheekbones had not been, in the Scotch manner, a little high in relief as well as in colour. Her apology was almost as abrupt as a command.

"I'm sorry to interrupt you, sir," she said; "but I had to follow Father Brown at once; it's nothing less than life or death."

Father Brown began to get to his feet in some disorder. "Why, what has happened, Maggie?" he said.

"James has been murdered, for all I can make out," answered the girl, still breathing hard from her rush. "That man Glass has been with him again; I heard them talking through the door quite plain. Two separate voices; for James speaks low, with a burr, and the other voice was high and quavery."

"That man Glass?" repeated the priest in some perplexity.

"I know his name is Glass," answered the girl, in great impatience. "I heard it through the door. They were quarrelling—about money, I think—for I heard James say again and again, 'That's right, Mr. Glass,' or 'No, Mr. Glass,' and then, 'Two and three, Mr. Glass.' But we're talking too much; you must come at once, and there may be time yet."

"But time for what?" asked Dr. Hood, who had been studying the young lady with marked interest. "What is there about Mr. Glass and his money troubles that should impel such urgency?"

"I tried to break down the door and couldn't," answered the girl shortly. "Then I ran round to the back-yard, and managed to climb on to the window-sill that looks into the room. It was all dim, and seemed to be empty, but I swear I saw James lying huddled up in a corner, as if he were drugged or strangled."

"This is very serious," said Father Brown, gathering his errant hat and umbrella and standing up; "in point of fact, I was just putting your case before this gentleman, and his view——"

"Has been largely altered," said the scientist gravely. "I do not think this young lady is so Celtic as I had supposed. As I have nothing else to do, I will put on my hat and stroll down the town with you."

In a few minutes all three were approaching the dreary tail of the MacNabs' street; the girl with the stern and breathless stride of the mountaineer, the criminologist with a lounging grace (which was not without a certain leopard-like swiftness), and the priest at an energetic trot entirely devoid of distinction. The aspect of this edge of the town was not entirely without justification for the doctor's hints about desolate moods and environments. The scattered houses stood farther and farther apart in a broken string along the seashore, the afternoon was closing with a premature and partly lurid twilight; the sea was of an inky purple and murmuring ominously. In the scrappy back garden of the MacNabs which ran down towards the sand, two black, barren-looking trees stood up like demon hands held up in astonishment, and as Mrs. MacNab ran down the street to meet them with lean hands similarly spread, and her fierce face in shadow, she was a little like a demon herself. The doctor and the priest made scant reply to her shrill reiterations of her daughter's story, with more disturbing details of her own, to the divided vows of vengeance against Mr. Glass for murdering, and against Mr. Todhunter for being murdered, or against the latter for having dared to want to marry her daughter, and for not having lived to do it. They passed through the narrow passages in the front of the house until they came to the lodger's door at the back, and there Dr. Hood, with the trick of an old detective, put his shoulder sharply to the panel and burst in the door.

It opened on a scene of silent catastrophe. No one seeing it, even for a flash, could doubt that the room had been the theatre of some thrilling collision between two, or perhaps more, persons. Playing-cards lay littered across the table or fluttered about the floor as if a game had been interrupted. Two wine-glasses stood ready for wine on a side-table, but a third lay smashed in a star of crystal upon the carpet. A few feet from it lay what looked like a long knife or short sword, straight, but with an ornamental and pictured handle; its dull blade just caught a grey glint from the dreary window behind, which showed the black trees against the leaden level of the sea. Towards the opposite corner of the room was rolled a gentleman's silk top hat, as if it had just been knocked off his head; so much so, indeed, that one almost looked to see it still rolling. And in the corner behind it, thrown like a sack of potatoes, but corded like a railway trunk, lay Mr. James Todhunter, with a scarf across his mouth, and six or seven ropes knotted round his elbows and ankles. His brown eyes were alive and shifted alertly.

Dr. Orion Hood paused for one instant on the door mat and drank in the whole scene of voiceless violence. Then he stepped swiftly across the carpet, picked up the tall silk hat, and gravely put it upon the head of the yet pinioned Todhunter. It was so much too large for him that it almost slipped down on to his shoulders.

"Mr. Glass's hat," said the doctor, returning with it and peering into the inside with a pocket lens. "How to explain the absence of Mr. Glass and the presence of Mr. Glass's hat? For Mr. Glass is not a careless man with his clothes. This hat is of a stylish shape and systematically brushed and burnished, though not very new. An old dandy, I should think."

"But, good heavens!" called out Miss MacNab, "aren't you going to untie the man first?"

"I say 'old' with intention, though not with certainty," continued the expositor; "my reason for it might seem a little far-fetched. The hair of human beings falls out in very varying degrees, but almost always falls out slightly, and with the lens I should see the tiny hairs in a hat recently worn. It has none, which leads me to guess that Mr. Glass is bald. Now when this is taken with the high-pitched and querulous voice which Miss MacNab described so vividly (patience, my dear lady, patience), when we take the hairless head together with the tone common in senile anger, I should think we may deduce some advance in years. Nevertheless he was probably vigorous, and he was almost certainly tall. I might rely in some degree on the story of his previous appearance at the window, as a tall man in a silk hat, but I think I have more exact indication. This wine-glass has been smashed all over the place, but one of its splinters lies on the high bracket beside the mantelpiece. No such fragment could have fallen there if the vessel had been smashed in the hand of a comparatively short man like Mr. Todhunter."

"By the way," said Father Brown, "might it not be as well to untie Mr. Todhunter?"

"Our lesson from the drinking vessels does not end here," proceeded the specialist. "I may say at once that it is possible that the man Glass was bald or nervous through dissipation rather than age. Mr. Todhunter, as has been remarked, is a quiet, thrifty gentleman, essentially an abstainer. These cards and wine cups are no part of his normal habit; they have been produced for a particular companion. But, as it happens, we may go farther. Mr. Todhunter may or may not possess this wine-service, but there is no appearance of his possessing any wine. What, then, were these vessels to contain? I would at once suggest some brandy or whisky, perhaps of a luxurious sort, from a flask in the pocket of Mr. Glass. We have thus something like a picture of the man, or at least of the type: tall, elderly, fashionable, but somewhat frayed, certainly fond of play and strong waters, and perhaps rather too fond of them. Mr. Glass is a gentleman not unkown on the fringes of society."

"Look here," cried the young woman, "if you don't let me pass to untie him I'll run outside and scream for the police."

"I should not advise *you*, Miss MacNab," said Dr. Hood gravely, "to be in any hurry to fetch the police. Father Brown, I seriously ask you to compose your flock, for their sakes, not for mine. Well, we have seen something of the figure and quality of Mr. Glass; what are the chief facts known of Mr. Todhunter? They are substantially three: that he is economical, that he is more or less wealthy, and that he has a secret. Now surely it is obvious that there are the three chief marks of the kind man who is blackmailed. And surely it is equally obvious that the faded finery, the profligate habits and the shrill irritation of Mr. Glass are the unmistakable marks of the kind of man who blackmails him. We have the two typical figures of a tragedy of hush money; on the one hand, the respectable man with a mystery, on the other, the west-end vulture with a scent for a mystery. These two men have met here to-day and have quarrelled, using blows and a bare weapon."

"Are you going to take those ropes off?" asked the girl stubbornly.

Dr. Hood replaced the silk hat carefully on the side-table, and went across to the captive. He studied him intently, even moving him a little and half-turning him round by the shoulders, but he only answered:

"No, I think these ropes will do very well till your friends the police bring the handcuffs."

Father Brown, who had been looking dully at the carpet, lifted his round face and said, "What do you mean?"

The man of science had picked up the peculiar dagger-sword from the carpet and was examining it intently as he answered:

"Because you find Mr. Todhunter tied up," he said, "you all jump to the conclusion that Mr. Glass had tied him up; and then, I suppose, escaped. There are four objections to this. First, why should a gentleman so dressy as our friend Glass leave his hat behind him, if he left of his own free will? Second," he continued, moving towards the window, "this is the only exit, and it is locked on the inside. Third, this blade here has a tiny touch of blood at the point, but there is no wound on Mr. Todhunter. Mr. Glass took that wound away with him, dead or alive. Add to all this primary probability. It is much more likely that the blackmailed person would try to kill his incubus, rather than that the blackmailer would try to kill the goose that lays his golden eggs. There, I think, we have a pretty complete story."

"But the ropes?" inquired the priest, whose eyes had remained open with a rather vacant admiration.

"Ah, the ropes," said the expert with a singular intonation. "Miss MacNab very much wanted to know why I did not set Mr. Todhunter free from his ropes. Well, I will tell her. I did not do it because Mr. Todhunter can set himself free from them at any minute he chooses."

"What?" cried the audience in quite different notes of astonishment.

"I have looked at all the knots on Mr. Todhunter," reiterated Hood quietly. "I happen to know something about knots; they are quite a branch of criminal science. Every one of those knots he has made himself and could loosen himself; not one of them would have been made by an enemy really trying to pinion him. The whole of this affair of the ropes is a clever fake, to make us think him the victim of the struggle instead of the wretched Glass, whose corpse may be hidden in the garden or stuffed up the chimney."

There was a rather depressed silence; the room was darkening, the sea-blighted boughs of the garden trees looked leaner and blacker than ever, yet they seemed to have come nearer to the window. One could almost fancy they were sea-monsters like crakens or cuttlefish, writhing polypi who had crawled up from the sea to see the end of this tragedy, even as *he*, the villain and victim of it, the terrible man in the tall hat, had once crawled up from the sea. For the whole air was dense with the morbidity of blackmail, which is the most morbid of human things, because it is a crime concealing a crime; a black plaster on a blacker wound.

The face of the little Catholic priest, which was commonly complacent and even comic, had suddenly become knotted with a curious frown. It was not the blank curiosity of his first innocence. It was rather that creative curiosity which comes when a man has the beginnings of an idea. "Say it again, please," he said in a simple, bothered manner; "do you mean that Todhunter can tie himself up all alone and untie himself all alone?"

"That is what I mean," said the doctor.

"Jerusalem!" ejaculated Brown suddenly, "I wonder if it could possibly be that!"

He scuttled across the room rather like a rabbit, and peered with quite a new impulsiveness into the partially covered face of the captive. Then he turned his own rather fatuous face to the company. "Yes, that's it!" he cried in a certain excitement. "Can't you see it in the man's face? Why, look at his eyes!"

Both the Professor and the girl followed the direction of his glance. And though the broad black scarf completely masked the lower half of Todhunter's visage, they did grow conscious of something struggling and intense about the upper part of it.

"His eyes do look queer," cried the young woman, strongly moved. "You brutes; I believe it's hurting him!"

"Not that, I think," said Dr. Hood, "the eyes have certainly a singular expression. But I should interpret those transverse wrinkles as expressing rather such slight psychological abnormality——"

"Oh, bosh!" cried Father Brown, "can't you see he's laughing?"

"Laughing!" repeated the doctor, with a start, "but what on earth can he be laughing at?"

"Well," replied the Reverend Brown apologetically, "not to put too fine a point on it, I think he is laughing at you. And indeed, I'm a little inclined to laugh at myself, now I know about it."

"Now you know about what?" asked Hood, in some exasperation.

"Now I know," replied the priest, "the profession of Mr. Todhunter."

He shuffled about the room looking at one object after another, with what seemed to be a vacant stare, and then invariably bursting into an equally vacant laugh, a highly irritating process for those who had to watch it. He laughed very much over the hat, still more uproariously over the broken glass, but the blood on the sword point sent him into mortal convulsions of amusement. Then he turned to the fuming specialist.

"Dr. Hood," he cried enthusiastically, "you are a great poet! You have called an uncreated being out of the void. How much more god-like that is than if you had only ferreted out the mere facts! Indeed, the mere facts are rather commonplace and comic by comparison."

"I have no notion what you are talking about," said Dr. Hood rather haughtily; "my facts are all inevitable, though necessarily incomplete. A place may be permitted to intuition, perhaps (or poetry if you prefer the term), but only because the corresponding details cannot as yet be ascertained. In the absence of Mr. Glass——"

"That's it, that's it," said the little priest, nodding quite eagerly, "that's the first idea to get fixed; the absence of Mr. Glass. He is so extremely absent I suppose," he added reflectively, "that there was never anybody so absent as Mr. Glass."

"Do you mean he is absent from the town?" demanded the doctor.

"I mean he is absent from everywhere," answered Father Brown; "he is absent from the Nature of Things, so to speak."

"Do you seriously mean," said the specialist with a smile, "that there is no such person?"

The priest made a sign of assent. "It does seem a pity," he said.

Orion Hood broke into a contemptuous laugh. "Well," he said, "before we go on to the hundred and one other evidences, let us take the first proof we found; the first fact we fell over when we fell into this room. If there is no Mr. Glass, whose hat is this?"

"It is Mr. Todhunter's," replied Brown.

"But it doesn't fit him," cried Hood impatiently. "He couldn't possibly wear it!"

Father Brown shook his head with ineffable mildness. "I never said he could wear it," he answered. "I said it was his hat. Or, if you insist on a shade of difference, a hat that is his."

"And where is the shade of difference?" asked the criminologist with a slight sneer.

"My good sir," cried the mild little man, with his first movement akin to impatience, "if you will walk down the street to the nearest hatter's shop, you will see that there is, in common speech, a difference between a man's hat and the hats that are his."

"But a hatter," protested Hood, "can get money out of his stock of new hats. What could Todhunter get out of this one old hat?"

"Rabbits," replied Father Brown promptly.

"What?" cried Dr. Hood.

"Rabbits, ribbons, sweetmeats, goldfish, rolls of coloured paper," said the reverend gentleman with rapidity. "Didn't you see it all when you found out the faked ropes? It's just the same with the sword. Mr. Todhunter hasn't got a scratch on him, as you say; but he's got a scratch in him, if you follow me."

"Do you mean inside Mr. Todhunter's clothes?" inquired Miss MacNab sternly.

"I do not mean inside Mr. Todhunter's clothes," said Father Brown. "I mean inside Mr. Todhunter."

"Well, what in the name of Bedlam *do* you mean?"

"Mr. Todhunter," explained Father Brown placidly, "is learning to be a professional conjurer, as well as juggler, ventriloquist, and expert in the rope trick. The conjuring explains the hat. It is without traces of hair, not because it is worn by the prematurely bald Mr. Glass, but because it had never been worn by anybody. The juggling explains the three glasses, which Todhunter was teaching himself to throw up and catch in rotation. But, being only at the stage of practice, he smashed one glass against the ceiling. And the juggling also explains the sword, which it was Mr. Todhunter's professional pride and duty to swallow. But, again, being at the stage of practice, he very slightly grazed the inside of his throat with the weapon. Hence he has a wound inside him, which I am sure (from the expression of his face) is not a serious one. He was also practising the trick of a release from ropes, like the Davenport Brothers, and he was just about to free himself when we all burst into the room. The cards, of course, are for card tricks, and they are scattered on the floor because he had just been practising one of those dodges of sending them flying through the air. He merely kept his trade secret, because he had to keep his tricks secret, like any other conjurer. But the mere fact of an idler in a top hat having once looked in at his back window, and been driven away by him with great indignation, was enough to set us all on a wrong track of romance, and make us imagine his whole life overshadowed by the silk-hatted spectre of Mr. Glass."

"But what about the two voices?" asked Maggie, staring.

"Have you never heard a ventriloquist?" asked Father Brown. "Don't you know they speak first in their natural voice, and then answer themselves in just that shrill, squeaky, unnatural voice that you heard?"

There was a long silence, and Dr. Hood regarded the little man who had spoken with a dark and attentive smile. "You are certainly a very ingenious person," he said; "it could not have been done better in a book. But there is just one part of Mr. Glass you have not succeeded in explaining away, and that is his name. Miss MacNab distinctly heard him so addressed by Mr. Todhunter."

The Rev. Mr. Brown broke into a rather childish giggle. "Well, that," he said, "that's the silliest part of the whole silly story. When our juggling friend here threw up the three glasses in turn, he counted them aloud as he caught them, and also commented aloud when he failed to catch them. What he really said was 'One, two, and three—missed a glass; one, two—missed a glass.' And so on."

There was a second of stillness in the room, and then every one with one accord burst out laughing. As they did so the figure in the corner complacently uncoiled all the ropes and let them fall with a flourish. Then, advancing into the middle of the room with a bow, he produced from his pocket a big bill printed in blue and red, which announced that ZALADIN, the World's Greatest Conjurer, Contortionist, Ventriloquist, and Human Kangaroo, would be ready with an entirely new series of Tricks at the Empire Pavilion, Scarborough, on Monday next at eight o'clock precisely.

THE PARADISE OF THIEVES

The great Muscari, most original of the young Tuscan poets, walked swiftly into his favourite restaurant, which overlooked the Mediterranean, was covered by an awning and fenced by little lemon and orange trees. Waiters in white aprons were already laying out on white tables the insignia of an early and elegant lunch; and this seemed to increase a satisfaction that already touched the top of swagger. Muscari had an eagle nose like Dante, his hair and neckerchief were dark and flowing; he carried a black cloak, and might almost have carried a black mask, so much did he bear with him a sort of Venetian melodrama. He acted as if a troubadour had still a definite social office, like a bishop. He went as near as his century permitted to walking the world literally like Don Juan, with rapier and guitar.

For he never travelled without a case of swords, with which he had fought many brilliant duels, or without a corresponding case of his mandolin, with which he had actually serenaded Miss Ethel Harrogate, the highly-conventional daughter of a Yorkshire banker, on a holiday. Yet he was neither a charlatan nor a child; but a hot, logical Latin who liked a certain thing and was it. His poetry was as straightforward as anyone else's prose. He desired fame or wine or the beauty of women with a torrid directness inconceivable among the cloudy ideals or cloudy compromises of the north; to vaguer races his intensity smelt of danger or even crime. Like fire or the sea, he was too simple to be trusted.

The banker and his beautiful English daughter were staying at the hotel attached to Muscari's restaurant; that was why it was his favourite restaurant. A glance flashed round the room told him at once, however, that the English party had not descended. The restaurant was glittering, but still comparatively empty. Two priests were talking at a table in a corner, but Muscari (an ardent Catholic) took no more notice of them than of a couple of crows. But from a yet farther seat, partly concealed behind a dwarf tree golden with oranges, there rose and advanced towards the poet a person whose costume was the most aggressive opposite to his own.

This figure was clad in tweeds of a piebald check, with a pink tie, a sharp collar and protuberant yellow boots. He contrived, in the true tradition of 'Arry at Margate, to look at once startling and commonplace. But as the Cockney apparition drew nearer, Muscari was astounded to observe that the head was distinctly different from the body. It was an Italian head, fuzzy, swarthy and very vivacious, that rose abruptly out of the standing collar like cardboard and the comic pink tie. In fact it was a head he knew. He recognised it, above all the dire erection of English holiday array, as the face of an old but forgotten friend named Ezza. This youth had been a prodigy at college, and European fame was promised him when he was barely fifteen; but when he appeared in the world he failed, first publicly as a dramatist and a demagogue, and then privately for years on end as an actor, a traveller, a commission agent or a journalist. Muscari had known him last behind the footlights; he was but too well attuned to the excitements of that profession, and it was believed that some moral calamity had swallowed him up.

"Ezza!" cried the poet, rising and shaking hands in a pleasant astonishment. "Well, I've seen you in many costumes in the green room; but I never expected to see you dressed up as an Englishman."

"This," answered Ezza gravely, "is not the costume of an Englishman, but of the Italian of the future."

"In that case," remarked Muscari, "I confess I prefer the Italian of the past."

"That is your old mistake, Muscari," said the man in tweeds, shaking his head. "And the mistake of Italy. In the sixteenth century we Tuscans made the morning: we had the newest steel, the newest carving, the newest chemistry. Why should we not now have the newest factories, the newest motors, the newest finance—and the newest clothes?"

"Because they are not worth having," answered Muscari. "You cannot make Italians really progressive; they are too intelligent. Men who see the short cut to good living will never go by the new elaborate roads."

"Well, to me Marconi, not D'Annunzio, is the star of Italy," said the other. "That is why I have become a Futurist—and a courier."

"A courier!" cried Muscari, laughing. "Is that the last of your list of trades? And whom are you conducting?"

"Oh, a man of the name of Harrogate, and his family, I believe."

"Not the banker in this hotel?" inquired the poet, with some eagerness.

"That's the man," answered the courier.

"Does it pay well?" asked the troubadour innocently.

"It will pay me," said Ezza, with a very enigmatic smile. "But I am a rather curious sort of courier." Then, as if changing the subject, he said abruptly, "He has a daughter—and a son."

"The daughter is divine," affirmed Muscari, "the father and son are, I suppose, human. But granted his harmless qualities, doesn't that banker strike you as a splendid instance of my argument? Harrogate has millions in his safes, and I have—the hole in my pocket. But you daren't say—you can't say—that he's cleverer than I, or bolder than I, or even more energetic. He's not clever; he's got eyes like blue buttons; he's not energetic, he moves from chair to chair like a paralytic. He's a conscientious, kindly old blockhead; but he's got money simply because he collects money, as a boy collects stamps. You're too strong-minded for business, Ezza. You won't get on. To be clever enough to get all that money, one must be stupid enough to want it."

"I'm stupid enough for that," said Ezza gloomily. "But I should suggest a suspension of your critique of the banker, for here he comes."

Mr. Harrogate, the great financier, did indeed enter the room, but nobody looked at him. He was a massive elderly man with a boiled blue eye and faded grey-sandy moustaches; but for his heavy stoop he might have been a colonel. He carried several unopened letters in his hand. His son Frank was a really fine lad, curly haired, sunburnt and strenuous; but nobody looked at him either. All eyes, as usual, were riveted, for the moment at least, upon Ethel Harrogate, whose golden Greek head and colour of the dawn seemed set purposely above that sapphire sea, like a goddess's. The poet Muscari drew a deep breath as if he were drinking something; as indeed he was. He was drinking the Classic; which his fathers made. Ezza studied her with a gaze equally intense and far more baffling.

Miss Harrogate was specially radiant and ready for conversation on this occasion; and her family had fallen into the easier Continental habit, allowing the stranger Muscari and even the courier Ezza to share their table and their talk. In Ethel Harrogate conventionality crowned itself with a perfection and splendour of its own. Proud of her father's prosperity, fond of her fashionable pleasures, a fond daughter but an arrant flirt, she was all these things with a sort of golden good-nature that made her very pride pleasing and her worldly respectability a fresh and hearty thing.

They were in an eddy of excitement about some alleged peril in the mountain path they were to attempt that week. The danger was not from rock and avalanche, but from something yet more romantic. Ethel had been earnestly assured that brigands, the true cutthroats of the modern legend, still haunted that ridge and held that pass of the Apennines.

"They say," she cried, with the awful relish of a schoolgirl, "that all that country isn't ruled by the King of Italy, but by the King of Thieves. Who is the King of Thieves?"

"A great man," replied Muscari, "worthy to rank with your own Robin Hood, signorina. Montano, the King of Thieves, was first heard of in the mountains some ten years ago, when people said brigands were extinct. But his wild authority spread with the swiftness of a silent revolution. Men found his fierce proclamations nailed in every mountain village; his sentinels, gun in hand, in every mountain ravine. Six times the Italian Government tried to dislodge him; and was defeated in six pitched battles as if by Napoleon."

"Now that sort of thing," observed the banker weightily, "would never be allowed in England; perhaps after all we had better choose another route. But the courier thought it perfectly safe."

"It is perfectly safe," said the courier contemptuously; "I have been over it twenty times. There may have been some old jail-bird called a King in the time of our grandmothers; but he belongs to history, if not to fable. Brigandage is utterly stamped out."

"It can never be utterly stamped out," Muscari answered, "because armed revolt is a reaction natural to southerners. Our peasants are like the mountains, rich in grace and green gaiety, but with the fires beneath. There is a point of human despair where the northern poor take to drink—and our own poor take to daggers."

"A poet is privileged," replied Ezza, with a sneer. "If Signor Muscari were English he would still be looking for highwaymen in Wandsworth. Believe me, there is no more danger of being captured in Italy than of being scalped in Boston."

"Then you propose to attempt it?" asked Mr. Harrogate, frowning.

"Oh, it sounds rather dreadful," cried the girl; turning her glorious eyes on Muscari. "Do you really think the pass is dangerous?"

Muscari threw back his black mane. "I know it is dangerous," he said. "I am crossing it to-morrow."

The young Harrogate was left behind for a moment, emptying a glass of white wine and lighting a cigarette, as the beauty retired with the banker, the courier and the poet, distributing peals of silvery satire. At about the same instant the two priests in the corner rose; the taller, a white-haired Italian, taking his leave. The shorter priest turned and walked towards the banker's son; and the latter was astonished to realise that though a Roman priest the man was an Englishman. He vaguely remembered meeting the priest at the social crushes of some of his Catholic friends. But the man spoke before his memories could collect themselves.

"Mr. Frank Harrogate, I think," he said. "I have had an introduction, but I do not mean to presume on it. The odd thing I have to say will come far better from a stranger. Mr. Harrogate, I say one word and go: take care of your sister in her great sorrow."

Even for Frank's truly fraternal indifference the radiance and derision of his sister still seemed to sparkle and ring; he could hear her laughter still from the garden of the hotel; and he stared at his sombre adviser in puzzledom.

"Do you mean the brigands?" he asked, and then, remembering a vague fear of his own, "or can you be thinking of Muscari?"

"One is never thinking of the real sorrow," said the strange priest. "One can only be kind when it comes."

And he passed promptly from the room, leaving the other almost with his mouth open.

A day or two afterwards a coach containing the company was really crawling and staggering up the spurs of the menacing mountain range. Between Ezza's cheery denial of the danger and Muscari's boisterous defiance of it, the financial family were firm in their original purpose; and Muscari made his mountain journey coincide with theirs. A more surprising feature was the appearance at the coast-town station of the little priest of the restaurant; he alleged merely that business led him also to cross the mountains of the midland. But young Harrogate could not but connect his presence with the mystical fears and warnings of yesterday.

The coach was a kind of commodious wagonette, invented by the modernist talent of the courier, who dominated the expedition with his scientific activity and breezy wit. The theory of danger from thieves was banished from thought and speech; though so far conceded in formal act that some slight protection was employed. The courier and the young banker carried loaded revolvers, and Muscari (with much boyish gratification) buckled on a kind of cutlass under his black cloak.

He had planted his person at a flying leap next to the lovely Englishwoman; on the other side of her sat the priest, whose name was Brown and who was fortunately a silent individual; the courier and the father and son were on the *banc* behind. Muscari was in towering spirits, seriously believing in the peril, and his talk to Ethel might well have made her think him a maniac. But there was something in the crazy and gorgeous ascent, amid crags like peaks loaded with woods like orchards, that dragged her spirit up along with his into purple preposterous heavens, with wheeling suns. The white road climbed like a white cat; it spanned sunless chasms like a tight-rope; it was flung round far-off headlands like a lasso.

And yet however high they went, the desert still blossomed like the rose. The fields were burnished in sun and wind with the colour of kingfisher and parrot and humming-bird; the hues of a hundred flowering flowers. There are no lovelier meadows and woodlands than the English; no nobler crests or chasms than those of Snowdon and Glencoe. But Ethel Harrogate had never before seen the southern parks tilted on the splintered northern peaks; the gorge of Glencoe laden with the fruits of Kent. There was nothing here of that chill and desolation that in Britain one associates with high and wild scenery. It was rather like a mosaic palace, rent with earthquakes; or like a Dutch tulip garden blown to the stars with dynamite.

"It's like Kew Gardens on Beachy Head," said Ethel.

"It is our secret," answered he, "the secret of the volcano; that is also the secret of the revolution—that a thing can be violent and yet fruitful."

"You are rather violent yourself," and she smiled at him.

"And yet rather fruitless," he admitted; "if I die to-night I die unmarried and a fool."

"It is not my fault if you have come," she said after a difficult silence.

"It is never your fault," answered Muscari; "it was not your fault that Troy fell."

As he spoke they came under overwhelming cliffs that spread almost like wings above a corner of peculiar peril. Shocked by the big shadow on the narrow ledge, the horses stirred doubtfully. The driver leapt to the earth to hold their heads, and they became ungovernable. One horse reared up to his full height—the titanic and terrifying height of a horse when he becomes a biped. It was just enough to alter the equilibrium; the whole coach heeled over like a ship and crashed through the fringe of bushes over the cliff. Muscari threw an arm round Ethel, who clung to him, and shouted aloud. It was for such moments that he lived.

At the moment when the gorgeous mountain walls went round the poet's head like a purple windmill, a thing happened which was superficially even more startling. The elderly and lethargic banker sprang erect in the coach and leapt over the precipice before the tilted vehicle could take him there. In the first flash it looked as wild as suicide; but in the second it was as sensible as a safe investment. The Yorkshireman had evidently more promptitude as well as more sagacity than Muscari had given him credit for. For he landed in a lap of land which might have been specially padded with turf and clover to receive him. As it happened, indeed, the whole company were equally lucky, if less dignified in their form of ejection. Immediately under this abrupt turn of the road was a grassy and flowery hollow like a sunken meadow; a sort of green velvet pocket in the long, green, trailing garments of the hills. Into this they were all tipped or tumbled with little damage, save that their smallest baggage and even the contents of their pockets were scattered in the grass around them. The wrecked coach still hung above, entangled in the tough hedge, and the horses plunged painfully down the slope. The first to sit up was the little priest, who scratched his head with a face of foolish wonder; Frank Harrogate heard him say to himself, "Now why on earth have we fallen just here?"

He blinked at the litter around him, and recovered his own very clumsy umbrella. Beyond it lay the broad sombrero fallen from the head of Muscari, and beside it a sealed business letter which, after a glance at the address, he returned to the elder Harrogate. On the other side of him the grass partly hid Miss Ethel's sunshade, and just beyond it lay a curious little glass bottle hardly two inches long. The priest picked it up; in a quick, unobtrusive manner he uncorked and sniffed it, and his heavy face turned the colour of clay.

"Heaven deliver us!" he muttered, "it can't be hers! Has her sorrow come on her already?" He slipped it into his own waistcoat pocket. "I think I'm justified," he said, "till I know a little more."

He gazed painfully at the girl, at that moment being raised out of the flowers by Muscari, who was saying, "We have fallen into heaven; it is a sign. Mortals climb up and they fall down; but it is only gods and goddesses who can fall upwards."

And indeed she rose out of the sea of colours so beautiful and happy a vision that the priest felt his suspicion shaken and shifted. "After all," he thought, "perhaps the poison isn't hers; perhaps it's one of Muscari's melodramatic tricks."

Muscari set the lady lightly on her feet, made her an absurdly theatrical bow, and then, drawing his cutlass, hacked hard at the taut reins of the horses, so that they scrambled to their feet and stood in the grass trembling. When he had done so a most remarkable thing occurred. A very quiet man, very poorly dressed and extremely sunburnt, came out of the bushes and took hold of the horses' heads. He had a queer-shaped knife, very broad and crooked, buckled on his belt; there was nothing else remarkable about him, except his sudden and silent appearance. The poet asked him who he was, and he did not answer.

Looking around him at the confused and startled group in the hollow, Muscari then perceived that another tanned and tattered man, with a short gun under his arm, was looking at them from the ledge just below, leaning his elbows on the edge of the turf. Then he looked up at the road from which they had fallen and saw, looking down on them, the muzzles of four other carbines and four other brown faces with bright but quite motionless eyes.

"The brigands!" cried Muscari, with a kind of monstrous gaiety. "This was a trap. Ezza, if you will oblige me by shooting the coachman first, we can cut our way out yet. There are only six of them."

"The coachman," said Ezza, who was standing grimly with his hands in his pockets, "happens to be a servant of Mr. Harrogate's."

"Then shoot him all the more," cried the poet impatiently; "he was bribed to upset his master. Then put the lady in the middle, and we will break the line up there—with a rush."

And, wading in wild grass and flowers, he advanced fearlessly on the four carbines; but finding that no one followed except young Harrogate, he turned, brandishing his cutlass to wave the others on. He beheld the courier still standing slightly astride in the centre of the grassy ring, his hands in his pockets; and his lean, ironical Italian face seemed to grow longer and longer in the evening light.

"You thought, Muscari, I was the failure among our schoolfellows," he said, "and you thought you were the success. But I have succeeded more than you and fill a bigger place in history. I have been acting epics while you have been writing them."

"Come on, I tell you!" thundered Muscari from above. "Will you stand there talking nonsense about yourself with a woman to save and three strong men to help you? What do you call yourself?"

"I call myself Montano," cried the strange courier in a voice equally loud and full. "I am the King of Thieves, and I welcome you all to my summer palace."

And even as he spoke five more silent men with weapons ready came out of the bushes, and looked towards him for their orders. One of them held a large paper in his hand.

"This pretty little nest where we are all picnicking," went on the courier-brigand, with the same easy yet sinister smile, "is, together with some caves underneath it, known by the name of the Paradise of Thieves. It is my principal stronghold on these hills; for (as you have doubtless noticed) the eyrie is invisible both from the road above and from the valley below. It is something better than impregnable; it is unnoticeable. Here I mostly live, and here I shall certainly die, if the gendarmes ever track me here. I am not the kind of criminal that 'reserves his defence,' but the better kind that reserves his last bullet."

All were staring at him thunderstruck and still, except Father Brown, who heaved a huge sigh as of relief and fingered the little phial in his pocket. "Thank God!" he muttered, "that's much more probable. The poison belongs to this robber-chief, of course. He carries it so that he may never be captured, like Cato."

The King of Thieves was, however, continuing his address with the same kind of dangerous politeness. "It only remains for me," he said, "to explain to my guests the social conditions upon which I have the pleasure of entertaining them. I need not expound the quaint old ritual of ransom, which it is incumbent upon me to keep up; and even this only applies to a part of the company. The Reverend Father Brown and the celebrated Signor Muscari I shall release to-morrow at dawn and escort to my outposts. Poets and priests, if you will pardon my simplicity of speech, never have any money. And so (since it is impossible to get anything out of them), let us seize the opportunity to show our admiration for classic literature and our reverence for Holy Church."

He paused with an unpleasing smile; and Father Brown blinked repeatedly at him, and seemed suddenly to be listening with great attention. The brigand captain took the large paper from the attendant brigand and, glancing it over, continued: "My other intentions are clearly set forth in this public document, which I will hand round in a moment; and which after that will be posted on a tree by every village in the valley, and every cross-road in the hills. I will not weary you with the verbalism, since you will be able to check it; the substance of my proclamation is this. I announce first that I have captured the English millionaire, the colossus of finance, Mr. Samuel Harrogate. I next announce that I have found on his person notes and bonds for two thousand pounds, which he has given up to me. Now since it would be really immoral to announce such a thing to a credulous public if it had not occurred, I suggest it should occur without further delay. I suggest that Mr. Harrogate senior should now give me the two thousand pounds in his pocket."

The banker looked at him under lowering brows, red-faced and sulky, but seemingly cowed. That leap from the falling carriage seemed to have used up his last virility. He had held back in a hang-dog style when his son and Muscari had made a bold movement to break out of the brigand trap. And now his red and trembling hand went reluctantly to his breast-pocket, and passed a bundle of papers and envelopes to the brigand.

"Excellent!" cried that outlaw gaily, "so far we are all cosy. I resume the points of my proclamation, so soon to be published to all Italy. The third item is that of ransom. I am asking from the friends of the Harrogate family a ransom of three thousand pounds; which I am sure is almost insulting to that family in its moderate estimate of their importance. Who would not pay triple this sum for another day's association with such a domestic circle? I will not conceal from you that the document ends with certain legal phrases about the unpleasant things that may happen if the money is not paid; but meanwhile, ladies and gentlemen, let me assure you that I am comfortably off here for accommodation, wine and cigars, and bid you for the present a sportsmanlike welcome to the luxuries of the Paradise of Thieves."

All the time that he had been speaking the dubious-looking men with carbines and dirty slouch hats had been gathering silently in such preponderating numbers that even Muscari was compelled to recognise his sally with the sword as hopeless. He glanced around him; but the girl had already gone over to soothe and comfort her father, for her natural affection for his person was as strong or stronger than her somewhat snobbish pride in his success. Muscari, with the illogicality of a lover, admired this filial devotion and yet was irritated by it. He slapped his sword back in the scabbard and went and flung himself somewhat sulkily on one of the green banks. The priest sat down within a yard or two, and Muscari turned his aquiline eye and nose on him in an instantaneous irritation.

"Well," said the poet tartly, "do people still think me too romantic? Are there, I wonder, any brigands left in the mountains?"

"There may be," said Father Brown agnostically.

"What do you mean?" asked the other sharply.

"I mean I am puzzled," replied the priest. "I am puzzled about Ezza or Montano or whatever his name is. He seems to me much more inexplicable as a brigand even than he was as a courier."

"But in what way?" persisted his companion. "Santa Maria! I should have thought the brigand was plain enough."

"I find three curious difficulties," said the priest in a quiet voice. "I should like to have your opinion on them. First of all I must tell you I was lunching in that restaurant at the seaside. As four of you left the room, you and Miss Harrogate went ahead, talking and laughing; the banker and the courier came behind, speaking sparely and rather low. But I could not help hearing Ezza say these words— 'Well, let her have a little fun; you know the blow may smash her any minute.' Mr. Harrogate answered nothing; so the words must have had some meaning. On the impulse of the moment I warned her brother that she might be in peril; I said nothing of its nature, for I did not know. But if it meant this capture in the hills, the thing is nonsense. Why should the brigand-courier warn his patron, even by a hint, when it was his whole purpose to lure him into the mountain-mousetrap? It could not have meant that. But if not, what is this other disaster, known both to courier and banker, which hangs over Miss Harrogate's head?"

"Disaster to Miss Harrogate!" ejaculated the poet, sitting up with some ferocity. "Explain yourself; go on."

"All my riddles, however, revolve round our bandit chief," resumed the priest reflectively. "And here is the second of them. Why did he put so prominently in his demand for ransom the fact that he had taken two thousand pounds from his victim on the spot? It had no faintest tendency to evoke the ransom. Quite the other way, in fact. Harrogate's friends would be far likelier to fear for his fate if they thought the thieves were poor and desperate. Yet the spoliation on the spot was emphasised and even put first in the demand. Why should Ezza Montano want so specially to tell all Europe that he had picked the pocket before he levied the blackmail?"

"I cannot imagine," said Muscari, rubbing up his black hair for once with an unaffected gesture. "You may think you enlighten me, but you are leading me deeper in the dark. What may be the third objection to the King of the Thieves?"

"The third objection," said Father Brown, still in meditation, "is this bank we are sitting on. Why does our brigand-courier call this his chief fortress and the Paradise of Thieves? It is certainly a soft spot to fall on and a sweet spot to look at. It is also quite true, as he says, that it is invisible from valley and peak, and is therefore a hiding-place. But it is not a fortress. It never could be a fortress. I think it would be the worst fortress in the world. For it is actually commanded from above by the common high-road across the mountains—the very place where the police would most probably pass. Why, five shabby short guns held us helpless here about half an hour ago. The quarter of a company of any kind of soldiers could have blown us over the precipice. Whatever is the meaning of this odd little nook of grass and flowers, it is not an entrenched position. It is something else; it has some other strange sort of importance; some value that I do not understand. It is more like an accidental theatre or a natural green-room; it is like the scene for some romantic comedy; it is like ..."

As the little priest's words lengthened and lost themselves in a dull and dreamy sincerity, Muscari, whose animal senses were alert and impatient, heard a new noise in the mountains. Even for him the sound was as yet very small and faint; but he could have sworn the evening breeze bore with it something like the pulsation of horses' hoofs and a distant halloing.

At the same moment, and long before the vibration had touched the less-experienced English ears, Montano the brigand ran up the bank above them and stood in the broken hedge, steadying himself against a tree and peering down the road. He was a strange figure as he stood there; for he had assumed a flapped fantastic hat and swinging baldric and cutlass in his capacity of bandit king, but the bright prosaic tweed of the courier showed through in patches all over him.

The next moment he turned his olive, sneering face and made a movement with his hand. The brigands scattered at the signal, not in confusion; but in what was evidently a kind of guerilla discipline. Instead of occupying the road along the ridge, they sprinkled themselves along the side of it behind the trees and the hedge, as if watching unseen for an enemy. The noise beyond grew stronger, beginning to shake the mountain road; and a voice could be clearly heard calling out orders. The brigands swayed and huddled, cursing and whispering, and the evening air was full of little metallic noises as they cocked their pistols or loosened their knives or trailed their scabbards over the stones. Then the noises from both quarters seemed to meet on the road above; branches broke, horses neighed, men cried out.

"A rescue!" cried Muscari, springing to his feet and waving his hat: "the gendarmes are on them! Now for freedom and a blow for it! Now to be rebels against robbers! Come, don't let us leave everything to the police; that is so dreadfully modern. Fall on the rear of these ruffians. The gendarmes are rescuing us; come, friends, let us rescue the gendarmes!"

And throwing his hat over the trees, he drew his cutlass once more and began to escalade the slope up to the road. Frank Harrogate jumped up and ran across to help him, revolver in hand, but was astounded to hear himself imperatively recalled by the raucous voice of his father, who seemed to be in great agitation.

"I won't have it," said the banker in a choking voice; "I command you not to interfere."

"But, father," said Frank very warmly, "an Italian gentleman has led the way. You wouldn't have it said that the English hung back."

"It is useless," said the older man, who was trembling violently, "it is useless. We must submit to our lot."

Father Brown looked at the banker; then he put his hand instinctively as if on his heart, but really on the little bottle of poison; and a great light came into his face like the light of the revelation of death.

Muscari meanwhile, without waiting for support, had crested the bank up to the road, and struck the brigand king heavily on the shoulder, causing him to stagger and swing round. Montano also had his cutlass unsheathed, and Muscari, without further speech, sent a slash at his head which he was compelled to catch and parry. But even as the two short blades crossed and clashed the King of Thieves deliberately dropped his point and laughed.

"What's the good, old man?" he said in spirited Italian slang; "this damned farce will soon be over."

"What do you mean, you shuffler?" panted the fire-eating poet. "Is your courage a sham as well as your honesty?"

"Everything about me is a sham," responded the ex-courier in complete good-humour. "I am an actor; and if I ever had a private character, I have forgotten it. I am no more a genuine brigand than I am a genuine courier. I am only a bundle of masks, and you can't fight a duel with that." And he laughed with boyish pleasure and fell into his old straddling attitude, with his back to the skirmish up the road.

Darkness was deepening under the mountain walls, and it was not easy to discern much of the progress of the struggle, save that tall men were pushing their horses' nozzles through a clinging crowd of brigands, who seemed more inclined to harass and hustle the invaders than to kill them. It was more like a town crowd preventing the passage of the police than anything the poet had ever pictured as the last stand of doomed and outlawed men of blood. Just as he was rolling his eyes in bewilderment, he felt a touch on his elbow, and found the odd little priest standing there like a small Noah with a large hat, and requesting the favour of a word or two.

"Signor Muscari," said the clerk, "in this queer crisis personalities may be pardoned. I may tell you without offence of a way in which you will do more good than by helping the gendarmes, who are bound to break through in any case. You will permit me the impertinent intimacy; but do you care about that girl? Care enough to marry her and make her a good husband, I mean?"

"Yes," said the poet quite simply.

"Does she care about you?"

"I think so," was the equally grave reply.

"Then go over there and offer yourself," said the priest: "offer her everything you can; offer her heaven and earth if you've got them. The time is short."

"Why?" asked the astonished man of letters.

"Because," said Father Brown, "her Doom is coming up the road."

"Nothing is coming up the road," argued Muscari, "except the rescue."

"Well, you go over there," said his adviser, "and be ready to rescue her from the rescue."

Almost as he spoke the hedges were broken all along the ridge by a rush of the escaping brigands. They dived into bushes and thick grass like defeated men pursued; and the great cocked hats of the mounted gendarmerie were seen passing along above the broken hedge. Another order was given; there was a noise of dismounting, and a tall officer with a cocked hat, a grey imperial and a paper in his hand appeared in the gap that was the gate of the Paradise of Thieves. There was a momentary silence, broken in an extraordinary way by the banker, who cried out in a hoarse and strangled voice, "Robbed! I've been robbed!"

"Why, that was hours ago," cried his son in astonishment, "when you were robbed of two thousand pounds."

"Not of two thousand pounds," said the financier, with an abrupt and terrible composure, "only of a small bottle."

The policeman with the grey imperial was striding across the green hollow. Encountering the King of Thieves in his path, he clapped him on the shoulder with something between a caress and a buffet and gave him a push that sent him staggering away. "You'll get into trouble, too," he said, "if you play these tricks."

Again to Muscari's artistic eye it seemed scarcely like the capture of a great outlaw at bay. Passing on, the policeman halted before the Harrogate group and said: "Samuel Harrogate, I arrest you in the name of the law for embezzlement of the funds of the Hull and Huddersfield Bank."

The great banker nodded with an odd air of business assent, seemed to reflect a moment, and before they could interpose took a half turn and a step that brought him to the edge of the outer mountain wall. Then, flinging up his hands, he leapt, exactly as he leapt out of the coach. But this time he did not fall into a little meadow just beneath; he fell a thousand feet below, to become a wreck of bones in the valley.

The anger of the Italian policeman, which he expressed volubly to Father Brown, was largely mixed with admiration. "It was like him to escape us at last," he said. "*He* was a great brigand if you like. This last trick of his I believe to be absolutely unprecedented. He fled with the company's money to Italy, and actually got himself captured by sham brigands in his own pay, so as to explain both the disappearance of the money and the disappearance of himself. That demand for ransom was really taken seriously by most of the police. But for years he's been doing things as good as that, quite as good as that. He will be a serious loss to his family."

Muscari was leading away the unhappy daughter, who held hard to him, as she did for many a year after. But even in that tragic wreck he could not help having a smile and a hand of half-mocking friendship for the indefensible Ezza Montano. "And where are you going next?" he asked him over his shoulder.

"Birmingham," answered the actor, puffing a cigarette. "Didn't I tell you I was a Futurist? I really do believe in those things if I believe in anything. Change, bustle and new things every morning. I am going to Manchester, Liverpool, Leeds, Hull, Huddersfield, Glasgow, Chicago—in short, to enlightened, energetic, civilised society!"

"In short," said Muscari, "to the real Paradise of Thieves."

THE MAN IN THE PASSAGE

Two men appeared simultaneously at the two ends of a sort of passage running along the side of the Apollo Theatre in the Adelphi. The evening daylight in the streets was large and luminous, opalescent and empty. The passage was comparatively long and dark, so each man could see the other as a mere black silhouette at the other end. Nevertheless, each man knew the other, even in that inky outline, for they were both men of striking appearance, and they hated each other.

The covered passage opened at one end on one of the steep streets of the Adelphi, and at the other on a terrace overlooking the sunset-coloured river. One side of the passage was a blank wall, for the building it supported was an old unsuccessful theatre restaurant, now shut up. The other side of the passage contained two doors, one at each end. Neither was what was commonly called the stage door; they were a sort of special and private stage doors, used by very special performers, and in this case by the star actor and actress in the Shakespearean performance of the day. Persons of that eminence often like to have such private exits and entrances, for meeting friends or avoiding them.

The two men in question were certainly two such friends, men who evidently knew the doors and counted on their opening, for each approached the door at the upper end with equal coolness and confidence. Not, however, with equal speed; but the man who walked fast was the man from the other end of the tunnel, so they both arrived before the secret stage door almost at the same instant. They saluted each other with civility, and waited a moment before one of them, the sharper walker, who seemed to have the shorter patience, knocked at the door.

In this and everything else each man was opposite and neither could be called inferior. As private persons, both were handsome, capable, and popular. As public persons, both were in the first public rank. But everything about them, from their glory to their good looks, was of a diverse and incomparable kind. Sir Wilson Seymour was the kind of man whose importance is known to everybody who knows. The more you mixed with the innermost ring in every polity or profession, the more often you met Sir Wilson Seymour. He was the one intelligent man on twenty unintelligent committees—on every sort of subject, from the reform of the Royal Academy to the project of bimetallism for Greater Britain. In the arts especially he was omnipotent. He was so unique that nobody could quite decide whether he was a great aristocrat who had taken up art, or a great artist whom the aristocrats had taken up. But you could not meet him for five minutes without realising that you had really been ruled by him all your life.

His appearance was "distinguished" in exactly the same sense; it was at once conventional and unique. Fashion could have found no fault with his high silk hat; yet it was unlike anyone else's hat—a little higher, perhaps, and adding something to his natural height. His tall, slender figure had a slight stoop, yet it looked the reverse of feeble. His hair was silver-grey, but he did not look old; it was worn longer than the common, yet he did not look effeminate; it was curly, but it did not look curled. His carefully pointed beard made him look more manly and militant rather than otherwise, as it does in those old admirals of Velasquez with whose dark portraits his house was hung. His grey gloves were a shade bluer, his silver-knobbed cane a shade longer than scores of such gloves and canes flapped and flourished about the theatres and the restaurants.

The other man was not so tall, yet would have struck nobody as short, but merely as strong and handsome. His hair also was curly, but fair and cropped close to a strong, massive head—the sort of head you break a door with, as Chaucer said of the Miller's. His military moustache and the carriage of his shoulders showed him a soldier, but he had a pair of those peculiar, frank, and piercing blue eyes which are more common in sailors. His face was somewhat square, his jaw was square, his shoulders were square, even his jacket was square. Indeed, in the wild school of caricature then current, Mr. Max Beerbohm had represented him as a proposition in the fourth book of Euclid.

For he also was a public man, though with quite another sort of success. You did not have to be in the best society to have heard of Captain Cutler, of the siege of Hong-Kong and the great march across China. You could not get away from hearing of him wherever you were; his portrait was on every other postcard; his maps and battles in every other illustrated paper; songs in his honour in every other music-hall turn or on every other barrel-organ. His fame, though probably more temporary, was ten times more wide, popular, and spontaneous than the other man's. In thousands of English homes he appeared enormous above England, like Nelson. Yet he had infinitely less power in England than Sir Wilson Seymour.

The door was opened to them by an aged servant or "dresser," whose broken-down face and figure and black shabby coat and trousers contrasted queerly with the glittering interior of the great actress's dressing-room. It was fitted and filled with looking-glasses at every angle of refraction, so that they looked like the hundred facets of one huge diamond—if one could get inside a diamond. The other features of luxury, a few flowers, a few coloured cushions, a few scraps of stage costume, were multiplied by all the mirrors into the madness of the Arabian Nights, and danced and changed places perpetually as the shuffling attendant shifted a mirror outwards or shot one back against the wall.

They both spoke to the dingy dresser by name, calling him Parkinson, and asking for the lady as Miss Aurora Rome. Parkinson said she was in the other room, but he would go and tell her. A shade crossed the brow of both visitors; for the other room was the private room of the great actor with whom Miss Aurora was performing, and she was of the kind that does not inflame admiration without inflaming jealousy. In about half a minute, however, the inner door opened, and she entered as she always did, even in private life, so that the very silence seemed to be a roar of applause, and one well deserved. She was clad in a somewhat strange garb of peacock green and peacock blue satins, that gleamed like blue and green metals, such as delight children and æsthetes, and her heavy, hot brown hair framed one of those magic faces which are dangerous to all men, but especially to boys and to men growing grey. In company with her male colleague, the great American actor, Isidore Bruno, she was producing a particularly poetical and fantastic interpretation of the *Midsummer Night's Dream,* in which the artistic prominence was given to Oberon and Titania, or in other words to Bruno and herself. Set in dreamy and exquisite scenery, and moving in mystical dances, the green costume, like burnished beetle-wings, expressed all the elusive individuality of an elfin queen. But when personally confronted in what was still broad daylight, a man looked only at the woman's face.

She greeted both men with the beaming and baffling smile which kept so many males at the same just dangerous distance from her. She accepted some flowers from Cutler, which were as tropical and expensive as his victories; and another sort of present from Sir Wilson Seymour, offered later on and more nonchalantly by that gentleman. For it was against his breeding to show eagerness, and against his conventional unconventionality to give anything so obvious as flowers. He had picked up a trifle, he said, which was rather a curiosity; it was an ancient Greek dagger of the Mycenaean Epoch, and might have been well worn in the time of Theseus and Hippolyta. It was made of brass like all the Heroic weapons, but, oddly enough, sharp enough to prick anyone still. He had really been attracted to it by the leaflike shape; it was as perfect as a Greek vase. If it was of any interest to Miss Rome or could come in anywhere in the play, he hoped she would——

The inner door burst open and a big figure appeared, who was more of a contrast to the explanatory Seymour than even Captain Cutler. Nearly six-foot-six, and of more than theatrical thews and muscles, Isidore Bruno, in the gorgeous leopard skin and golden-brown garments of Oberon, looked like a barbaric god. He leaned on a sort of hunting-spear, which across a theatre looked a slight, silvery wand, but which in the small and comparatively crowded room looked as plain as a pikestaff—and as menacing. His vivid, black eyes rolled volcanically, his bronzed face, handsome as it was, showed at that moment a combination of high cheekbones with set white teeth, which recalled certain American conjectures about his origin in the Southern plantations.

"Aurora," he began, in that deep voice like a drum of passion that had moved so many audiences, "will you——"

He stopped indecisively because a sixth figure had suddenly presented itself just inside the doorway—a figure so incongruous in the scene as to be almost comic. It was a very short man in the black uniform of the Roman secular clergy, and looking (especially in such a presence as Bruno's and Aurora's) rather like the wooden Noah out of an ark. He did not, however, seem conscious of any contrast, but said with dull civility: "I believe Miss Rome sent for me."

A shrewd observer might have remarked that the emotional temperature rather rose at so unemotional an interruption. The detachment of a professional celibate seemed to reveal to the others that they stood round the woman as a ring of amorous rivals; just as a stranger coming in with frost on his coat will reveal that a room is like a furnace. The presence of the one man who did not care about her increased Miss Rome's sense that everybody else was in love with her, and each in a somewhat dangerous way: the actor with all the appetite of a savage and a spoilt child; the soldier with all the simple selfishness of a man of will rather than mind; Sir Wilson with that daily hardening concentration with which old Hedonists take to a hobby; nay, even the abject Parkinson, who had known her before her triumphs, and who followed her about the room with eyes or feet, with the dumb fascination of a dog.

A shrewd person might also have noted a yet odder thing. The man like a black wooden Noah (who was not wholly without shrewdness) noted it with a considerable but contained amusement. It was evident that the great Aurora, though by no means indifferent to the admiration of the other sex, wanted at this moment to get rid of all the men who admired her and be left alone with the man who did not—did not admire her in that sense, at least; for the little priest did admire and even enjoy the firm feminine diplomacy with which she set about her task. There was, perhaps, only one thing that Aurora Rome was clever about, and that was one half of humanity—the other half. The little priest watched, like a Napoleonic campaign, the swift precision of her policy for expelling all while banishing none. Bruno, the big actor, was so babyish that it was easy to send him off in brute sulks, banging the door. Cutler, the British officer, was pachydermatous to ideas, but punctilious about behaviour. He would ignore all hints, but he would die rather than ignore a definite commission from a lady. As to old Seymour he had to be treated differently; he had to be left to the last. The only way to move him was to appeal to him in confidence as an old friend, to let him into the secret of the clearance. The priest did really admire Miss Rome as she achieved all these three objects in one selected action.

She went across to Captain Cutler and said in her sweetest manner: "I shall value all these flowers because they must be your favourite flowers. But they won't be complete, you know, without *my* favourite flower. *Do* go over to that shop round the corner and get me some lilies-of-the-valley and then it will be *quite lovely.*"

The first object of her diplomacy, the exit of the enraged Bruno, was at once achieved. He had already handed his spear in a lordly style like a sceptre to the piteous Parkinson, and was about to assume one of the cushioned seats like a throne. But at this open appeal to his rival there glowed in his opal eyeballs all the sensitive insolence of the slave; he knotted his enormous brown fists for an instant, and then, dashing open the door, disappeared into his own apartments beyond. But meanwhile Miss Rome's experiment in mobilising the British Army had not succeeded so simply as seemed probable. Cutler had indeed risen stiffly and suddenly, and walked towards the door, hatless, as if at a word of command. But perhaps there was something ostentatiously elegant about the languid figure of Seymour leaning against one of the looking-glasses, that brought him up short at the entrance, turning his head this way and that like a bewildered bulldog.

"I must show this stupid man where to go," said Aurora in a whisper to Seymour, and ran out to the threshold to speed the parting guest.

Seymour seemed to be listening, elegant and unconscious as was his posture, and he seemed relieved when he heard the lady call out some last instructions to the Captain, and then turn sharply and run laughing down the passage towards the other end, the end on the terrace above the Thames. Yet a second or two after, Seymour's brow darkened again. A man in his position has so many rivals, and he remembered that at the other end of the passage was the corresponding entrance to Bruno's private room. He did not lose his dignity; he said some civil words to Father Brown about the revival of Byzantine architecture in the Westminster Cathedral, and then, quite naturally, strolled out himself into the upper end of the passage. Father Brown and Parkinson were left alone, and they were neither of them men with a taste for superfluous conversation. The dresser went round the room, pulling out looking-glasses and pushing them in again, his dingy dark coat and trousers looking all the more dismal since he was still holding the festive fairy spear of King Oberon. Every time he pulled out the frame of a new glass, a new black figure of Father Brown appeared; the absurd glass chamber was full of Father Browns, upside down in the air like angels, turning somersaults like acrobats, turning their backs to everybody like very rude persons.

Father Brown seemed quite unconscious of this cloud of witnesses, but followed Parkinson with an idly attentive eye till he took himself and his absurd spear into the farther room of Bruno. Then he abandoned himself to such abstract meditations as always amused him—calculating the angles of the mirrors, the angles of each refraction, the angle at which each must fit into the wall . . . when he heard a strong but strangled cry.

He sprang to his feet and stood rigidly listening. At the same instant Sir Wilson Seymour burst back into the room, white as ivory. "Who's that man in the passage?" he cried. "Where's that dagger of mine?"

Before Father Brown could turn in his heavy boots, Seymour was plunging about the room looking for the weapon. And before he could possibly find that weapon or any other, a brisk running of feet broke upon the pavement outside, and the square face of Cutler was thrust into the same doorway. He was still grotesquely grasping a bunch of lilies-of-the-valley. "What's this?" he cried. "What's that creature down the passage? Is this some of your tricks?"

"My tricks!" hissed his pale rival, and made a stride towards him.

In the instant of time in which all this happened Father Brown stepped out into the top of the passage, looked down it, and at once walked briskly towards what he saw.

At this the other two men dropped their quarrel and darted after him, Cutler calling out: "What are you doing? Who are you?"

"My name is Brown," said the priest sadly, as he bent over something and straightened himself again. "Miss Rome sent for me, and I came as quickly as I could. I have come too late."

The three men looked down, and in one of them at least the life died in that late light of afternoon. It ran along the passage like a path of gold, and in the midst of it Aurora Rome lay lustrous in her robes of green and gold, with her dead face turned upwards. Her dress was torn away as in a struggle, leaving the right shoulder bare, but the wound from which the blood was welling was on the other side. The brass dagger lay flat and gleaming a yard or so away.

There was a blank stillness for a measurable time; so that they could hear far off a flower-girl's laugh outside Charing Cross, and someone whistling furiously for a taxicab in one of the streets off the Strand. Then the Captain, with a movement so sudden that it might have been passion or play-acting, took Sir Wilson Seymour by the throat.

Seymour looked at him steadily without either fight or fear. "You need not kill me," he said, in a voice quite cold; "I shall do that on my own account."

The Captain's hand hesitated and dropped; and the other added with the same icy candour: "If I find I haven't the nerve to do it with that dagger, I can do it in a month with drink."

"Drink isn't good enough for me," replied Cutler, "but I'll have blood for this before I die. Not yours—but I think I know whose."

And before the others could appreciate his intention he snatched up the dagger, sprang at the other door at the lower end of the passage, burst it open, bolt and all, and confronted Bruno in his dressing-room. As he did so, old Parkinson tottered in his wavering way out of the door and caught sight of the corpse lying in the passage. He moved shakily towards it; looked at it weakly with a working face; then moved shakily back into the dressing-room again, and sat down suddenly on one of the richly cushioned chairs. Father Brown instantly ran across to him, taking no notice of Cutler and the colossal actor, though the room already rang with their blows and they began to struggle for the dagger. Seymour, who retained some practical sense, was whistling for the police at the end of the passage.

When the police arrived it was to tear the two men from an almost apelike grapple; and, after a few formal inquiries, to arrest Isidore Bruno upon a charge of murder, brought against him by his furious opponent. The idea that the great national hero of the hour had arrested a wrongdoer with his own hand doubtless had its weight with the police, who are not without elements of the journalist. They treated Cutler with a certain solemn attention, and pointed out that he had got a slight slash on the hand. Even as Cutler bore him back across tilted chair and table, Bruno had twisted the dagger out of his grasp and disabled him just below the wrist. The injury was really slight, but till he was removed from the room the half-savage prisoner stared at the running blood with a steady smile.

"Looks a cannibal sort of chap, don't he?" said the constable confidentially to Cutler.

Cutler made no answer, but said sharply a moment after: "We must attend to the . . . the death . . ." and his voice escaped from articulation.

"The two deaths," came in the voice of the priest from the farther side of the room. "This poor fellow was gone when I got across to him." And he stood looking down at old Parkinson, who sat in a black huddle on the gorgeous chair. He also had paid his tribute, not without eloquence, to the woman who had died.

The silence was first broken by Cutler, who seemed not untouched by a rough tenderness. "I wish I was him," he said huskily. "I remember he used to watch her wherever she walked more than—anybody. She was his air, and he's dried up. He's just dead."

"We are all dead," said Seymour, in a strange voice, looking down the road.

They took leave of Father Brown at the corner of the road, with some random apologies for any rudeness they might have shown. Both their faces were tragic, but also cryptic.

The mind of the little priest was always a rabbit-warren of wild thoughts that jumped too quickly for him to catch them. Like the white tail of a rabbit, he had the vanishing thought that he was certain of their grief, but not so certain of their innocence.

"We had better all be going," said Seymour heavily; "we have done all we can to help."

"Will you understand my motives," asked Father Brown quietly, "if I say you have done all you can to hurt?"

They both started as if guiltily, and Cutler said sharply: "To hurt whom?"

"To hurt yourselves," answered the priest. "I would not add to your troubles if it weren't common justice to warn you. You've done nearly everything you could do to hang yourselves, if this actor should be acquitted. They'll be sure to subpoena me; I shall be bound to say that after the cry was heard, each of you rushed into the room in a wild state and began quarrelling about a dagger. As far as my words on oath can go, you might either of you have done it. You hurt yourselves with that; and then Captain Cutler must hurt himself with the dagger."

"Hurt myself!" exclaimed the Captain, with contempt. "A silly little scratch."

"Which drew blood," replied the priest, nodding. "We know there's blood on the brass now. And so we shall never know whether there was blood on it before."

There was a silence; and then Seymour said, with an emphasis quite alien to his daily accent: "But I saw a man in the passage."

"I know you did," answered the cleric Brown, with a face of wood; "so did Captain Cutler. That's what seems so improbable."

Before either could make sufficient sense of it even to answer, Father Brown had politely excused himself and gone stumping up the road with his stumpy old umbrella.

As modern newspapers are conducted, the most honest and most important news is the police news. If it be true that in the twentieth century more space was given to murder than to politics, it was for the excellent reason that murder is a more serious subject. But even this would hardly explain the enormous omnipresence and widely distributed detail of "The Bruno Case," or "The Passage Mystery," in the Press of London and the provinces. So vast was the excitement that for some weeks the Press really told the truth; and the reports of examination and cross-examination, if interminable, even if intolerable, are at least reliable. The true reason, of course, was the coincidence of persons. The victim was a popular actress; the accused was a popular actor; and the accused had been caught red-handed, as it were, by the most popular soldier of the patriotic season. In those extraordinary circumstances the Press was paralysed into probity and accuracy; and the rest of this somewhat singular business can practically be recorded from the reports of Bruno's trial.

The trial was presided over by Mr. Justice Monkhouse, one of those who are jeered at as humorous judges, but who are generally much more serious than the serious judges, for their levity comes from a living impatience of professional solemnity; while the serious judge is really filled with frivolity, because he is filled with vanity. All the chief actors being of a worldly importance, the barristers were well balanced; the prosecutor for the Crown was Sir Walter Cowdray, a heavy but weighty advocate of the sort that knows how to seem English and trustworthy, and how to be rhetorical with reluctance. The prisoner was defended by Mr. Patrick Butler, K.C., who was mistaken for a mere *flâneur* by those who misunderstand the Irish character—and those who had not been examined by him. The medical evidence involved no contradictions, the doctor whom Seymour had summoned on the spot, agreeing with the eminent surgeon who had later examined the body.

Aurora Rome had been stabbed with some sharp instrument such as a knife or dagger; some instrument, at least, of which the blade was short. The wound was just over the heart, and she had died instantly. When the first doctor saw her she could hardly have been dead for twenty minutes. Therefore when Father Brown found her she could hardly have been dead for three.

Some official detective evidence followed, chiefly concerned with the presence or absence of any proof of a struggle: the only suggestion of this was the tearing of the dress at the shoulder, and this did not seem to fit in particularly well with the direction and finality of the blow. When these details had been supplied, though not explained, the first of the important witnesses was called.

Sir Wilson Seymour gave evidence as he did everything else that he did at all—not only well, but perfectly. Though himself much more of a public man than the judge, he conveyed exactly the fine shade of self-effacement before the King's Justice; and though everyone looked at him as they would at the Prime Minister or the Archbishop of Canterbury, they could have said nothing of his part in it but that it was that of a private gentleman, with an accent on the noun. He was also refreshingly lucid, as he was on the committees. He had been calling on Miss Rome at the theatre; he had met Captain Cutler there; they had been joined for a short time by the accused, who had then returned to his own dressing-room; they had then been joined by a Roman Catholic priest, who asked for the deceased lady and said his name was Brown. Miss Rome had then gone just outside the theatre to the entrance of the passage, in order to point out to Captain Cutler a flower-shop at which he was to buy her some more flowers; and the witness had remained in the room, exchanging a few words with the priest. He had then distinctly heard the deceased, having sent the Captain on his errand, turn round laughing and run down the passage towards its other end, where was the prisoner's dressing-room. In idle curiosity as to the rapid movements of his friends, he had strolled out to the head of the passage himself and looked down it towards the prisoner's door. Did he see anything in the passage? Yes, he saw something in the passage.

Sir Walter Cowdray allowed an impressive interval, during

which the witness looked down, and for all his usual composure seemed to have more than his usual pallor. Then the barrister said in a lower voice, which seemed at once sympathetic and creepy: "Did you see it distinctly?"

Sir Wilson Seymour, however moved, had his excellent brains in full working order. "Very distinctly as regards its outline, but quite indistinctly—indeed not at all—as regards the details inside the outline. The passage is of such length that anyone in the middle of it appears quite black against the light at the other end." The witness lowered his steady eyes once more and added: "I had noticed the fact before, when Captain Cutler first entered it." There was another silence, and the judge leaned forward and made a note.

"Well," said Sir Walter patiently, "what was the outline like? Was it, for instance, like the figure of the murdered woman?"

"Not in the least," answered Seymour quietly.

"What did it look to you like?"

"It looked to me," replied the witness, "like a tall man."

Everyone in court kept his eyes riveted on his pen or his umbrella handle or his book or his boots or whatever he happened to be looking at. They seemed to be holding their eyes away from the prisoner by main force; but they felt his figure in the dock, and they felt it as gigantic. Tall as Bruno was to the eye, he seemed to swell taller and taller when all eyes had been torn away from him.

Cowdray was resuming his seat with his solemn face, smoothing his black silk robes and white silk whiskers. Sir Wilson was leaving the witness-box, after a few final particulars to which there were many other witnesses, when the counsel for the defence sprang up and stopped him.

"I shall only detain you a moment," said Mr. Butler, who was a rustic-looking person with red eyebrows and an expression of partial slumber. "Will you tell his lordship how you knew it was a man?"

A faint, refined smile seemed to pass over Seymour's features. "I'm afraid it is the vulgar test of trousers," he said. "When I saw daylight between the long legs I was sure it was a man, after all."

Butler's sleepy eyes opened as suddenly as some silent explosion.

"After all!" he repeated slowly. "So you did think first it was a woman?"

Seymour looked troubled for the first time. "It is hardly a point of fact," he said, "but if his lordship would like me to answer for my impression, of course I shall do so. There was something about the thing that was not exactly a woman and yet was not quite a man; somehow the curves were different. And it had something that looked like long hair."

"Thank you," said Mr. Butler, K.C., and sat down suddenly, as if he had got what he wanted.

Captain Cutler was a far less plausible and composed witness than Sir Wilson, but his account of the opening incidents was solidly the same. He described the return of Bruno to his dressing-room, the dispatching of himself to buy a bunch of lilies-of-the-valley, his return to the upper end of the passage, the thing he saw in the passage, his suspicion of Seymour, and his struggle with Bruno. But he could give little artistic assistance about the black figure that he and Seymour had seen. Asked about its outline, he said he was no art critic—with a somewhat too obvious sneer at Seymour. Asked if it was a man or a woman, he said it looked more like a beast—with a too obvious snarl at the prisoner. But the man was plainly shaken with sorrow and sincere anger, and Cowdray quickly excused him from confirming facts that were already fairly clear.

The defending counsel also was again brief in his cross-examination; although (as was his custom) even in being brief, he seemed to take a long time about it. "You used a rather remarkable expression," he said, looking at Cutler sleepily. "What do you mean by saying that it looked more like a beast than a man or a woman?"

Cutler seemed seriously agitated. "Perhaps I oughtn't to have said that," he said, "but when the brute has huge humped shoulders like a chimpanzee, and bristles sticking out of its head like a pig——"

Mr. Butler cut short his curious impatience in the middle. "Never mind whether its hair was like a pig's," he said; "was it like a woman's?"

"A woman's!" cried the soldier. "Great Scott, no!"

"The last witness said it was," commented the counsel, with unscrupulous swiftness. "And did the figure have any of those serpentine and semi-feminine curves to which eloquent allusion has been made? No? No feminine curves? The figure, if I understand you, was rather heavy and square than otherwise?"

"He may have been bending forward," said Cutler, in a hoarse and rather faint voice.

"Or again, he may not," said Mr. Butler, and sat down suddenly for the second time.

The third witness called by Sir Walter Cowdray was the little Catholic clergyman, so little compared with the others, that his head seemed hardly to come above the box, so that it was like cross-examining a child. But unfortunately Sir Walter had somehow got it into his head (mostly by some ramifications of his family's religion) that Father Brown was on the side of the prisoner, because the prisoner was wicked and foreign and even partly black. Therefore, he took Father Brown up sharply whenever that proud pontiff tried to explain anything; and told him to answer yes or no, and tell the plain facts without any jesuitry. When Father Brown began, in his simplicity, to say who he thought the man in the passage was, the barrister told him that he did not want his theories.

"A black shape was seen in the passage. And you say you saw the black shape. Well, what shape was it?"

Father Brown blinked as under rebuke; but he had long known the literal nature of obedience. "The shape," he said, "was short and thick, but had two sharp, black projections curved upwards on each side of the head or top, rather like horns, and——"

"Oh! the devil with horns, no doubt," ejaculated Cowdray, sitting down in triumphant jocularity. "It was the devil come to eat Protestants."

"No," said the priest dispassionately; "I know who it was."

Those in court had been wrought up to an irrational but real sense of some monstrosity. They had forgotten the figure in the dock and thought only of the figure in the passage. And the figure in the passage, described by three capable and respectable men who had all seen it, was a shifting nightmare: one called it a woman, and the other a beast, and the other a devil. . . .

The judge was looking at Father Brown with level and piercing eyes. "You are a most extraordinary witness," he said, "but there is something about you that makes me think you are trying to tell the truth. Well, who was the man you saw in the passage?"

"He was myself," said Father Brown.

Butler, K.C., sprang to his feet in an extraordinary stillness, and said quite calmly: "Your lordship will allow me to cross-examine?" And then, without stopping, he shot at Brown the apparently disconnected question: "You have heard about this dagger; you know the experts say the crime was committed with a short blade?"

"A short blade," assented Brown, nodding solemnly like an owl, "but a very long hilt."

Before the audience could quite dismiss the idea that the priest had really seen himself doing murder with a short dagger with a long hilt (which seemed somehow to make it more horrible), he had himself hurried on to explain.

"I mean daggers aren't the only things with short blades. Spears have short blades. And spears catch at the end of the steel just like daggers, if they're that sort of fancy spear they have in theatres; like the spear poor old Parkinson killed his wife with, just when she'd sent for me to settle their family troubles—and I came just too late, God forgive me! But he died penitent—he just died of being penitent. He couldn't bear what he'd done."

The general impression in court was that the little priest, who was gabbling away, had literally gone mad in the box. But the judge still looked at him with bright and steady eyes of interest; and the counsel for the defence went on with his questions, unperturbed.

"If Parkinson did it with that pantomime spear," asked Butler, "he must have thrust from four yards away. How do you account for signs of struggle, like the dress dragged off the shoulder?" He had slipped into treating this mere witness as an expert; but no one noticed it now.

"The poor lady's dress was torn," said the witness, "because it was caught in a panel that slid to just behind her. She struggled to free herself, and as she did so Parkinson came out of the prisoner's room and lunged with the spear."

"A panel?" repeated the barrister in a curious voice.

"It was a looking-glass on the other side," explained Father Brown. "When I was in the dressing-room I noticed that some of them could probably be slid out into the passage."

There was another vast and unnatural silence, and this time it was the judge who spoke. "So you really mean that when you looked down that passage, the man you saw was yourself—in a mirror?"

"Yes, my lord; that was what I was trying to say," said Brown, "but they asked me for the shape; and our hats have corners just like horns, and so I———"

The judge leaned forward, his old eyes yet more brilliant, and said in specially distinct tones: "Do you really mean to say that when Sir Wilson Seymour saw that wild what-you-call-him with curves and a woman's hair and a man's trousers, what he saw was Sir Wilson Seymour?"

"Yes, my lord," said Father Brown.

"And you mean to say that when Captain Cutler saw that chimpanzee with humped shoulders and hog's bristles, he simply saw himself?"

"Yes, my lord."

The judge leaned back in his chair with a luxuriance in which it was hard to separate the cynicism and the admiration. "And can you tell us why," he asked, "you should know your own figure in a looking-glass, when two such distinguished men don't?"

Father Brown blinked even more painfully than before; then he stammered: "Really, my lord, I don't know . . . unless it's because I don't look at it so often."

THE HEAD OF CAESAR

There is somewhere in Brompton or Kensington an interminable avenue of tall houses, rich but largely empty, that looks like a terrace of tombs. The very steps up to the dark front doors seem as steep as the sides of pyramids; and one would hesitate to knock at the door, lest it should be opened by a mummy. But a yet more depressing feature in the grey façade is its telescopic length and changeless continuity. The pilgrim walking down it begins to think he will never come to a break or a corner; but there is one exception— a very small one, but hailed by the pilgrim almost with a shout. There is a sort of mews between two of the tall mansions, a mere slit like the crack of a door by comparison with the street, but just large enough to permit a pigmy ale-house or eating-house, still allowed by the rich to their stable-servants, to stand in the angle. There is something cheery in its very dinginess and something free and elfin in its very insignificance. At the feet of those grey stone giants it looks like a lighted house of dwarfs.

Anyone passing the place during a certain autumn evening itself almost fairy-like might have seen a hand pull aside the red half-blind which (along with some large white lettering) half hid the interior from the street, and a face peer out not unlike a rather innocent goblin's. It was, in fact, the face of one with the harmless human name of Brown, formerly priest of Cobhole in Essex, and now working in London. His friend Flambeau, a semi-official investigator, was sitting opposite him, making his last notes of a case he had cleared up in the neighbourhood. They were sitting at a small table, close up to the window, when the priest pulled the curtain back and looked out. He waited till a stranger in the street had passed the window, to let the curtain fall into its place again. Then his round eyes rolled to the blind white lettering on the window above his head, and then strayed to the next table, at which sat only a navvy with beer and cheese, and a young girl with red hair and a glass of milk. Then (seeing his friend put away the pocket-book), he said softly:

"If you've got ten minutes, I wish you'd follow that man with the false nose."

Flambeau looked up in surprise; but the girl with the red hair also looked up, and with something that was stronger than astonishment. She was simply and even loosely dressed in light brown sacking stuff; but she was a lady, and even, on a second glance, a rather needlessly haughty one: "The man with the false nose!" repeated Flambeau. "Who's he?"

"I haven't a notion," answered Father Brown. "I want you to find out; I ask it as a favour. He went down there"—and he jerked his thumb over his shoulder in one of his undistinguished gestures—"and can't have passed three lamp-posts yet. I only want to know the direction."

Flambeau gazed at his friend for some time, with an expression between perplexity and amusement; and then, rising from the table, squeezed his huge form out of the little door of the dwarf tavern, and melted into the twilight.

Father Brown took a small book out of his pocket and began to read steadily; he betrayed no consciousness of the fact that the red-haired lady had left her own table and sat down opposite him. At last she leaned over and said in a low, strong voice: "Why do you say that? How do you know it's false?"

He lifted his rather heavy eyelids, which fluttered in considerable embarrassment. Then his dubious eye roamed again to the white lettering on the glass front of the public-house. The young woman's eyes followed his, and rested there also, but in pure puzzledom.

"No," said Father Brown, answering her thoughts. "It doesn't say 'Sela,' like the thing in the psalms; I read it like that myself when I was wool-gathering just now; it says 'Ales.'"

"Well?" inquired the staring young lady. "What does it matter what it says?"

His ruminating eye roved to the girl's light canvas sleeve, round the wrist of which ran a very slight thread of artistic pattern, just enough to distinguish it from a working dress of a common woman and make it more like the working dress of a lady art-student. He seemed to find much food for thought in this; but his reply was very slow and hesitant. "You see, madam," he said, "from outside the place looks—well, it is a perfectly decent place—but ladies like you don't—don't generally think so. They never go into such places from choice, except——"

"Well?" she repeated.

"Except an unfortunate few who don't go in to drink milk."

"You are a most singular person," said the young lady. "What is your object in all this?"

"Not to trouble you about it," he replied, very gently. "Only to arm myself with knowledge enough to help you, if ever you freely ask my help."

"But why should I need help?"

He continued his dreamy monologue. "You couldn't have come in to see *protégées*, humble friends, that sort of thing, or you'd have gone through into the parlour . . . and you couldn't have gone in because you were ill, or you'd have spoken to the woman of the place, who's obviously respectable . . . besides, you don't look ill in that way, but only unhappy. . . . This street is the only original long lane that has no turning; and the houses on both sides are shut up. . . . I could only suppose that you'd seen somebody coming whom you didn't want to meet; and found the public-house was the only shelter in this wilderness of stone. . . . I don't think I went beyond the

licence of a stranger in glancing at the only man who passed immediately after. .... And as I thought he looked like the wrong sort ...
and you looked like the right sort ... I held myself ready to help if
he annoyed you; that is all. As for my friend, he'll be back soon; and
he certainly can't find out anything by stumping down a road like
this. .... I didn't think he could."

"Then why did you send him out?" she cried, leaning forward
with yet warmer curiosity. She had the proud, impetuous face that
goes with reddish colouring and a Roman nose, as it did in Marie
Antoinette.

He looked back at her steadily for the first time, and said, "Because I hoped you would speak to me."

She looked back at him for some time with a heated face, in
which there hung a red shadow of anger; then, despite her anxi-
eties, humour broke out of her eyes and the corners of her mouth,
and she answered almost grimly: "Well; if you're so keen on my
conversation, perhaps you'll answer my question." After a pause she
added, "I had the honour to ask you why you thought the man's
nose was false."

"The wax always spots like that just a little in this weather," answered Father Brown, with entire simplicity.

"But it's such a *crooked* nose," remonstrated the red-haired girl.

The priest smiled in his turn. "I don't say it's the sort of nose one
would wear out of mere foppery," he admitted. "This man, I think,
wears it because his real nose is so much nicer."

"But why?" she insisted.

"What is the nursery-rhyme?" observed Brown absent-mindedly.
"There was a crooked man and he went a crooked mile. .... That
man, I fancy, has gone a very crooked road by following his nose."

"Why, what's he done?" she demanded, rather shakily.

"I don't want to force your confidence by a hair," said Father
Brown, very quietly. "But I think you could tell me more about that
than I can tell you."

The girl sprang to her feet and stood quite quietly, but with
clenched hands, like one about to stride away; then her hands loosened slowly, and she sat down again. "You are more of a mystery

than all the others," she said desperately; "but I feel there might be a heart in your mystery."

"What we all dread most," said the priest, in a low voice, "is a maze with *no* centre. That is why atheism is only a nightmare."

"I will tell you everything," said the red-haired girl doggedly, "except why I am telling you; and that I don't know."

She picked at the darned table-cloth and went on: "You look as if you knew what isn't snobbery as well as what is; and when I say that ours is a good old family, you'll understand it is a necessary part of the story; indeed, my chief danger is in my brother's high and dry notions, *noblesse oblige,* and all that. Well, my name is Christabel Carstairs; and my father was that Colonel Carstairs you've probably heard of, who made the famous Carstairs Collection of Roman coins. I could never describe my father to you; the nearest I can say is that he was very like a Roman coin himself. He was as handsome and as genuine and as valuable and as metallic and as out of date. He was prouder of his Collection than of his coat-of-arms—nobody could say more than that. His extraordinary character came out most in his will. He had two sons and one daughter. He quarrelled with one son, my brother Giles, and sent him to Australia on a small allowance. He then made a will leaving the Carstairs Collection, actually with a yet smaller allowance, to my brother Arthur. He meant it as a reward, as the highest honour he could offer, in acknowledgment of Arthur's loyalty and rectitude and the distinctions he had already gained in mathematics and economics at Cambridge. He left me practically all his pretty large fortune; and I am sure he meant it in contempt.

"Arthur, you may say, might well complain of this; but Arthur is my father over again. Though he had some differences with my father in early youth, no sooner had he taken over the Collection than he became like a pagan priest dedicated to a temple. He mixed up these Roman halfpence with the honour of the Carstairs family in the same stiff, idolatrous way as his father before him. He acted as if Roman money must be guarded by all the Roman virtues. He took no pleasures; he spent nothing on himself; he lived for the Collection. Often he would not trouble to dress for his simple meals; but pottered about among the corded brown paper parcels (which no one else was allowed to touch) in an old brown dressing-gown. With its rope and tassel and his pale, thin, refined face, it made him look like an old ascetic monk. Every now and then, though he would appear dressed like a decidedly fashionable gentleman; but that was only when he went up to the London sales or shops to make an addition to the Carstairs Collection.

"Now, if you've known any young people, you won't be shocked if I say that I got into rather a low frame of mind with all this; the frame of mind in which one begins to say that the Ancient Romans were all very well in their way. I'm not like my brother Arthur; I can't help enjoying enjoyment. I got a lot of romance and rubbish where I got my red hair, from the other side of the family. Poor Giles was the same; and I think the atmosphere of coins might count in excuse for him; though he really did wrong and nearly went to prison. But he didn't behave any worse than I did; as you shall hear.

"I come now to the silly part of the story. I think a man as clever as you can guess the sort of thing that would begin to relieve the monotony for an unruly girl of seventeen placed in such a position. But I am so rattled with more dreadful things that I can hardly read my own feelings; and don't know whether I despise it now as a flirtation or bear it as a broken heart. We lived then at a little seaside watering-place in South Wales, and a retired sea-captain living a few doors off had a son about five years older than myself, who had been a friend of Giles's before he went to the Colonies. His name does not affect my tale; but I tell you it was Philip Hawker because I am telling you everything. We used to go shrimping together, and said and thought we were in love with each other; at least he certainly said he was, and I certainly thought I was. If I tell you he had bronzed curly hair and a falconish sort of face, bronzed by the sea also, it's not for his sake, I assure you, but for the story; for it was the cause of a very curious coincidence.

"One summer afternoon, when I had promised to go shrimping along the sands with Philip, I was waiting rather impatiently in the front drawing-room, watching Arthur handle some packets of coins he had just purchased and slowly shunt them, one or two at a time, into his own dark study and museum which was at the back of the house. As soon as I heard the heavy door close on him finally I made a bolt for my shrimping-net and tam-o'-shanter, and was just going to slip out when I saw that my brother had left behind him one coin that lay gleaming on the long bench by the window. It was a bronze coin, and the colour, combined with the exact curve of the Roman nose and something in the very lift of the long, wiry neck, made the head of Cæsar on it the almost precise portrait of Philip Hawker. Then I suddenly remembered Giles telling Philip of a coin that was like him, and Philip wishing he had it. Perhaps you can fancy the wild, foolish thoughts with which my head went round; I felt as if I had had a gift from the fairies. It seemed to me that if I could only run away with this, and give it to Philip like a wild sort of wedding-ring, it would be a bond between us for ever; I felt a thousand such things at once. Then there yawned under me, like the pit, the enormous, awful notion of what I was doing; above all, the unbearable thought, which was like touching hot iron, of what Arthur would think of it. A Carstairs a thief; and a thief of the Carstairs treasure! I believe my brother could see me burned like a witch for such a thing. But then, the very thought of such fanatical cruelty heightened my old hatred of his dingy old antiquarian fussiness and my longing for the youth and liberty that called to me from the sea. Outside was strong sunlight with a wind; and a yellow head of some broom or gorse in the garden rapped against the glass of the window. I thought of that living and growing gold calling to me from all the heaths of the world—and then of that dead, dull gold and bronze and brass of my brother's growing dustier and dustier as life went by. Nature and the Carstairs Collection had come to grips at last.

"Nature is older than the Carstairs Collection. As I ran down the streets to the sea, the coin clenched tight in my fist, I felt all the Roman Empire on my back as well as the Carstairs pedigree. It was not only the old lion argent that was roaring in my ear, but all the eagles of the Cæsars seemed flapping and screaming in pursuit of me. And yet my heart rose higher and higher like a child's kite, until

I came over the loose, dry sand-hills and to the flat wet sands, where Philip stood already up to his ankles in the shallow shining water, some hundred yards out to sea. There was a great red sunset; and the long stretch of low water, hardly rising over the ankle for half a mile, was like a lake of ruby flame. It was not till I had torn off my shoes and stockings and waded to where he stood, which was well away from the dry land, that I turned and looked round. We were quite alone in a circle of sea-water and wet sand; and I gave him the head of Cæsar.

"At the very instant I had a shock of fancy: that a man far away on the sand-hills was looking at me intently. I must have felt immediately after that it was a mere leap of unreasonable nerves; for the man was only a dark dot in the distance; and I could only just see that he was standing quite still and gazing, with his head a little on one side. There was no earthly logical evidence that he was looking at me; he might have been looking at a ship, or the sunset, or the seagulls, or at any of the people who still strayed here and there on the shore between us. Nevertheless, whatever my start sprang from was prophetic; for, as I gazed, he started walking briskly in a bee-line towards us across the wide wet sands. As he drew nearer and nearer I saw that he was dark and bearded, and that his eyes were marked with dark spectacles. He was dressed poorly but respectably in black, from the old black top hat on his head to the solid black boots on his feet. In spite of these he walked straight into the sea without a flash of hesitation, and came on at me with the steadiness of a travelling bullet.

"I can't tell you the sense of monstrosity and miracle I had when he thus silently burst the barrier between land and water. It was as if he had walked straight off a cliff and still marched steadily in mid-air. It was as if a house had flown up into the sky or a man's head had fallen off. He was only wetting his boots; but he seemed to be a demon disregarding a law of Nature. If he had hesitated an instant at the water's edge it would have been nothing. As it was, he seemed to look so much at me alone as not to notice the ocean. Philip was some yards away with his back to me, bending over his net. The stranger came on till he stood within two yards of me, the water washing half-way up to his knees. Then he said, with a clearly modulated and rather mincing articulation: 'Would it discommode you to contribute elsewhere a coin with a somewhat different superscription?'

"With one exception there was nothing definably abnormal about him. His tinted glasses were not really opaque, but of a blue kind common enough, nor were the eyes behind them shifty, but regarded me steadily. His dark beard was not really long or wild; but he looked rather hairy, because the beard began very high up in his face, just under the cheek-bones. His complexion was neither sallow nor livid, but on the contrary rather clear and youthful; yet this gave a pink-and-white wax look which somehow (I don't know why) rather increased the horror. The only oddity one could fix was that his nose, which was otherwise of a good shape, was just slightly turned sideways at the tip; as if when it was soft it had been tapped on one side with a toy hammer. The thing was hardly a deformity; yet I cannot tell you what a living nightmare it was to me. As he stood there in the sunset-stained water, he affected me as some hellish sea-monster just risen roaring out of a sea like blood. I don't know why a touch on the nose should affect my imagination so much. I think it seemed as if he could move his nose like a finger. And as if he had just that moment moved it.

" 'Any little assistance,' he continued, with the same queer, priggish accent, 'that may obviate the necessity of my communicating with the family.'

"Then it rushed over me that I was being blackmailed for the theft of the bronze piece; and all my merely superstitious fears and doubts were swallowed up in one overpowering practical question. How could he have found out? I had stolen the thing suddenly and on impulse; I was certainly alone; for I always made sure of being unobserved when I slipped out to see Philip in this way. I had not, to all appearance, been followed in the street; and if I had, they could not 'X-ray' the coin in my closed hand. The man standing on the sand-hills could no more have seen what I gave Philip than shoot a fly in one eye, like the man in the fairy tale.

" 'Philip,' I cried helplessly, 'ask this man what he wants.'

"When Philip lifted his head at last from mending his net he looked rather red, as if sulky or ashamed; but it may have been only the exertion of stooping and the red evening light; I may have only had another of the morbid fancies that seemed to be dancing about me. He merely said gruffly to the man: 'You clear out of this.' And, motioning me to follow, set off wading shoreward without paying further attention to him. He stepped on to a stone breakwater that ran out from among the roots of the sand-hills, and so struck homeward; perhaps thinking our incubus would find it less easy to walk on such rough stones, green and slippery with seaweed, than we, who were young and used to it. But my persecutor walked as daintily as he talked; and he still followed me, picking his way and picking his phrases. I heard his delicate, detestable voice appealing to me over my shoulder, until at last, when we had crested the sand-hills, Philip's patience (which was by no means so conspicuous on most occasions) seemed to snap. He turned suddenly, saying, 'Go back. I can't talk to you now.' And, as the man hovered and opened his mouth, Philip struck him a buffet on it that sent him flying from the top of the tallest sand-hill to the bottom. I saw him crawling out below, covered with sand.

"This stroke comforted me somehow, though it might well increase my peril; but Philip showed none of his usual elation at his own prowess. Though as affectionate as ever, he still seemed cast down; and before I could ask him anything fully, he parted with me at his own gate, with two remarks that struck me as strange. He said that, all things considered, I ought to put the coin back in the Collection; but that he himself would keep it 'for the present.' And then he added, quite suddenly and irrelevantly, 'You know Giles is back from Australia?' "

The door of the tavern opened and the gigantic shadow of the investigator Flambeau fell across the table. Father Brown presented him to the lady in his own slight, persuasive style of speeches, mentioning his knowledge and sympathy in such cases; and almost without knowing, the girl was soon reiterating her story to two listeners. But Flambeau, as he bowed and sat down, handed the priest a small slip of paper. Brown accepted it with some surprise and read on it: "Cab to Wagga Wagga, 379, Mafeking Avenue, Putney." The girl was going on with her story.

"I went up the steep street to my own house with my head in a whirl; it had not begun to clear when I came to the doorstep, on which I found a milk-can—and the man with the twisted nose. The milk-can told me the servants were all out; for, of course, Arthur, browsing about in his brown dressing-gown in a brown study, would not hear or answer a bell. Thus there was no one to help me in the house, except my brother, whose help must be my ruin. In desperation I thrust two shillings into the horrid thing's hand, and told him to call again in a few days, when I had thought it out. He went off sulking, but more sheepishly than I had expected—perhaps he had been shaken by his fall—and I watched the star of sand splashed on his back receding down the road with a horrid vindictive pleasure. He turned a corner some six houses down.

"Then I let myself in, made myself some tea, and tried to think it out. I sat at the drawing-room window looking on to the garden, which still glowed with the last full evening light. But I was too distracted and dreamy to look at the lawns and flower-pots and flower-beds with any concentration. So I took the shock the more sharply because I'd seen it so slowly.

"The man or monster I'd sent away was standing quite still in the middle of the garden. Oh, we've all read a lot about pale-faced phantoms in the dark; but this was more dreadful than anything of that kind could ever be. Because, though he cast a long evening shadow, he still stood in warm sunlight. And because his face was not pale, but had that waxen bloom still upon it that belongs to a barber's dummy. He stood quite still, with his face towards me; and I can't tell you how horrid he looked among the tulips and all those tall, gaudy, almost hothouse-looking flowers. It looked as if we'd stuck up a wax-work instead of a statue in the centre of our garden.

"Yet almost the instant he saw me move in the window he turned and ran out of the garden by the back garden gate, which stood open and by which he had undoubtedly entered. This renewed timidity on his part was so different from the impudence with which he had walked into the sea, that I felt vaguely comforted. I fancied, perhaps, that he feared confronting Arthur more than I knew. Anyhow, I settled down at last, and had a quiet dinner alone (for it was against the rules to disturb Arthur when he was rearranging the museum), and, my thoughts a little released, fled to Philip and lost themselves, I suppose. Anyhow, I was looking blankly, but rather pleasantly than otherwise, at another window, uncurtained, but by this time black as a slate with the final night-fall. It seemed to me that something like a snail was on the outside of the window-pane. But when I stared harder, it was more like a man's thumb pressed on the pane; it had that curled look that a thumb has. With my fear and courage reawakened together, I rushed at the window and then recoiled with a strangled scream that any man but Arthur must have heard.

"For it was not a thumb; any more than it was a snail. It was the tip of a crooked nose, crushed against the glass; it looked white with the pressure; and the staring face and eyes behind it were at first invisible and afterwards grey like a ghost. I slammed the shutters together somehow, rushed up to my room, and locked myself in. But even as I passed, I could almost swear I saw a second black window with something on it that was like a snail.

"It might be best to go to Arthur after all. If the thing was crawling close all round the house like a cat, it might have purposes worse even than blackmail. My brother might cast me out and curse me for ever; but he was a gentleman, and would defend me on the spot. After ten minutes' curious thinking, I went down, knocked at the door and then went in: to see the last and worst sight.

"My brother's chair was empty; and he was obviously out. But the man with the crooked nose was sitting waiting for his return, with his hat still insolently on his head, and actually reading one of my brother's books under my brother's lamp. His face was composed and occupied, but his nose-tip still had the air of being the most mobile part of his face, as if it had just turned from left to right like an elephant's proboscis. I had thought him poisonous enough while he was pursuing and watching me. But I think his unconsciousness of my presence was more frightful still.

"I think I screamed loud and long; but that doesn't matter. What

I did next does matter: I gave him all the money I had, including a good deal in papers which, though it was mine, I dare say I had no right to touch. He went off at last, with hateful, tactful regrets all in long words; and I sat down, feeling ruined in every sense. And yet I was saved that very night by a pure accident. Arthur had gone off suddenly to London, as he so often did, for bargains; and returned, late but radiant, having nearly secured a treasure that was an added splendour even to the family Collection. He was so resplendent that I was almost emboldened to confess the abstraction of the lesser gem; but he bore down all other topics with his overpowering projects. Because the bargain might still miss fire any moment, he insisted on my packing at once and going up with him to lodgings he had already taken in Fulham, to be near the curio-shop in question. Thus, in spite of myself, I fled from my foe almost in the dead of night—but from Philip also. . . . My brother was often at the South Kensington Museum, and, in order to make some sort of secondary life for myself, I paid for a few lessons at the Art Schools. I was coming back from them this evening, when I saw the abomination of desolation walking alive down the long straight street; and the rest is as this gentleman has said.

"I've got only one thing to say. I don't deserve to be helped; and I don't question or complain of my punishment; it is just, it ought to have happened. But I still question, with bursting brains, how it can have happened. Am I punished by miracle? or how *can* anyone but Philip and myself know I gave him a tiny coin in the middle of the sea?"

"It is an extraordinary problem," admitted Flambeau.

"Not so extraordinary as the answer," remarked Father Brown, rather gloomily. "Miss Carstairs, will you be at home if we call at your Fulham place in an hour and a half hence?"

The girl looked at him; and then rose and put her gloves on. "Yes," she said, "I'll be there"; and almost instantly left the place.

That night the detective and the priest were still talking of the matter as they drew near the Fulham house, a tenement strangely mean even for a temporary residence of the Carstairs family.

"Of course the superficial, on reflection," said Flambeau, "would think first of this Australian brother who's been in trouble before, who's come back so suddenly, and who's just the man to have shabby confederates. But I can't see how he can come into the thing by any process of thought, unless——"

"Well?" asked his companion patiently.

Flambeau lowered his voice. "Unless the girl's lover comes in too, and he would be the blacker villain. The Australian chap did know that Hawker wanted the coin. But I can't see how on earth he could know that Hawker had got it; unless Hawker signalled to him or his representative across the shore."

"That is true," assented the priest, with respect.

"Have you noted another thing?" went on Flambeau eagerly, "this Hawker hears his love insulted; but doesn't strike till *he's got to the soft sand-hills,* where he can be victor in a mere sham-fight. If he'd struck amid rocks and sea, he might have hurt his ally."

"That is true again," said Father Brown, nodding.

"And now, take it from the start. It lies between few people, but at least three. You want one person for suicide; two people for murder; but at least three people for blackmail."

"Why?" asked the priest softly.

"Well, obviously," cried his friend, "there must be one to be exposed; one to threaten exposure; and one at least whom exposure would horrify."

After a long ruminant pause, the priest said, "You miss a logical step. Three persons are needed as ideas. Only two are needed as agents."

"What can you mean?" asked the other.

"Why shouldn't a blackmailer," asked Brown, in a low voice, "threaten his victim with himself? Suppose a wife became a rigid teetotaller *in order* to frighten her husband into concealing *his* pub-frequenting, and then wrote him blackmailing letters in another hand, threatening to tell his wife! Why shouldn't it work? Suppose a father forbade a son to gamble, and then, following him in a good disguise, threatened the boy with his own sham paternal strictness! Suppose—but here we are, my friend."

"My God!" cried Flambeau, "you don't mean——"

An active figure ran down the steps of the house and showed under the golden lamplight the unmistakable head that resembled the Roman coin. "Miss Carstairs," said Hawker without ceremony, "wouldn't go in till you came."

"Well," observed Brown confidentially, "don't you think it's the best thing she can do to stop outside—with you to look after her? You see, I rather guess you have guessed it all yourself."

"Yes," said the young man, in an undertone, "I guessed on the sands and now I know; that was why I let him fall soft."

Taking a latchkey from the girl and the coin from Hawker, Flambeau let himself and his friend into the house, and passed into the outer parlour. It was empty of all occupants but one. The man whom Father Brown had seen pass the tavern was standing against the wall as if at bay; unchanged, save that he had taken off his black coat and was wearing a brown dressing-gown.

"We have come," said Father Brown politely, "to give back this coin to its owner." And he handed it to the man with the nose.

Flambeau's eyes rolled. "Is this man a coin-collector?" he asked.

"This man is Mr. Arthur Carstairs," said the priest positively, "and he is a coin-collector of a somewhat singular kind."

The man changed colour so horribly that the crooked nose stood out on his face like a separate and comic thing. He spoke, nevertheless, with a sort of despairing dignity. "You shall see, then," he said, "that I have not lost all the family qualities."

And he turned suddenly and strode into an inner room, slamming the door.

"Stop him!" shouted Father Brown, bounding and half falling over a chair; and, after a wrench or two, Flambeau had the door open. But it was too late. In dead silence Flambeau strode across and telephoned for doctor and police.

An empty medicine bottle lay on the floor. Across the table the body of the man in the brown dressing-gown lay amid his burst and gaping brown paper parcels; out of which poured and rolled, not Roman, but very modern English coins.

The priest held up the bronze head of Cæsar. "This," he said, "was all that was left of the Carstairs Collection."

After a silence he went on, with more than common gentleness: "It was a cruel will his wicked father made, and you see he did resent it a little. He hated the Roman money he had, and grew fonder of the real money denied him. He not only sold the Collection bit by bit, but sank bit by bit to the basest ways of making money— even to blackmailing his own family in a disguise. He blackmailed his brother from Australia for his little forgotten crime (that is why he took the cab to Wagga Wagga in Putney), he blackmailed his sister for the theft he alone could have noticed. And that, by the way, is why she had that supernatural guess when he was away on the sand-dunes. Mere figure and gait, however distant, are more likely to remind us of somebody than a well-made-up face quite close."

There was another silence. "Well," growled the detective, "and so this great numismatist and coin-collector was nothing but a vulgar miser."

"Is there so great a difference?" asked Father Brown, in the same strange, indulgent tone. "What is there wrong about a miser that is not often as wrong about a collector? What is wrong, except... thou shalt not make thyself any graven image; thou shalt not bow down to them nor serve them, for I... but we must go and see how the poor young people are getting on."

"I think," said Flambeau, "that, in spite of everything, they are probably getting on very well."

THE PURPLE WIG

Mr. Edward Nutt, the industrious editor of *The Daily Reformer,* sat at his desk, opening letters and marking proofs to the merry tune of a typewriter, worked by a vigorous young lady.

He was a stoutish, fair man, in his shirt-sleeves; his movements were resolute, his mouth firm and his tones final; but his round, rather babyish blue eyes had a bewildered and even wistful look that rather contradicted all this. Nor indeed was the expression altogether misleading. It might truly be said of him, as of many journalists in authority, that his most familiar emotion was one of continuous fear; fear of libel actions, fear of lost advertisements, fear of misprints, fear of the sack.

His life was a series of distracted compromises, between the proprietor of the paper (and of him), who was a senile soap-boiler with three ineradicable mistakes in his mind, and the very able staff he had collected to run the paper; some of whom were brilliant and experienced men and (what was even worse) sincere enthusiasts for the political policy of the paper.

A letter from one of these lay immediately before him; and rapid and resolute as he was, he seemed almost to hesitate before opening it. He took up a strip of proof instead, ran down it with a blue eye, and a blue pencil, altered the word "adultery" to the word "impropriety," and the word "Jew" to the word "Alien," rang a bell and sent it flying upstairs.

Then with a more thoughtful eye he ripped open the letter from his more distinguished contributor, which bore a postmark of Devonshire, and ran as follows:

"DEAR NUTT,—As I see you're working Spooks and Dooks at the same time, what about an article on that rum business of the Eyres of Exmoor; or as the old women call it down here, the Devil's Ear of Eyre? The head of the family, you know, is the Duke of Exmoor; he is one of the few really stiff old Tory aristocrats left, a sound old crusted tyrant it is quite in our line to make trouble about. And I think I'm on the track of a story that will make trouble.

"Of course I don't believe in the old legend about James I; and as for you, you don't believe in anything, not even in journalism. The legend, you'll probably remember, was about the blackest business in English history—the poisoning of Overbury by that witch's cat Frances Howard, and the quite mysterious terror which forced the King to pardon the murderers. There was a lot of alleged witchcraft mixed up with it; and the story goes that a man-servant listening at a keyhole heard the truth in a talk between the King and Carr; and the bodily ear with which he heard grew large and monstrous as by magic, so awful was the secret. And though he had to be loaded with lands and gold and made an ancestor of dukes, the elf-shaped ear is still re-current in the family. Well, you don't believe in black magic; and if you did, you couldn't use it for copy. If a miracle happened in your office, you'd have to hush it up, now so many bishops are agnostics. But that is not the point. The point is that there really *is* something queer about Exmoor and his family; something quite natural, I dare say, but quite abnormal. And the Ear is in it somehow, I fancy; either a symbol or a delusion or a disease or something. Another tradition says that Cavaliers just after James I began to wear their hair long only to cover the ear of the first Lord Exmoor. This also is no doubt fanciful.

"The reason I point it out to you is this: It seems to me that we make a mistake in attacking aristocracy entirely for its champagne and diamonds. Most men rather admire the nobs for having a good time, but I think we surrender too much when we admit that aristocracy has made even the aristocrats happy. I suggest a series of articles pointing out how dreary, how inhuman, how downright diabolist, is the very smell and atmosphere of some of these great houses. There are plenty of instances; but you couldn't begin with a better one than the Ear of the Eyres. By the end of the week I think I can get you the truth about it.—Yours ever, FRANCIS FINN."

Mr. Nutt reflected a moment, staring at his left boot; then he called out in a strong, loud and entirely lifeless voice, in which every syllable sounded alike: "Miss Barlow, take down a letter to Mr. Finn, please."

"DEAR FINN,—I think it would do; copy should reach us second post Saturday.—Yours, E. NUTT."

This elaborate epistle he articulated as if it were all one word; and Miss Barlow rattled it down as if it were all one word. Then he took up another strip of proof and a blue pencil, and altered the word "supernatural" to the word "marvellous," and the expression "shoot down" to the expression "repress."

In such happy, healthful activities did Mr. Nutt disport himself, until the ensuing Saturday found him at the same desk, dictating to the same typewriter, and using the same blue pencil on the first instalment of Mr. Finn's revelations. The opening was a sound piece of slashing invective about the evil secrets of princes, and despair in the high places of the earth. Though written violently, it was in excellent English; but the editor, as usual, had given to somebody else the task of breaking it up into sub-headings; which were of a spicier sort, as "Peeress and Poisons," and "The Eerie Ear," "The Eyres in their Eyrie," and so on through a hundred happy changes. Then followed the legend of the Ear, amplified from Finn's first letter, and then the substance of his later discoveries, as follows.

"I know it is the practice of journalists to put the end of the story at the beginning and call it a headline. I know that journalism largely consists in saying 'Lord Jones Dead' to people who never knew that Lord Jones was alive. Your present correspondent thinks that this, like many other journalistic customs, is bad journalism; and that *The Daily Reformer* has to set a better example in such things. He proposes to tell his story as it occurred, step by step. He will use the real names of the parties, who in most cases are ready to confirm his testimony. As for the headlines, the sensational proclamations—they will come at the end.

"I was walking along a public path that threads through a private Devonshire orchard and seems to point towards Devonshire cider, when I came suddenly upon just such a place as the path suggested. It was a long, low inn, consisting really of a cottage and two barns; thatched all over with the thatch that looks like brown and grey hair grown before history. But outside the door was a sign which called it the Blue Dragon; and under the sign was one of those long rustic tables that used to stand outside most of the free English inns, before teetotallers and brewers between them destroyed freedom. And at this table sat three gentlemen, who might have lived a hundred years ago.

"Now that I know them all better, there is no difficulty about disentangling the impressions; but just then they looked like three very solid ghosts. The dominant figure, both because he was bigger in all three dimensions, and because he sat centrally in the length of the table, facing me, was a tall, fat man dressed completely in black, with a rubicund, even apoplectic visage, but a rather bald and rather bothered brow. Looking at him again, more strictly, I could not exactly say what it was that gave me the sense of antiquity, except the antique cut of his white clerical necktie and the barred wrinkles across his brow.

"It was even less easy to fix the impression in the case of the man at the right end of the table, who, to say truth, was as commonplace a person as could be seen anywhere, with a round, brown-haired head and a round snub nose, but also clad in clerical black, of a stricter cut. It was only when I saw his broad curved hat lying on the table beside him that I realised why I connected him with anything ancient. He was a Roman Catholic priest.

"Perhaps the third man, at the other end of the table, had really more to do with it than the rest, though he was both slighter in physical presence and more inconsiderate in his dress. His lank limbs were clad, I might also say clutched, in very tight grey sleeves and pantaloons; he had a long, sallow, aquiline face which seemed somehow all the more saturnine because his lantern jaws were imprisoned in his collar and neckcloth more in the style of the old stock; and his hair (which ought to have been dark brown) was of an odd dim, russet colour which, in conjunction with his yellow face, looked rather purple than red. The unobtrusive yet unusual colour was all the more notable because his hair was almost unnaturally healthy and curling, and he wore it full. But, after all analysis, I incline to think that what gave me my first old-fashioned impression was simply a set of tall, old-fashioned wine-glasses, one or two lemons, and two church-warden pipes. And also, perhaps, the old-world errand on which I had come.

"Being a hardened reporter, and it being apparently a public inn, I did not need to summon much of my impudence to sit down at the long table and order some cider. The big man in black seemed very learned, especially about local antiquities; the small man in black, though he talked much less, surprised me with a yet wider culture. So we got on very well together; but the third man, the old gentleman in the tight pantaloons, seemed rather distant and haughty, until I slid into the subject of the Duke of Exmoor and his ancestry.

"I thought the subject seemed to embarrass the other two a little; but it broke the spell of the third man's silence most successfully. Speaking with restraint and with the accent of a highly educated gentleman, and puffing at intervals at his long church-warden pipe, he proceeded to tell me some of the most horrible stories I have ever heard in my life: how one of the Eyres in the former ages had hanged his own father; and another had his wife scourged at the cart tail through the village; and another had set fire to a church full of children, and so on.

"Some of the tales, indeed, are not fit for a public print; such as the story of the Scarlet Nuns, the abominable story of the Spotted

Dog, or the thing that was done in the quarry. And all this red roll of impieties came from his thin, genteel lips rather primly than otherwise, as he sat sipping the wine out of his tall, thin glass.

"I could see that the big man opposite me was trying, if anything, to stop him; but he evidently held the old gentleman in considerable respect, and could not venture to do so at all abruptly. And the little priest at the other end of the table, though free from any such air of fear or embarrassment, looked steadily at the table, and seemed to listen to the recital with great pain—as well he might.

" 'You don't seem,' I said to the narrator, 'to be very fond of the Exmoor pedigree.'

"He looked at me a moment, his lips still prim, but whitening and tightening; then he deliberately broke his long pipe and glass on the table and stood up, the very picture of a perfect gentleman with the flaming temper of a fiend.

" 'These gentlemen,' he said, 'will tell you whether I have cause to like it. The curse of the Eyres of old has lain heavy on this country, and many have suffered from it. They know there are none who have suffered from it as I have.' And with that he crushed a piece of the fallen glass under his heel, and strode away among the green twilight of the twinkling apple-trees.

" 'That is an extraordinary old gentleman,' I said to the other two; 'do you happen to know what the Exmoor family has done to him? Who is he?'

"The big man in black was staring at me with the wild air of a baffled bull; he did not at first seem to take it in. Then he said at last, 'Don't you know who he is?'

"I reaffirmed my ignorance, and there was another silence; then the little priest said, still looking at the table, 'That is the Duke of Exmoor.'

"Then, before I could collect my scattered senses, he added equally quietly, but with an air of regularising things: 'My friend here is Doctor Mull, the Duke's librarian. My name is Brown.'

" 'But,' I stammered, 'if that is the Duke, why does he damn all the old dukes like that?'

" 'He seems really to believe,' answered the priest called Brown, 'that they have left a curse on him.' Then he added, with some irrelevance, 'That's why he wears a wig.'

"It was a few moments before his meaning dawned on me. 'You don't mean that fable about the fantastic ear?' I demanded. 'I've heard of it, of course, but surely it must be a superstitious yarn spun out of something much simpler. I've sometimes thought it was a wild version of one of those mutilation stories. They used to crop criminals' ears in the sixteenth century.'

" 'I hardly think it was that,' answered the little man thoughtfully, 'but it is not outside ordinary science or natural law for a family to have some deformity frequently reappearing—such as one ear bigger than the other.'

"The big librarian had buried his big bald brow in his big red hands, like a man trying to think out his duty. 'No,' he groaned. 'You do the man a wrong after all. Understand, I've no reason to defend him, or even keep faith with him. He has been a tyrant to me as to everybody else. Don't fancy because you see him sitting simply here that he isn't a great lord in the worst sense of the word. He would fetch a man a mile to ring a bell a yard off—if it would summon another man three miles to fetch a matchbox three yards off. He must have a footman to carry his walking-stick; a body servant to hold up his opera-glasses——'

" 'But not a valet to brush his clothes,' cut in the priest, with a curious dryness, 'for the valet would want to brush his wig too.'

"The librarian turned to him, and seemed to forget my presence; he was strongly moved, and, I think, a little heated with wine. 'I don't know how you know it, Father Brown,' he said, 'but you are right. He lets the whole world do everything for him—except dress him. And that he insists on doing in a literal solitude like a desert. Anybody is kicked out of the house without a character who is so much as found near his dressing-room door.'

" 'He seems a pleasant old party,' I remarked.

" 'No,' replied Dr. Mull quite simply; 'and yet that is just what I mean by saying you are unjust to him after all. Gentlemen, the Duke does really feel the bitterness about the curse that he uttered just now. He does, with sincere shame and terror, hide under that purple wig something he thinks it would blast the sons of man to see. I know it is so; and I know it is not a mere natural disfigurement, like a criminal mutilation, or a hereditary disproportion in the features. I know it is worse than that; because a man told me who was present at a scene that no man could invent, where a stronger man than any of us tried to defy the secret, and was scared away from it.'

"I opened my mouth to speak, but Mull went on in oblivion of me, speaking out of the cavern of his hands. 'I don't mind telling you, Father, because it's really more defending the poor Duke than giving him away. Didn't you ever hear of the time when he very nearly lost all the estates?'

"The priest shook his head; and the librarian proceeded to tell the tale as he had heard it from his predecessor in the same post, who had been his patron and instructor, and whom he seemed to trust implicitly. Up to a certain point it was a common enough tale of the decline of a great family's fortunes; the tale of a family lawyer. This lawyer, however, had the sense to cheat honestly, if the expression explains itself. Instead of using funds he held in trust, he took advantage of the Duke's carelessness to put the family in a financial hole, in which it might be necessary for the Duke to let him hold them in reality.

"The lawyer's name was Isaac Green, but the Duke always called him Elisha; presumably in reference to the fact that he was quite bald, though certainly not more than thirty. He had risen very rapidly, but from very dirty beginnings; being first a 'nark' or informer, and then a money-lender: but as solicitor to the Eyres he had the sense, as I say, to keep technically straight until he was ready to deal the final blow. The blow fell at dinner; and the old librarian said he should never forget the very look of the lampshades and the decanters, as the little lawyer, with a steady smile, proposed to the great landlord that they should halve the estates between them. The sequel certainly could not be overlooked; for the Duke, in dead silence, smashed a decanter on the man's bald head, as suddenly as I had seen him smash the glass that day in the orchard. It left a red triangular scar on the scalp, and the lawyer's eyes altered, but not his smile.

"He rose tottering to his feet, and struck back as such men do strike. 'I am glad of that,' he said, 'for now I can take the whole estate. The law will give it to me.'

"Exmoor, it seems, was white as ashes, but his eyes still blazed. 'The law will give it you,' he said, 'but you will not take it. . . . Why not? Why, because it would be the crack of doom for me; and if you take it *I shall take off my wig*. . . . Why, you pitiful plucked fowl, anyone can see your bare head. But no man shall see mine and live.'

"Well, you may say what you like and make it mean what you like. But Mull swears it is the solemn fact that the lawyer, after shaking his knotted fists in the air for an instant, simply ran from the room and never reappeared in the country-side. And since then Exmoor has been feared more for a warlock than even for a landlord and a magistrate.

"Now Dr. Mull told his story with rather wild theatrical gestures, and with a passion I think at least partisan. I was quite conscious of the possibility that the whole was the extravagance of an old braggart and gossip. But before I end this half of my discoveries, I think it due to Dr. Mull to record that my two first inquiries have confirmed his story. I learned from an old apothecary in the village that there was a bald man in evening dress, giving the name of Green, who came to him one night to have a three-cornered cut on his forehead plastered. And I learnt from the legal records and old newspapers that there was a lawsuit threatened, and at least begun, by one Green against the Duke of Exmoor."

Mr. Nutt, of *The Daily Reformer,* wrote some highly incongruous words across the top of the copy, made some highly mysterious marks down the side of it, and called to Miss Barlow in the same loud, monotonous voice, "Take down a letter to Mr. Finn."

"DEAR FINN,—Your copy will do, but I have had to headline it a bit; and our public would never stand a Romanist priest in the story—you must keep your eye on the suburbs. I've altered him to Mr. Brown, a Spiritualist.—Yours, E. NUTT."

A day or two afterwards found the active and judicious editor examining, with blue eyes that seemed to grow rounder and rounder, the second installment of Mr. Finn's tale of mysteries in high life. It began with the words:

"I have made an astounding discovery. I freely confess it is quite different from anything I expected to discover, and will give a much more practical shock to the public. I venture to say, without any vanity, that the words I now write will be read all over Europe, and certainly all over America and the Colonies. And yet I heard all I have to tell before I left this same little wooden table in this same little wood of apple-trees.

"I owe it all to the small priest Brown; he is an extraordinary man. The big librarian had left the table, perhaps ashamed of his long tongue, perhaps anxious about the storm in which his mysterious master had vanished: anyway, he betook himself heavily in the Duke's tracks through the trees. Father Brown had picked up one of the lemons and was eyeing it with an odd pleasure.

" 'What a lovely colour a lemon is!' he said. 'There's one thing I don't like about the Duke's wig—the colour.'

" 'I don't think I understand,' I answered.

" 'I dare say he's got good reason to cover his ears, like King Midas,' went on the priest, with a cheerful simplicity which somehow seemed rather flippant under the circumstances. 'I can quite understand that it's nicer to cover them with hair than with brass plates or leather flaps. But if he wants to use hair, why doesn't he make it look like hair? There never was hair of that colour in this world. It looks more like a sunset-cloud coming through the wood. Why doesn't he conceal the family curse better, if he's really so ashamed of it? Shall I tell you? It's because he isn't ashamed of it. He's proud of it.'

" 'It's an ugly wig to be proud of—and an ugly story,' I said.

" 'Consider,' replied this curious little man, 'how you yourself really feel about such things. I don't suggest you're either more snobbish or more morbid than the rest of us: but don't you feel in a vague way that a genuine old family curse is rather a fine thing to have? Would you be ashamed, wouldn't you be a little proud, if the heir of the Glamis horror called you his friend; or if Byron's family had confided, to you only, the evil adventures of their race? Don't be too hard on the aristocrats themselves if their heads are as weak as ours would be, and they are snobs about their own sorrows.'

" 'By Jove!' I cried, 'and that's true enough. My own mother's family had a banshee; and, now I come to think of it, it has comforted me in many a cold hour.'

" 'And think,' he went on, 'of that stream of blood and poison that spirted from his thin lips the instant you so much as mentioned his ancestors. Why should he show every stranger over such a Chamber of Horrors unless he is proud of it? He doesn't conceal his wig, he doesn't conceal his blood, he doesn't conceal his family curse, he doesn't conceal the family crimes—*but*——'

"The little man's voice changed so suddenly, he shut his hand so sharply, and his eyes so rapidly grew rounder and brighter like a waking owl's, that it had all the abruptness of a small explosion on the table.

" 'But,' he ended, '*he does really conceal his toilet.*'

"It somehow completed the thrill of my fanciful nerves that at that instant the Duke appeared again silently among the glimmering trees, with his soft foot and sunset-hued hair, coming round the corner of the house in company with his librarian. Before he came within earshot, Father Brown had added quite composedly, 'Why does he really hide the secret of what he does with the purple wig? Because it isn't the sort of secret we suppose.'

"The Duke came round the corner and resumed his seat at the head of the table with all his native dignity. The embarrassment of the librarian left him hovering on his hind legs, like a huge bear. The Duke addressed the priest with great seriousness. 'Father Brown,' he said, 'Doctor Mull informs me that you have come here to make a request. I no longer profess an observance of the religion of my fathers; but for their sakes and for the sake of the days when we met before, I am very willing to hear you. But I presume you would rather be heard in private.'

"Whatever I retain of the gentleman made me stand up. Whatever I have attained of the journalist made me stand still. Before this paralysis could pass, the priest had made a momentarily detaining motion. 'If,' he said, 'your Grace will permit me my real petition, or if I retain any right to advise you, I would urge that as many people as possible should be present. All over this country I have found hundreds, even of my own faith and flock, whose imaginations are poisoned by the spell which I implore you to break. I wish we could have all Devonshire here to see you do it.'

" 'To see me do what?' asked the Duke, arching his eyebrows.

" 'To see you take off your wig,' said Father Brown.

"The Duke's face did not move; but he looked at his petitioner with a glassy stare which was the most awful expression I have ever seen on a human face. I could see the librarian's great legs wavering under him like the shadows of stems in a pool; and I could not banish from my own brain the fancy that the trees all around us were filling softly in the silence with devils instead of birds.

" 'I spare you,' said the Duke in a voice of inhuman pity. 'I refuse. If I gave you the faintest hint of the load of horror I have to bear alone, you would lie shrieking at these feet of mine and begging to know no more. I will spare you the hint. You shall not spell the first letter of what is written on the altar of the Unknown God.'

" 'I know the Unknown God,' said the little priest, with an unconscious grandeur of certitude that stood up like a granite tower. 'I know his name; it is Satan. The true God was made flesh and dwelt among us. And I say to you, wherever you find men ruled merely by mystery, it is the mystery of iniquity. If the devil tells you something is too fearful to look at, look at it. If he says something too terrible to hear, hear it. If you think some truth unbearable, bear it. I entreat your Grace to end this nightmare now and here at this table.'

" 'If I did,' said the Duke in a low voice, 'you and all you believe, and all by which alone you live, would be the first to shrivel and perish. You would have an instant to know the great Nothing before you died.'

" 'The cross of Christ be between me and harm,' said Father Brown. 'Take off your wig.'

"I was leaning over the table in ungovernable excitement; in listening to this extraordinary duel half a thought had come into my head. 'Your Grace,' I cried, 'I call your bluff. Take off that wig, or I will knock it off.'

"I suppose I can be prosecuted for assault, but I am very glad I did it. When he said, in the same voice of stone, 'I refuse,' I simply sprang on him. For three long instants he strained against me as if he had all hell to help him; but I forced back his head until the hairy cap fell off it. I admit that, whilst wrestling, I shut my eyes as it fell.

"I was awakened by a cry from Mull, who was also by this time at the Duke's side. His head and mine were both bending over the bald head of the wigless Duke. Then the silence was snapped by the librarian exclaiming: 'What can it mean? Why, the man had nothing to hide. His ears are just like everybody else's.'

" 'Yes,' said Father Brown, 'that is what he had to hide.'

"The priest walked straight up to him; but strangely enough did not even glance at his ears. He stared with an almost comical seriousness at his bald forehead; and pointed to a three-cornered cicatrice, long healed, but still discernible. 'Mr. Green, I think,' he said politely, 'and he did get the whole estate after all.'

"And now let me tell the readers of *The Daily Reformer* what I think the most remarkable thing in the whole affair. This transformation-scene, which will seem to you as wild and purple as a Persian fairy tale, has been (except for my technical assault) strictly legal and constitutional from its first beginnings. This man with the odd scar and the ordinary ears is not an impostor. Though (in one sense) he wears another man's wig and claims another man's ear, he has not stolen another man's coronet. He really is the one and only Duke of Exmoor. What happened was this. The old Duke really had a slight malformation of the ear, which really was more or less hereditary. He really was morbid about it; and it is likely enough that he did invoke it as a kind of curse in the violent scene (which undoubtedly happened) in which he struck Green with the decanter. But the contest ended very differently. Green pressed his claim and got the estates; the dispossessed nobleman shot himself and died without issue. After a decent interval the beautiful English Government revived the 'extinct' peerage of Exmoor, and bestowed it, as is usual, on the most important person, the person who had got the property.

"This man used the old feudal fables—probably, in his snobbish soul, really envied and admired them. So that thousands of poor English people tremble before a mysterious chieftain with an ancient destiny and a diadem of evil stars—when they are really trembling before a gutter-snipe who was a pettifogger and a pawnbroker not twelve years ago. I think it very typical of the real case against our aristocracy as it is, and as it will be till God sends us braver men."

Mr. Nutt put down the manuscript and called out with unusual sharpness, "Miss Barlow, please take down a letter to Mr. Finn.

"DEAR FINN,—You must be mad; we can't touch this. I wanted vampires and the bad old days and aristocracy hand-in-hand with superstition. They like that. But you must know the Exmoors would never forgive this. And what would our people say then, I should like to know! Why, Sir Simon is one of Exmoor's greatest pals; and it would ruin that cousin of the Eyres that's standing for us at Bradford. Besides, old Soap-Suds was sick enough at not getting his peerage last year; he'd sack me by wire if I lost him it with such lunacy as this. And what about Duffey? He's doing us some rattling articles on 'The Heel of the Norman.' And how can he write about Normans if the man's only a solicitor? Do be reasonable.—Yours, E. NUTT."

As Miss Barlow rattled away cheerfully, he crumpled up the copy and tossed it into the waste-paper basket; but not before he had, automatically and by mere force of habit, altered the word "God" to the word "circumstances."

THE STRANGE CRIME
OF JOHN BOULNOIS

Mr. Calhoun Kidd was a very young gentleman with a very old face, a face dried up with its own eagerness, framed in blue-black hair and a black butterfly tie. He was the emissary in England of the colossal American daily called *The Western Sun*—also humorously described as the "Rising Sunset." This was in allusion to a great journalistic declaration (attributed to Mr. Kidd himself) that "he guessed the sun would rise in the west yet if American citizens did a bit more hustling." Those, however, who mock American journalism from the standpoint of somewhat mellower traditions forget a certain paradox which partly redeems it. For while the journalism of the States permits a pantomimic vulgarity long past anything English, it also shows a real excitement about the most earnest mental problems, of which English papers are innocent, or rather incapable. The *Sun* was full of the most solemn matters treated in the most farcical way. William James figured there as well as "Weary Willie," and pragmatists alternated with pugilists in the long procession of its portraits.

Thus when a very unobtrusive Oxford man named John Boulnois wrote in a very unreadable review called *The Natural Philosophy Quarterly* a series of articles on alleged weak points in Darwinian evolution, it fluttered no corner of the English papers; though Boulnois's theory (which was that of a comparatively stationary universe visited occasionally by convulsions of change) had some rather faddy fashionableness at Oxford, and got so far as to be named "Catastrophism." But many American papers seized on the challenge as a great event; and the *Sun* threw the shadow of Mr. Boulnois quite gigantically across its pages. By the paradox already noted, articles of valuable intelligence and enthusiasm were presented with headlines apparently written by an illiterate maniac; headlines such as "Darwin Chews Dirt; Critic Boulnois Says He Jumps the Shocks"—or "Keep Catastrophic, Says Thinker Boulnois." And Mr. Calhoun Kidd, of *The Western Sun,* was bidden to take his butterfly tie and lugubrious visage down to the little house outside Oxford where Thinker Boulnois lived in happy ignorance of such a title.

That fated philosopher had consented, in a somewhat dazed manner, to receive the interviewer, and had named the hour of nine that evening. The last of a summer sunset clung about Cumnor and the low wooded hills; the romantic Yankee was both doubtful of his road and inquisitive about his surroundings; and, seeing the door of a genuine feudal old-country inn, The Champion Arms, standing open, he went in to make inquiries.

In the bar parlour he rang the bell, and had to wait some little time for a reply to it. The only other person present was a lean man with close red hair and loose horsey-looking clothes, who was drinking very bad whisky, but smoking a very good cigar. The whisky, of course, was the choice brand of The Champion Arms; the cigar he had probably brought with him from London. Nothing could be more different than his cynical *négligé* from the dapper dryness of the young American; but something in his pencil and open notebook, and perhaps in the expression of his alert blue eye, caused Kidd to guess, correctly, that he was a brother journalist.

"Could you do me the favour," asked Kidd, with the courtesy of his nation, "of directing me to the Grey Cottage, where Mr. Boulnois lives, as I understand?"

"It's a few yards down the road," said the red-haired man, removing his cigar; "I shall be passing it myself in a minute, but I'm going on to Pendragon Park to try and see the fun."

"What is Pendragon Park?" asked Calhoun Kidd.

"Sir Claude Champion's place—haven't you come down for that, too?" asked the other pressman, looking up. "You're a journalist, aren't you?"

"I have come to see Mr. Boulnois," said Kidd.

"I've come to see Mrs. Boulnois," replied the other. "But I shan't catch her at home." And he laughed rather unpleasantly.

"Are you interested in Catastrophism?" asked the wondering Yankee.

"I'm interested in catastrophes; and there are going to be some," replied his companion gloomily. "Mine's a filthy trade, and I never pretend it isn't."

With that he spat on the floor; yet somehow in the very act and instant one could realise that the man had been brought up as a gentleman.

The American pressman considered him with more attention. His face was pale and dissipated, with the promise of formidable passions yet to be loosed; but it was a clever and sensitive face; his clothes were coarse and careless, but he had a good seal ring on one of his long, thin fingers. His name, which came out in the course of talk, was James Dalroy; he was the son of a bankrupt Irish landlord, and attached to a pink paper which he heartily despised, called *Smart Society*, in the capacity of reporter and of something painfully like spy.

Smart Society, I regret to say, felt none of that interest in Boulnois on Darwin which was such a credit to the heads and hearts of *The Western Sun*. Dalroy had come down, it seemed, to snuff up the scent of a scandal which might very well end in the Divorce Court, but which was at present hovering between Grey Cottage and Pendragon Park.

Sir Claude Champion was known to the readers of *The Western Sun* as well as Mr. Boulnois. So were the Pope and the Derby Winner; but the idea of their intimate acquaintanceship would have struck Kidd as equally incongruous. He had heard of (and written about, nay, falsely pretended to know) Sir Claude Champion, as "one of the brightest and wealthiest of England's Upper Ten"; as the great sportsman who raced yachts round the world; as the great traveller who wrote books about the Himalayas, as the politician who swept constituencies with a startling sort of Tory Democracy, and as the great dabbler in art, music, literature, and, above all, acting. Sir Claude was really rather magnificent in other than American eyes. There was something of the Renascence Prince about his omnivorous culture and restless publicity; he was not only a great amateur, but an ardent one. There was in him none of that antiquarium frivolity that we convey by the word "dilettante."

That faultless falcon profile with purple-black Italian eyes, which had been snap-shotted so often both for *Smart Society* and *The Western Sun*, gave everyone the impression of a man eaten by ambition as by a fire, or even a disease. But though Kidd knew a great deal about Sir Claude—a great deal more, in fact, than there was to know—it would never have crossed his wildest dreams to connect so showy an aristocrat with the newly-unearthed founder of Catastrophism, or to guess that Sir Claude Champion and John Boulnois could be intimate friends. Such, according to Dalroy's account, was nevertheless the fact. The two had hunted in couples at school and college, and, though their social destinies had been very different (for Champion was a great landlord and almost a millionaire, while Boulnois was a poor scholar and, until just lately, an unknown one), they still kept in very close touch with each other. Indeed, Boulnois's cottage stood just outside the gates of Pendragon Park.

But whether the two men could be friends much longer was becoming a dark and ugly question. A year or two before, Boulnois had married a beautiful and not unsuccessful actress, to whom he was devoted in his own shy and ponderous style; and the proximity of the household to Champion's had given that flighty celebrity opportunities for behaving in a way that could not but cause painful and rather base excitement. Sir Claude had carried the arts of publicity to perfection; and he seemed to take a crazy pleasure in being equally ostentatious in an intrigue that could do him no sort of honour. Footmen from Pendragon were perpetually leaving bouquets for Mrs. Boulnois; carriages and motorcars were perpetually calling at the cottage for Mrs. Boulnois; balls and masquerades perpetually filled the grounds in which the baronet paraded Mrs. Boulnois, like the Queen of Love and Beauty at a tournament. That very evening, marked by Mr. Kidd for the exposition of catastrophism, had been marked by Sir Claude Champion for an open-air rendering of *Romeo and Juliet*, in which he was to play Romeo to a Juliet it was needless to name.

"I don't think it can go on without a smash," said the young man with red hair, getting up and shaking himself. "Old Boulnois may be squared—or he may be square. But if he's square he's thick—what you might call cubic. But I don't believe it's possible."

"He is a man of grand intellectual powers," said Calhoun Kidd, in a deep voice.

"Yes," answered Dalroy. "But even a man of grand intellectual powers can't be such a blighted fool as all that. Must you be going on? I shall be following myself in a minute or two."

But Calhoun Kidd, having finished a milk and soda, betook himself smartly up the road towards the Grey Cottage, leaving his cynical informant to his whisky and tobacco. The last of the daylight had faded; the skies were of a (dark green-grey like slate, studded here and there with a star, but lighter on the left side of the sky, with the promise of a rising moon.

The Grey Cottage, which stood entrenched, as it were, in a square of stiff, high thorn-hedges, was so close under the pines and palisades of the Park that Kidd at first mistook it for the Park Lodge. Finding the name on the narrow wooden gate, however, and seeing by his watch that the hour of the "Thinker's" appointment had just struck, he went in and knocked at the front door. Inside the garden hedge, he could see that the house, though unpretentious enough, was larger and more luxurious than it looked at first, and was quite a different kind of place from a porter's lodge. A dog-kennel and a beehive stood outside like symbols of old English country life; the moon was rising behind a plantation of prosperous pear trees; the dog that came out of the kennel was reverend-looking and reluctant to bark; and the plain, elderly man-servant who opened the door was brief but dignified.

"Mr. Boulnois asked me to offer his apologies, sir," he said, "but he has been obliged to go out suddenly."

"But see here, I had an appointment," said the interviewer, with a rising voice. "Do you know where he went to?"

"To Pendragon Park, sir," said the servant rather sombrely, and began to close the door.

Kidd started a little. "Did he go with Mrs.—with the rest of the party?" he asked rather vaguely.

"No, sir," said the man shortly; "he stayed behind, and then went out alone." And he shut the door, brutally, but with an air of duty not done.

The American, that curious compound of impudence and sensitiveness, was annoyed. He felt a strong desire to hustle them all along a bit and teach them business habits; the hoary old dog and the grizzled, heavy-faced old butler with his prehistoric shirt-front, and the drowsy old moon, and, above all, the scatter-brained old philosopher who couldn't keep an appointment.

"If that's the way he goes on, he deserves to lose his wife's purest devotion," said Mr. Calhoun Kidd. "But perhaps he's gone over to make a row. In that case I reckon a man from *The Western Sun* will be on the spot."

And turning the corner by the open lodge-gates, he set off, stumping up the long avenue of black pine-woods that pointed in abrupt perspective towards the inner gardens of Pendragon Park. The trees were as black and orderly as plumes upon a hearse; there were still a few stars. He was a man with more literary than direct natural associations; the word "Ravenswood" came into his head repeatedly. It was partly the raven colour of the pine-woods; but partly also an indescribable atmosphere almost described in Scott's great tragedy; the smell of something that died in the eighteenth century; the smell of dank gardens and broken urns; of wrongs that will never now be righted; of something that is nonetheless incurably sad because it is strangely unreal.

More than once, as he went up that trim, black road of tragic artifice, he stopped startled, thinking he heard steps in front of him. He could see nothing in front but the twin sombre walls of pine and the wedge of starlit sky above them. At first he thought he must have fancied it or been mocked by a mere echo of his own tramp. But as he went on he more and more inclined to conclude, with the remains of his reason, that there really were other feet upon the road. He thought hazily of ghosts; and was surprised how swiftly he could see the image of an appropriate and local ghost, one with a face as white as Pierrot's, but patched with black. The apex of the triangle of dark-blue sky was growing brighter and bluer, but he did not realise as yet that this was because he was coming nearer to the lights of the great house and garden. He only felt that the atmosphere was growing more intense; there was in the sadness more violence and secrecy—more—he hesitated for the word, and then said it with a jerk of laughter—Catastrophism.

More pines, more pathway slid past him, and then he stood rooted as by a blast of magic. It is vain to say that he felt as if he had got into a dream; but this time he felt quite certain that he had got into a book. For we human beings are used to inappropriate things; we are accustomed to the clatter of the incongruous; it is a tune to which we can go to sleep. If one appropriate thing happens, it wakes us up like the pang of a perfect chord. Something happened such as would have happened in such a place in a forgotten tale.

Over the black pine-wood came flying and flashing in the moon a naked sword, such a slender and sparkling rapier as may have fought many an unjust duel in that ancient park. It fell on the pathway far in front of him and lay there glistening like a large needle. He ran like a hare and bent to look at it. Seen at closer quarters, it had rather a showy look; the big red jewels in the hilt and guard were a little dubious. But there were other red drops upon the blade which were not dubious.

He looked round wildly in the direction from which the dazzling missile had come, and saw that at this point the sable façade of fir and pine was interrupted by a smaller road at right angles; which, when he turned it, brought him in full view of the long, lighted house, with a lake and fountains in front of it. Nevertheless, he did not look at this, having something more interesting to look at.

Above him, at the angle of the steep green bank of the terraced garden, was one of those small picturesque surprises common in the old landscape gardening; a kind of small round hill or dome of grass, like a giant mole-hill, ringed and crowned with three concentric fences of roses and having a sundial in the highest point in the centre. Kidd could see the finger of the dial stand up dark against the sky like the dorsal fin of a shark; and the vain moonlight clinging to that idle clock. But he saw something else clinging to it also, for one wild moment—the figure of a man.

Though he saw it there only for a moment, though it was outlandish and incredible in costume, being clad from neck to heel in tight crimson, with glints of gold, yet he knew in one flash of moonlight who it was. That white face flung up to heaven, clean-shaven and so unnaturally young, like Byron with a Roman nose, those black curls already grizzled—he had seen the thousand public portraits of Sir Claude Champion. The wild red figure reeled an instant against the sundial; the next it had rolled down the steep bank and lay at the American's feet, faintly moving one arm. A gaudy unnatural gold ornament on the arm suddenly reminded Kidd of *Romeo and Juliet*; of course, the tight crimson suit was part of the play. But there was a long red stain down the bank from which the man had rolled; that was no part of the play. He had been run through the body.

Mr. Calhoun Kidd shouted and shouted again. Once more he seemed to hear phantasmal footsteps, and started to find another figure already near him. He knew the figure, and yet it terrified him. The dissipated youth who had called himself Dalroy had a horribly quiet way with him; if Boulnois failed to keep appointments that had been made, Dalroy had a sinister air of keeping appointments that hadn't. The moonlight discoloured everything; against Dalroy's red hair his wan face looked not so much white as pale green.

All this morbid impressionism must be Kidd's excuse for having cried out, brutally and beyond all reason, "Did you do this, you devil?"

James Dalroy smiled his unpleasing smile; but before he could speak, the fallen figure made another movement of the arm, waving vaguely towards the place where the sword fell; then came a moan, and then it managed to speak.

"Boulnois . . . Boulnois, I say . . . Boulnois did it . . . jealous of me . . . he was jealous, he was, he was . . ."

Kidd bent his head down to hear more, and just managed to catch the words:

"Boulnois . . . with my own sword . . . he threw it . . ."

Again the falling hand waved towards the sword, and then fell rigid with a thud. In Kidd rose from its depths all that acrid humour that is the strange salt of the seriousness of his race.

"See here," he said sharply and with command, "you must fetch a doctor. This man's dead."

"And a priest, too, I suppose," said Dalroy, in an undecipherable manner. "All these Champions are papists."

The American knelt down by the body, felt the heart, propped up the head, and used some last efforts at restoration; but before the other journalist reappeared, followed by a doctor and a priest, he was already prepared to assert they were too late.

"Were you too late also?" asked the doctor, a solid, prosperous-looking man, with conventional moustache and whiskers, but a lively eye, which darted over Kidd dubiously.

"In one sense," drawled the representative of the *Sun*. "I was too late to save the man, but I guess I was in time to hear something of importance. I heard the dead man denounce his assassin."

"And who was the assassin?" asked the doctor, drawing his eyebrows together.

"Boulnois," said Calhoun Kidd, and whistled softly.

The doctor stared at him gloomily with a reddening brow; but he did not contradict. Then the priest, a shorter figure in the background, said mildly: "I understood that Mr. Boulnois was not coming to Pendragon Park this evening."

"There again," said the Yankee grimly, "I may be in a position to give the old country a fact or two. Yes, *sir,* John Boulnois was going to stay in all this evening; he fixed up a real good appointment there with me. But John Boulnois changed his mind; John Boulnois left his home abruptly and all alone, and came over to this derned Park an hour or so ago. His butler told me so. I think we hold what the all-wise police call a clue—have you sent for them?"

"Yes," said the doctor. "But we haven't alarmed anyone else yet."

"Does Mrs. Boulnois know?" asked James Dalroy; and again Kidd was conscious of an irrational desire to hit him on his curling mouth.

"I have not told her," said the doctor gruffly. "But here come the police."

The little priest had stepped out into the main avenue, and now returned with the fallen sword, which looked ludicrously large and theatrical when attached to his dumpy figure, at once clerical and commonplace. "Just before the police come," he said apologetically. "Has anyone got a light?"

The Yankee journalist took an electric torch from his pocket, and the priest held it close to the middle part of the blade, which he examined with blinking care. Then, without glancing at the point or pommel, he handed the long weapon to the doctor.

"I fear I'm no use here," he said, with a brief sign. "I'll say good-night to you, gentlemen." And he walked away up the dark avenue towards the house, his hands clasped behind him and his big head bent in cogitation.

The rest of the group made increased haste towards the lodge-gates, where an inspector and two constables could already be seen in consultation with a lodge-keeper. But the little priest only walked slower and slower in the dim cloister of pine, and at last stopped dead, on the steps of the house. It was his silent way of acknowledging an equally silent approach; for there came towards him a presence that might have satisfied even Calhoun Kidd's demands for a lovely and aristocratic ghost. It was a young woman in silvery satins of a Renascence design; she had golden hair in two long shining ropes, and a face so startlingly pale between them that she might have been chryselephantine—made, that is, like some old Greek statues, out of ivory and gold. But her eyes were very bright, and her voice, though low, was confident.

"Father Brown?" she said.

"Mrs. Boulnois?" he replied gravely. Then he looked at her and immediately said: "I see you know about Sir Claude."

"How do you know I know?" she asked steadily.

He did not answer the question, but asked another: "Have you seen your husband?"

"My husband is at home," she said. "He has nothing to do with this."

Again he did not answer; and the woman drew nearer to him, with a curiously intense expression on her face.

"Shall I tell you something more?" she said, with a rather fearful smile. "I don't think he did it, and *you* don't either."

Father Brown returned her gaze with a long, grave stare, and then nodded, yet more gravely.

"Father Brown," said the lady, "I am going to tell you all I know, but I want you to do me a favour first. Will you tell me *why* you haven't jumped to the conclusion of poor John's guilt, as all the rest have done? Don't mind what you say: I—I know about the gossip and the appearances that are against him."

Father Brown looked honestly embarrassed, and passed his hand across his forehead. "Two very little things," he said. "At least, one's very trivial and the other very vague. But such as they are, they don't fit in with Mr. Boulnois being the murderer."

He turned his blank round face up to the stars and continued absent-mindedly: "To take the vague idea first. I attach a good deal of importance to vague ideas. All those things that 'aren't evidence' are what convince me. I think a moral impossibility the biggest of all impossibilities. I know your husband only slightly, but I think this crime of his, as generally conceived, something very like a moral impossibility. Please do not think I mean that Boulnois could not be so wicked. Anybody can be wicked—as wicked as he chooses. We can direct our moral wills; but we can't generally change our instinctive tastes and ways of doing things. Boulnois might commit a murder, but not this murder. He would not snatch Romeo's sword from its romantic scabbard; or slay his foe on the sundial as on a kind of altar; or leave his body among the roses; or fling the sword away among the pines. If Boulnois killed anyone he'd do it quietly and heavily, as he'd do any other doubtful thing—

take a tenth glass of port, or read a loose Greek poet. No, the romantic setting is not like Boulnois. It's more like Champion."

"Ah!" she said, and looked at him with eyes like diamonds.

"And the trivial thing was this," said Brown. "There were finger-prints on that sword; finger-prints can be detected quite a time after they are made if they're on some polished surface like glass or steel. These were on a polished surface. They were half-way down the blade of the sword. Whose prints they were I have no earthly clue; but why should anybody hold a sword half-way down? It was a long sword, but length is an advantage in lunging at an enemy. At least, at most enemies. At all enemies except one."

"Except one!" she repeated.

"There is only one enemy," said Father Brown, "whom it is easier to kill with a dagger than a sword."

"I know," said the woman. "Oneself."

There was a long silence, and then the priest said quietly but abruptly: "Am I right, then? Did Sir Claude kill himself?"

"Yes," she said, with a face like marble. "I saw him do it."

"He died," said Father Brown, "for love of you?"

An extraordinary expression flashed across her face, very different from pity, modesty, remorse, or anything her companion had expected: her voice became suddenly strong and full. "I don't believe," she said, "he ever cared about me a rap. He hated my husband."

"Why?" asked the other, and turned his round face from the sky to the lady.

"He hated my husband because ... it is so strange I hardly know how to say it ... because ..."

"Yes?" said Brown patiently.

"Because my husband wouldn't hate him."

Father Brown only nodded, and seemed still to be listening: he differed from most detectives in fact and fiction in a small point—he never pretended not to understand when he understood perfectly well.

Mrs. Boulnois drew near once more with the same contained glow of certainty. "My husband," she said, "is a great man. Sir

Claude Champion was not a great man: he was a celebrated and successful man. My husband has never been celebrated or successful; and it is the solemn truth that he has never dreamed of being so. He no more expects to be famous for thinking than for smoking cigars. On all that side he has a sort of splendid stupidity. He has never grown up. He still liked Champion exactly as he liked him at school; he admired him as he would admire a conjuring trick done at the dinner table. But he couldn't be got to conceive the notion of *envying* Champion. *And Champion wanted to be envied.* He went mad and killed himself for that."

"Yes," said Father Brown. "I think I begin to understand."

"Oh, don't you see?" she cried. "The whole picture is made for that—the place is planned for it. Champion put John in a little house at his very door, like a dependent—to make him *feel* a failure. He never felt it. He thinks no more about such things than—than an absent-minded lion. Champion would burst in on John's shabbiest hours or homeliest meals with some dazzling present or announcement or expedition that made it like the visit of Haroun Alraschid, and John would accept or refuse amiably, with one eye off, so to speak, like one lazy schoolboy agreeing or disagreeing with another. After five years of it John had not turned a hair; and Sir Claude Champion was a monomaniac."

"And Haman began to tell them," said Father Brown, "of all the things wherein the king had honoured him; and he said, 'All these things profit me nothing while I see Mordecai the Jew sitting in the gate.'"

"The crisis came," Mrs. Boulnois continued, "when I persuaded John to let me take down some of his speculations and send them to a magazine. They began to attract attention, especially in America; and one paper wanted to interview him. When Champion (who was interviewed nearly every day) heard of this late little crumb of success falling to his unconscious rival, the last link snapped that held back his devilish hatred. Then he began to lay that insane siege to my own love and honour which has been the talk of the shire. You will ask me why I allowed such atrocious attentions. I answer that I could not have declined them except by explaining to my husband,

and there are some things the soul cannot do, as the body cannot fly. Nobody could have explained to my husband. Nobody could do it now. If you said to him in so many words, 'Champion is stealing your wife,' he would think the joke a little vulgar: that it could be anything but a joke—that notion could find no crack in his great skull to get in by. Well, John was to come and see us act this evening, but just as we were starting he said he wouldn't; he had got an interesting book and a cigar. I told this to Sir Claude, and it was his death-blow. The monomaniac suddenly saw despair. He stabbed himself, crying out like a devil that Boulnois was slaying him; he lies there in the garden dead of his own jealousy to produce jealousy; and John is sitting in the dining-room reading a book."

There was another silence, and then the little priest said: "There is only one weak point, Mrs. Boulnois, in all your very vivid account. Your husband is not sitting in the dining-room reading a book. That American reporter told me he had been to your house, and your butler told him Mr. Boulnois had gone to Pendragon Park, after all."

Her bright eyes widened to an almost electric glare; and yet it seemed rather bewilderment than confusion or fear. "Why, what *can* you mean?" she cried. "All the servants were out of the house, seeing the theatricals. And we don't keep a butler, thank goodness!"

Father Brown started and spun half round like an absurd teetotum. "What, what?" he cried, seeming galvanised into sudden life. "Look here—I say—can I make your husband hear if I go to the house?"

"Oh, the servants will be back by now," she said, wondering.

"Right, right!" rejoined the cleric energetically, and set off scuttling up the path towards the Park gates. He turned once to say: "Better get hold of that Yankee, or 'Crime of John Boulnois' will be all over the Republic in large letters."

"You don't understand," said Mrs. Boulnois. "He wouldn't mind. I don't think he imagines that America really is a place."

When Father Brown reached the house with the beehive and the drowsy dog, a small and neat maid-servant showed him into the dining-room, where Boulnois sat reading by a shaded lamp, exactly as his wife described him. A decanter of port and a wine-glass were at his elbow; and the instant the priest entered he noted the long ash stand out unbroken on his cigar.

"He has been here for half an hour, at least," thought Father Brown. In fact, he had the air of sitting where he had sat when his dinner was cleared away.

"Don't get up, Mr. Boulnois," said the priest, in his pleasant, prosaic way. "I shan't interrupt you a moment. I fear I break in on some of your scientific studies."

"No," said Boulnois. "I was reading *The Bloody Thumb.*" He said it with neither frown nor smile, and his visitor was conscious of a certain deep and virile indifference in the man which his wife had called greatness. He laid down a gory yellow "shocker" without even feeling its incongruity enough to comment on it humorously. John Boulnois was a big, slow-moving man with a massive head, partly grey and partly bald, and blunt, burly features. He was in shabby and very old-fashioned evening dress, with a narrow triangular opening of shirt-front: he had assumed it that evening in his original purpose of going to see his wife act Juliet.

"I won't keep you long from *The Bloody Thumb* or any other catastrophic affairs," said Father Brown, smiling. "I only came to ask you about the crime you committed this evening."

Boulnois looked at him steadily, but a red bar began to show across his broad brow; and he seemed like one discovering embarrassment for the first time.

"I know it was a strange crime," assented Brown, in a low voice. "Stranger than murder perhaps—to you. The little sins are sometimes harder to confess than the big ones—but that's why it's so important to confess them. Your crime is committed by every fashionable hostess six times a week: and yet you find it stuck to your tongue like a nameless atrocity."

"It makes one feel," said the philosopher slowly, "such a damned fool."

"I know," assented the other, "but one often has to choose between feeling a damned fool and being one."

"I can't analyse myself well," went on Boulnois, "but sitting in that chair with that story I was as happy as a schoolboy on a half-holiday. It was security, eternity—I can't convey it . . . the cigars were within reach . . . the matches were within reach . . . the *Thumb* had four more appearances to . . . it was not only a peace, but a plentitude. Then that bell rang, and I thought for one long mortal minute that I couldn't get out of that chair—literally, physically, muscularly couldn't. Then I did it like a man lifting the world, because I knew all the servants were out. I opened the front door, and there was a little man with his mouth open to speak and his notebook open to write in. I remembered the Yankee interviewer I had forgotten. His hair was parted in the middle, and I tell you that murder——"

"I understand," said Father Brown. "I've seen him."

"I didn't commit murder," continued the Catastrophist mildly, "but only perjury. I said I had gone across to Pendragon Park and shut the door in his face. That is my crime, Father Brown, and I don't know what penance you would inflict for it."

"I shan't inflict any penance," said the clerical gentleman, collecting his heavy hat and umbrella with an air of some amusement; "quite the contrary. I came here specially to let you off the little penance which would otherwise have followed your little offence."

"And what," asked Boulnois, smiling, "is the little penance I have so luckily been let off?"

"Being hanged," said Father Brown.

A NOTE ON THE TYPE

The principal text of this Modern Library edition
was set in a digitized version of Janson, a typeface that
dates from about 1690 and was cut by Nicholas Kis,
a Hungarian working in Amsterdam. The original matrices have
survived and are held by the Stempel foundry in Germany.
Hermann Zapf redesigned some of the weights and sizes for
Stempel, basing his revisions on the original design.

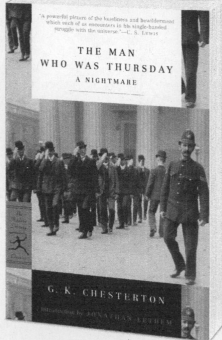